Point of Crisis

Alex Fletcher Book Four

a novel by

Steven Konkoly

Copyright Information

stevekonkoly@striblingmedia.com

Work by Steven Konkoly

The Black Flagged Series

Black Ops/Political /Conspiracy/Action thrillers

"Daniel Petrovich, the most lethal operative created by the Department of Defense's Black Flag Program, protects a secret buried in the deepest vaults of the Pentagon. A secret that is about to unravel his life."

ALPHA: A Black Ops Thriller (Book 1)
REDUX: A Black Ops Thriller (Book 2)
APEX: A Black Ops Thriller (Book 3)
VEKTOR: A Black Ops Thriller (Book 4)
OMEGA: A Black Ops Thriller (Book 5)
COVENANT: A Black Ops Thriller (Book 4.5) — Novella

The Alex Fletcher Books

Suspense/Action/Adventure/Conspiracy thrillers

"Alex Fletcher, Iraq War veteran, has read the signs for years. With his family and home prepared to endure an extended disaster, Alex thinks he's ready for anything. ***He's not even close.****"*

The Jakarta Pandemic (Book 1)
The Perseid Collapse (Book 2)
Event Horizon (Book 3)
Point of Crisis (Book 4)
Dispatches (Book 5)

The Zulu Virus Chronicles
Bioweapons/Conspiracy/Action thrillers

"Something sinister has arrived in America's heartland. Within 24 hours, complete strangers, from different walks of life will be forced to join together to survive the living nightmare that has been unleashed."

Hot Zone (Book 1)
Kill Box (Book 2)
Fire Storm (Book 3)

Fractured State Series
Near-future Black ops/Conspiracy/Action thrillers

"2035. A sinister conspiracy unravels. A state on the verge of secession. A man on the run with his family."

Fractured State (Book 1)
Rogue State (Book 2)

To my family.

The reasons I write.

"Point of Crisis"

A fixed point in the "Malthusian Catastrophe," where population levels exceed the food production and distribution capacity of a system—resulting in a crisis that can only be regulated by famine, war or disease.

– From Thomas Malthus's Essay on the Principle of Population (1798).

A list of military/government acronyms and definitions used throughout *The Alex Fletcher Books* is available at the back of the book.

Point of Crisis

Prologue

EVENT +2 Days

Space Fence "Site Alpha"
Kwajalein Island, Republic of the Marshall Islands

Technical Sergeant Marla Quinn typed the last lines of code into the Joint Space Operations Center (JSpOC) interface and pressed *return.* Her strained face relaxed, revealing the early stages of a grin.

"Frank, we're connected to Vandenberg," she said, turning to find the Raytheon contractor responsible for engineering the bypass.

An air force sergeant seated near the door shrugged his shoulders. "He left with the rest of the civilians a minute ago."

"You've got to be kidding me?" Quinn muttered, turning back to the computer station.

She had been so busy typing code that she hadn't noticed the exodus. The contractors had worked tirelessly with the station's U.S. Air Force personnel to figure out a way to package the post-"event" Space Fence data and deliver it to the Joint Space Operations Center at Vandenberg Air Force Base. Under normal conditions, the information streamed continuously to the California base, but two days ago, at 20:58 local time, the Joint Space Operations Center stopped accepting data. Less than thirty minutes later, the U.S Air Force garrison on Kwajalein Island went into lockdown.

Her fingers returned to the keyboard, typing the last string of commands that would route 593.7 terabytes of orbital tracking data through dozens of satellites, on a circuitous path to reach Vandenberg's central processing mainframe. She was surprised that Frank left the room. He was well aware that she was minutes away from rebooting the system and testing his program.

"Did he say where they were going?" she asked.

"Negative. Manuel poked his head in and said everybody needed to see something. You know these guys. They interpret the term 'appointed place of duty' pretty loosely," he said.

"They've busted their asses for thirty-six hours straight on this, so I don't care if they're hitting golf balls into the atoll. Can you run out and look for Frank? I'd hate for him to miss this."

"Just send it. It's not like the computer's gonna pour him a glass of Johnnie Walker Blue to celebrate."

"I'll type," Quinn said. "You find out what's so important."

She wouldn't be surprised if they had been called to another "closed" security briefing. Several of the contractors held security clearances higher than their commanding officer, and they'd spent considerable time behind closed doors since the "event." The new Space Fence system had applications far beyond tracking the flight paths of more than twenty thousand orbital objects. The powerful S-band frequency radar used by Site Alpha could detect smaller objects than the previous VHF version, providing the United States with the capability to track China's latest fleet of previously undetectable microsatellites. That was all she knew—and all they were going to tell her. She typed the rest of the code and held her pinkie finger above the return key.

"Marla, get out here now!" said the duty sergeant, suddenly appearing in the operations center door.

"Hold on," she said, tapping the key. "What the fuck is the big deal?"

"Something happened to the navy ship. Something bad," he said, disappearing.

Quinn stood up, mostly annoyed, but partly frightened. The USS *Paul Hamilton*, one of the U.S. Navy's Ballistic Missile Defense (BMD) capable Arleigh Burke class destroyers, arrived at the recently constructed naval facility two months ago. The ship's mission was unknown to the station, but it didn't take a War College degree to figure out that it had something to do with Site Alpha's unadvertised tracking capabilities. Yelling erupted in the hallway, and she dashed through the door, colliding with Frank DeMillo.

"Did you send the data?" he asked, wiping beads of sweat from his forehead.

"I started the sequence a couple seconds ago. Sorry, I didn't think you—"

"We need to get out of here," he said, grabbing her arm.

The door leading outside crashed open, spilling bright light and another civilian into the hallway.

"It's fucking gone, Frank! They sank the *Hamilton*!"

"Let's go," he said, grabbing her wrist and pulling her away from the door.

She wrestled her arm away from DeMillo and sprinted past the panicked contractor. They were out of their minds. A swell of warm, muggy air enveloped her like a shroud when she stepped out of the climate-controlled building, instantly creating droplets of perspiration on her face and neck. Two men dressed in khaki pants and polo shirts stood around a telescope, one frantically adjusting the knobs; the other staring at the horizon with binoculars.

"Dan! What the hell happened?" she asked.

The overweight, balding man behind the scope turned to face her. "The *Hamilton* took off at full speed, zigzagging east. Anti-torpedo maneuver. Less than a minute later, we saw a massive geyser engulf the ship. When the spray cleared, the ship was in two pieces. Went down within seconds. Un-fucking believable. We need to get clear of this building ASAP," he said, picking up the telescope.

The second man lowered his binoculars.

"Dan?"

"What?"

"Do the Chinese have nuke-tipped SLCMs?"

"Of course they do," said Frank, walking briskly toward her.

"I don't think running will make any difference," he said, pointing toward the Pacific Ocean.

In the distance, a faintly visible smoke trail arced skyward, lazily tipping at the apex of its trajectory and disappearing. Quinn back-stepped toward the door, shielding her eyes from the sun while searching for the object. She found it. A small, gray dot at a forty-five-degree altitude above the horizon. One of the civilians pulled her across the grass, toward the western fence line. They had reached the corner of the two-story operations building when the fifteen-kiloton warhead attached to the DongHai 10 (DH-10) cruise missile detonated directly above Kwajalein Island.

EVENT +3 Days

Naval Base Kitsap-Bangor
Bangor, Washington

David Grant turned his passenger-burdened SUV left onto Sturgeon Street, still not sure what to make of the cars headed in the opposite direction. Whenever one of the "boomers" graced Delta Pier with a visit, every contractor at the naval base's Intermediate Maintenance Facility (IMF) flocked north to take advantage of the submarine's short stay. He recognized enough of the passing faces to guess that his group would soon join the exodus back to Building 7000.

"This isn't looking good," stated Bob Pearson from the passenger seat.

"No, it's not," muttered Grant.

He eased the vehicle onto Sea Lion Road, mindful of the men crammed into the back seat, and headed north along the eastern shore of Hood Canal. Through the dense underbrush and trees lining the road, he caught distant glimpses of the lush, emerald Toandos Peninsula. They passed two cars on the brief coastline stretch before the road turned sharply inland, leading to the Enclave.

Established several years ago as an independent security zone within the naval base, the Enclave featured an illuminated, double-layered, electrified fence that extended from the tip of Bangor Lake to the Explosive Handling Wharf north of Delta Pier. Protected by an elite battalion of Security Force Marines, access to the Enclave was firmly restricted to the submarine crew and authorized naval base support personnel—on a case-by-case basis. His carload of electrical engineers had been granted eight days to inspect and test critical circuits aboard USS *Maine* (SSBN 741), to confirm beyond a shadow of a doubt that the boat's $110-million-dollar EMP-hardening upgrade had been worth the money.

Three days into their assessment, Grant's team hadn't found any reason to suggest that the Ohio Class ballistic missile submarine was anything less than one hundred percent mission capable. Of course, he was still five long days away from putting his stamp of approval on the final report. The boat had been hooked to shore power while berthed at Delta Pier, and despite the somewhat limited effects of the EMP throughout the Pacific Northwest, he'd insisted on a full inspection. Equipment malfunctions several hundred feet below the ocean's surface tended to be catastrophic.

"She's gone! Slow down, Dave," said one of the men from the back seat.

Grant gently applied the brakes, pulling even with a break in the trees. *Son of a bitch.* Delta Pier's southwestern-facing berth was empty. He couldn't believe SUBPAC would put her to sea without finishing the inspections. His team was one of several dozen IMF crews scouring the submarine for evidence of EMP damage. Without a completed systems assessment, the admiral was taking a serious risk with a key strategic asset. The implications of SUBPAC's decision didn't escape him.

A car travelling in the opposite direction pulled even with his SUV, partially blocking their view. He recognized the driver—one of IMF's master electricians.

"Marines have the Enclave locked down. We're headed back to the shop."

"Did they say why?" asked Dave, instantly realizing the silliness of his question.

"They're not very talkative today—or any day."

"The boat's gone," said Dave, pointing past the car.

The car's occupants craned their heads toward the sliver of water between the trees. The electrician shook his head slowly and met Dave's eyes.

"They must have been in a hurry to get her out of the Sound."

"A big hurry," replied Dave.

EVENT +3 Days

USS GRAVELY (DDG 107)
Atlantic Ocean

Chief Fire Controlman Warren Jeffries visually confirmed the aft Vertical Launch System (VLS) status on the Combat Information Center's (CIC) Fire Control Systems screen, before sliding behind Petty Officer Clark's seat at the dedicated C2BMC (Command, Control, Battle Management and Communications) console. He rested both of his hands on the back of Clark's chair and leaned forward, watching the digital display for any changes to *Graveley*'s launch orders.

"Same as it's been for the past two hours, Chief," said Clark, "not that it matters on our end."

Chief Jeffries patted Clark's shoulder. "I know, but we can't fuck this up. This may be our only chance at payback."

Clark was referring to the fact that no buttons would be pushed in CIC to carry out the mission. They would continue to function as a Launch-On-Remote platform, controlled by the Missile Defense Agency. The only key difference between today and every other day *Gravely* spent assigned to the Homeland Ballistic Missile Defense (HBMD) mission was that the ship was plying through the Atlantic Ocean at twenty knots. Typically, they were tied securely to the dedicated BMD pier at Naval Station Norfolk—like the day of the "event."

He'd never forget the terror of reaching the flight deck and seeing the naval station in flames. Across the water, the city of Hampton burned fiercely, reflecting bright yellow off the churned-up water of Hampton Roads. Confusion reigned for the next several minutes as the engineering duty section tried to restore power to the drifting ship.

The thermal effects of the blast had burned the mooring lines, weakening them significantly for the inbound 117-mile-per-hour air blast recorded by the ship's anemometer. Without the lines to keep her in place, the prevailing winds and the tide pushed the 9,200-ton warship lazily into Hampton Roads, sending her toward the mouth of the James River. Tugboats from the naval station responded with fifteen minutes, barely in time to keep *Gravely* from hitting the southern Hampton Roads Beltway Tunnel entrance.

Most of the ship's EMP fail-safes rebooted by the time they nestled against Pier 14, restoring the critical mission systems that had been automatically disabled to save them. Once pierside, the crew spent the next ninety-three minutes frantically conducting underway checks. *Gravely* had orders to get underway at 0730, with whatever crew she could muster.

At 0729, with frantic family members lining the pier, *Gravely* sounded one prolonged blast, followed by three short blasts on the ship's horn as the gray ship backed into Hampton Roads with 182 of her 380 crewmembers. Most of the officers and senior enlisted personnel never arrived, including the captain.

After six days of steaming evasive patterns in an assigned patrol station east of Cape May, New Jersey, *Gravely* received a warning order preparing them for the remote launch of the ship's twenty modified antisatellite-capable SM-3 missiles. Jeffries' only mission in life for the past eight hours had been to ensure the successful launch of those missiles.

The orders contained no information regarding the missiles' targets, but enough information had surfaced since the event to suggest they would be used against satellites owned and operated by the People's Republic of China. Long-range, unencrypted transmissions between Russian Federation Space Agency stations and the International Space Station (ISS) indicated damage to the station consistent with the detonation of a thermonuclear weapon in Low Earth Orbit over the United States. Coincidentally, the Chinese Space Station (CSS) had changed orbital location three days prior to the event and was several hundred miles further away from the ISS than normal.

The crew was eager to connect the dots, and more than willing to launch the missiles. They had woken to a nightmare on Monday morning—left with the hellish image of their world on fire and no way to contact their families. The ship had set the strictest emissions-control conditions after cruising over the Chesapeake Bay Tunnel, eliminating all transmissions. *Gravely* was in receive-only mode, hidden from electronic observation until she fired her full complement of twenty Light Exo-

Atmospheric Projectiles (LEAPs) into orbit over the continental United States.

"Captain's in CIC!" yelled a sailor seated at a console near the entrance.

Lieutenant Commander Gayle Thompson rushed across CIC to the C2BMC console, bumping into the back of the first chair. Her eyes were several minutes away from making the adjustment between the bright sunlight of the ship's bridge and the catacomb-like darkness of the ship's nerve center. Thompson, previously the Combat Systems Officer, had been the senior officer present onboard *Gravely* when they got underway, designating her the ship's acting commanding officer.

"How are we looking, Chief?" she said, sounding out of breath.

"Green lights across the board, ma'am. As long as the ship doesn't sink in the next few seconds, we'll get some payback," said Jeffries.

"Don't say that," she said.

"About the payback?"

"The other part. The C2 link is working?"

"It's transmitting the countdown time and all of the launch data. I've been watching it like a hawk. We've got this one, ma'am. Go watch over the new ensigns on the bridge."

"I feel like they're keeping an eye on me. I've spent my last three years down here."

"Lieutenant Mosely's keeping us out of trouble," said Jeffries.

"Barely," grumbled Mosely. "Skylight One-One is still downloading surface tracks. All clear. No maritime bands on the 'Slick 32' or contacts of interest detected by

TACTAS (Tactical Towed-Array Sonar)."

"Nothing coming into the Delaware Channel?" Thompson asked.

"Nothing, ma'am. We would have picked up any commercial radar transmissions."

"Hard to believe nothing's heading in to Philly," Jeffries remarked.

"Eerie. TAO, I'm headed back to the bridge. I'd like a countdown over the 1MC. The crew needs to know that their nation is back in the fight," said Thompson.

"Excellent, ma'am," said Mosely, nodding in their direction.

"Captain's out of CIC!" Jeffries heard, followed by the thunk of the hatch closing.

"Chief, you want to do the honors?" asked Lieutenant Mosely.

"Negative, sir. I need to keep an eye on this. It's all you."

"Roger that, Chief. T-minus seventy seconds. Look alive," he said to the half-manned CIC.

The ship-wide countdown proceeded smoothly according to the time provided by Missile Defense Agency data. At zero, Jeffries detected a slight tremor, which was quickly swallowed by the normal vibrations felt on a warship plying through the water. He turned to watch the Aegis System Display screen at the front of CIC, which showed a live closed-circuit camera image of the rear VLS cells. One hatch after another sprang open, belching fire thirty feet into the air and boosting one of the SM-3 missiles skyward. Cheers filled CIC as the last missile left its canister.

EVENT +3 Days

ISS Mission Control, Russian Federal Space Agency Korolev, Russian Federation

Alexei Belenkin barked at the mission control specialists before returning the phone to his ear.

"Damn it, we need more warning than this!" he said.

"This is all the warning you get!" insisted the Aerospace Defense Force general.

"We can't execute a Debris Avoidance Maneuver with the push of a button. This has to be planned carefully! We're not playing a fucking video game here!"

"I know how rocket boosters work, Doctor Belenkin! I spent most of my career in the Strategic Rocket Forces. You press a button, and they launch!"

"It's not that simple," stated Belenkin.

"Well, simplify the procedure, or risk losing the station. You need to move the ISS as far out of its current orbit as practical."

"I'm not getting any warnings about orbital debris from our sensors, General. This is too radical of an order—even from you."

"In about sixty-four seconds, Low Earth Orbit may very well become uninhabitable. I have no official authority over you, Doctor. This is a courtesy call before I contact Moscow. By the time they call to issue the order, it may be too late. Do what you need to do."

"Can you at least tell me what we're dealing with?"

"You scientists always need a damn explanation."

"We don't follow orders blindly, General."

"Satellite early warning systems detected one hundred twenty sea-based missile launches fitting anti-satellite trajectory profiles. Ground-based space-tracking radars indicate sudden, drastic changes to U.S. military satellite orbits. Our best guess is they're going for every Chinese satellite in Low Earth Orbit while trying to save their own. Good luck," said the general, leaving Belenkin holding a disconnected line.

"Mother of Russia," muttered Belenkin, placing the phone in its cradle.

If the Americans hit the Chinese satellites, they would instantly create hundreds of thousands of pieces of debris, effectively rendering portions of Low Earth Orbit (LEO) completely uninhabitable to satellites and manned space missions. The debris from the Chinese satellites, located at different altitudes and orbital planes, would eventually strike other satellites, triggering the Kessler Syndrome, which would pulverize everything in that orbital range. Navigating in Low Earth Orbit could become hazardous to the point of impossible, with millions of pieces travelling in unpredictable directions at relative speeds in excess of 20,000 kilometers per hour. He wasn't sure there was any point to moving the station. They would have no way to reach it again.

"Alexei! What are your orders?"

He thought about the situation for a few seconds. They had to try to save the abandoned station.

"Boost the station as high as possible for now. We need to get her out of the busiest orbital altitudes—immediately."

Ian Kharitonov, senior mission orbital specialist, turned to his section of personnel and nodded.

"Do it!" he said, scattering the men and women to their control stations.

Belenkin watched the screens for the next several

seconds, waiting to see the mission parameters change. Kharitonov turned his head from his monitor.

"Secondary thrusters on Zvezda Service Module activated. Maneuvering the station into position for primary thruster activation."

"Thank you, Ian," Belenkin said, staring with disbelief at the overhead screens.

"Alexei, what the hell happened?"

"I think the Americans just started World War III."

Part I

"Reassess"

Chapter 1

EVENT +5 Days

Limerick, Maine

Jeffrey Brown steadied his hands on a thick branch and surveyed Old Middle Road with powerful binoculars. Sitting in a climber's harness fifty feet above the ground, he could simultaneously watch the entrance to Gelder Pond and observe several hundred yards of road in either direction. His view through the leaves and branches was far from perfect—but clear lines of sight worked both ways. Since it was practically impossible to identify passengers inside the tactical vehicles, he saw no reason to risk detection by selecting a more exposed site. His job was simple. Estimate enemy troop strength at the compound and identify exploitable patterns. He didn't need an unobstructed view to accomplish that mission.

A low rumbling drew his attention west, his magnified view of the road competing with wavering green foliage. He spotted the rising dust trail before the vehicles—two fast-moving tactical vehicles, tan camouflage pattern, full turret configuration.

Son of a bitch.

Brown watched as they approached, hoping they would continue toward Limerick. A random military patrol didn't represent a showstopper. He wasn't surprised when they veered onto Gelder Pond Lane, tires screeching.

Scratch Eli's plan.

He pressed the remote transmit button attached to his tactical vest. "Relay One, this is Overwatch. SPOTREP. Two Matvees approached from the west and turned into compound. Estimated enemy strength at compound follows. Three, possibly four Matvees with turret-mounted weapons. Possible addition of squad-sized unit. Maximum of twelve. Minimum of six based on previous observations. Number of personnel at compound estimated at eighteen. Overwatch remains unobserved. How copy? Over."

A short delay preceded the next station's recitation of his report. They must be writing his words down verbatim. Finally. Their first few attempts at repeating his top-of-the-hour reports had been abysmal. He shuddered to think what might reach Eli's ears after passing through four or five relay stations.

"Solid copy, Relay One. Send the message. Out."

Brown lifted himself by the anchor lines and shifted in his harness, finding a slightly less uncomfortable position. He unconsciously glanced at his watch and shook his head. 0722. Fourteen hours until he climbed down and occupied OP Bravo for the night. A long fourteen hours. Leaning into the tree, he closed his eyes and took a few deep breaths—listening. A few minutes later, the familiar throttling of a diesel engine echoed through the trees. One of the tactical vehicles sped into sight and skidded onto Old Middle Road, heading for Limerick.

Interesting.

Chapter 2

EVENT +5 Days

Sanford, Maine

"Jackson, I need you down from the turret," said Alex.

He'd visited Harrison Campbell's farm twice while writing an informational piece about the York County Readiness Brigade. Once to formally interview selected militia leadership, the second time to attend one of the organization's public potluck dinners. He remembered that the main house and barn sat close to a quarter mile back from the road, hidden by a deep stretch of pine trees.

"Stop in front of the mailbox, but stay off the property. I'll walk it in from the fence."

"Walk it where?"

"Past those trees," said Alex.

The Matvee stopped in front of a deeply rutted dirt lane. Gently winding around a cattail-infested pond, the road disappeared into a dark stand of pines. He had no doubt they were watching his vehicle from a concealed position in the distant forest scrub.

"I don't know, sir. You're awfully exposed on the approach. Once you get in the trees, we can't do shit for you."

"I'll be fine. These are the good guys."

"You willing to bet your life on that, sir?"

He considered the marine's question, before grabbing the door handle. Deeper examination of Homeland's Recovery Zone protocols reinforced the critical importance of partnering with Campbell's organization. Failure to secure the brigade's cooperation could lead to severe consequences for the people of southern Maine—his family included.

"I don't have a choice. Grady needs these people on his side before Homeland starts calling the shots."

"I'll park this rig across the street, pointing *that* way," said Corporal Lianez, nodding toward the forest. "Say the word, and we roll up guns blazing."

"I'll send regular updates. Every ten minutes or so. If you don't hear from me and I don't respond to your call—guns blazing," Alex said, stepping out of the vehicle.

"Sounds like a plan. Sir, you forgot your rifle!" yelled Lianez.

"I won't need it," he said, shutting the door on the marine's continued protest.

His earpiece crackled.

"Sir, you cannot—"

"Lianez, Jackson, radio check. Over."

"This is Jackson. Lima Charlie. Lianez. Lima Charlie. Captain, I need you to take—"

"Keep the channel clear for further instructions. Out," Alex said, walking briskly down the dirt road.

He could feel Lianez pounding the steering wheel behind him but didn't turn to confirm it. Leaving a rifle behind ranked just below gut-punching your own mother on a Marine's exhaustive list of rules and conventions. Purposefully walking into an unknown situation without your rifle wasn't even on that list—it hovered in the gray area between negligent and insane.

In this case, Captain Fletcher made a one-time exception to the rule. Ditching the rifle was a calculated act. Combined with the Matvee visibly idling across the street, he sent a not-so-subtle message to Harrison Campbell: *I come in peace, but retain the ability to wreck your shit at a moment's notice.* Diplomacy—with the threat of violence.

Roughly fifty paces into the forest, he started to question Campbell's security measures. He hadn't expected a guard post at the fence along the main road, but allowing him to get this close to their headquarters seemed a little careless.

"Hands above your head!" yelled a female voice from his right.

A woman dressed in woodland camouflage appeared from a concealed position behind a fallen tree, pointing an AR-15-style rifle at his head. He detected movement on the left side of the road. Purposeful, no doubt. Just to let him know that she wasn't alone.

"You and your friend know this is private property?" she asked.

"Yes, ma'am. We have no intention of violating your rights."

"But here you are—with a firearm."

"Goes with the territory. I need to speak with Harrison Campbell. I didn't see any other way to get in touch."

"Who are you, exactly?"

"Captain Alex Fletcher. United States Marine Corps. I've met with Harrison before, in a different capacity."

"I didn't realize the Marines were authorized to wear

jeans and a T-shirt under their body armor," she said.

"I'm not part of the regular Marine Corps. Something *very* different. Something Mr. Campbell needs to hear about immediately."

"You said Alex Fletcher? Captain?" she said, shifting her nonfiring hand to a radio mounted on her vest.

"Provisional Captain. Regional Recovery Zone One."

"Regional what?"

"Regional Recovery Zone One, formerly known as the state of Maine. Pass that along."

After a hushed conversation, punctuated by distrusting looks, the woman lowered her rifle.

"You're cleared to approach the gate. Gary will escort you to the barn," she stated.

He waited several seconds for another sentry to materialize from the landscape. The severe-looking woman stared at him impassively.

"Where's Gary?"

"At the gate. Follow the yellow brick road," she said, pointing deeper in the forest.

"Right," he said, frowning. "You're not going to take my pistol?"

"Harrison says you're legit. That's all I need to hear—Captain. I'd keep it in your holster, though."

"Thanks for the sage advice—Miss?"

"Nunya."

"Nunya?"

"Nunya business."

"Ex-military?"

"Ex-husbands."

"Fair enough. Make sure your team doesn't glass my Marines. They're a little edgy."

"I'll keep that in mind," she said.

Alex reported his progress to Lianez and hiked around a shallow turn, running into the headquarters' primary security barrier. Chest-high timber bunkers flanked the dirt road, supporting a metal gate constructed of three-inch-thick welded galvanized pipes. A strip of road spikes lay across the road thirty feet ahead of the gate. A tall, bearded man in camouflage stepped around the rightmost bunker. He slung his rifle and extended a hand.

"Gary Powers. Brigade training officer."

He gladly accepted the friendly gesture. "Alex Fletcher. My job is a little hard to explain."

"Sounds like it. I'll be right back, Danny," he said to someone out of sight.

"I'll be here," replied a voice from the second bunker.

"How is the brigade holding up so far?" Alex asked.

"Better than expected given the scope of the disaster. The coastal chapters were hit hard. Not much we can do east of the 95. It's still too early to figure out exactly where we can fit into the bigger scheme of things. Right now, we're running basic supplies to an empty storefront in downtown Sanford, waiting for the mayor's office to kick off a countywide relief effort," Powers said, raising an eyebrow.

"You don't sound convinced," said Alex.

"It's too big in scope, and it's eating up our reserves. We've spent the past four years promising people localized support, by chapter."

"But you're the York County Readiness Brigade," said Alex.

"Which is why we can't turn down the mayor's request for help."

"I'm sure he's well aware of that."

"More than you know. Our history in the county has

seen its share of ups and downs. Greg Hoode has been good to us, so it's time to return the favor. Unfortunately, the brigade's stockpile is suited for a short-term crisis—even shorter with half of it going to the mayor."

"Harrison didn't anticipate an EMP attack coupled with a tsunami?"

Powers laughed. "Probably my fault as training officer, right?" His brief moment of levity settled into a distant stare. "Harrison painted some pretty rosy pictures during our public suppers. Picturesque fields filled with families living in quaint tents. Everyone chasing butterflies and cooking over campfires. Temporarily. When the families start showing up—and they will show up—I'm not sure what we can do for them in the long run. Two months from now, every wood-burning stove in New England will be running full time to beat the cold. I'm not optimistic about our future here once the snow starts falling."

"I might be able to help out with that, but it's going to take a leap of faith. Even then, I don't know," said Alex.

"Regional Recovery Zone?" said Powers.

"See if you can get someone to fill in for you at the gate. You'll want to hear what I have to say."

"We're a little shorthanded at headquarters. Everyone's pulling guard duty. Even Harrison," he said.

"Trust me, this affects you just as much as Harrison."

Powers nodded as they broke out of the woods, radioing the request ahead of their arrival. The red, two-story barn dwarfed the gray Cape Cod-style home hidden under a canopy of mature elms. An armed sentry sat in a chair on the porch, searching the tree line behind them with binoculars. They followed the dirt road around the house and past a second guard, who eyed them warily before jogging toward the forest. Three cars sat against the far edge of a dirt parking lot, next to the barn.

"Harrison's expecting us inside. You've been here before?"

"Twice. I wrote an article for *New England Magazine* a few years ago, which featured aspects of the brigade. I also did a couple of blog articles focused on militia groups. I interviewed Harrison, Glen Cuskelly and Kevin McCulver."

"I took over McCulver's position a year and a half ago," said Powers.

"Is he still with the brigade?" Alex asked.

"No. He, uh—"

"He liked to play with explosives, and we don't put up with that kind of nonsense," interrupted Harrison Campbell from the doorway. "Gary steered the training cadre back on the right path. Made a ton of improvements on top of that. Good to see you again, Alex, or should I address you as captain?" he said, shaking Alex's hand.

"Still Alex."

"You might want to pick one uniform and stick with it. It's less confusing that way," said Campbell, looking him up and down.

"I'm hoping to straddle the fence as long as possible," said Alex.

"Stay on that fence too long, and someone will pull you down on the wrong side."

Powers closed the door behind them, drawing Glen Cuskelly's attention away from one of the maps on the wall. Campbell led them to the makeshift operations center in the far right corner of the barn, beyond the rough-cut wooden benches.

"We just brewed a fresh pot of coffee. You look like you could use a cup—or two," said Campbell.

"I'm past the point where coffee will make a difference, but I'll take you up on the offer."

"You remember Glen."

"Of course," said Alex, nodding at the solemn-faced former artillery officer.

"So, what can we do for Captain Fletcher?" said Campbell, grabbing the coffee pot and an extra mug.

"I'll get to that in a minute. First, I need to warn you about something. Long story short, there's a rogue militia unit running around southern Maine. Eventually, you're gonna run into them."

"Eli Russell's group?" asked Campbell.

"You know about him?"

"He killed our Limerick deputy. Massacred the whole family."

"Jesus. I'm sorry."

"How did you find out about him?" asked Cuskelly.

"He tried to kill my family. Attacked my house in Limerick with a platoon-sized force."

"Limerick?" asked Campbell.

"My parents live on Gelder Pond. That was our bug-out plan. Now it's filled with several hundred bullet holes."

"How's your family?"

"They're fine, but barely."

"Thank God for that. And Eli?"

"He escaped with maybe a dozen men. Paid a heavy price for the attack. Twenty-nine KIA."

"Twenty-nine? What the hell did you have at the house, a platoon of Marines?" said Powers.

"We were ready for them. The Marines showed up

after most of Eli's crew was dead or wounded. Those fuckers brought a Browning M1919A6. In good working order, too. I put that out of action first."

"He used to show that thing off when he was part of the brigade. I'm not sure when he acquired it, but I guarantee it wasn't a legal transaction," said Campbell.

"Well, it's mine now. I have it covering a 180-degree arc in front of my house."

Powers looked puzzled. "Why the hell would he attack you?"

"We'll get into that. Why didn't anyone mention his group during our interviews?"

Cuskelly winced. "That was my call. I didn't want to draw any more negative attention to the word 'militia' in southern Maine. We had just spent the better part of a year culling the ranks. All part of rebuilding our image."

"And putting the brigade back on the right path," Campbell added. "It wasn't a PR stunt."

"Either way, Eli was one of the first to go, and he wasted no time putting together his own crew. We basically fed him recruits for a year."

Campbell poured Alex a cup of coffee.

"We still do. Anyone we turn down, he welcomes with open arms, including felons. The Maine Liberty Militia ranks swelled with jailbirds after Eli's youngest brother was released from the state."

"Fuck me. Another Russell to worry about?" said Alex, waving off a sugar packet.

"Nope. Jimmy got served an epic portion of karma a few days ago. One of my scouting teams found him dead at the Milton Mills Bridge, along with most of his platoon. Ambushed, from what I could tell."

Alex froze, the hot coffee burning his tongue. After a

long swallow, he cleared his throat. "I led the group that killed those men."

Cuskelly tensed, signaling a mood shift at the table. Alex detected it immediately, belatedly recognizing the implications of his statement.

"Why would you be hunting down militia less than a day after the event?" asked Campbell.

"It's not like that. My son is a freshman—*was* a freshman—at Boston University. My neighbor's daughter was at Boston College, and his jeep survived the EMP. We teamed up with a third neighbor to drive down and get the kids back. The turnpike was blocked by the military, so we traced the border until we arrived at Milton Mills. They refused to let us pass, so we shot our way through."

Campbell didn't look convinced. "Then how did you end up as *Captain* Fletcher? Last time we spoke, you were out of the Marine Corps."

"I was, but circumstances in Boston led to my appointment as a provisional captain," he said, pulling the badge out of his vest and handing it to Campbell.

"Date of issue 21AUG2019. Captain (PROV). 1st BTN, 25TH," Campbell read. "The reserve battalion out of Devens?"

"The same. Half of the battalion was at Devens for summer training when the EMP hit. They received orders to draw gear and head to Boston. The commanding officer was one of my platoon commanders in Iraq. Wounded by the same RPG that put me in a level-five treatment facility for three months. He offered me a provisional appointment because the battalion is short on militia group analysts. Ever hear of a group called the Liberty Boys?"

"If I recall, they appeared at the outset of the Revolutionary War. Sort of a colonial intelligence network."

"Apparently, they never went away. Homeland had extensive files on the Liberty Boys, right down to existing members within the reserve battalion. They were detained immediately after the EMP. How long has Eli's group operated?"

"A few years. Maybe less," said Campbell.

"Homeland doesn't have anything on his group. Eli is listed as former York County Militia."

"Eli flies below the radar. Everything's word of mouth," said Powers.

"Do they have files on us?" Campbell asked.

Alex nodded slowly.

"Homeland's been spying on us all along. Those lying sacks of shit," uttered Campbell.

"Probably have someone on the inside," said Powers.

"I don't think so," Alex said. "They'd have a file on Eli Russell's crew if they had an inside man."

"Says Mr. Homeland," stated Campbell. "It's time to ask the million-dollar question. Why are you really here?"

"I need your help. Lieutenant Colonel Sean Grady, commanding officer of 1st Battalion, 25th Marine Infantry Regiment, is coming to Maine, ahead of thousands of soldiers, airmen, relief workers, FEMA crews and Homeland bureaucrats. Here's the deal, Grady's problem with the Liberty Boys in Boston escalated out of control. Trust in the government is at an all-time low, compounded by the fact that nobody really knows what happened Monday morning."

"Or nobody is telling us," said Randy.

"Fair enough. Colonel Grady's battalion is tasked to

provide security for recovery operations in York County."

"Security for who?"

"Primary focus will be on Recovery Zone assets, which include assigned personnel, infrastructure, essential equipment."

"Military units operating on U.S. soil? I don't like it," said Powers.

"Nobody does, which is why I'm asking for your help. People trust the brigade, if you—"

"I can't in good conscience support a blatant violation of the Insurrection Act," said Campbell.

"Congress legally modified it with the 2015 Defense Authorization Bill," said Alex.

"I don't care what those fucking idiots did. They jammed that down our throats when nobody was looking. Supporting a military security apparatus in York County won't sit well with the people. Everybody knows where we stand on this," said Campbell.

"Which is why they will listen when you cautiously accept the invitation to integrate some of your members with my provisional security team."

"I think you need to catch up on some sleep, Mr. Fletcher. I can't ask my people to accompany Homeland security patrols. Helping out local law enforcement and Maine guard units is slippery enough," stated Campbell.

"I completely understand what you're saying, but you're not seeing the big picture. I've been to Boston and back. Grade A clusterfuck across the board. Everybody is headed north—right now. Here's *our* problem. The primary Recovery Zone plan holds most of these refugees south of the New Hampshire border."

"Sounds like a benefit," said Powers.

"Only if the primary RZ remains viable, from a

security standpoint. The alternate plan eliminates the southern Security Area and establishes the Saco River as the new Security Area border, extending west to New Hampshire."

"What happens to southern Maine in the second scenario?" asked Cuskelly.

"It becomes one big refugee camp."

"And Colonel Grady's mission?" Campbell queried.

"Moved north of the Saco River."

"The people?"

Alex shook his head. "They get to contend with a million-plus refugees looking for food and shelter at the outset of a long New England winter. If the primary RZ is dismantled, I'm packing up and heading north with my golden ticket," Alex said, holding up his badge. "Without one of these, you'll be reclassified as a refugee. We have to make a partnership work."

He let the personal ramifications sink in before continuing.

"Homeland is coming. Nothing can change that. As insane as this may sound, we need to do everything in our power to keep them here. If they pack up and head north, the only thing separating you and your families from millions of desperate New Englanders will be the rifle in your hands."

Campbell stared at him for an uncomfortable length of time. If he refused, the follow-up conversation promised to be twice as painful. Alex would have to secure Campbell's promise that the brigade would remain neutral throughout the Recovery Zone, in both action and word. Then he'd have to sell the value of that promise to Lieutenant Colonel Grady, who ultimately decided the brigade's fate. Based on Grady's experience in Boston,

Alex wasn't optimistic about a friendly handshake solution.

"What do you need from us?" Campbell asked.

"Not much—for now. The first order of business is Milton Mills. My guess is the bridge is still open for business."

"It is, but the dead bodies have kept traffic to a minimum."

"Let's reinstate the checkpoint at Milton Mills. Six on each bridge at all times. I'll provide a tactical vehicle, four Marines, food, shelter and communications. You provide the rest. I'll set the ROE, which will be strict. The security detail will withdraw if fired upon. Agreed?"

"We're stretched pretty thin. Dave Littner has most of the Berwick chapter stationed at the major law enforcement checkpoints south of Route 202."

"Have Littner redeploy all of his assets to Milton Mills."

"That's a lot more than you requested," said Cuskelly.

"There's a reason. I need a reputable third party to investigate a possible mass murder at the church on Foxes Ridge Road. Eli's brother was running some kind of scam, where he let people across the border and stole their cars. I found a dozen or more cars with out-of-state plates in the church parking lot. The classrooms behind the chapel were stuffed with luggage and personal effects. I don't think any of the travelers made it past the church. Have Littner's people search the woods and document everything they find."

"What happened to Jimmy's crew at the church?"

"I put an end to their operation."

"Just you and a few neighbors?" said Campbell, cocking his head slightly.

"They weren't expecting trouble from this side of the border, and we got lucky."

"You're gonna have to deal with Eli at some point. He's been travelling from town to town, spreading rumors about government assassination teams and the impending Homeland takeover. The people are starting to listen."

"Then we need to shut him down immediately," said Alex.

Cuskelly nodded. "We know where to find him."

"He's not in Parsonsfield," Alex said. "The trailer and barn burned to the ground yesterday. Probably right after the attack on my house. He's not at his house in Waterboro either. We checked."

"I doubt he'll show up for any more town hall meetings either. I'll put the word out to my network, in case he slips up and makes a public appearance," Campbell promised. "My guess is he'll lay low for a while. If we're lucky, he'll try to kill you again."

"What does unlucky look like?"

"He starts blowing shit up. Fomenting an insurgency—"

"And still tries to kill you," added Cuskelly.

"Option number one sounds marginally better," said Alex.

"Either way," Campbell said, "he won't stop until you're dead."

"Then we'll have to work together to make sure that doesn't happen. The assassination of a key provisional Recovery Zone security officer won't sit well with Lieutenant Colonel Grady."

"I assume you'll need more than a border checkpoint and some scattered intelligence on Eli Russell?"

"A few more things," answered Alex, taking a long sip of coffee.

Chapter 3

EVENT +5 Days

Bridgton, Maine

Welcome to Bridgton, The Maine Place for All Seasons. Incorporated 1794.

Eli Russell twisted his body in the front passenger seat and eased the .45 Colt Commander out of his hip holster.

Welcome indeed.

"Gentlemen, let's pass all of the rifles back, keeping them low. Safeties engaged. Magazines removed. We want the rifles in plain sight within the rear storage compartment. Gotta be a checkpoint up here somewhere."

"You want us to clear the rifles?"

"Negative. Keep the first rounds chambered, in case we need to put them into action pronto-like."

"What about the pistols?" asked one of the men in the back seat.

"Keep them in their holsters. They won't fuck with us for carrying pistols."

"It's illegal to transport a loaded firearm without a concealed carry permit," said the man.

"Thanks for the gun law update, mister helper. You want to shut up and let me run the show?"

"Yes, sir."

"Good. If you haven't noticed, there's a bit of a different situation going on nowadays, something to do with a fucking EMP attack! Keep your hands where they can see them, and don't say a word unless asked a question. They'll be glad to see responsible folks like us helping out," said Eli, passing his rifle between the seats.

The turn straightened onto a long stretch of tree-flanked road, revealing the roadblock. A few hundred feet ahead, an oversized pickup truck and a white police car blocked both lanes of Route 93, squeezed between two guardrails. The cruiser's blue strobe lights started flashing.

"Slow us down a little more," Eli said, tracking their approach to the roadblock.

"I don't know about this," said his driver nervously.

"We'll be fine, Griz. I may ask you to vouch for me."

"I can do that."

John Barry, aka "Grizzly," had eagerly joined his organization after the town hall meeting in Limerick. He'd led Eli to Ken Haskell, who'd been more than happy to play a role in keeping Limerick safe from government assassination teams. Haskell had identified one of the young women riding in Nathan Russell's silver BMW SUV. "One of the Fletcher kids or something like that. They live out on Gelder Pond." Less than an hour later, "Deputy" Eli Russell and Jeffrey Brown had paid the Fletchers a little visit, scoping out their compound.

Grizzly followed the police officer's hand signals, easing the car to a stop about twenty feet in front of the blockade. Two men dressed in civilian clothes and tactical gear shuffled between the vehicles, approaching Eli's SUV with rifles aimed into the cabin. The police officer trailed them by several feet, keeping his pistol pointed at

Eli through the windshield. A fourth shooter stood behind the pickup truck's hood, aiming a bipod-supported, optics-equipped assault rifle at them. Eli hated feeling this helpless, but it was the only way to gain enough trust to talk his way into town. The riflemen split up, drawing even with the front doors and covering the men in the SUV.

"No sudden movements," whispered Eli.

The police officer approached Eli from an oblique angle, partially obscured from his sight by the doorframe.

"Shut the car down! Hands out of the vehicle!"

"Boys. Hands out the windows. Slowly," said Eli.

He nodded at Grizzly before turning his body far enough to rest his hands, palms up, on the top of the doorframe.

"This is a no-fucking-around situation, gentlemen. If you move your hands, you're dead. Understand?"

"Yes, sir," said Eli.

Once the men in the SUV settled, the riflemen closed the distance, peering deeper into the vehicle.

"I have four military-style rifles in the cargo compartment. I see at least one shoulder holster!" yelled the rifleman on the driver's side of the vehicle.

"You have about five seconds to explain why you were driving into town with this shit," said the police officer.

"My name is Eli Russell, and I'm the founder of the Maine Liberty Militia."

"Never heard of it," replied the officer.

"We're based out of York County."

"You're coming from the wrong direction."

"We were just up in Lovell, warning them about the government takeover down south."

"Why do you need military-style hardware to spread the word?" asked the rifleman, waving his AR at the back of the SUV.

"In case we're attacked. The government has been killing local law enforcement and militia members down south, softening the area for whatever they have planned. We've lost over forty men since the supposed EMP. I put the rifles in back because I didn't want to alarm you."

"We haven't heard about any attacks down south," said the officer.

"It doesn't surprise me. York County sheriff's deputies started to disappear right after the EMP. Mostly the ones under contract with the small townships. The state police and regular departments seem fine, but something fishy is definitely happening in the rural areas. Checkpoints like this along the border have been wiped out. I was personally asked by the state police to send my people to one of the more obscure border crossings. None of them returned."

"What happened?" asked the rifleman.

"They were killed in Milton Mills, right on the New Hampshire border. I lost twelve men, including my brother. I recognized the tactics from my time as a military advisor in Central America in the '80s. We tracked down the government black ops team to a small lakeside property in Limerick. I lost twenty-nine men trying to take that house. They had it fortified with light machine guns and sandbag bunkers inside."

"If I raise the York County Sheriff's Department on the radio, can they verify any of this?"

"I would hope so. Just be careful about identifying yourself. You never know who's listening,

Officer...Hoyt," Eli said, reading the policeman's name badge.

"I want all of you out of the car while I make the call. Leave your pistols on your seats," he said, turning to the rifleman next to him. "Verify they're unarmed and sit them in front of the SUV. Hands on their heads."

Fifty minutes later, Eli's arms shook with fatigue as he held on to the last vestige of a forced neutral expression. He'd imagined killing both of them so many times over the past hour that he'd exhausted his mental inventory of gruesomely painful deaths. Not an easy feat given the vast amount of time he dedicated to visualizing novel ways to torture and kill people. It had become sort of a game for him. He'd see a woman buying cigarettes at the gas station and picture burning her to a crisp with a can of hairspray and a lighter. Teenager gives him a dirty look at the Foodmart and winds up a discarded pile of body parts on the cellar floor next to Eli's table saw. It was harmless entertainment. For now.

Officer Hoyt stepped out of his cruiser and walked up to Eli. "You can lower your hands. The guys up in Lovell said you made a good impression, and I ran your scenario through the Cumberland County Sheriff's Department. A state police bulletin was passed two days ago warning departments about targeted violence against rural deputies. Source of that information was the York County Sheriff's Department. This is the kind of information we need at the local level," grumbled the officer.

"That's why I'm making the rounds. Nobody has heard about this, and it's only a matter of time before the violence spreads north," said Eli, noticing a slight relaxation in the guards' postures.

"State police were a little tight-lipped about your border massacre claim, but county dispatch picked up a request for a mobile crime scene unit. Destination, Milton Mills. Sorry about your brother," he said.

The guard slung his rifle and stepped forward, extending a hand.

"Ron Bevins. Chief selectman for the Town of Bridgton. Sorry about the crappy treatment, but we've had some problems with people travelling through town."

Eli took his hand and used it to rise up on his unsteady legs. "I understand. Trust but verify. Didn't Reagan say that?"

"He did," said Bevins, helping the rest of Eli's crew to their feet. "So, what can we do for you? I'm afraid the town is a little overwhelmed right now. We're about triple our normal population due to the summer crowd."

"I might be able to help you with that. I assume most of those folks have no way to get home?"

"The ones with working vehicles took off right after it happened. Some hiked it out. The grocery stores and restaurants have been picked clean. We're on borrowed time before things start breaking down."

"It's already starting," said Officer Hoyt. "We won't have patrol officers at these roadblocks next week."

Eli fought to suppress the grin pulling at his facial muscles. He was looking at a textbook coup d'état opportunity. An entire town under his control if he played it right.

"Here's what I'm thinking. I can give you some well-trained, trustworthy men to help man the roadblocks. Free up a few of your police officers. We'd keep my people on the periphery of town so they don't spook anyone. Militia is still kind of a dirty word for a lot of folks."

"It would be a big help," said Officer Hoyt, looking at Bevins.

"I can see something like this passing muster with the rest of the selectmen, as long as your men stay out of town. You're right about people being a little worried about militia."

"Lots of folks still see us as mutant biker zombies. Mad Max types. We'll work under the direct supervision of your roadblock crews, staying on the outskirts of town. If you need us to do more, we can talk about that later. There's only one favor I would ask of you."

"Sure," said Bevins.

"Would you be willing to schedule one town hall meeting for me to address the people? I'm not going to bullshit you. I'm looking for recruits. It's a good gig for anyone with previous law enforcement or military experience. All I need is fifteen minutes to address whoever shows up. I'll come unarmed, dressed however you'd like."

"I don't want you panicking the town," said Bevins.

"I'll keep the York County stories to myself. Scaring people into joining the militia isn't the best way to go about business. I'll tell them what we do, leaving out the part about staffing the checkpoints."

"It's probably not a bad idea to have some trained folks at the checkpoints, especially if the patrol officers are needed elsewhere. How long can your people stay?"

"As long as they're needed. If I get enough volunteers from town, I can run a two-week training course and give some of them back. Might give you the boost you need to cover any inbound routes you're missing."

"We have a few smaller roads on the other side of Highland Lake that don't get much traffic," said Bevins.

"I'd like to put someone on Sam Ingalls Road, west of here. People crossing the border from New Hampshire are bound to find that road eventually. Same with King Hills down south. We have seven checkpoints, all staffed twenty-four hours a day by at least one member of the department. This would be a big help, Ron," said Officer Hoyt. "If Mr. Russell can get his people here later today or tomorrow, they could work with our officers at each checkpoint for a few days. Sort of a trial period."

"You give me the thumbs-up, and I'll have ten men here in a few hours."

"We'll have to run it by the chief. He'll have some reservations."

"I understand his position. Tell him my men can start out unarmed until he's comfortable with them. Let's say three men. If it works out, we can expand the program. Baby steps, gentlemen. I get it."

"I'll take this back to the chief and the rest of the selectmen," said Bevins. "Do you want to come back around five? Give us some time to work this out?"

"If you don't mind, we'll wait. That way, if your chief has any questions, we're not far away. We'd planned to be out all day. Got some MREs and plenty of water."

"Sounds good," said Bevins. "I'll be back."

"No hurry," said Eli, turning to Officer Hoyt. "I'll pull the car back to the town line so we don't interfere with your duties. If you need us, just flash the high beams."

"Will do," said Hoyt, turning to walk to his patrol car.

The man with the bipod-equipped rifle lifted the weapon off the pickup truck's hood and made room for Ron Bevins and Officer Hoyt. He kept the sight fixed on

Eli as the pickup truck's engine roared.

Trust but verify.

Chapter 4

EVENT +5 Days

Sanford, Maine

Alex searched the trees on the left side of the deserted two-lane road for signs of the airport's boundary fence. He used to drive into Sanford using this route when he worked in pharmaceutical sales, and remembered that the tree line opened to a massive, flat expanse of land containing Sanford Seacoast Regional Airport. The airport had never impressed him, just another stop for Cessna-type aircraft or maybe something a little bigger. He'd been surprised to learn that the airport had a reinforced 6,300-foot runway, suitable for use by a United States Air Force C-17B (Globemaster III) military transport aircraft. The runway had been hardened in 2016, using federal grants.

Uncle Sam has been busy since the Jakarta Pandemic.

The forest thinned, yielding a vast, sun-browned field of low-cut scrub grasses separated from the road by a barb-wire-topped, chain-link fence. Not much standing between the public and the airfield. Alex imagined that Maine's 133rd Engineering Battalion had a few upgrades planned for the perimeter—especially given Regional Recovery Zone security protocols. He had spent most of the night on the battalion's SIPRNet (Secret Internet Protocol Routing Network) connection, digging through the hundreds of classified documents in an attempt to understand the scope and impact of the RRZ's deployment to southern Maine.

The picture was complicated, but one thing became crystal clear. Once the president of the United States activated the National Recovery Plan, you wanted to be *inside* one of the RRZ security zones—for reasons he tried to impress on Harrison Campbell. You especially didn't want to end up in one of the FEMA camps outside the RRZ. The documents painted a rosy picture of the United States' "upgraded" capacity to implement and administer a sprawling system of refugee camps, but time and time again, history proved otherwise. Alex intended to do everything in his power to keep his family and friends inside the security zone.

They drove past an enormous vacant parking lot connecting a Super Walmart with a Home Depot. He planned to visit The Home Depot on the way back, to secure some plywood for their windows and two toilets. They had stacked enough boards in the barn to barricade the first-floor windows against intruders, but the Maine Liberty Militia's sustained fusillade had shattered close to every window in the house. Since the event blast wave had been negligible in Sanford, he didn't feel bad commandeering the wood, along with a few other repair supplies needed to patch up the holes.

Three olive-drab flatbed trucks converged on Route 109 from a road beyond the parking lot. Without stopping, the loaded vehicles turned right and accelerated, pouring black exhaust above the convoy. From a distance, the trucks resembled the Mk23 MTVRs

(Medium Tactical Vehicle Replacement) used by Grady's battalion.

Where the hell did they come from?

His tactical overview of organic RRZ units indicated that the 1136th Transportation Company based out of Sanford had M1078 MTVs—but their headquarters was four miles west of here. As Alex's vehicle passed the fire station, he matched the street sign to the vehicle's tactical display. The digital map confirmed that Eagle Road was a dead end.

Interesting.

"Looks like they know where they're going," said Alex.

"Let's hope, sir," said Lianez. "I'll tuck in right behind them."

"Make sure to stop at the gate so we can figure out where we need to go. I'm not exactly sure where we're supposed to check in, but I assume there's a base commander or something like that," said Alex, fumbling with the door. "How do you open the windows?"

"You don't, sir. This is an integrated projectile and blast resistant design."

"Really? How the hell did I miss that?"

"Most officers don't figure it out until they want to shoot something from that seat. I had one platoon commander who insisted we were messing with him. Every time he got in the damn vehicle, he fucked around with that door."

"It was kind of silly-like," said Jackson over the PRC-153 Intra-Squad Radio (ISR).

"I'm sure he had every reason to trust the two of you to steer him in the right direction," said Alex, smirking. "So, how the hell does the crew defend the vehicle?"

"You leave that up to me, sir," said Jackson.

"Not even a gun port?"

"Fucks with the blast-resistant dynamics," said Lianez.

"What are you, a vehicle engineer?"

"Mechanical engineering degree at Northeastern."

"You're kidding."

"Negative, sir."

"I stumbled into the Einstein Battalion," Alex muttered.

"Lianez is the exception to the rule. Most of us are good ol'-fashioned New England hicks. No G.I. Bill for me. I do this shit for free," said Jackson.

"Good, because I have a feeling your next paycheck is going to be late," said Alex. "Really late."

They followed the convoy to a security checkpoint at the entrance to a large parking lot. A white commercial sign with "Seacoast Aviation" in red letters protruded from the ground next to an improvised waist-level sandbag emplacement. A group of soldiers dressed in full combat gear cleared out of the way, giving the MTVs a wide berth. They stayed on the sides of the gravel road, waving Alex's vehicle through.

"Do you want me to stop, sir?"

Alex examined the door again. They weren't kidding; there was no way to talk to the soldiers without opening the door.

"Just keep going and park us next to those Humvees. At least with those, you could roll down the windows," said Alex.

"Sounds like old-timer talk, sir," said Lianez.

"No wonder Grady gave you guys up without hesitation," he said. "Stay with the vehicle. Don't go making friends."

"We're not in the business of making friends, sir."

"Good. Until I'm one hundred percent sure this operation is legit, I got one foot out the door," he said, shutting the hatch and walking toward Seacoast Aviation's passenger terminal.

The last of the military trucks passed through a wide gate next to the terminal, disappearing behind the corrugated metal structure. Alex stopped next to one of the parked Humvees and stared through the fence at the other side of the closest tarmac. An olive-drab tractor with a post-hole digger attachment worked next to a group of soldiers wearing ACU pants, T-shirts and combat helmets. A cluster of flatbed trucks carrying sheets of rolled fencing sat in front of an empty hangar at the end of the tarmac. From what he could tell by the posts that had been installed along the far edge of the asphalt, engineers were fencing off a section of the airport.

A tall soldier in ACUs and a patrol cap emerged from the open terminal door, holding an M4 carbine at low ready. Alex turned to face him, slowly removing the identification card from the front pouch of his tactical vest. He kept his hands off his rifle.

"Sir, I need to see some ID," said the sergeant.

Alex noticed a second soldier pointing her rifle at him through the doorway.

"I'm a provisional captain with 1st Battalion, 25th Marine Infantry Regiment," said Alex, handing his badge to the sergeant.

He gave it a quizzical examination. "Never seen one of these before. Captain, we have a provo marine! Showed up in a Matvee!"

"Good timing," said a voice from the other side of the door. "Get him in here."

With the female soldier's rifle still trained on him, Alex stepped inside the dark, sweltering terminal. Two rows of dark orange connected plastic seats sat pushed against the left wall. A rectangular folding table occupied the center of the room, covered with ruggedized military laptops and dozens of cables. Four haggard-looking soldiers crowded around the table in folding chairs, typing and talking into headsets.

"The captain's in the last office," said the soldier, handing Alex the ID card.

"You can stop pointing that at me now," said Alex.

The pasty-faced, sweat-covered specialist didn't blink.

"You want to call her off? This is the second time I've had a rifle pointed at my head today."

"You can stand down, Crosby," said the sergeant.

The woman flipped the selector switch on her rifle to safe and let the rifle dangle across her body armor by its sling. She was the only soldier in the terminal wearing the MTV (Modular Tactical Vest), which added at least thirty pounds to a soldier or marine's standard load out.

"Why are you the only one wearing the MTV?" asked Alex.

"Because she thinks the Chinese are gonna drop from the sky and take the airport," stated one of the soldiers working on a laptop.

"Crosby plans to take them all out," announced another soldier.

She shook her head and muttered a few expletives.

"You might be on to something, Crosby," said Alex, silencing her colleagues.

Alex walked down the shadowy hallway, passing two pitch-black, empty offices. Light from the outside filled the third office, rendering the space useable. A desk chair scraped the floor inside the office, followed by muttering.

"Where the fuck is this guy?"

A dark-haired soldier charged out of the doorway, stopping himself before barreling into Alex.

"Shit. Sorry about that. Did they run your ID?"

"The sergeant gave it a once-over," said Alex.

"Goddamn it," he muttered, extending a hand. "Captain Rick Adler. Commanding officer, 262nd Engineering Company out of Westbrook."

"Captain Alex Fletcher. United States Marine Corps. Provisional."

"Provo, huh? I just cracked the code on all of this shit. Mind if I grab your ID?"

"Sure," said Alex, handing it over again.

"Follow me," he said, storming down the hallway.

"Listen up! We talked about provisional ID cards! You have to scan them at this computer and send the e-file to my desk. Easy enough?"

The table of lethargic soldiers nodded and responded with wary, "Yes, sirs."

"That way, I know if I'm dealing with a civilian construction engineer sent by battalion, or…" He swiped Alex's card and read the screen. "Huh. Let's talk in my office."

Alex wasn't sure how to interpret Adler's sudden need for privacy. Once inside the spacious, ghastly hot office, Adler shut the door and offered him a drink from a water cooler behind his modular desk.

"Room temperature. All of our juice is going to the comms gear, though it's awfully tempting to run a line to the cooler."

Alex took a sip.

"You could make hot cocoa with this," he said,

finishing the thin paper cup.

"Without the central air-conditioning, the building is basically one big convection oven. Tin roof. Fucking miserable. It's worse in the hangars."

"Really?" said Alex, immediately eliminating the possibility of bringing his family to the hangar.

Adler slid Alex's ID card across the desk. "This card identifies you as the airport's MIF."

"MIF?"

"Most Important Fucker. Congratulations. Until an EMIF arrives—your wish is my command." At Alex's questioning look, Adler explained, "Even More Important Fucker. I'm still cracking the code on this Regional Recovery Zone shit, but the hierarchy is well defined. Security and Intelligence is at the top of the food chain."

"You didn't know about the Category Five response protocols?"

"Negative. I can only assume that knowledge was kept at the battalion commander and above level. I had a sealed pod kept under lock and key at the unit armory—to be opened under certain circumstances. Suspected EMP was one of those circumstances. I found this laptop computer and a ROTAC satphone, along with instructions for tapping into the battalion's SIPRNet through DTCS. We never used DTCS before Monday, now it's the only way to communicate over any appreciable distance."

"We used real radios in my day, and if you didn't have comms—you didn't have comms. Portable sat-gear was borderline *Star Wars* shit, even at the battalion level," said Alex.

"Even today it's not widely issued to regular units

below the battalion level."

"Then why does it seem like every soldier and Marine has one?"

"Good question. DTCS came to life in 2011. Too late to make a big difference in the War on Terror, but the Pentagon pushed it."

"I don't blame them. I lost several Marines in Iraq because of shitty comms."

"That was the big selling point. One hundred percent worldwide coverage at all times. I studied the system a year ago in one of my Staff and Command courses. One case study after another where DTCS-enabled sat-gear could have saved lives. Made sense to me, except it was never rolled out below company level. Then the DTCS budget was drastically expanded in 2016."

"And they were issued along with helmets in boot camp."

"No. That was a big point of discussion during last year's summer training. None of the guard or reserve units saw them. Neither did their active-duty counterparts."

"Then where did the radios come from?"

"Category Five response load outs. We had a secure conex box set inside one of the buildings. I assume it was EMP hardened, like a Faraday cage. The keys and combinations needed to access the conex box were located in my secure pod."

"What was in the container?"

"Dozens of ROTAC handhelds, heavier duty communications gear, computers, router equipment, night-vision devices, motion sensors, cameras—everything I needed for my role at Sanford Seacoast Regional Airport. Quite a coincidence, right? Especially given the fact that the conex box was delivered over two years ago."

"I'm discovering a lot of these post-Jakarta Pandemic coincidences," said Alex.

"Like the runway out there?" asked Adler.

"Makes you wonder."

"I wouldn't wonder too loudly. My initial Category Five orders also involved sending two soldiers home—booted from the company. Stripped of all rank and privileges, like they were criminals."

"Militia?"

"Likely militia involvement."

"The orders said that?"

"Negative. I called Colonel Hanson over ROTAC to confirm the orders, looking for an explanation. His orders came with a few more details. He lost a total of eight from the battalion. All with suspected or confirmed ties to Maine militia groups."

"That's interesting given my role here," said Alex.

Adler stared at him for a moment, his expression flashing from doubt to panic. "Look, I'm in this for the long haul. Part of the team. I just can't help making the connections to—"

"Rick, what are you talking about?"

Adler cocked his head. "Let's just say I get worried when I see the label 'security and intelligence' accompanied by 'provide unrestricted access.' Call me paranoid."

"What else did my ID badge tell you?"

"That's the extent of it, but what else do you need? It's more or less a carte blanche declaration, which is why it struck me as odd. The RRZ protocols are thick, delineating relationships, authority, this and that. Typical government bullshit. I have to go through ten layers of nonsense to move one of the airport's porta-shitters ten feet to the left."

"It didn't say what type of security? I was under the impression that the Marine battalion was an area security unit for southern Maine. Almost like MPs."

"You have one of the least defined security clearances I've ever seen. It set off my internal alarm. Let's leave it at that."

"I think you might want to heed your spider sense. You never know who you're talking to, or who's listening."

"I hear you. Keep it zipped and do your job," said Adler.

"Especially when the Recovery Zone personnel start to arrive. Any idea when that might start?"

"My first priority is to build a security barrier around the cluster of hangars and commercial buildings across the tarmac. I assume the RRZ folks will start rolling in once it's finished."

"That'll be one long line of EMIFs," said Alex.

"I won't have to worry about that. A company of Rangers from the 2nd Ranger Battalion is scheduled to arrive tomorrow, along with a headquarters element from the 75th Ranger Regiment. They'll take over physical security and general airport operations while I harden the perimeter. After that, it's a nonstop parade of aircraft and vehicles. 4th Brigade Combat Team, 10th Mountain Division has been assigned to RRZ border control and FEMA camp security. They're bringing part of the division's Aviation Brigade. Blackhawks and Chinooks. You won't recognize this place by next week."

"The entire Brigade Combat Team?"

"That's the plan. Advanced elements left Fort Drum this morning."

"I need to secure hangar space for my battalion—before it's standing room only. Something out of the way, with quick access to a gate," said Alex.

Captain Adler stood up and walked to the window, pointing across the main runway.

"See those long hangars? Two in front, along the taxiway, and one partially hidden behind them?"

"Got it," said Alex, feeling the heat pour through the thin glass as he neared.

"We cleared the aircraft out yesterday. The hangars have their own gate and access road. Easy in, easy out. A straight shot down Airport Road to Route 109. How much room do you need?"

"I'll take all three hangars," said Alex, staring past the waves of superheated air rising from the asphalt runway.

"Why not? First come, first serve. Perfect timing, too. Your conex boxes arrived on that convoy. I'll send them over to the hangars," he said, nodding at the three trucks Alex had followed into the airport.

"Were the conex boxes delivered to another airport?"

"This is where it gets really interesting. They're dragging container after container out of an old business park behind Walmart. Started two days ago."

"Want to take bets on when that business park was abandoned?" Alex asked wryly.

"About the same time the runway was reinforced. I had a talk with the mayor," said Adler. "The company that owned the business park let the leases expire on several local businesses between 2015 and 2016. They may have bought out a few of the longer term leases."

"I'm starting to get a bad feeling about this," said Alex.

"Starting?"

Alex considered the implications raised by his conversation with Adler. One thing was certain. The federal government had been planning for a catastrophic, national-scale disaster since 2015, possibly earlier. The complexity of the Category Five Response Plan was mind-boggling. Hundreds, possibly thousands of active duty and reserve military commanders received orders governing and coordinating the deployment of their units. Countless thousands of equipment containers had been pre-staged across the United States for the express purpose of supporting Category Five requirements—or the Federal Recovery Plan.

The relationship between the two looked hazy. Declaration of a Category Five Event triggered specific military missions, like Lieutenant Colonel Grady's immediate deployment to Boston, but it also appeared to set the Federal Recovery Plan wheels in motion. Adler received orders to secure the airport and start building an inner perimeter, all tasks designed to support the Regional Recovery Zone. Maybe the declaration of a Category Five Event was synonymous with the activation of the Federal Recovery Plan. He didn't know, and he was too exhausted to give it any more thought. He'd oversee the delivery of his battalion's conex boxes to the distant hangars and head back to Limerick after he had a look at the contents.

Chapter 5

EVENT +5 Days

Limerick, Maine

Kate checked her watch and shook her head.

Where the hell is he?

Alex had been gone for nearly five hours, two hours longer than he had estimated. His absence was conspicuous given the circumstances. At first she had been angry, but now she was worried that he had run into trouble with the supposedly friendly militia group. Or worse, he had decided to ignore her repeated warnings about staying away from Eli Russell's base camp and had been ambushed. She sensed a presence in the bathroom doorway.

"I'm sure he's fine, Kate," said Tim Fletcher, Alex's dad and Kate's father-in-law.

"He should have been back already," she said, mopping at the hardened mixture of drywall dust on the tile floor.

"We'd know if something was wrong. The Marines would get a distress call and respond."

"Unless they were taken out by an IED or a coordinated ambush. Six hours without a phone call?"

"I'll have Staff Sergeant Evans check in on them.

Looking good in here," Tim said, glancing at the entire mudroom.

"Aside from the missing toilet, cracked sink and bullet holes," she said.

"It's coming along. The first floor is clear of debris and drywall dust. We'll put the kids to work on the upstairs after lunch. Tomorrow, we'll start on the outside. If Alex can find plywood and heavy-duty hinges, we'll fashion some crude hurricane shutters that can be pulled shut from the inside. It won't look pretty, but we'll be back in business in a few weeks."

"I don't know." Kate sighed. "Alex doesn't seem optimistic about this whole Recovery Zone thing."

"I suppose we could make a go of it back at the Scarborough house. Put a little distance between ourselves and the border."

"We need to move away from the population centers, especially Portland. Plus, the house will be one giant mold spore in a few weeks. The water went up to the ceiling. I'd only recommend our house in an absolute emergency."

"Well, if the situation deteriorates, we'll have to consider it."

"Worse than this?" she said, and they both laughed.

Kate lowered her voice to a whisper. "Emily overheard Ed talking to Charlie and Linda about their place up in Belgrade. Maybe we should consider relocating—at least until the Marines destroy this militia group."

"Who's to say the situation is any better up north?" Tim whispered back.

"It has to be better than living in fear of a murderous lunatic," she said.

"We're in pretty good hands here. I'd rather take my chances with what I know, and I didn't get the impression that Charlie had a big place up there. Sounded like a cozy, four-season lake cottage. We have seventeen mouths to feed here. This is our best bet, if we can make it work."

"This Colonel Grady character can yank the Marines away at a moment's notice."

"We need to discuss this—with everyone. Figure out the options. For now, we have to press on with the repairs. Winter won't wait for us to make a decision."

"I know," Kate said. "I really want this to work."

"Why don't you take a break? Grab a sandwich and a beer," Tim said, taking the mop. "There's a cooler at the bottom of the stairs. I got the rest of this."

"We probably shouldn't be drinking alcohol in front of the Marines. At the very least we should keep it on the down low. Most of them haven't spoken with their own families since this started. I'd be pretty pissed if I was ordered to protect someone else's family while they tipped back beers."

"I didn't think of it that way," said Tim.

"We've barely had time to process the basics, especially after what happened yesterday. I'm not saying we have to walk around like this is the end of the world, but…"

Kate stopped, realizing that their situation was about as close to the "apocalypse" as anyone could reasonably expect in their lifetime. "What kind of sandwiches?"

"Grilled cheese…from the bullet-riddled grill in the backyard."

"Last of the cheese?"

"Last of anything we couldn't throw in the freezer. The refrigerator took one too many broadsides; may she rest in peace," Tim said, stepping into the mudroom bathroom.

Kate let go of the mop and grabbed her rifle from one of the coat hooks in the mudroom. She slung it over her shoulder and let it hang in the "shoulder-ready" position behind her back, where it was out of the way but readily accessible. The rifle no longer felt like a cold, alien object. It still caught on furniture and clunked against the walls, but she'd come to terms with the fact that the rifle wasn't dangerous unless she released the safety and pulled the trigger.

The kitchen looked spotless, if you could overlook a few structural problems. Split cabinets, cracked backsplash tile, missing chunks of drywall, painted-over bloodstains, and bullet-peppered furniture to name a few. Still, it was a radical improvement over this morning. She could live with the cosmetic damage, especially if it meant they could stay. The realities of evacuating the house weighed heavily on her mind.

They had designed the compound with resilience and redundancy in mind. "The rule of threes." Three sources or layers for each of their basic needs. Water provided by a well, pumped out of the pond, or collected in fifty-gallon, food-grade drums from the gutters during a rainstorm. Food supplied by their garden and fields, supplemented when necessary by the vast stores in the basement, with the year-round option of fishing, trapping or hunting. Security had multiple layers. Communications. Heating. Power. Whenever practical, they sought long-term solutions with multiple backups. If they left Gelder Pond, their survival plan would have to fit into a car—shared by another family.

"Hungry?" asked Samantha Walker, appearing from

the deck with a platter of sandwiches.

"Starving."

"I'm taking these down to the critical care ward," she said. "Why don't you grab one?"

"I'll get one off the grill after everyone has eaten. How's Ed doing?"

"He'll be fine. I'm worried about the Thorntons. Linda's foot is destroyed, and Charlie's calf muscle is torn. Neither of them can walk unaided. It leaves them a little vulnerable as a family," she said.

"They'll have to stay put for now. We can move them into the great room now that it's clean. Air them out a little."

"I'm not sure they'll want to leave the basement."

"Safer?"

"That, and it's about thirty degrees cooler."

"Doesn't sound bad. Where are the kids?" asked Kate, staring into the empty screen porch.

"Cooling off in the cellar," offered Samantha.

"They don't want to be upstairs, either," said Kate. "I don't blame them."

"It'll be a while before anyone feels safe up here—or anywhere."

"I'm not opposed to moving mattresses into the basement—or cellar. Whatever you New Englanders call it," Kate said, winking.

"I thought you were from the Midwest. Don't they call it a storm cellar there?" asked Samantha.

"New Jersey. Princeton area. We called it a basement. I think storm cellars were separate from the house. Alex might know."

"Have you heard from your parents?"

Kate shook her head slowly. "I've tried on Alex's

military satphone, but they're not picking up. Alex gave my dad a satphone for Christmas three years ago. I think it went back in the box after Alex showed him how to set it up."

"Family Christmas gatherings with Alex must be…interesting."

"It gets interesting, and a little tense, depending on what he tries to sneak by the censors. He gave our eight-year-old nephew a folding Gerber knife, magnetic compass and SureFire light for his birthday. The knife part went over well, as you can imagine."

Samantha stifled a laugh. "I imagine it gets worse."

"Much worse," said Kate, her smile fading.

"I'm sure your parents are fine, Kate."

"I hope so. You better get those down to the troops. I'll grab the next batch," she said, purposely steering the conversation away from family.

"See you in a few," said Samantha, disappearing into the basement.

Kate took a deep breath and eyed the Iridium phone on the kitchen counter. She'd been unable to reach her brother, Robbie, which made her nervous. She could see her parents having no clue and keeping the satphone uncharged in the original box, but Robbie had gladly accepted Alex's gift of the phone and a basic calling plan. They'd even tested it out once a year, at Alex's insistence. He lived in a suburb of Concord, New Hampshire, less than eighty miles away from Limerick.

They'd discussed coming to the compound if something happened, but he seemed hell-bent on taking his family to their camp in the White Mountains. After the Jakarta Pandemic, he made some basic modifications to the rustic structure, including a small solar-power setup, enough to run the well pump and a few lights. Alex had convinced him to store a few months of food in the house and keep enough firewood for an entire winter season. The cabin represented a possible refuge if they couldn't stay in Limerick. Then again, she wasn't sure if leaving the state was an option anymore. Alex no longer seemed to think so.

He'd woken in a dark mood today, after a long night on the military laptop, forcing his way through morning pleasantries before departing with the Marines. He looked uncommitted gearing up for the trip. She suspected he had uncovered something he wasn't ready to share. Now he was overdue from his outing. She'd ask Staff Sergeant Evans to give him a call over ROTAC.

Kate washed her hands in the sink and instinctively opened one of the cabinet doors to retrieve a glass for a drink of water. She stopped herself halfway, remembering that none of the glassware or plates had survived the gun battle. She looked anyway. The inside was bare; the shattered pieces thoroughly removed by the teenage cleanup crew that had scoured the rest of the first floor. She guessed that Amy had another set hiding inside one of the plastic storage bins in the basement. Kate spotted a stack of red plastic cups on the kitchen table, next to a pile of paper plates and plastic utensils.

One of the Marines stepped out of the dining room, holding a motion sensor transceiver like it was a dead rat.

"This one is wrecked, too, ma'am. I made a few more adjustments to the sensor perimeter."

"You guys don't have to mess with that stuff. Why don't you grab a plate and get some lunch. I'll let Staff Sergeant Evans know, so all of you can eat some real food."

"I'll take you up on that in a minute, ma'am."

"You can call me Kate."

"Yes, ma'am. So, we moved some of the sensors to direct most of the coverage east and north along the most likely attack vectors—same routes they used before. We'll put an LP/OP lakeside, so we won't need sensors to the west."

"LP/OP?"

"Listening post, observation post. Basically, two Marines trying to stay awake all night. With night vision, it'll be nearly impossible for anything to get across the lake undetected. Plus, we'll have one of the Matvees next to the house, in a position to cover the western tree line."

"What about the south?"

"The south is their least likely approach vector. It's three hundred fifty feet to the trees, across open ground," he said, pointing out of the dining room window. "They could mix it up in the barley field, but they'd have no real cover. We'll have two Matvees in a position to watch that sector, plus your husband's .30-caliber machine gun. Even if someone managed to crawl to the edge of the barley, they'd have another two hundred plus feet to go before they reached the house. That's what we call machine-gun-assisted suicide."

"Clever. We'll have our own rotation in the house, watching the sensors. Sounds like we should be fine."

"You're in good hands. We won't let anything through," said the marine.

"Thank you. I'm terrible with names," said Kate. "Corporal?"

"Corporal Derren, ma'am."

"Sorry about that. Thank you, Corporal Derren," she said. "Do you have family near Fort Devens?"

"I have a two-year-old daughter named Liz. She's with my wife in Greenfield. I hope."

"Alex—Captain Fletcher—said they were sending trucks out to pick up the military families, bringing them to Devens."

"That's what Staff Sergeant Evans said. Even if the truck showed up, she might not be there. She has a huge family in Amherst, which isn't far away. They would have come for her by now."

"I'm glad to hear that. It doesn't seem fair that you were sent to Boston without contacting your families."

"This is just part of the deal for us. Plus, there was no way to contact them anyway," he said, matter-of-factly. "They don't have a satphone."

"We'll say a prayer for them, Corporal Derren."

"It's about all we can do right now," he said, placing the transceiver on the table.

"I'll let the chef know we have some more mouths to feed."

"Thank you, ma'am. I just have a few more things to check and I'll be out to grab some chow."

"Thank you for doing this. I'm not going to pretend to know how hard it is for you, being away from your family, but I just wanted you to know that we'll never forget this."

Derren nodded, maintaining a stoic façade. This wasn't fair to the Marines at all, and as far as she was concerned, it was an unsustainable situation. She wouldn't blame any of them for taking one of the tactical vehicles and driving out of here before the battalion arrived. Kate knew they wouldn't. She married a Marine twenty years ago, and nothing got in the way of duty, which was why she felt so uneasy about her husband's provisional position in Lieutenant Colonel Grady's battalion. The Fletcher family couldn't afford a shift in Alex's priorities. Not now.

Chapter 6

EVENT +5 Days

Main Operating Base "Sanford"
Regional Recovery Zone 1

Alex wiped the sweat off his face with his forearm and sighed. The heat index inside the hangar had to be over a hundred degrees, with one hundred percent humidity. Home sweet home for 1st Battalion. He waited for Grady to answer his ROTAC call.

"I'm in the middle of a briefing, Alex. Did you secure my hangar space?"

"Affirmative, sir. More than enough room for the Marines, vehicles and equipment. I have three conex boxes sitting in one of the hangars."

"Conex boxes?"

"Maybe conex isn't the right description. I'm guessing each one is twenty feet by eight by eight, equipped with a biometric scanner."

"Sounds like a regular-sized shipping container. Stand by."

Alex shrugged his shoulders at Corporal Lianez, who stood in front of the closest eight-foot-tall gray container pushed against the back wall of the corrugated metal hangar. A few minutes later, Grady responded.

"Alex, I'm sending you two sets of combinations for

each container in a text message to your ROTAC. Have one of the Marines show you how to retrieve it. The first set will disable the biometric sensor. The second will open them. I need you to inventory the equipment and post a full-time guard at the hangar. The boxes can't be locked once opened. Security feature."

"I don't have enough Marines to post a 24/7 watch at the airport. I'll open the boxes when Gunny Deschane arrives from Brunswick."

"Negative. Gunny is still a few days out. I need to know what's in the boxes."

"You didn't know about the boxes?"

"Alex, I have to go. Inventory the contents and send a detailed report. Do not leave the gear unattended. Out."

"Did you know they pre-staged the entire RRZ's load out in secret warehouses near the airport?" asked Alex.

The ROTAC display read "No Lock."

"Motherfucker," he muttered.

"Sir?" said Lianez.

"Nothing. Grady's sending the combinations via text message. I assume you know how to retrieve messages?"

"It's just like a cell phone, sir," he said, walking over to show Alex.

"We'll need to call Staff Sergeant Evans and set up a full-time watch rotation. The boxes can't be locked once they're opened."

"What's inside, sir?"

"Either the colonel doesn't know or he won't tell me," Alex said, handing the radio to Lianez.

A few minutes later, they had opened the first box, finding the airtight vessel filled with grayish-blue scale MARPAT uniforms, helmet covers, rucksacks, body armor carriers, tactical load-bearing gear—enough to refit the entire battalion. The container emitted a strong disinfectant smell, which he figured was some sort of chemical preservative or pest repellent. Possibly both. Presumably, the uniforms had been packed with no foreseeable use date, so it made sense to protect them for long-term storage.

"Ever seen this camo pattern before?" Alex asked Lianez.

"Negative. Looks like a dedicated urban pattern. Pretty useless in the native environment out there," said Lianez, pointing to the trees beyond the main runway.

Alex rubbed the material between his fingers, staring deeper into the container.

Unless Homeland wants us to stand out.

He pulled a packet labeled "manifest" from a metal folder attached to the inside of the door and ripped the sealed plastic covering. The first line item on the packing inventory disturbed him: Marine *Corps Combat Utility Uniform, MARPAT: Federal Security pattern. 800 Units. Size adjustable.*

Federal Security? He couldn't wait to see what was in the rest of the containers. No wonder Grady had hung up on him.

"Does it say what the pattern is?" asked Lianez.

"Negative," Alex muttered. "Can I trust the two of you to check out the other hangars, without shooting someone? I'll dig through the rest of this shit," said Alex, hoping to somehow secure the containers before they returned.

"That's hurtful, sir. I do have feelings."

"Nice try. The Marine Corps doesn't issue feelings, so I know you don't have any. Just do a quick walkthrough.

Make sure we don't have any squatters. Looks like there's a small office in each hangar. Close them up when you're done."

He held out a ring of keys, which Lianez swiped from his hand.

"Roger that, sir."

By the time Alex entered the final combination for the second container, the Matvee had sped to the adjacent hangar. The keypad LED turned green, and the hinged front door hissed, releasing its airtight seal. Instead of a disinfectant smell, the second container reeked of gun lubricant.

This should be interesting.

Alex pulled on the heavy gray metal doors, swinging each half hard enough to hit the sides of the container.

"Whoa."

The box resembled an armory, filled front to back with four sliding weapons racks. A two-foot-wide passage ran down the center of the rows, leading to the rear of the container. Alex took a small flashlight from one of the pouches on his vest and illuminated the darker recesses beyond the racks. Dark green ammunition crates filled the far end, stacked from bottom to top and strapped to the container. He pulled on one of the weapons racks, which eased out of the container on heavily greased tracks attached to the floor and ceiling.

Welcome, Kmart shoppers.

The fifteen-foot-long, reinforced metal gun rack bowed slightly when fully extended, prompting Alex to push it most of the way back into the container. He didn't want to break the sliding mechanism and not be able to get this rack out of sight. The contents would raise questions. He counted the rifles as it slid inside. One hundred mint condition MR556SDs, counting both sides of the rack. Recognizable by their hexagon-shaped, partially integrated suppressors, each rifle was fitted with an ACOG sight, forty-five-degree-mounted reflex sights for Close Quarters Battle (CQB), vertical front grip and the AN/PEQ-15 Advanced Target Pointer Illuminator Aiming Device.

He directed the light down the next rack, seeing the same rifles.

Why the hell would they need rifles designed to accept specially adapted suppressors? And why would they need two hundred of them?

The third rack contained an even more bizarre choice of weapon. Compact and futuristic-looking MP-7 Personal Defense Weapons (PDW) fitted with reflex sights. The MP-7 fired a unique 4.6X30mm cartridge, capable of punching a hole through a Kevlar helmet at one hundred yards and defeating most Level IIIA body armor at similar ranges. The armor-penetrating projectile gave a concealable, submachine-gun-sized weapon the comparable power of a combat rifle. A thick, cylindrical suppressor sat in the rack next to each MP-7. Definitely not something seen at the Marine infantry level. More like Delta Force or Devgru.

The final rack held a variety of mountable optics, including night vision and infrared scopes. Forty M-27 Infantry Automatic Rifles (IAR) with 3.5X Squad Day Optics crowded the far end of the rolling frame. The M-27 had replaced the Marine infantry fire team's belt-fed M249 Squad Automatic Weapon several years ago. The IAR was basically a heavier-barreled version of the standard issue HK416, equipped with a bipod. Nothing out of the ordinary here, though the night optics seemed a bit over the top for a unit already carrying night-vision goggles.

Something about the equipment didn't make sense. It resembled the type of load out he'd expect for a high-impact, special-purpose unit, not infantry Marines repurposed for area security. He was almost afraid to open the third container, leery that he might find something that would force the immediate evacuation of the Limerick compound. He could still pull it off while the bulk of the battalion was stuck in New Hampshire. Head north, away from the epicenter of RRZ control, and slip into Canada. Maybe hop over to New Hampshire and try to link up with Kate's brother. All options still on the table—for now.

Alex walked to the front of the last container. He felt flushed, almost nervous. Part of him wanted to find something incriminating in the third conex box. Something to give him the excuse he needed to get as far away from this as possible. He knew on a gut level that nothing good could come of the RRZ. If the government didn't restore limited power and essential services by late November, a scant three months away, nothing short of a one-hundred-mile-long, twenty-foot-tall, electrified fence could keep hundreds of thousands of refugees from swarming north ahead of the winter.

Even with FEMA's prophetically suspicious pre-staging of supplies, there was no way the government could support massive refugee camps throughout the winter. Not without permanent heated structures, which would take far too long to construct given the scope of the EMP damage. Then again, maybe FEMA had socked away several thousand wood-burning stoves. He doubted it. Once winter hit, the situation would fall apart. RRZ leadership would be faced with some tough choices, pack up and head north—or look for other options. He didn't plan on being around to implement the protocols the RRZ "Authority" would undoubtedly follow. One glimpse inside these containers told him everything he needed to know about where this was headed.

He punched in the codes for the third container and waited for the seal to release. After a prolonged hiss, he swung the doors wide, not sure what to expect. Rows of locked equipment boxes lined the walls, leaving enough space in the middle to walk to the end. Military nomenclature on the first few boxes identified sophisticated night-vision goggles. GPNVG-18. Panoramic night-vision goggles, doubling a soldier's field of vision from standard NVGs. Special Operations gear. He thought about it for a moment; if the battalion had forty or fifty sets, they could conduct swift, vehicle-based night operations. The additional field of vision provided by the panoramic NVGs would give drivers the situational awareness needed to maneuver in tighter spaces, like forests.

The pieces were coming together. Suppressed weapons. Strange uniforms. A heavy emphasis on night operations. Fuck if it didn't sound like 1st Battalion, 25th Marines was being reequipped as some kind of internal security group, capable of snatch-and-grab operations. No wonder Adler had freaked out.

He detected a faint high-pitched squeal behind him and spun with his rifle ready for action. An unfamiliar soldier wearing ACUs and a heavily modified tactical load out skidded to a stop on an obviously spray-painted, green and tan camouflage-patterned mountain bike.

"Nice ride," said Alex, lowering his rifle.

"Spray painted it myself."

"Couldn't tell."

"Tech Sergeant David Gedmin. 22nd Special Tactics Squadron."

"Combat Controller? You're a long way from home," said Alex.

"Tell me about it. I just wanted to check in before it got crazy around here," he said, dismounting the bike and peeking into the hangar.

"Captain Alex Fletcher. United States Marines. I'm acting as a forward liaison for 1st Battalion, 25th Infantry Regiment. How long do we have until it gets hectic?"

"Forty-eight hours, tops. We have two C-130s rolling in within the hour to deliver a more robust air traffic control package. Radar, generators, fuel, and more personnel. Once that's up and running, the RRZ gets the green light for full deployment. We'll have air traffic 24/7."

"I thought air control was your job?" joked Alex.

"Combat air control. Higher stress, lower volume. This is more like combining a runway at Logan with the flight deck of a carrier."

"Sounds like fun."

"Sounds like a clusterfuck. Are you taking all three of these hangars?"

"Yeah. I have a Marine battalion with a motor transport element, and we need quick access to a gate. We'll be coming and going at all hours."

"Well, you picked the right spot for that, plus you'll be out of the way. I'd base your ready vehicles in the rear hangar so they don't get boxed in. The taxiway in front of your hangars will get busy," he said, his eyes shifting past Alex's left shoulder, no doubt having just caught a glimpse of the equipment.

"Thanks for the heads-up. I expect the full battalion to arrive within three days with the bulk of our vehicles. I have a platoon-size element heading down from Brunswick. Should be here by tomorrow."

"Reservists?"

"Reserve infantry battalion out of Fort Devens. The Marines are spread out all over New England."

"Nifty rifles for a reserve unit," Gedmin said, nodding at the middle container.

The doors had partially opened, exposing several of the suppressed combat rifles.

"Tell me about it. The containers came out of one of the secret stashes pre-staged around the airport."

"Lots of secrets," he said, glancing from the rifles to Alex with a grimace.

"How did you end up at Sanford Seacoast Regional Airport? I assume you didn't ride that bike from Seattle," said Alex.

"A Humvee pulled up to my house at three in the morning on Monday. I got fifteen minutes to pack up and say good-bye to my family. Less than an hour after that, I was sitting on a government Learjet taking off from McChord Field, headed here. The whole squadron was deployed."

"Any word on what happened?"

Gedmin shook his head. "Mum's the word from higher echelon stations. Any news on your end?"

"Nothing official, but it's pretty obvious that we're dealing with an EMP."

"What do you think about the Homeland broadcasts claiming a near-Earth object landed off the coast?"

"I've just returned from Boston. Witnesses reported

seeing a messy contrail headed out over the water, like the one in Siberia several years ago. I'm inclined to believe what they're saying, but the rest?"

"We thought it might be a limited nuclear attack. Something the government is to keep under wraps while they figure out how to retaliate. Maybe North Korea?"

"Funny you say that. My father picked up several HAM broadcasts claiming that our entire ballistic missile sub fleet has been deployed. Bangor Naval Base, up in your neck of the woods, supposedly emptied out yesterday."

"I wish they'd tell us something. Anything."

"They won't. Not if there's a nuclear option on the table. How were things back west? My dad heard reports that the EMP effects weren't as bad in the Pacific Northwest."

"We still had power at the house when the Humvees arrived. I have no idea if any of our cars worked. I barely got a chance to kiss my girls. The ride over looked about the same, but that's not saying much for three in the morning. I can't even remember if the stoplights were flashing. What about Boston?"

"Devastated by whatever hit offshore. No power. Near total anarchy," said Alex.

"Jesus," Gedmin said. "None of this really makes sense. A nuclear blast at ground level doesn't cause widespread EMP effects. Very localized, as in you won't be around to try to start your car anyway. This is something else," he said, looking at the sky.

"I'd keep that to yourself," said Alex, walking over to the first container and opening the doors. "Care to take a guess what pattern?"

"Digital urban? Looks like you got one of the

containers earmarked for Manhattan."

"Federal Security pattern."

"Interesting," said Gedmin.

"That's an understatement," Alex said, thinking about something Adler had said when he first arrived. "Do you have Adler on ROTAC?"

"Yeah," said Gedmin, unsnapping the radio from his combat rig. "Preset four. Just hold down the numeric key and it'll lock onto Adler's radio."

Alex pressed "4" and listened.

"Captain Adler."

"Rick, this is Captain Fletcher, using Tech Sergeant Gedmin's radio."

"Sorry about the intrusion. I sent him out to meet you. Figured you'd need to coordinate tarmac activity."

"Quick question about the arrival of my conex boxes."

"Send it," said Adler.

"It was awfully fortunate that I arrived when I did. This isn't the kind of gear you'd want lying around unattended. Can you shed any light on this coincidence?"

"The incidence of coincidence around here defies explanation."

"Sounds like a tongue twister. Would it help if I paid a visit to the guard unit hauling these boxes?"

"I've already looked under that rock. They receive orders from the North Pole and deliver the requested containers."

"Santa Claus, huh?"

"May as well be," said Adler. "This has been a 'monkey see, monkey do' operation from minute one. Not much thought required."

"Likely by design. I'll stop by on the way out."

"I'll keep the water room temperature for you," said Adler.

Alex handed the radio back.

"Did your gear arrive as soon as you touched down?"

"The truck was idling next to the field," said Gedmin.

"Did you have your ROTAC with you on the flight, or was it part of the waiting load out?"

"It was issued at McChord."

Alex pulled his tactical radio out of its pouch. "Do you think they could track these phones?"

"I don't see why not. It's all satellite based."

"I'd be careful what you said on these regarding any theories you might have."

"Roger that, sir. Good advice."

"And you didn't see anything unusual in these containers," said Alex.

"Of course not, sir. Advanced combat rifles with integral suppressor systems is precisely what I would expect for a reservist infantry battalion."

Technical Sergeant Gedmin pedaled across the taxiway as the Matvee returned. Lianez parked the vehicle in front of the hangar bay holding the containers.

"All clear. We shut the hangars and locked the doors," he said, holding out the keys.

His eyes went straight for the second container. "Are those for us?"

"I really hope not."

Chapter 7

EVENT +5 Days

Limerick, Maine

Ryan Fletcher balanced his bandaged left hand against the shredded drywall and moved his folding chair with his good hand to the window facing the pond. Careful not to topple over, he slid the chair under the windowsill and lowered his weight cautiously, balancing on his right leg until he was fairly certain he wouldn't end up on the floor. His leg throbbed from the trip up two flights of stairs, but he didn't have a choice. One of the tactical vehicles had sped away a few minutes ago, taking three of the Marines out of the perimeter, and nobody else volunteered to leave the basement.

He felt guilty as soon as the thought passed through his mind. He couldn't fault any of them for seeking refuge below ground. The house had become a shooting gallery. What his dad called a "bullet-rich environment." He'd thought the phrase was funny—until yesterday. Ryan didn't blame them at all.

The stairs creaked, and he lifted a pair of binoculars to scan the tree line. He stared vacantly at the trees, catching the occasional glimmering streak of reflected sunlight from the pond. The hardwood floor announced a presence in the bedroom doorway.

"I brought you an extra sandwich," said his mom.

"I thought you came up here to chase me into the basement," he said, lowering the binoculars and twisting in the chair.

His mom looked worn out and dazed, in a grizzled, survivor kind of way. Dressed in filthy khaki pants and one of his dad's old woodland MARPAT blouses, she sat on the edge of the bare mattress behind him, forcing a smile across her lightly bruised and cut face.

"Nothing would make me happier than knowing you're tucked away in the convalescent ward with the Walkers and Thorntons," she said, handing him the tinfoil-wrapped grilled cheese.

He ripped open the package and started to stuff one of Nana's grilled cheese marvels into his mouth.

"She does make a mean grilled cheese," said Kate.

"Yours are good too, Mom," Ryan said, purposely slowing his consumption rate.

"Uh-huh. How's your hand?" she said, unslinging her AR-15 and laying it on the bed.

"It should be fine," he said, holding it out to show her. "A scratch."

She took the bandaged hand and examined it suspiciously. "Staff Sergeant Evans said he could see your knuckle. Like, the actual bone."

"Barely. The bullet tore some skin away. Hurts like hell, but not a big deal. Nothing a little ibuprofen can't take care of."

"And your leg?"

"I can manage," Ryan said, looking away.

"You look like you're in a lot of pain. One of the Marines can give you some stronger painkillers."

"I can't take any of those. I felt sluggish during the

attack yesterday, still drugged up from Boston. I can manage the pain."

"When your dad gets back, I want you in the basement resting up."

"I'm not going down into the morgue, Mom."

"Ryan, you've been through enough. You need to take it easy."

"This is the perfect job for me. I'm resting and helping. Seriously."

"You're probably cutting off the blood flow to your injured leg on that chair, and it's hot up here," she said.

"I have a full CamelBak, and there's a little breeze flowing through the windows. I win."

"You can't win against a worried mom. I'll have the cleaning crew bring you one of the dining room chairs."

"Is everyone going to be up here?"

"Even Chloe," she whispered, "so be nice."

"What do you mean? She's the one that's been ignoring *me* since we got back," he whispered back.

"She's embarrassed about what happened in Boston. Just be nice. I know a thing or two about how women think, and I can tell she still wants to be your *friend,*" she said, miming air quotes.

"What does that mean?"

"Call it a mother's intuition…and a few loose lips among the adults."

He felt like breaking into a sweat. He didn't think any of them suspected he had been dating Chloe for most of the summer. They'd spent a lot of time together in high school, mostly as friends, but had drifted apart during her last year in high school. Most of the senior girls dated other seniors or guys in college, so he didn't dwell on it. She left for Boston College with a hug and a warm smile, excited to start a new life. Ryan spent his senior year badly missing her. They'd always had a few minutes here and there in school. Their occasional jog on the weekends. Walking over to her driveway to catch her getting out of her car. He didn't realize how much she meant to him until she was gone.

When it came time to apply to colleges, he tried to play it cool. No way he could fill out an application to Boston College. That would look desperate. He had the grades to get into at least two or three competitive schools in Boston that wouldn't raise any suspicion about his intentions. Northeastern and Boston University put him on Chloe's side of the Charles River and an easy "T" ride away.

Ryan put applications in the mail for Dartmouth, NYU and Fordham University, with the secret hope that he didn't get accepted. NYU panned out, but it didn't take much effort on his part to convince his parents that he should stay closer to home, "especially after the pandemic." Acceptance to Boston University sealed the deal, and he eagerly awaited the start of his freshman year in Boston. Then this happened. It was time to change the subject.

"How's Dad? Any word on why the Marines left?"

"He's fine. They have to keep a twenty-four-hour guard at one of the hangars. Three Marines and one of the vehicles."

"Now we're down to nine?"

"We're lucky to have them here at all."

"If they keep pulling Marines away, we won't be able to defend ourselves from another attack."

"Your dad has Marines arriving from the reserve company in Brunswick. He expects them to arrive by tomorrow. We'll be fine here," she said, resting her hand on his shoulder. "Or wherever we end up."

"Do you think it'll ever go back to normal?"

"I think we'll be looking at a different normal," Kate said.

"I'm not going back to college."

"Why not?"

"If this is the new normal, what's the point?" he said, touching the rifle leaned against the wall next to the window.

"It won't be like this for long. Things got back to normal after the pandemic," she reminded him.

"Dad doesn't seem to think it'll get better."

"He told you that?" she asked, rubbing her eyes and yawning.

"No, but he's too quiet," Ryan replied. "He only gets like that when he's worried."

"We all have plenty to worry about, especially your mother," she said, staring at the damaged sandbags under the other window.

He squeezed her hand, remembering every detail of yesterday's battle.

"The bullets started coming through the barrier at the end. Not fast enough to break through my BDU's, but I could feel it. Like being snapped by a thick rubber band."

"Are you trying to give me a panic attack?"

"I'm trying to get you out of here, unless you have another grilled cheese sandwich," Ryan said, winking.

"I'll send Nana up with one. She looks like she could use a nap," Kate said, pressing the mattress.

"Mom, no," Ryan whined.

"Then I'll send it up with Chloe instead."

He shook his head and resumed his survey of the western approach.

"Is that a yes or a no?"

"It's a yes. You guys are relentless."

"Part of my job description, young man. I'll see what I can arrange," she said, and he heard her get up.

"Mom?"

"Yeah?"

He paused, momentarily unsure why he had said her name. A few seconds passed before he figured it out.

"I love you, Mom. And thanks for the sandwich."

Kate leaned over and kissed him on the top of his head. "I love you too, Ryan. We're all really proud of you."

"Thanks, Mom," he said, holding back tears.

He'd overheard his dad talking with Staff Sergeant Evans about the worsening situation inside and outside the United States. The "new normal" was a nightmare landscape dominated by violence and power. He'd seen nothing to refute this belief, which was why he couldn't sit in the basement. Someone fully vested in their safety had to watch over them. His dad trusted the Marines, but they had families too, and every one of them wanted to get back home to see them. Ryan couldn't risk their safety on a possible conflict of interest. He pulled the HK416 closer to the windowsill and adjusted his leg. He'd stay up here all day and night if necessary.

Chapter 8

EVENT +5 Days

Route 160
Porter, Maine

Eli tightened his grip on the SUV's grab handle as Grizzly veered onto the unmarked dirt road, skidding the tires.

"Take it easy."

"Sorry, Eli. I figured if anyone was following us, that'd throw them off our trail," said Grizzly.

"You about threw *us* off the trail," Eli said, laughing at his own joke.

Nobody else made a sound.

"No fucking sense of humor in any of you. Like a funeral parlor all day," he muttered.

The vehicle slowed to twenty miles per hour, which was barely safe on what amounted to a well-worn jeep trail through the woods. They could have continued along Route 160 to their usual turnoff, but he wanted to see if this path connected with Porterfield Road. He'd noticed this turnoff on their way out to Brownfield, but couldn't match it to anything on their maps or GPS displays. With vehicles regularly entering and exiting Porterfield Road at the Route 160 junction, they were bound to attract the wrong kind of attention, especially when they kicked off the juicy part of his plan. He needed a less conspicuous route for everyday use, one they could easily block if necessary.

"We've got about a mile to go if it breaks through," he said.

"Got it, Eli."

"Why don't we stick with *sir*? That goes for all of you," he said.

"Yes, sir," they all mumbled.

Better—barely. He watched their track on the handheld GPS screen, encouraged that they continued west toward Porterfield Road. If this was a private driveway, it was one long-ass private driveway—and whoever lived at the end of it would die horribly. He'd been itching to hurt someone or something since they started out in the morning, but he'd promised himself that he'd wait. The situation at the roadblock outside of Bridgton might not have gone so smoothly if his clothes had been covered in blood—and boy, did they go smoothly.

He could barely believe his luck. The chief of police had been less receptive to the idea, but Eli had won them over with tales of how his men were handpicked, only vetted and screened ex-military or law enforcement at first. The rest were recommended and vouched for by fully vested members of the militia group. All total bullshit, but he'd make sure his people looked the part when they reported for duty at the checkpoints.

The chief had positively swooned over his offer to keep the men unarmed. He'd been on the fence until Eli had suggested it. No firearms unless they were issued by the Bridgton police or by authorized checkpoint personnel. Good ol' Ron Bevins, the town's chief selectman, had insisted on that point. He wanted permission to arm Eli's volunteers if necessary. Too good to be true. Bevins was in for one hell of a surprise in a few days.

On top of it all, the town council gave him an hour to speak at the high school. The turnout hadn't exactly broken any records, but he left with nine names, their souls to be collected tomorrow and never returned to Bridgton. He had it all worked out.

Grizzly eased the SUV into a shallow turn as the trees thinned and a field of corn appeared on their right. The GPS unit indicated they were driving at a forty-five-degree angle to Porterfield Road, which lay directly ahead. The SUV slowed at the junction and stopped as soon as it hit the pavement.

"What are you doing?" said Eli.

"I thought you might want to mark the location on your GPS or fashion some kind of sign."

"Can I just for once be the one to give the orders to my own fucking militia?"

"Sorry, sir. I just wasn't sure we'd find this spot again, since the other groups didn't report finding a road that broke through."

"I know you're new, Griz, but you're thinking too much, and you're making assumptions. We all know what happens when you make assumptions, right?"

"You make an ass out of you and me. Really sorry about that."

"No, you have it wrong. I don't make an ass out of anyone, especially me. I'm never the ass."

"That's right, Eli. I mean, sir. That's just the saying. 'You' means me—the one saying the quote. I didn't mean you were the one making an ass out of you and—"

"You all right, Griz? You're starting to sound like a

mental patient. I already marked the coordinates. Let's go."

The engine revved, but the SUV stayed in place.

"You need to put the car in drive. Jesus Christ, did you have a stroke or something?"

"Just nervous, sir."

Eli shook his head. "Nervous about what?"

He could tell Grizzly wanted to say something but held his tongue. Griz was learning pretty quickly, which was more than Eli could say for the majority of his undisciplined crew. He took one of the handheld radios out of the cup holder and raised it to his ear.

"Liberty North, this is Liberty Actual, approaching your position. Stand by to authenticate."

"This is Liberty North. Read you loud and clear. Authenticate Lucky Town."

"I authenticate Local Hero. Over."

"Welcome back, sir."

"Good job on the RT procedure. Picture perfect. Any traffic since we left?"

"Negative. The special-purpose group kept everyone corralled north while they went house to house. How did you get onto Porterfield from the north?"

"Small jeep trail I saw on 160. I marked the coordinates. We'll probably make a few adjustments to Liberty North's location so we can keep an eye on it," he said, glaring at Grizzly.

"Copy that. You should be able to see us right about now," said the sentry post.

A pair of headlights shined through a cluster of thick bushes next to a dilapidated gray barn. Four flashes.

"Flash them back. Three times."

"Track number three," said Grizzly.

"That's right. You a fan of The Boss?"

"Hell, I grew up on The Boss—sir. Used to drive down to Hartford once a year to see him. Fourteen shows."

"No shit? Hit the lights, Griz, before they light us up."

"Yes, sir," he said, flashing the high beams three times.

"Secondary authentication complete," said Liberty North.

They passed a small clearing on the left with a mobile home and an aboveground pool in the front yard before reaching the checkpoint. An F-150-sized pickup truck sat hidden in the brush, parked at a narrow angle to the two-lane road. If they had failed the first authentication sequence, the F-150 would have raced onto the bumpy pavement, blocking their path. Eli waved at one of the sentries standing near the road with a pump-action shotgun, who saluted him.

Now that's what I'm talking about. Someone with a little discipline.

"Good job, boys. Liberty Actual, out."

Eli turned back to Grizzly. "I'm putting you in charge of the daily security code. Different album every day. Pick the track. One member from each group leaving the compound gets the information, along with the sentries. Changes every twenty-four hours, with the morning swap out. The light trick is a little insurance policy, in case the group is compromised. If we were under duress, you could have flashed twice or six times. Bam! They would have opened fire without warning."

"Pretty clever, sir."

"Eli. Any man that's seen The Boss fourteen times can call me by my first name. I've only seen him twice."

Ten minutes later, after passing two more hidden

checkpoints, they pulled up to the farmhouse. McCulver stood up from one of the rocking chairs and met him at the foot of the covered porch's stairs.

"How'd we do?" Eli asked over the hood of the SUV.

"Long day, but we cleared out the properties all the way to Kennard Hill Road, then circled back toward Route 160 and vacated those premises. The York County sheriff's cruiser came in handy."

"Any trouble?"

"No," said McCulver, "but Jimmy's guys are, uh—a little out of control."

"How so?" Eli asked, guiding McCulver onto the porch so the men getting out of the SUV wouldn't hear.

"They're a little quick to pull the trigger. We didn't bring anyone back to help out with the farm work."

"Well, we don't have enough people to watch over prisoners anyway. Not yet," said Eli, sensing there was more.

"And they don't take orders very well. Not from me, at least. We had some delays while they toyed around with some of the survivors. If we weren't short on personnel, I would have killed them on the spot. Looks like some prison habits rubbed off on them."

"You better watch that," snarled Eli, tensing his fists.

"I'm only bringing it up because it's a liability. We had eight homesteads to clear on Porterfield, and these sick fucks spent an hour in the first house."

"I'll have a talk with them," said Eli.

"Good, because they're multiplying. They took two of the minivans out this afternoon and collected more 'Vikings,' as they like to say. They came back with seven recruits, all armed to the teeth and about as scary looking as Jimmy's crew."

"That's good news," said Eli.

"If you can control them. I meant absolutely no disrespect toward your brother, but this is a dangerous group. We have to watch them closely, or we could have a 'situation' on our hands. I'll feel more comfortable when we've doubled our numbers," said McCulver.

"You think they might mutiny?"

"How much time did you spend with them before all of this happened?"

"Not much. Jimmy kept a close leash on—"

"And Jimmy's dead. If you'd seen what they did to that family, we wouldn't be having this discussion."

"If they'd disobeyed my orders, I would have killed them," stated Eli.

McCulver squinted, clearly considering his next words. Eli knew what he wanted to say. The question was whether McCulver had the good sense to keep it to himself. Eli didn't care what kind of collateral damage Jimmy's 'Vikings' did during their assigned operations, as long as they obeyed orders and accomplished the mission. He hoped Kevin was wrong about the possibility of a mutiny. He'd need their help.

"I have an idea that will keep them occupied while we build up the core militia group. I'll show you inside," McCulver said, opening the front door to the farmhouse. "How was your foray along the 302?"

He chose those words wisely, Eli thought to himself. McCulver continued to impress him, even if he sensed a touch of insubordination.

"Unbelievably productive. We signed up an entire town."

McCulver paused, searching his face for a sign that he was joking.

"They just don't know it yet," continued Eli.

"Sounds interesting," he said, directing Eli to the dining room.

A large-scale map of southern Maine covered half of the rectangular table, along with scattered notebooks and pencils.

"Which town?"

"Bridgton. Met with the town council and the chief of police about helping them train up some of their folks to help man their checkpoints. Told them we can train them in basic firearms procedures, military-style cover and concealment. Enough to handle their own needs."

"That must have been one of your best performances. Sorry I missed it."

"Well, most of it was spent on my knees with a gun to my head, but it worked out better than I anticipated," Eli said, circling Bridgton on the map with one of the pencils. "Shit, it was like winning the lottery."

"I presume we get something out of the deal?"

"While we train their people at our compound," he said, winking, "we'll provide them with men, on a trial basis, to work at each checkpoint. If it all works out, this will get their police officers back into a patrol role within the town. They're having a bit of a problem handling the summer crowd. I was more than happy to help out."

"They bought off on having armed militia in town?"

"Only at the checkpoints, and our folks will be unarmed."

"Unarmed?"

"To build trust," he said, grinning wickedly.

"You got me, Eli. What am I missing? I figure this isn't your charitable side flaring up."

"Am I that easy to read?"

"Not for the good people of Bridgton, apparently."

Eli pounded the table, laughing. "And I thought everyone's sense of humor faded away with the electricity. You should have seen the car ride today. Holy Jesus, I was riding around with a bunch of stiffs."

"So what exactly am I missing?"

"You're missing the part where we simultaneously execute half of Bridgton's police force and take over the town."

McCulver studied the map, tracing roads from Bridgton toward the coast.

"How do you see Bridgton fitting into all of this in the long run? It can't be our new base of operations. Too exposed."

"I figured we'd get as many new recruits as possible, even if we have to conscript folks. Grab enough people to work the fields. Probably take as much equipment as possible. Tractors. Buses. Any of the public works stuff that'll still run," said Eli.

"So, you don't want to hold on to the town permanently?" said McCulver.

"Like you said, it'll just make us targets. We'll keep it long enough to get what we need."

McCulver placed his finger on a point halfway between Sebago Lake and Portland.

"Did you know there's a state correctional facility in Windham?"

"Jimmy spent some time there."

"So did most of the guys in his crew. They think we might be able to solve our recruiting problem with a trip to the facility. Might be a solution to our manpower issues."

"I assume the prison guards won't let me set up a

booth in the cafeteria to take volunteers," said Eli.

"Probably not." McCulver laughed. "But I wouldn't be completely surprised if the guards haven't taken off already. They spent over a hundred million dollars rebuilding the entire men's facility three years ago, and everything's automated, completely dependent on electricity. Once the juice stops flowing to the system, every secure door in that facility goes into countdown mode. Thirty minutes until every secure door opens permanently. I guarantee the corrections officers are keeping a close eye on the backup generator's fuel supply. We just need to get there before the doors open, or we'll miss the recruiting opportunity."

"Then what the fuck are we waiting for? Let's get some eyes on that prison."

Chapter 9

EVENT +5 Days

Limerick, Maine

Alex kissed Emily on the forehead and stroked her hair for a few seconds. "Good night, sweetie. I love you."

"I love you too, Dad. When is Ryan coming down?"

"Really soon."

"Can you send him down now?"

"He should be down in a few minutes."

"Is everyone going to sleep down here?"

"Most of us will be upstairs, keeping an eye on the house, but Nana and Grandpa will be down here. The old people need their sleep," he said, and his daughter laughed.

"I heard that," said his mother, who was propped up on an air mattress next to the door leading out of the "bunker." The 20-gauge shotgun leaned against the wall next to the mattress.

"What about the Thorntons and Mr. Walker?"

"They've been down here all night. We're airing them out for a while. You're in good hands down here, sweetie. Nobody can get in here without going through all of us first."

"I wish you and Mom could sleep down here."

"Me too, but you're safer with us upstairs. You have Ethan and Kevin sound asleep right next to you."

"I'm not asleep," said Ethan.

"You should be asleep," said Alex.

"I'm not either," Kevin chimed in.

"Great. Well, your cousins can attest to Nana's skill with a shotgun, and so can I."

Emily sighed. "I wish there were more Marines."

"Nana's like three Marines combined," he said, and they laughed.

"Watch where you're going with that," said his mom, Amy Fletcher.

"We'll have more Marines here in a few days," he said and kissed Emily again. "Love you."

"Love you, too, Daddy."

"Love you, guys."

"Love you, Uncle Alex," Kevin and Ethan mumbled.

"Things will get back to normal. I promise," Alex said and stepped away.

Samantha Walker and her three children appeared in the doorway.

"See? The basement's filling up fast," he said and walked over to the door to greet her. "We have a bunch of camping mattresses for the kids. Blankets, sleeping bags, non-shot-up pillows—a couple of overprotective grandparents. I think the kids will be fine down here."

"Perfect. Thank you," said Samantha, stepping through the door with her family.

"I only charge ten dollars an hour," said Alex's mom.

"I brought a nineteen-year-old. Do I get a discount?"

"Can she use a shotgun?"

"Not yet," said Chloe.

"Seven dollars."

"Deal," said Samantha.

"They can take whatever makes them comfortable," Alex offered. "I don't think we'll be spending much time down here tonight."

"Probably not," Samantha said, leading her kids into the candlelit room.

"Abby, thanks for hooking up my laptop to the video receivers. From what I understand, you're running the tech show around here."

"Pretty much," said Samantha's daughter.

"She was the only one that could read your writing," said Amy.

"Funny, Mom. I'll see you upstairs in a few."

Alex walked over to the bulkhead and flashed his light at the metal doors, confirming that they were latched to the ringbolts imbedded in the basement floor. No matter how hard anyone tried, the doors would not swing open unless he detached the thick metal retaining rods from the bolts. Satisfied that the basement was secure, he walked upstairs into the kitchen, which was lit by a combination of candles and green chemlights donated by the Marines. Staff Sergeant Evans sat at the kitchen island, scrolling through the ruggedized tablet he had removed from the Matvee. His face glowed from the soft red screen.

"Are the Marines settled in for the night?"

"Yes, sir. I have the vehicles positioned to give 360-degree coverage, two Marines in each vehicle. We set up an LP/OP at the entrance to Gelder Pond Lane. I had them move into position after dark. They have clear lines of sight down the eastern side of the road in front of your property and the road leading to the western side. Ideally, we'd have another along the pond, but I'm the only one left. I'll be on the thirty-cal up in the master bedroom. I can cover nearly 270 degrees around the house from that room."

"Perfect. I'll come by around zero-two-hundred to give you a break."

"I should be fine, sir."

"When's the last time you caught any meaningful sleep?"

"It's been a while," Evans admitted.

"I'll at least bring you and your Marines some coffee."

"Sounds like a fair deal."

"Thank you, Staff Sergeant. This means a lot to me, my family—all of us," said Alex.

"I'm just glad we can help out while we're here. I'd want someone doing that for me," said Evans.

"Anything you need, please don't hesitate to ask. I know you guys are temporarily assigned under my command, but I consider this to be a personal favor that you're doing—"

Evans started to protest.

"Nope. I don't want to hear any arguments to the contrary. My house is your house. Seriously."

"Well, I don't—"

"Staff Sergeant?" Alex said, shaking his head. "You need something, you ask, or send someone who doesn't mind asking."

"Thank you, sir. I was going to say, that between your mother and your wife, we haven't had to ask. They've been really generous. Very much appreciated."

"Good, then I'll expect you to catch up on some sleep tonight," said Alex, patting him on the back.

"I wouldn't go that far, sir."

"We'll see."

"I'll get out of your way," said Evans, grabbing his tablet and rifle.

"Good night, Staff Sergeant."

"Night, sir."

Alex walked into the great room, searching for a seat. Unsurprisingly, half of the group appeared to be asleep. Breathing deeply, Ed Walker lay on an air mattress pushed under the windows to the right. He was turned on one side; his bandaged hip off the mattress. Linda and Charlie sat side by side on the leather couch, with their bandaged legs resting on small pillows on the coffee table. The soft, flickering glow of candlelight from one of the end tables exposed Charlie's gaping mouth, though his buzz-saw-like snoring left little doubt about his status. Linda hit her husband's shoulder.

"What? What happened?" he said, jolted out of a shallow sleep.

"I just figured out why we got kicked out of the basement," said Linda.

"What do you mean?" asked Charlie.

"You sound like a foghorn."

"It's not that bad," he countered.

"It's pretty bad, my friend," Alex said. "I'm starting to wonder how we still have the Jeep."

"He probably scared everyone away," added Ed.

"I used those nose strips," said Charlie.

"I hope you stocked up, for Linda's sake," said Kate.

She sat cross-legged on the floor, leaning against the bullet-peppered wall to the left. She was partially concealed in the shadow cast by the La-Z-Boy occupied by his father. In the dim light, the room almost looked normal, except for the numerous dark splotches in the drywall and the various rifles leaned against the furniture or walls. Alex unslung his rifle and hung it on the wood-burning stove, taking a seat in one of the folding chairs set up around the coffee table.

"Sam should be right up," said Alex. "She was getting the kids settled."

"What about Ryan? He's been up in his perch long enough," said Kate.

"I'll have a talk with him. I don't think Emily will fall asleep without him in the basement."

"I'd sleep better knowing he was upstairs," said Ed. "He saved our skins yesterday."

"I wonder where he gets that from?" said Linda.

"Runs in the family," said Kate. "Alex's dad served two tours in Vietnam as a Marine lieutenant."

"I didn't know your dad was in 'Nam. You should have said something, Alex," said Charlie.

"He's pretty much read every book and watched every documentary on the Vietnam War—twice," said Linda.

"More than that," added Charlie.

"Dad clams up pretty quick when the subject is brought up, except around his Marine Corps buddies," said Alex.

"That seems to run in the family too," commented Kate.

"Charlie, we can talk history anytime. Did Alex tell you about this rifle?" said Tim Fletcher, lifting his rifle off the floor and setting it in front of the lounger.

"Now he's mister talkative," said Alex.

"That's not from Vietnam, is it?" asked Charlie.

"Damn right it is. I used this as a military advisor. Tracked it down by serial number when they switched over to those plastic guns."

"He got a congressman involved," said Alex.

"He was a TBS classmate," said Tim.

Charlie twisted on the couch, trying to get a better look at the rifle. He grimaced in pain when his foot shifted on the pillow and slid to the surface of the table.

"I got it," said Alex, lifting the bandaged leg high enough to replace the pillow. "How are you feeling?"

"A deep, throbbing pain has replaced the holy shit agony I was feeling most of yesterday. The pain pills help."

Alex examined Linda's foot. The hospital had provided a large, easily removable splint, which enclosed the bandages covering her ankle.

"What about you, Mrs. Rambo?" asked Alex.

"I'm still at the holy fuck level most of the time," she said.

"Me too," said Ed.

"You guys taking your pain meds?"

"No," said Linda. "They give me a headache."

"I'll take them off your hands," said Ed.

"Probably not a great idea right now," said Alex. "Let's talk it over with Corporal Allen when he makes his rounds. He has some stronger stuff, if necessary. If you can't sleep, let me know, and we'll get you something."

"I won't have any trouble sleeping," said Ed, "as long as I'm not in the same room as Foghorn Leghorn."

"Can I get a separate room?" said Linda.

"Everybody's ganging up on me again," Charlie whined.

The basement door slid open, revealing Samantha Walker and Amy Fletcher. Alex's mom carried the shotgun in the crook of her elbow.

"We good for a few minutes?" asked Alex.

"I think so. I told them we'd be at the top of the stairs," said Samantha, sitting on the single step leading into the great room.

Alex's mother joined her, leaning the shotgun against the half wall separating the kitchen from the sunken great room. "First things first. We made it," said Alex, pausing to let the words sink in. "We're all here, more or less in one piece. The kids are fine. Given the curveball we were thrown, I'd say we've done pretty damn well as a team."

"I'll second that," said Charlie, followed by hushed agreement from everyone.

"With that said, we still have a long way to go."

"I can't imagine it getting any worse," said Ed.

"Jesus. What the hell else could they throw at us? They left twenty-nine bodies behind," said Samantha.

"I'm more concerned with the bigger picture. I have a few things I want to share with you. Information I've gathered over the past forty-eight hours. When you add it to the HAM radio broadcasts, we—"

"The bigger picture doesn't have everyone hiding in the basement," Kate cut in. "What's going on with the group that attacked us?"

"The leader has disappeared for now. I spoke with members of the York County Readiness Brigade and—"

"Another militia group? Screw that. I don't want to see any of those people around here," said Samantha.

"I'm not bringing them here. I thought they might be able to shed some light on this Russell character. Apparently, they forgot to mention him during both of my interviews a few years ago."

"How convenient," Samantha said. "I wouldn't trust them."

"I'm not trusting anybody outside of our group."

"What about Colonel Grady?" whispered Tim Fletcher.

"I trust his Marines. I'll let them take care of Mr. Russell and whatever's left of his crew when we find them. Right now, I feel pretty good about our security situation."

"Until Grady pulls them away," said Ed.

"He's bought off on using our property as a rapid-response, forward operating base. We'll have double the number of Marines here within a week. They'll either set up a tent for their headquarters or use the barn. Either way, they'll have to leave Marines behind to guard the headquarters—and us."

"That's good news," said his dad.

"It is..." Alex said, hesitating.

He wasn't sure how much of the big-picture doom-and-gloom scenario he should share with the group. Several situations ran through his head, many of which resulted in abandoning the compound before the weather turned. All would require serious planning and consideration.

"What's the bad news?" Charlie prompted.

"The bad news is that we have to plan for the possibility of leaving this house," said Alex.

"Because of the militia?" asked his mom.

"That's one scenario, but not the most likely. I'm more concerned with the refugee situation. I just can't see how it will work, even with several thousand soldiers in place to guard the borders and patrol the camps. If the broadcasts we've been hearing over the HAM radio are true, word will spread, and the rest of the Boston area will empty. Nobody will want to be near a big city with a possible nuclear escalation on the table. There's no way in hell FEMA can take care of a million-plus people. Winter will make it worse."

"We're off the beaten path out here. I would think most of the people would make their way to the 95 corridor. There's nothing out here."

"I would tend to agree with that, but if the situation deteriorates, the Recovery Zone border will shift north, taking everything with it."

"Including you," stated Kate bitterly.

"It's a Catch-22. We definitely need the Marines here until the Maine Liberty Militia has been neutralized."

"Which hopefully won't be very long," said Linda.

"Currently, they're the biggest internal threat to stability within the Recovery Zone. I don't see an issue convincing Grady to allocate considerable resources to solving the problem."

"Then we won't need the Marines forever, though they're welcome to stay, even if you're not part of the battalion," said Kate.

"Yes…and no. If the Recovery Zone border is moved north, everyone south of the border suddenly joins the refugee population," said Alex.

"What does that mean, exactly?" Ed asked cautiously.

"It means that without this golden ticket," he said, holding up his ID card, "we might not be allowed to cross the Saco River. That's the fallback boundary."

"That's bullshit!" Ed sputtered.

"That's the reality of the situation and why we need to put a lot of thought into this. If I give up my status and we stay, we might not be able to flee north if the situation gets out of control here."

"Then we need to get out of here as soon as possible," Ed said. "Charlie?"

"We can always head up to Belgrade. It'll be tight, but everyone's welcome. That includes all of us," said Charlie.

"We'd make it work," affirmed Linda.

"You can't go anywhere right now, Ed. How are you going to sit in a car for four hours?" said Samantha.

"We have time," said Alex, "but we need to figure out how to do this logistically and start making preparations. We have two cars and seventeen people, four of whom can't walk. I don't anticipate any of you getting around on your own without crutches for at least a month. Linda will probably be longer."

"*If* I can even use the foot again," she said, sounding dismal for the first time Alex could remember.

"I'll see what I can do about getting you to an orthopedic surgeon. Maybe one at Bridgton Hospital. They won't be jammed with casualties like Sanford or the coastal hospitals. I remember them having an orthopedic group."

"You should get on that as soon as possible," said Kate.

"I will," he said.

"I guess there isn't a huge downside to working with the Marines, at least through the winter. If the situation stabilizes, you could part ways in the spring," said Kate.

"If they'll let me. Just saying. We need to plan for any contingency, including the sudden revocation of my ID card. I'm not one hundred percent sure what I'm dealing with."

"What do you mean?" asked Charlie.

"Maybe this isn't the best time," Alex whispered.

"I thought you trusted them," said Samantha.

"I do, but they follow orders, and I've seen a few things that make me wonder about Homeland's plans for the battalion. I opened a large shipping container at the airport, which held enough uniforms to outfit the entire unit."

"That doesn't sound so bad. I'm sure the Marines could use a change of clothes," said Samantha.

"It doesn't sound bad until you find out that the container had been secretly stored for years in a fenced-off warehouse complex near the airport and that the uniforms are a strange pattern, labeled 'Federal Security.' I saw that on the manifest."

"Jesus," said Tim. "That's not a good sign."

"Right. And that's just the tip of the iceberg. The second container held racks of weapons not found at the infantry battalion level. Rifles with integral suppressors. MP-7 submachine guns. Advanced night-vision optics."

Ed asked, "What does that mean, in layman's terms?"

"I don't know, but these are the types of weapons you'd expect to find in a very slick, low-profile special operations unit. It means the battalion may be tasked to do more than Colonel Grady advertised, or knows about. If it turns into a secret police operation, we're out of here."

The room fell silent for several moments as the gravity of Alex's statement settled.

"Either way, we have to prepare this place for winter," said Tim.

"Right. We'll have to work on both plans at the same time. If possible, I'd like to take a trip to your place up north, Charlie. Make sure it's still a viable option. A lake house with solar panels might not remain unoccupied for long after an EMP attack."

"Anyone thinking they're getting a bargain with the solar panels will be in for a rude awakening. The whole system is probably fried."

"That's something we'll have to consider. We can disassemble the system in the basement and bring any of the parts we'll need, but I'm not sure about the solar panels. Were yours disconnected?"

Charlie shook his head.

"Then the panels are probably dead," said Alex.

"What about borrowing one of the tactical vehicles for a run?" Ed suggested.

"It's possible, but we'd probably have to do it now, before the battalion arrives. I can't see commandeering one of their vehicles for a full-day side trip once they're fully operational."

"I don't think that's a good idea," said Kate. "Offloading gear from a military vehicle will draw way too much attention. Guaranteed to be pillaged at that point."

"This is all stuff we need to start game-planning," said Alex.

"Timeline?" asked Tim.

"I think we should be ready to roll, if necessary, by the end of September. Plan on multiple trips. I'll do what I can to get some support, either civilian or military. For now, it's all hands on deck getting the outside of the house patched up. I picked up plenty of caulk and materials to plug the holes."

"What about the toilets?" Charlie asked. "The pain pills cause constipation, but that ain't gonna last forever."

"Good God," muttered Linda, shaking her head.

"Hey! Just giving everyone fair warning. That camping toilet ain't gonna cut it when the time comes."

"Thank you, Charlie," said Alex. "Top priority tomorrow morning. I brought full replacements from

Home Depot."

"Toilets, shutters, caulking," said Kate.

"And sleep. In that order," said Alex.

Part II

"Rearm"

Chapter 10

EVENT +7 Days

Maine State Correctional Facility
Windham, Maine

Eli Russell leaned forward in the front seat of the SUV and examined the Maine State Correctional Facility's main parking lot as they approached the intersection at Mallison Falls Road. The lot looked deserted, sprinkled with cars abandoned after the event. He barely recognized the place. He'd visited his brother here on a few occasions in late 2009, long before the one-hundred-million-dollar upgrade. From what he could tell, few of the old buildings had survived the overhaul. He waved Grizzly on, pushing his convoy of six vehicles across the empty rural road.

"Liberty Two, this is Actual. Start your approach," he said, releasing a second, smaller convoy along a jeep trail due east of the prison.

"Copy. Patriot Two inbound to target."

"Liberty Three, proceed to secondary target and execute your mission. You should be able to disable the tower without engaging the personnel inside. The front parking lot is empty and completely obscured from the building by a tall row of bushes," said Eli.

McCulver's voice answered. "Copy. We're making the

turn off Elm Street. ETA thirty seconds."

Everything was falling into place. The special-purpose group, aka Jimmy's Vikings, had scouted the area surrounding the prison before settling in for a long day of surveillance. One of the first things they noticed driving River Road was a communications tower rising several stories above the trees. Thinking it was an odd location for a cell phone tower, they followed a few back roads to the tower, discovering the Cumberland County Regional Communications Center. A quick drive through the parking lot confirmed the presence of a running generator, which meant the center was fully operational. Since the communications center provided long-range emergency dispatch services to dozens of towns in the county, Eli thought it wise to disable the center prior to the attack on the prison.

McCulver suggested knocking the tower out with small explosive charges rather than trying to storm the building. The last thing they needed was a plea for help broadcast to every law enforcement officer in the county. With the tower destroyed, the dispatchers inside posed little threat to the operation. The only problem with McCulver's plan was that it required him to blow up the tower and race to the prison in order to handle the explosives. Eli couldn't rely on any of the men in the convoy to properly set and safely detonate the charges required to breach the back gate and the utility bays leading to the generator.

The whole plan hinged on McCulver's unique skill-set, which left Eli feeling a little uneasy. Moving forward, McCulver would train an apprentice. The Maine Liberty Militia was one stray bullet away from losing its biggest force multiplier—an unacceptable risk given their overall plan.

Eli's convoy cruised through the parking lot, passing the facility's single authorized pedestrian entrance, which had been sealed from the lot by a rolling razor-wire-topped gate. Recent correctional "guests" within Jimmy's group speculated that the few correctional officers on duty would congregate in the futuristic steel and glass administrative building. The correctional custody units beyond the building no longer contained their own control rooms, cutting down on the number of officers required to staff the prison.

All inmate movement was monitored and directed from a single control center located in that building, giving the officers little reason to be elsewhere, especially with the inmate population locked in their cells. Night shifts were reduced even further due to automation, explaining the paucity of vehicles in the parking lot. Jimmy's men estimated they'd be up against a few dozen officers, most of whom had little to no practical firearms training.

Once inside, they should have little difficulty mopping up the staff if they decided to stay and defend the prison. Eli planned to leave the front entrance unopposed, to encourage the guards' swift departure. If he could take the prison without losing any men—all the better.

Grizzly turned the SUV left toward the end of the parking lot, where the asphalt transitioned to a hard-packed gravel road that followed the prison's eastern fence line to the loading bays and a utility garage. Yesterday, one of the bay doors had been left open for several hours, presumably to release excess diesel fumes from the generator they had pinpointed to one of the buildings next to the garage. If they could catch one of the doors open this morning, they wouldn't have to wait for McCulver. As they raced down the fence, the second convoy appeared, trailing a column of dust as it barreled toward the garage.

"This is Liberty Two. I just saw one of the loading bay doors slam shut. Looks like they know we're here. Over."

Damn closed-circuit cameras!

"This is Actual. Proceed with caution, and wait for Liberty Three. Do not try to open any of the doors without explosives. Never know what's waiting on the other side."

They'd have to do this the hard way.

The westbound convoy crossed ahead of Eli's SUV, screeching to a stop on the pavement outside of the corrugated metal garage building. His convoy sped past the loading area, following a tight dirt road around the security fence until it connected with a paved road that cut right down the middle of the facility. They accelerated toward the gate at the end of the road, stopping several feet in front of the gate. A closed-circuit television camera mounted to the underside of the adjacent building panned in their direction, no doubt filling every screen in the control room. Eli stuck his compact AR-15 out of the passenger window and fired three bullets into the boxy, plastic contraption, shattering it.

He opened his car door and walked up to the gate, shaking it. Sturdy, but far from indestructible. He was tempted to have one of the vehicles ram the gate, but the thought of disabling a car right in front of the primary breach point chased the idea away. Unobstructed vehicle access along this road was critical to his plan. He had no reason to hurry inside the gate, since they couldn't access any of the secure prison areas until thirty minutes after the generator was destroyed.

If McCulver is right about the automated lock system.

He was rarely wrong. They were probably better off waiting at a standoff distance, anyway. The guards had access to military-grade weapons, and there was no reason to tempt any of them to play Rambo.

"Liberty One. Form a defensive perimeter around the vehicles, focused on the building to our right. We don't want any surprises while we're waiting," he said into his radio.

The primary assault team took cover behind the SUVs, aiming at the windows and doors along the building, while one man from each vehicle watched the opposite direction. A few days of vehicle drills had paid off. The men actually looked like they knew what they were doing.

Three nearly simultaneous cracks hit Eli's ears, followed by a slight tremor.

"Liberty Actual, this is Liberty Three. The tower is down. I say again, the tower is down. En route to first breach point," said McCulver.

"Hot damn, Liberty Three!" he said into the radio, unable to contain his excitement.

This was going down like a real military operation.

"Copy, en route to first breach point."

Eli reached through the passenger window and grabbed a pair of binoculars sitting on the dashboard. He focused the wide field of view on the administrative building at the end of the road three hundred yards away. Beyond the fence, the utility road was flanked on both sides by gray, one-story correctional units, which fed into the recreation fields lining the prison's perimeter fence. The units were connected by a long security hallway, which meant they would have to be careful on their approach. Enterprising guards could catch them in a lethal crossfire on the way to the administrative building. If Liberty Two didn't breach the utility garage soon, the guards could work their way to the adjacent building, forcing Liberty One to retreat. Worse than that, they could keep Liberty Two from disabling the generator, severely complicating the operation.

At that point, they would be forced to use bolt cutters on the fence, which would put them on foot looking for an entrance leading to the generator room that could be forced open. Everything depended on McCulver, who should be arriving any minute to blow a hole in one of the garage bay doors.

***

Dave Camp magnified the camera feed and counted the men visible near the vehicles.

Jesus. They have a fucking army out there.

This was entirely too much. He needed to get the hell out of here before it was too late. Most of his shift took off as soon as it became apparent that they were dealing with more than a downed power line. The first wave crammed into the few vehicles that worked, heading out before shift change at 6:30. A few vanished on foot over the next hour or two, slipping out of the utility garage and walking east to River Road. He watched them peek nervously over their shoulders until they were out of sight, but never said a word.

He notified Casey Norton, the nightshift captain, when motion sensors triggered cameras in the main garage next to the administrative building. Three guards tried to hotwire one of the facility's fifteen-passenger prisoner transport vans, but were stopped by Norton, with the seemingly reluctant help of the remaining officers. Norton surprised them all by offering to drive the rest of the shift home in the van, if that's what they wanted. Five guards, including the three caught stealing the van, took him up on the offer. When Norton returned with the vehicle around ten in the morning, they were down to fourteen correctional officers and Stanley Collier, the deputy warden, who rode his bike to the prison.

He should have taken Norton up on the offer to leave but didn't have any compelling reason to go. His shared apartment in Westbrook was most likely stripped of any food, and his family lived north of Waterville, well outside of Norton's advertised delivery range. The prison offered a secure bed, food, and access to the dispatch center across the street, which seemed to be the only way anyone was communicating after the event. At the time, it seemed like the best deal available. The idea of an armed attack against the prison never crossed his mind. Nobody wasted time thinking about how to break into a prison, which was why the group of men on his monitor scared him.

"I have about fifteen heavily armed men at the back gate. They're wearing camouflage and carrying assault rifles. I'm not sure what they're waiting for."

"Did you say fifteen?" asked Collier.

"More than that. I can't see the whole group from this angle and distance. They shot up the camera at the gate," said Camp, pointing toward one of the center images on the sixty-inch flat-screen monitor above his station.

He shifted his hand left, highlighting a different screen.

"I have at least twelve more outside of Vendor

Services. They're playing with one of the delivery bays," added Camp.

"Can you see what they're doing?"

"Trying to get in," said one of the guards watching on a different screen.

"Jesus, these guys are heavily armed. I don't think we can hold them off if they get inside," said Collier.

"Not armed with batons and pepper spray. We need to access the armory, Stan, before it's too late," said a thick, gray-haired guard standing in the control room's doorway. "My people are getting nervous."

"Casey, they can't get into any of the buildings directly connected with the correctional areas," said Collier.

"They're in!" yelled Camp, drawing everyone to the surveillance station.

A cloud of smoke rose above the building as men poured into the delivery bay. One of the vehicles backed out of the delivery lot and sped along the fence toward the back of the facility. He'd missed whatever they'd done to the door.

Shit!

"You were saying?" said Norton.

"Did they use explosives?" Collier asked.

"I didn't see," said Camp. "But the smoke wasn't there a second ago."

"Stan! If they take out the generator, we'll have a big problem on our hands in about thirty minutes."

"They don't know how the system works," stated Collier.

"You willing to bet your life on that?" asked the shift captain. "They seem pretty organized to me. I bet that car racing toward the back is carrying enough explosives to blow the gate and a few of the external doors."

An out-of-breath guard ran into the control room. "The dispatch tower across the street is down! That's what we heard! The whole thing fell over. What the fuck is going on?"

"That's it, Stan. We have fifteen officers on duty, including you. It's not enough if they get inside. I'm opening the armory," said the shift captain.

"Even if they manage to trigger the thirty-minute lockdown fail-safe, they can't get into the administrative building. We're safe here."

"With nine hundred pissed-off prisoners on the loose?"

"They'll run for the gate," said Collier.

"They've been drinking out of their toilets for the last several days. We haven't exactly been taking good care of them."

"What else could we do? The facility isn't equipped to handle this kind of an emergency. Orders from the governor were clear. Hold the prisoners until—"

"Until what?"

"I don't know. They're working on something," said Collier.

"They're working on something, all right. The state can manage to deliver diesel for the generator, but they can't be bothered to feed the inmates?"

Collier shrugged his shoulders. "What do you want from me?"

"I want you to give me the keys to the armory. Whether we stay or go, we need weapons," said the captain.

"We can't take the weapons out of here. They're state property," stated Collier.

"What if they got another team out there waiting for us to leave?"

"I don't know!"

"You better start thinking really hard about the situation. You think none of these fuckers knows where you live? I guarantee your home address is public knowledge in the high-security unit."

"What, I just issue weapons and drop everyone off at home?" said Collier. "How am I going to explain that one to the governor's office?"

A muted thud echoed in the room, followed by a brief second of darkness before the emergency lighting activated.

"Set your watches," grumbled the shift captain. "Thirty minutes until we no longer have the option of leaving."

Camp thought about Norton's input for a few seconds. *What the fuck was he waiting for?* He'd give the deputy warden one more chance before walking out on his own—with or without a firearm. If he headed west, he could hide along the banks of the Presumpscot River until these inmates cleared the area, maybe warn a few of the folks living in South Windham. With nine hundred prisoners on the loose, the nearby houses were sure to be attacked, along with the residents inside.

"We need to get out of here, sir," said Camp, standing up from his computer station. "Cameras show the front is clear. Our van is in the parking lot. They obviously don't know the van works. We could make a quick getaway."

"Damn it, all right. Get all of your men back to admin," said Collier.

"They're already here. I just need to get into the armory."

Collier balked, grimacing at the suggestion before nodding.

"The keys are in my office safe."

***

Sammy Vaughn heard a car door slam, freezing him in place. He twisted slowly onto his stomach and faced uphill, scanning the row of vehicles facing the road behind him. The parking lot sat twenty feet higher than Vaughn's position, on an incline that restricted his view of the parking lot. Pressed into the grass at the base of a tree, he could only see the tops of the tallest vehicles. A powerful engine started as he scanned for signs of movement. It sounded like a diesel. He focused on the top of the big-ass, gray passenger van he had seen when he was running across the parking lot to the trees.

Has to be the van.

"Liberty Actual, this is Overwatch. I have a vehicle starting in the parking lot. I think it's the prison van."

"This is Actual. Can you confirm how many are in the van?"

"Negative. Not without giving my position away. Hold on. It's backing up. I should have a solid visual when it drives out of the lot. I could hit them with the IED. No point in letting them raise the alarm."

"Negative. Without the dispatch tower, they'd be talking to themselves. Do not trigger the IED. We can't afford to waste any explosives," said Eli.

"Roger that," Vaughan said, slipping the radio into one of his cargo pockets.

When the top of the van disappeared, he grabbed his binoculars and sprinted to a second stand of trees closer to the exit, making sure to stay as low to the ground as possible. He'd been extremely lucky with the van. If he hadn't been lying prone on the ground, scanning the road, the guards might have spotted him. Vaughn raised the binoculars and waited for the van to appear beyond the parked cars at the end of the lot. When the van cleared the cars, speeding toward Mallison Falls Road, the first thing he noticed was Casey Norton's shit-eating grin—plainly visible through the open front passenger window.

That fucker still works here?

Vaughn ceased thinking about his duties to the Maine Liberty Militia. He barely registered the fact that every seat in the van was filled with guards. He stood up and pulled the handheld detonator from one of his tactical vest pouches, flicking the on/off switch. McCulver had showed him exactly how to detonate the ten-pound pipe bomb sitting in the gravel next to the entrance. He locked eyes with Norton and nodded.

Adios, bitch.

The thought conflicted with Norton's face, which grinned at him behind the iron sights of an assault rifle. Vaughn never heard the shot that evacuated his skull. The van screeched onto the road as Vaughn's body dropped, triggering the pipe bomb.

***

Eli pulled McCulver away from the fence, pushing him behind the open SUV door.

"Take it easy! I'm working with shit that goes bang, all right? That was the pipe bomb. Sounds like Vaughn doesn't like to follow orders."

"Watch what you say about Vaughn, motherfucker," said one of Jimmy's psychopaths, who was crouched between the first and second vehicles.

"Just saying," said McCulver.

"Overwatch, this is Liberty Actual. Report your status. Over."

Nothing. Eli tried again, with no response.

"Shit. Stay here. I can't afford to have you shot or blown up," he said, muttering curses as he walked briskly toward the back of the convoy.

He couldn't wait to get rid of Jimmy's idiots. His brother had trained capable soldiers, but they were mouthy and insubordinate, two traits he could ill afford to cultivate. He'd pawn them off on the town of Bridgton, along with the rest of their miscreant friends in the prison. Ironically, he needed the Vikings on this raid, to immediately identify the problem recruits. Anyone singled out by his brother's men as a "must have" would become a "must go." Eli would keep the serious recruiting prospects for the regular ranks.

"Joe, I want you to head around front with your team and see what the fuck is going on with Vaughn. Watch yourself. I need to know if the gray Maine State Corrections van is still in the parking lot."

"Got it," said the team leader, directing his men to load up the rear SUV.

Less than a minute later, Eli's radio crackled.

"Liberty Actual, this is Liberty One-Six. Vaughn is dead. One bullet through the forehead. No van in sight."

McCulver shrugged his shoulders and mouthed, "The bomb?"

"What about the bomb?" radioed Eli.

"Blew a nice little crater in the asphalt, but that's about it. No sign of any vehicle damage. Over."

"Copy all. Park your car in a discreet location and keep an eye on the approaches. Engage any vehicles entering the parking lot. Out."

Eli shook his head. "Sounds like the guards hightailed it out of here. Blow the fucking gate," he said, turning to the man crouched between the cars. "Sorry about Vaughn. Fuckers got a lucky shot off. Dead before he hit the ground."

"Any guards left inside?" asked the man with a look of pure hatred and murder on his face.

Eli checked his watch. "I guess we'll find out for sure in about thirteen minutes."

Chapter 11

EVENT +7 Days

Maine State Correctional Facility
Windham, Maine

Two gray prison buses idled outside of the gate, just beyond the reach of the disorganized gaggle of prisoners Eli had selected for the final test. Surveying the group, he was mostly satisfied with the result of their prison raid. Within fifty-two minutes of arriving at the facility, he stood in front of seventy-three men and eight women with the potential to join his militia. The process had been simple.

Instead of wasting time trying to break into the administrative building, most of the inmates sought the next logical point of egress from the facility. The back gate. The prison's jogging track and basketball court were situated in the massive open area at the rear of the facility, adjacent to the gate, which meant most prisoners watched trucks going in and out of the gate all day. Eli started honking the SUV's horn when the first gray uniforms appeared on the utility road deep within the facility. Within moments, the word spread, sending a steady stream of desperate, starving prisoners in their direction.

He'd planned the next stage carefully, having no

intention of putting his men in direct contact with several hundred criminals. Using bolt cutters, he created a rectangular opening in the western fence, visible to the prisoners from the gate. As the prisoners approached, Eli addressed them with his megaphone, congratulating them on their liberation and asking them to wait between two of the nearby buildings if they were interested in joining the Maine Liberty Militia. If not, they were directed toward the western fence line and told to immediately vacate the area.

"We provide food, shelter and a chance to bear arms against the tyrannical forces that left you here to die." This tagline snagged one hundred and seventeen prisoners, including five that were immediately squeezed through the gate to join the Vikings. He had to keep those crazy fuckers happy one way or the other until he was done with them.

Once the prisoner exodus thinned, he lined the candidates up, single file, thirty feet from the gate and called them forward one at a time for a quick visual inspection and interview. He spent no more than ten seconds on each prisoner, quickly determining three things. Did they look physically fit enough for the militia? He couldn't have any more winded warriors creeping through the forest. What crimes did they commit? He didn't want any child molesters or skinheads. Did they have any prior firearms or military experience? The less ammo he wasted developing basic marksmanship skills, the better.

If they passed muster, they were sent to the left and told to sit in the shade. The rest were pointed toward the hole in the western fence. Throughout the process, Kevin McCulver stood on the hood of Eli's SUV, warning them to stay back from the fence until called forward. The presence of two dozen heavily armed men visible through the chain links kept the process orderly.

Eli walked up to the gate with the bullhorn, ready for the final phase of his selection process. He needed to establish an iron grip for their integration to work, but he had to do it right or risk losing the entire group. How do you take eighty-one criminals from different cell blocks and bring them together in a way that doesn't cause an implosion? He had a theory.

"Candidates. The buses are ready, but we have a problem. I can only take seventy-two of you," said Eli.

Grumbling picked up in the group, followed quickly by the question he had hoped they would ask.

"How does that work?" said an overly muscular, towering inmate at the front of the group.

"I'll let all of you figure it out. I only have a few rules. Nobody gets on the bus until you're down to seventy-two, and nobody leaves without getting on the bus."

"What the fuck do you mean?" muscle man said, gripping the fence.

"He means you're not coming along for the ride," said a female voice behind the man.

Before muscle man could turn around, a woman jumped on his back, straddling him with both legs and locking his chin back with her left forearm. Her right hand rapidly pounded the back of his neck, causing his legs and arms to go slack. She jumped off as he toppled to the ground, landing on her feet. Holding a bloodied, makeshift knife over her head, she yelled at the prisoners, "One down, eight to go. Who's next?"

Nobody in the front of the group took her up on the offer, but a scuffle broke out toward the rear. Two men and a woman bolted for the western fence line, followed by a few more. Eli raised the bullhorn.

"Rule number three. If anyone escapes, everyone dies," he said, watching the group spring into action and swarm after the small group trying to get away.

"Liberty One-Five. Block the exit," he said into his radio.

The SUV on the dirt road next to the opening in the fence pulled forward, blocking their only way out of the facility.

"I don't think it would have mattered," said McCulver as the horde enveloped the runners.

"Probably not. Look at that crazy bitch," said Eli, pointing to the woman that had stabbed muscle man.

She stalked a group of three women that had purposely fallen behind the pack.

"We don't need any more psychopaths in the group," whispered McCulver, glancing around furtively.

"We don't need another *insubordinate* psychopath in the group," Eli countered. "A highly loyal one might come in handy. Let's see how this plays out."

He watched in awe as she tackled the closest woman and jammed the knife into her back using a powerful icepick-style grip. Several strikes later, the woman pinned under her stopped thrashing. The two survivors of the ambush sprinted into the throng of prisoners in a desperate attempt to disappear. Eli flipped the selector switch on his rifle and fired several bullets over the group. The frenzy stopped just as quickly as it started, and the group made room for Eli to see their handiwork. He counted five lifeless bodies on the ground, at their feet. Six including the woman killed on the fringes of the gang. Seven in total.

"I count seven. Close enough for government work. Form up at the gate," he said over the bullhorn.

They gathered in a more orderly formation this time, attempting to create rows behind the men and women brave enough to stand in front. His little trick worked like a charm. Create a little adversity amongst the recruits. Have them solve a problem together and *abracadabra!* Instant discipline! Just like boot camp—except for the killing each other part. All part of the new world order. Necessary for the greater good, or something like that. He didn't plan to get too highbrow with his philosophy. As long as they followed orders, he didn't care what they believed in.

"Welcome to the Maine Liberty Militia. You're all provisional recruits, still subject to *dismissal*," he said, raising an eyebrow. "You're part of my militia, and we have a lot of work to do. I don't have time to deal with problems. I simply cut them out like cancer or pick them off like a scab. Simple rules. Follow orders and take your training seriously. You do that, and we'll get along fine. If you try to escape or harm one of my soldiers, you'll be killed on the spot. No questions. If this group of recruits gets out of hand, meaning I detect an air of insubordination, defiance, noncooperation or disobedience, I'll be looking for a twenty-percent reduction the next time around. How many is that, Miss Killer?"

"Fourteen."

"Fourteen," he said, waiting for the number to sink in. "That won't be a pretty sight. Does everyone understand the rules?"

The group responded with different levels of enthusiasm and volume.

"As a group, using the words 'yes, sir,' does everyone understand my rules?"

A more coherent response filled Eli's ears. Good enough.

"Load 'em up, Kevin," he said, pulling the gate open.

Chapter 12

EVENT +8 Days

Limerick, Maine

Kate aligned the rechargeable screwdriver with the barrel hinge and drove the three-inch stainless steel screws flush with the hardware. She repeated the process for the remaining three screws, handing the screwdriver to Alex, who was situated across the plywood on a second ladder. Kate kept the board pushed against the window frame while he adjusted the right hinge, trying to place it level with the other hinge. Over the past two days, the two of them had managed to construct makeshift hurricane shutters for all of the second-story windows, depleting most of the plywood supply.

Alex planned to acquire more materials tomorrow, after resuming his duties at the airport, or wherever Grady's orders took him. It had been nice having Alex around during the past two days. Despite the fact that they were guarded 24/7 by a squad of Marines, the two days together had returned a comforting sense of normalcy to their lives. She hoped his duties would be manageable on a part-time schedule. The kids needed him here. *She* needed him here.

"Looks good," said Alex, clipping the screwdriver to his belt with a D-ring.

"Let's see."

They grabbed the board near the bottom corners and lifted, swinging the heavy board upward and outward. The hinges didn't move as they lowered the board back in place. Crude but effective. The board covered the window but was far from airtight, with half-inch to quarter-inch spaces lining the sides. Once the weather turned, they'd have to attach some type of commercial weather stripping—anything to block the cold drafts that would pour through these cracks. For now, they needed the ability to keep the rain from pouring directly into the house. They could refine the process later.

"Not bad at all," she said, glancing past Alex at a row of open hurricane shutters along the back of the house.

Inside, Alex's dad would attach a two-foot garden stake to the bottom of the board with a small hinge, providing a way to push open the board and prop it open against the windowsill. The only disadvantage was that the shutter could not be opened far enough to provide fire at distant targets. Even if they used bigger stakes and pushed the shutters open further, a single bullet to the propping mechanism could close the shutter. If they were attacked, Alex said they could rip some of the shutters out of the wood and reinstall them later. It wasn't an optimal solution, but they had to balance the need for security with the necessity of keeping the rain, wind and snow out of the house.

"We could start a business," joked Alex, starting down the ladder. "There's certainly no shortage of work."

When they reached the bottom, Alex's dad was waiting with a worried look. Kate saw her husband didn't seem to notice.

"That's it. Second floor is finished with two hours to

spare. It's time for an adult beverage," said Alex, turning his attention from the ladder to his dad. "What's wrong?"

"Charlie picked up some bad news on the HAM radio. Ed sounds like he's ready to leave tonight."

"Shit. They're in no shape to go anywhere right now. What did they hear?" said Alex.

Kate stepped off the ladder and joined them, hoping they hadn't wasted two days.

"A northern Maine militia group has started a full-time broadcast, warning Maine citizens that Homeland just dissolved the state government. They claim that the governor had a falling out with the Regional Recovery Zone Authority and—"

"They used those words? Regional Recovery Zone Authority?" said Alex.

"That's what Charlie said."

"Why is that a big deal?" asked Kate. Alex used the term regularly.

"Unless we're missing federal broadcasts over AM or FM radio, the words Regional Recovery Zone shouldn't be in the average citizen's vernacular," said Alex.

"They've been scanning those channels too. Nothing so far," said his dad.

"Then whoever is broadcasting over the HAM radio must have a contact in the governor's office or one of the reserve military units up north. I heard about the RRZ plan for the first time standing in Colonel Grady's operations center. This was a closely held secret."

"Not anymore," said Kate.

"Especially if what we're hearing is true," said Alex. "From what I could tell, the RRZ administration planned to work closely with state and local officials to minimize impact on the designated area. Abolishing local government isn't one of the steps," said Alex.

"But the RRZ Authority is ultimately in charge?"

"Technically, yes. Once the Federal Recovery Plan is authorized and activated, RRZ infrastructure supersedes local government."

"What about in an area like Boston?" asked Tim. "Who's in charge there?"

"I would assume it's the same situation. Each RRZ is responsible for recovery projects within a designated geography, with some overlap. We're in RRZ#1, New England North, responsible for recovery projects in Rhode Island, Connecticut, Massachusetts, Vermont, New Hampshire and Maine. RRZ#2, New England West, is located halfway between Catskill and Poughkeepsie, New York, west of the Hudson. Its primary purpose is to shelter refugees fleeing west out of Connecticut, Rhode Island and Massachusetts. Unfortunately, they're going to get crushed by runoff. RRZ#3, Tri-State Region, was originally based on Long Island."

"They got slammed by a tsunami from the south," said Kate.

"Right. They lost a majority of the gear earmarked for RRZ#3. They're still trying to determine if Long Island is a viable location for the RRZ, given the physical damage."

"How does that make sense?" asked Kate.

Alex shrugged his shoulders. "My guess is they have a fleet of supply ships, similar to the DoD's maritime prepositioning ships. Roll-on, roll-off capable, high-capacity vessels, probably based out of Norfolk or Philadelphia. The MPS squadrons used by the military carried a shit ton of equipment. Each squadron carried enough gear to support a Marine Air Ground Task Force for thirty days—fuel, ammo, food, water. Everything. I'd be shocked if they didn't have something similar."

"By the time they deploy something like that, it'll be too late," Kate said. "The people will be on the move."

Tim nodded. "Then it's all a question of whether the runoff will head north or south. Navigating through the Allegheny and the Appalachian Mountains won't be an option for most."

"The nearest RRZ south of Long Island is the Delaware Peninsula, but you'd be travelling through some seriously congested areas to get there, and you'd be competing with millions of people from Baltimore and D.C.," said Alex.

"But people won't know about the RRZ starting out. Right?" asked Kate. "It's eight days after the event, and FEMA's still not advertising. They'll look at a map and start walking. I'd want to avoid major population areas, but I'd be concerned about winter."

"Either way, this could spiral out of control if just a quarter of the people went north," said Tim.

"I mean, we all know FEMA can't do a goddamn thing right in the first place. I hate to say it, Alex, but I think it might be a wise idea to finish up the patchwork and start arranging a contingency plan."

"First we need to talk Charlie and Ed down off the ledge. We're not in any danger, yet. Not with a brigade from the 10th Mountain Division arriving tomorrow," said Alex.

"It might be time to take Ed's Jeep on a trip to Belgrade," said Tim.

"And a few other places," said Alex.

Kate didn't like the sound of Tim's idea, not with Russell's militia on the loose. They had no idea if he had people in Limerick looking for Ed's Jeep or the silver BMW SUV. All it would take was one random sighting to initiate an attack, far from the safety of their guarded compound or an armored vehicle.

"Promise you won't take a trip like that without talking to me first," said Kate.

"I promise," Alex said, but she didn't believe him.

Chapter 13

EVENT +9 Days

Sanford, Maine

Alex's tactical vehicle slowed as they passed Goodall Hospital. Tents swarmed the wide, grassy areas surrounding the main driveway, blocking their view of the parking lots. He leaned close to Lianez's face and peered through the thick, bullet-resistant glass of the driver's side window, straining to catch a glimpse beyond the tents.

"Jackson, what do you have in the hospital parking lot?" he yelled into the turret.

"Packed with vehicles. People milling around, camping in and around their cars. Looks like a tailgate, except nobody looks to be in the partying mood."

"Can't imagine why," Staff Sergeant Evans remarked from one of the back seats.

He'd decided to bring Evans on the trip to meet with Harrison Campbell in Sanford before heading to the airport. Alex figured the militia leader needed to meet some of the Marines tasked with the "internal security" mission. To give them a human face. The sooner he pictured the battalion's Marines as men and women with the same needs and fears as his own, the better. Same thing the other way around. Eventually, members of the York County Readiness Brigade would ride in vehicles and man checkpoints alongside 1st Battalion Marines. Integration of the two groups was critical to establishing and maintaining trust. Until then, Campbell was taking an enormous leap of faith.

He followed the Mousam River for a few blocks, passing under the long shadows of several windowless four-story brick buildings, fading relics of a prosperous era in Sanford's distant past. Alex was pleased to see people on the streets as they approached Main Street. Logically, he understood that none of them were out for coffee and a morning stroll, but on a deeper, emotional level, the sight of people encouraged him. This distant feeling of contentment faded quickly with the realization that the people avoided eye contact with the vehicle, hurrying their steps to increase the distance. He understood their concerns perfectly.

"Take a left at the intersection and pull up behind that row of cars," he directed. "We're in the empty place next to the coffee shop. Jackson, down from the turret. No point in sending the wrong message to the good folks of Sanford."

"Looks like they already got the message," said Evans, nodding at a group of people walking briskly away from the park across the street from the coffee shop.

"Yeah. We have our work cut out for us. There's Campbell," he said, pointing toward the park.

A small group of men in woodland camouflage appeared as the group gathered in the park dispersed. They wore black baseball caps with "YCRB" stenciled in white across the crown and carried military-style rifles.

"Lianez and Jackson will keep an eye on our ride home. Report any vehicles that approach the intersection, and take notes. I want license plate, make and model. I saw a stack of Maine license plates in the church by Milton Mills. Probably lifted from cars throughout southern Maine."

"I don't think the state police have internet access," said Evans.

"Probably not, but I'm willing to bet Homeland has an active license plate database. Never know, we might get lucky and stumble on one of Russell's guys. If I were him, I'd be out looking around, very incognito-like."

"Driving a car these days ain't exactly incognito, sir," said Lianez.

"True, but it's worth a shot."

"Copy, sir. Staff Sergeant, you want us out of the Matvee?"

"Affirmative. Kind of hard to keep an eye on Uncle Sam's property sitting inside one of these buckets. Post yourselves on the sidewalk. Weapons slung."

"Roger, Staff Sergeant," said Lianez.

"Sidearms only—for us," said Alex.

"You're killing me, sir."

"We have a 30,000-pound armored vehicle backing us up. We'll be fine. Let's go."

They met Harrison and his entourage in the middle of Main Street.

"Harrison, this is Staff Sergeant Evans. He drew the short straw and got stuck with me. His family's in Worcester," said Alex.

"Pleased to meet you, Mr. Campbell," said Evans, shaking his hand.

"Likewise. Welcome to Maine. I wish it were under different circumstances," said Harrison. "Any news from your family?"

"They're trying to evacuate military families to Devens

or Hanscom Air Force Base. I haven't heard anything definitive. It's wait and see, sir," said Evans.

"I'm afraid we're in one big wait-and-see holding pattern for now. We'll say a prayer for their safe arrival, Staff Sergeant."

"Thank you, sir."

"Harrison. Please call me Harrison. Only these yahoos call me sir, and I wish they wouldn't," he said, nodding at his own group.

"This is Margaret and Sheldon Klein. Neighbors, good friends and longstanding members of the militia. You're getting two for the price of one out at the airport. Both highly capable and deadly serious. Probably not what you expected, but this way I don't have to tear someone away from family."

"Works for me. Welcome aboard," said Alex, shaking their hands.

They looked uneasy, which he expected.

"I brought some communications gear so you can talk freely with Harrison. I assume you have gear to transfer?"

"Our gear is loaded in one of the cars," said Margaret, glancing at Harrison, "but we'd like to bring the car onto the base."

"I don't see a problem with that. We can sneak it through the back gate," said Alex.

"Perfect. I have to concede an ulterior motive for assigning the Kleins to the airport. Their son just started his junior year at U.C. Davis. Plant Sciences major. The Kleins own a hundred and thirty-three acres down the road, which he planned to turn into some kind of organic, sustainable farm. They were hoping there might be a way to communicate with their son. I figured the airport would be the best place for that."

"Sounds like your son would be a critical asset to New England's recovery. I can't make any promises, but stranger things have happened. Fortunately for your son, the EMP effects seem less pronounced on the West Coast," said Alex.

"We heard the same thing over the radio," said Harrison, turning to the Kleins. "See?"

"I've confirmed it through my sources," said Alex.

"We've heard some other disturbing things via HAM. Reports of naval assets scrambling out of port. Stuff passed from Europe about hundreds of satellites burning up in orbit, or more meteorites. Nobody knows."

"My dad heard the same things," said Alex. "You want to step inside? I'd hate to tarnish your reputation any further."

"I'm not too worried. People have pretty much made up their minds about Harrison Campbell. We need to work on *your* reputation, which starts right here with a pat on the back and a cup of coffee next door, unless Marines don't drink straight coffee anymore. I'm afraid the espresso-chino machine is out of order."

"If they're open, we'd be more than happy to give up our latte habit for the morning," said Alex.

"Good, because it happens that the mayor walked in a few minutes ago, and I think we should run the idea of a joint recruiting station by him," said Harrison.

"Sounds like you know this hearts and minds game better than I do."

"You're not doing so bad, Captain Fletcher. Approaching the brigade was a smart move. Buys you some legitimacy right away," said Harrison.

Alex smiled. "And I thought I was being slick about this."

"You're about as slick as sandpaper, which is why we're standing here. Speaking of slick, let's head inside before the mayor starts sliding through the town. No pun intended," he said, motioning toward the coffee shop.

"He can't be that bad," said Alex.

"He really isn't, but he's a career politician, and politics is a game of give and take, with an emphasis on the take. Don't make any promises you can't keep."

"I really don't have that much to offer," said Alex.

"That badge you're carrying says different. It wouldn't hurt if you'd start wearing a full Marine uniform. This civilian-slash-military hybrid style will only confuse people," said Harrison.

"Hallelujah," said Staff Sergeant Evans.

Harrison led them through the front door of the mostly empty coffee shop. A heavy blond woman in jeans and a red coffee-shop-logo T-shirt stood in front of the mahogany service bar, talking to the mayor. At least Alex assumed he was the mayor.

Who else would dress in gray slacks and matching blazer over a light blue button-down oxford?

The two of them stopped talking as they filed into the shop. For a moment, the mayor looked terrified, as if he suspected they had come to arrest him. Alex guessed that was how most of the people in town felt with the military busy at the airport.

It would only get worse later today, when elements of the 10th Mountain Division started pouring into Sanford. Hundreds of vehicles, from Stryker AFVs (Armored Fighting Vehicles) to L-ATVs (Light Combat Tactical-All Terrain Vehicles), would stream into town from points west. At the same time, the skies above would roar from the continuous flow of heavy transport aircraft transporting the rest of the 4th Brigade Combat Team from Wheeler-Sack Army Airbase near Fort Drum to their new home, Regional Recovery Zone #1, New England North. The mayor was about to find himself at the epicenter of attention.

"Are you all right with these weapons in here, Terry?" asked the mayor, watching them closely while addressing the owner.

"They wouldn't be breaking the law even before all this craziness happened. Open carry is perfectly legal and acceptable in my place of business. Keeps out the riff-raff," said the woman.

"That's my Terry," said Harrison, walking forward to give her a quick hug.

"Just saying that you have the right to keep firearms out of here, if you want to," said the Mayor.

"Seeing as we're not exactly flush with customers, I'll keep the current policy intact," she said.

"Free coffee and you're empty?" said Harrison, looking at the sign on the door.

"Nobody's in the sipping coffee mood, I guess, and a few of the patrons might have slipped out the side door when your armored car arrived," she said, winking at Alex.

"Sorry about that, ma'am," said Alex. "That's about as low profile as it gets for us right now."

"The mayor might have scared a few away himself," she said, winking at the man in the sport coat.

"Good to see you down here, Harrison."

"Same to you, Mayor. I don't want to hold you up, but I thought you might want to meet a few new friends of mine. This is provisional Captain Alex Fletcher, United States Marine Corps, and Staff Sergeant Evans. They're attached to 1st Battalion, 25th Marines, reserve unit out of Fort Devens, Massachusetts. Captain Fletcher is from Maine."

"Greg Hoode, mayor of Sanford and the most uninformed man in the county. Provisional captain? Sorry, let's take a seat. Terry, the coffee's on me," he said, eliciting a few laughs.

"It's good to see you giving the people a place to pretend things are normal," added Alex.

"For a few minutes, anyway. People are worried, especially about the lack of information. It's been nine days, and nobody has a clue what happened," said Terry.

"Information is scarce at this point, at all levels. Why don't you grab a seat since we scared away most of your customers. I can't think of a better place to start spreading what little knowledge I have."

"I think I'll take you up on that," she said, walking around the counter. "Coffee's self-serve."

After grabbing coffee, they settled around one of the larger tables and finished the introductions. Curious faces stared through the windows, refilling the park across the street. Eager nods and smiles had replaced the distrust and fear broadcast through the town square upon their arrival. Sitting down with the mayor in one of the town's central gathering places had been a stroke of genius. Campbell knew what he was doing.

"So, *provisional* captain? I've never heard of this," said the mayor.

"Neither had I until a few days ago. I was basically recruited by the commanding officer of the battalion in Boston."

"You were down in Boston?" he asked, looking incredulous. "I heard the city turned into a war zone."

"Boston suffered an incredible amount of blast and tsunami damage from the asteroid or meteorite that hit off the coast. The situation spiraled out of control, as you can imagine," Alex said, hoping to end that part of the discussion.

He preferred to dodge the uncomfortable task of explaining how the same battalion headed to Sanford and a long-standing militia group ended up in a protracted, low-intensity conflict throughout the city over a basic misunderstanding. He was doing his best to prevent a repeat of the same disaster in southern Maine.

"So...what can you tell me about the situation in Maine?" asked the mayor, leaning back and sipping his coffee. "The National Guard unit based right here in Sanford set up roadblocks on the approaches. I can't get in anymore. They've been busy hauling tons of supplies out of secret stockpiles. People are getting nervous."

"Has anyone from FEMA or Homeland talked to you about the airport?"

"No. I'm completely in the dark about this Recovery Zone thing."

"Where did you hear that term?" asked Alex. "I'm more curious than anything. I haven't talked to a single person within the military command structure that knew about the stockpiles around the airport prior to the disaster."

"I put it together when Diane Ellis came out to one of the roadblocks to talk to me. She's in charge of the 1136th Transportation Detachment based right here in Sanford. Diane said the whole Recovery Zone headquarters area was off-limits to civilian personnel. Acted really funny about it, like when a friend tells you they can't help out when you know they can. I asked her how big of an area that was, and she wouldn't say. Diane and I went to high school together. Twenty years, and I've never seen her look that spooked. Something fishy is going on out there."

"Everyone's pretty spooked at this point," said Alex. "As for the airport, all I can really tell you is that the 1136th, along with an engineering company from Westbrook, are turning Sanford Seacoast Airport into a Recovery Zone headquarters. Within the next few days, it's going to get extremely busy and crowded around the airport."

"And your people are all right with this?" asked the mayor, shifting his focus to Harrison.

"I don't see us having much choice in the matter. They're coming whether we like it or not. Captain Fletcher has asked me to integrate a limited number of my people into a provisional security platoon. Checkpoint duties, patrolling—I'll have the Kleins at the airport, serving as a direct liaison," he said, nodding at Margaret and Sheldon. "I'd rather be directly involved than shut out of the equation."

"I just wonder if it might be a better idea to hold off until we know what we're dealing with," said the mayor. "No offense, Captain Fletcher."

Alex shrugged his shoulders. "None taken. It's Harrison's call."

"Do you mind if I share some of the less rosy picture you painted a few days ago out at my house?" Harrison asked.

The mayor looked surprised. "You showed him your headquarters?"

"Alex interviewed members of the brigade a few years ago. He knew where to find us," said Harrison.

"I'm still not understanding how you got wrapped into this role," said the mayor, raising an eyebrow and shifting his glance to Alex.

"Neither do I. Providence, I guess. It's a long story that goes back to 2003, in Iraq."

"I don't have that long. What were you saying, Harrison?"

"Captain Fletcher travelled to Brookline and back from Scarborough, all within the first four days after the event. He lends a particularly credible, firsthand perspective to the equation. The bottom line is that we have a mass exodus heading to Maine."

"State police closed the borders within twelve hours of the event," the mayor said. "Cars are backed up for miles on the 95. Same with Route 4 and Route 9 headed into the Berwicks. One of their deputy commanders gave me the grand tour a few days ago."

"You saw the tip of the iceberg—the people with functioning cars," Alex informed them. "The rest left the greater Boston area on foot. We had to take side roads to get back to Maine because every major route was jammed with people. Trust me, the RRZ may be the only thing that prevents southern Maine from being swallowed whole. Picture a million-plus people marching down the roads, looking for food and water."

"Fuck," muttered the mayor.

"Greg, I didn't take you for a cussing man," said Harrison.

"I'm not a drinking man either, but I could use a little pick-me-up right about now. Can this mystical RRZ hold the line at the border?"

"I don't know, and frankly, that's pretty much out of our hands. My direct concern is the state of affairs inside the RRZ," said Alex, leaning back and taking a long sip of his dark roast.

"Oh boy, here comes the pitch," said the mayor. "And I thought I was going to work you guys over."

"We're not here to work you over. Quite the opposite. Harrison suggested we run something by you, as a professional courtesy, which may or may not be how the RRZ runs business around here in the future."

"You make it sound like they're taking over," said the mayor.

"According to the Federal Recovery Plan, the RRZ is under federal jurisdiction. All part of the 2015 Defense Authorization Bill," said Alex.

"Just the airport."

Alex shook his head, glancing at Harrison.

"Southern Maine?"

"Everything. Everywhere," said Alex.

"The people won't stand for it," said the mayor.

"The people have to stand for it, at least until the government figures out the refugee situation."

"Harrison, I can't believe you're still seated. This goes against everything you've preached for as long as I remember."

"I tried to warn people," said Campbell.

"To be fair, nobody could have predicted that the East Coast would get hit by an asteroid," said the mayor.

"Somebody figured it out," said Alex. "EMPs are a man-made phenomenon."

The table became uncomfortably silent, each mind likely racing with a different conspiracy theory. Alex knew he was walking on thin ice at this point, especially with Staff Sergeant Evans. Even a vague hint that the United States might have played a part in the catastrophe might be too much for him. Alex broke the quiet with his final pitch.

"Here's the deal, Mayor Hoode. If the internal security situation goes sideways in southern Maine, the government will move the MOB out of the southern zone to—"

"MOB?" said the mayor.

"Main Operating Base. Sanford Airport. Right now, everyone in Maine is classified RRZ Internal. Everyone outside is classified RRZ External. *External* gets you a cot in a FEMA tent—if you're lucky. Not a great prospect with winter a few months away. If the RRZ relocates the MOB to a northern location, everyone south of the new boundary will be redesignated *external.* Southern Maine will be thrown to the wolves, as millions stream north to the new border somewhere north of here. Can I count on you to remain neutral, at a minimum, while you're making rounds through the community? I'm not asking you to promote the RRZ; I just don't see a point to encouraging peoples' fear of the unknown. Especially right now."

The mayor furrowed his brow and ran a hand through his thinning brown hair. After a theatrical exhale, he forced a smile.

"All right. I'm on board. I have to do what's best for the people, and I don't see a better option. The town has been lucky so far. We've had some petty theft and a few fights related to the crisis, but beyond that, it's been quiet," he said, standing and shaking their hands.

"The quieter the better, for all of us," Alex said.

They all thanked the shopkeeper, insisting on leaving money, which she refused. Once outside, the mayor turned to Harrison.

"What we're you going to ask me when we first sat down?"

"I almost forgot. Captain Fletcher and I plan to run a joint recruiting station out of the storefront next door. Anyone interested can join the Marines as a provisional recruit or join my brigade. No pressure, just options," said Harrison.

"Volunteers will train together at the airport, forming a joint platoon, maybe a full company, if we can drum up enough business," Alex explained. "They'd be trained for basic military police duties and based at the airport or Forward Operating Bases within the southern zone. Ideally, units like these would constitute the bulk of forces visible within the RRZ."

"The rest would be invisible?" the mayor asked.

"That's the idea."

"Can *I* join the provisional Marines? Sounds like the best deal in town," he said, and they all laughed.

"You'd have to resign as mayor," said Alex.

"Well, I guess that's off the table."

"If you happened to mention the recruiting station during your rounds today, we'd be eternally grateful," said Harrison.

"How grateful?"

Another round of laughter ensued.

"I could improve the supply situation at the storefront, but I think you should focus your goodwill efforts on Sanford. A countywide effort is too broad," said Alex.

"Damn, gentlemen. I feel like I'm out of my league here. Now Harrison's working me through you. I'm sure as hell glad this isn't an election year. I'd be afraid for my job," he said, chuckling for a moment before settling his gaze on Alex.

"Sounds like a deal. *We'll* focus on the town."

Staff Sergeant Evans whispered into his tactical microphone, activating Lianez and Jackson, who were standing on the sidewalk near the corner of the building. The two Marines walked toward the Matvee, adjusting their rifles.

"Everything okay?" the mayor asked.

"Car inbound from the north," Evans reported.

"Everything's fine. We just haven't seen many cars on the road," said Alex. "Starting to become a rare sight."

A gray hatchback slowed at the intersection across from the park, easing onto Washington Street. The vehicle carried two male passengers, who stared at Alex's group for a moment before nodding uncomfortably. Once past the coffee shop, the car picked up speed, heading in the direction of the airport. Lianez walked onto the road and raised a pair of binoculars, passing the license plate information to Jackson. On any other day before the event, the car and its occupants wouldn't have drawn any attention, but given that they'd seen a grand total of three other functioning automobiles this morning, its presence was notable.

"Recognize either of those men?" Alex asked.

"Can't say I do, but we have more than twenty thousand citizens. Bound to be a few I don't know," the mayor said.

After another round of handshakes, the mayor crossed the road to mingle with the group that lingered at the edge of the park near the street. The mayor pointed back at them and patted a young man on the shoulder.

Hard at work already.

Alex wasn't sure what to make of the mayor's promise, but he couldn't afford to have the man running around town repeating stories about secret warehouses and black helicopters, even if the stories proved to be true.

"What do you think?" Harrison asked him.

"I think we're better off than before we walked into the coffee shop."

"Let's hope so. What's the next step to getting this place up and running as a recruiting station?"

"We should take a trip to the airport. I need to issue your group several radios. Enough for you, the station and the Kleins. We'll need to talk regularly once we start gathering recruits."

"My men at the Milton Mills checkpoint could use one too so we can coordinate a rotation. They've been on their own for four days. I've been checking on them once a day, but they're starting to wear thin," said Harrison. "They could use that backup you promised."

"I'll dispatch a vehicle with some of the Marines that have trickled in from the Brunswick detachment. We'll stock them up with MREs and anything else they might need. How many do you have assigned to the storefront?"

"Three at all times, mostly to safeguard the supplies. My plan is to set up a tent and a few tables outside the hospital, where we can assess need from a distance. Otherwise, this will turn into a free-for-all."

"Plan on that happening within a week. I'll give you two Marines here, and we'll adjust accordingly as the situation unfolds. If it starts getting hectic, we'll send people out the back door, where they'll get a quick pitch from our designated recruiters."

"Sounds easy enough," said Harrison.

"Don't count on it."

Chapter 14

EVENT +9 Days

Acton, Maine

"Slow down here, Gene. I want to see if the state police are still at the church," said Harrison Campbell.

"How far up the road?" Gene McCall, the driver, asked.

"Should be coming up pretty fast. It's a little white church buried in the trees," Harrison said, picking up the olive green handheld ROTAC unit given to him by Alex Fletcher.

One of the Marines at the airport hangar had enabled two dedicated "call sign" channels on all of the radios assigned to Campbell's group. The primary channel, designated "Patriot Five Bravo," was structured for internal York County Readiness Brigade communications. He'd been instructed to use this for command and control with his militia units. Alex was upfront about the fact that Marines at the airport would monitor all internal transmissions.

The second channel, "Patriot Five Charlie," was a blind-response link to the battalion's broadcast ROTAC net, giving Harrison's people the capability to carry on conversations over the battalion's primary tactical ROTAC channel, but not listen to exchanges initiated outside of Patriot Five Charlie. They would use this radio net to report intelligence or request assistance when required. The ROTAC in the armored vehicle following them was directly monitoring both channels. He selected Patriot Five Bravo and pressed "lock," waiting a few seconds before speaking, like he was instructed.

"Guardian One-Zero, I need to make a quick stop at a church up on our right to talk with state police investigators."

"Roger. Do you want us to proceed to the checkpoint?"

"Negative. We should probably show our faces together until I get you settled in with my folks."

"Copy. We'll stay right behind you."

The trees opened, exposing a weather-beaten, single-steeple church. A stark white van marked "MOBILE CRIME LAB" sat next to a dilapidated gazebo behind the neglected structure. Parked cars with cracked and shattered windows appeared beyond the church. Something had happened here.

"This is it."

Gene took the turn carefully, easing the sedan over a partially exposed corrugated steel drainage pipe and onto a long gravel driveway. He had no idea when the police arrived at the site, since he had purposely avoided Foxes Ridge Road until Alex procured an official military escort. If Alex wasn't exaggerating about what had transpired here, he didn't think the state investigators would be too keen on having armed militia show up unannounced, especially with dead militia strewn about the scene.

"What do you think they found?" asked Gene.

"I don't know for sure. Captain Fletcher reported finding Eli Russell's people out here the day after the event. Claims they were stealing cars and executing the occupants in the woods. Jimmy's crew was supposedly running the show. I had Dave Littner get one of the troopers to take a look. Looks like they found something."

Gene grimaced and shook his head slowly. Harrison knew what he was thinking. Gene had been in the brigade long enough to know that Eli's brother had formed a group within the Maine Liberty Militia. The stories circulated over whispers and shifty glances at the shit-ball taverns and out-of-the-way cocktail lounges in York County. Dark stories about initiation ceremonies, disappearances, murders…worse. Stuff you wanted to immediately "unhear," because you never knew who was playing pool or sipping from a pitcher a few stools over. He hoped the news was true. The world was a better place without Jimmy, or *any* of the Russells.

"How does Captain Fletcher know Jimmy was involved?"

"Eli staged an attack on Captain Fletcher's house in Limerick, nearly killing his family. Retribution for what happened here. He didn't say, but I get the impression that they captured some of Eli's men."

McCall gave him a doubtful look.

"Have you verified that he was attacked?"

"I didn't ask to see his house, if that's what you mean. He had details about Eli Russell that aren't public knowledge."

"From what you've told me, Homeland appears to have cornered the market on information that isn't public knowledge. Just saying. He seems to be on the up and up, but you never know, especially now."

"I know. It's something to keep a sharp eye on. Looks

like we've attracted some attention," said Harrison, nodding toward the crime scene van.

A trooper holding a shotgun at port arms approached their car, motioning for them to stop. He didn't look happy to see them. Neither did the crime scene team standing outside of the doorway to the church's one-story annex. Dressed in navy blue coveralls, gray booties, and elbow-length gloves, the group comprised of two men and a woman glared at them as they edged up to the yellow crime scene tape barrier. Harrison grabbed the radio again.

"Guardian One-Zero, I might need an assist on this one."

"I was wondering. On my way over," Staff Sergeant Taylor said, and the front passenger door of the Matvee swung open.

"Keep your hands where that trooper can see them," said Harrison, studying the parking lot scene.

Something definitely happened here.

He counted nine cars parked against the white building, all with out-of-state license plates. All of them appeared undamaged, with the notable exception of the vehicle closest to the building's entrance. The shiny black SUV showed clear evidence of a sustained shootout. All of the windows were shattered, littering the worn asphalt with hundreds of light blue safety glass particles. Small holes circled by chipped paint peppered the driver's side doors and rear cargo area panels, leading to the rear left tire, which sagged into the pavement. A faint red stain traced down the siding panels located directly in front of the vehicle, extending below the hood. He didn't see any bodies, shell casings or markings in the parking lot.

"I need you to back your car up immediately. This is

still an active crime scene," said the trooper.

"We're the ones that called this in. York County Readiness Brigade," said Harrison, keeping his hands plainly visible on the dashboard.

"Doesn't matter. I need you out of here."

"We're operating with 1st Battalion, 25th Marines based out of Sanford Airport."

Staff Sergeant Taylor jumped down from the vehicle and called out to the trooper over the hood of the Matvee. "Officer, they're with me. They just have a few questions for your investigators," he said, squeezing between the two vehicles. "Staff Sergeant Taylor. I'm part of the Recovery Zone security battalion."

"The what?" asked the trooper, still keeping most of his attention directed toward the sedan.

"Internal security for southern Maine. Any way we could get a word with your crime scene team?"

"Hold on," he said and waved the team over.

"Do you mind if Mr. Campbell and Mr. McCall get out of their vehicle?" said Taylor.

The trooper hesitated for a moment before answering. "Sure. I don't suppose that's a problem. Keep any weapons in the car."

Harrison didn't feel like getting into a Maine firearms law discussion with the young trooper, so he nodded, placing his pistol on the dashboard. He had Gene do the same, under the watchful eye of the nervous trooper. The three officers ducked under the yellow tape and joined them in front of Campbell's car.

"Harrison Campbell. York County Readiness Brigade," he said, nodding a greeting. "I received the initial report about this place and had one of my people call it in. Looks like something big went down here."

"Detective Jane Berry. Maine State Evidence Response Team," the woman said. "We can't share any information with the public at this time. You shouldn't even be here." She turned to the trooper. "We need to barricade the driveway closer to the road."

Before anyone responded, Staff Sergeant Taylor stepped forward. "Detective, Mr. Campbell and members of his unit are working on behalf of the Regional Recovery Zone security team. We're hoping to uncover any patterns or tactics that might assist with our security mission."

"Doesn't matter, Staff Sergeant. I was told to report directly to my boss in Augusta on this one. Plus, I don't know a thing about this…Recovery Zone?" said Berry.

"What about the bridge at Milton Mills?" Harrison asked.

"We retrieved the bodies yesterday afternoon. Your people had already contaminated the crime scene beyond the point of investigation."

"My people didn't touch the bodies," said Harrison.

"The bodies didn't stack themselves," Berry muttered. "Either way, it doesn't matter. We're in cleanup mode here. We'll be gone in a few hours, but the area will remain off limits, and I expect you to observe that. Someone from the state police will be in touch to take statements."

"Thank you for your time, Detective. Based on what I heard, this couldn't have been an easy scene to process, on any level," said Harrison.

She stared at him with a neutral expression. "Who exactly reported this to you?"

"One of the RRZ internal security officers," said Harrison, keeping the title as vague as possible.

"Where can I find this unnamed security officer?"

"Ma'am, if you have a card, I'll pass it along to him," said Staff Sergeant Taylor.

"You're really not going to give me that information?"

"That's correct, ma'am. He'll either contact you, or you can report to the RRZ's Main Operating Base at Sanford Seacoast Airport and place a request in person with a representative from 1st Battalion, 25th Marines. They'll pass the request along. We should head to the bridge, gentlemen."

Detective Berry bristled at his rebuff, placing her hands on her hips and tightening her jaw. "Maybe I should contact Augusta and request that the entire bridge area be designated a crime scene."

"We both have better things to do than step on each other's toes," said Taylor.

"I don't think you have the authority to step on my toes, Staff Sergeant."

Harrison was interested in Taylor's reaction to her challenge. It would tell him a lot about the future of their collaboration with the Marines. If he threatened her with his authority, he'd be concerned.

"Honestly, ma'am, the command and control situation is a little nebulous right now, so I have no idea whether I have the authority to step on your toes. I'm not a big fan of toe stomping anyway."

Taylor passed Campbell's litmus test, which hadn't altogether surprised him. Like Staff Sergeant Evans, Taylor came across as a thoughtfully sharp, independent decision maker. Somewhat surprisingly, all of the Marines he'd encountered during the course of the day had defied the rowdy, impulsive jarhead stereotype. They carried themselves as restrained, competent professionals, giving him a little more confidence in his decision to assist the Marines with their security function. Taylor's response to the detective had been perfect.

"Neither am I. Like you said. Better things to do," she said, removing a business card from her pocket. "I'd appreciate a chance to talk to your security officer. I've never seen anything like this before. And I never want to see it again."

"I'm guessing none of us do," said Taylor.

Harrison was about to reinforce Taylor's sentiment when a deep, rhythmic thumping filled the air, intensifying rapidly. They all started to search the sky for the source of the sound.

"Blackhawks. Really close," said Taylor. "Probably the lead elements of the 10th Mountain Division."

"How many can we expect?" yelled Detective Berry.

"Helicopters?"

"No. Soldiers!"

"Several thousand, but you didn't hear that from me!" said Taylor. "Not that it's going to be a secret for very long."

A UH-60 Blackhawk raced over the treetops behind the church, blowing a wall of dead leaves, grass and dust through the parking lot. The roar crescendoed as a second Black Hawk appeared at the eastern end of the church clearing, passing directly overhead and bathing them in debris. A few moments later, another thundered over the church. Within seconds the thumping started to abate, drifting east toward Sanford.

"I hope you were done," said Harrison.

"I get the feeling it doesn't matter," said Detective Berry, staring east. "Are they all going to Sanford Airport?"

"Be glad you're stationed up north. It's about to get really crowded down here," said Taylor.

Chapter 15

EVENT +9 Days

Milton Mills Crossing
Acton, Maine

The road straightened in front of Harrison's sedan, giving way to a long stretch of white picket fence next to the road. A yellow house sat at the back of a sparse green lawn, overrun with patches of dead crabgrass. Two figures stood in the shadows on the farmer's porch. The Boyds. A few days ago, he'd knocked on their door to let them know that the militia unit at the bridge was friendly. Without a doubt, the Boyds had heard the gunfire that left Jimmy Russell rotting in the sun. Curtis Boyd had smiled nervously through his partially opened front door, obviously eager to close it again.

He didn't blame Mr. Boyd. Strange men with guns almost always spelled trouble, regardless of their intentions. Harrison was well aware of this perception, which was why he'd shifted the brigade's focus away from its previously unhealthy fixation on guns. Guns and the citizens' 2nd Amendment right to bear arms would always occupy a fundamental role in the brigade's mission; they just wouldn't be the "face" of his militia. The York County Readiness Brigade's primary mission was to support the citizens. If that mission required firearms, so be it.

The couple vanished through the front door, likely responding to the second vehicle in their small convoy. Nobody was happy to see military vehicles.

"We have a problem," stated Gene, slowing the car.

Harrison turned his attention back to the road. The stop sign at the intersection of Foxes Ridge Road and French Street caught his eye first, followed immediately by four soldiers in full combat body armor and protective helmets standing next to it. The soldiers kept their weapons trained on the sedan as Gene stopped more than fifty feet from the intersection. One of the men clad in Universal Camouflage Pattern ACUs beckoned them forward with one hand, letting his rifle hang from its sling. Harrison quit holding his breath when the entire fire team lowered their weapons. He twitched when Staff Sergeant Taylor's voice broadcast over the ROTAC.

"I'm going to pull alongside you, Mr. Campbell. Looks like 3rd Brigade Combat Team dropped us a gift."

"Feel free to pull in front of me."

Two of the soldiers jogged toward the sedan as Taylor's Matvee pulled forward. Harrison remained in his seat, waiting for the staff sergeant to fully defuse the situation. Under a tree next to the bridge, a tight cluster of militia members lay face down with their hands laced over the backs of their heads. Two soldiers stood watch over them, pointing their rifles at the group.

Son of a bitch!

He reached for the door handle.

"Harrison," hissed Gene. "Not a good idea right now. This'll all get sorted out in a minute."

He withdrew his hand from the door, infuriated to see

his own people being treated like criminals. Alex should have sent one of the Marine vehicles to Milton Mills three days ago, like he had promised. Now he'd have to deal with Dave Littner, who was already the most vocal government conspiracy theorist in the brigade.

Shit—the soldiers have them eating dirt right where Jimmy's crew spent six days decomposing.

Littner would be out-of-control mad. Harrison would be lucky to keep the Berwick chapter intact, let alone willing to collaborate with Fletcher's Marines.

"Staff Sergeant Taylor?" he yelled through the driver's side window.

"I see it, Mr. Campbell. That's my first priority," said the marine, kneeling next to the window. "I'll have them on their feet in thirty seconds."

"They're lying right where Russell's people were piled up. I need you to support them, no matter how nasty they get toward the soldiers. We're in this together."

"Understood," he said, giving them a thumbs-up. "I was planning on kicking ass and taking names anyway. Follow me, gentlemen."

Taylor met the two soldiers in front of the vehicles, speaking energetically while pointing toward the captive militia. Harrison grabbed his rifle from the back seat and stepped out of the car, instructing Gene to stay behind for now. As soon as he shut the car door, the soldiers at the stop sign raised their rifles and ran forward, screaming at him. The two men in front of Staff Sergeant Taylor backed up and crouched, pointing their M4 carbines at his head. Harrison froze, adrenaline coursing through his body. An angry chorus of, "Drop your rifle!" and, "On the ground now!" bombarded his senses, barely penetrating the wave of anger and betrayal radiating from his core. Taylor jarred him out of an extremely dangerous state of mind.

"Are you fucking stupid, Specialist?" barked Taylor, stepping between Harrison and the rifle barrels. "You clearly saw that he's with me, right? How the fuck could you interpret this any other way."

"Ease off my soldiers, asshole! They're doing their job. Civilians are not authorized to carry weapons in the RRZ!" said a sergeant arriving from the stop sign.

"Is this the stupid squad?" Taylor snapped. "Do you think I just met this man a few seconds ago? Mr. Campbell commands the York County Readiness Brigade."

"Militia is no exception. We're under strict orders to confiscate weapons from non-RRZ-authorized personnel."

"The men and women you're holding at gunpoint are working at the request of my commanding officer. They're authorized."

"Prove it, or they're not going anywhere. Including Mr. Campbell."

"Harrison, why don't you get inside my vehicle until I get this squared away. We've got a shit-for-brains epidemic, and I'd hate for you to get infected."

"He doesn't go anywhere," said the sergeant, raising his rifle.

"Munoz, Kennedy—you copying this?" Taylor said into his helmet mic.

A few seconds passed. "If one of these soldiers shoots Mr. Campbell or any of his people and I am unable to issue orders, your last mission is to assist members of the York County Readiness Brigade in a tactical withdrawal to FOB Lakeside. Assume *all* ground personnel in the area to be hostile."

Harrison wished Littner and his crew could hear this. It would go a long way toward keeping them on board with Captain Fletcher's plan.

"Sounds like the Marines live in shit-talk city," grunted one of the privates.

"The *private* needs to keep his cock holster shut," said Taylor.

The soldier took a step forward, but stopped when a staff sergeant raced into the group.

"Jesus. How many NCOs does it take to lead a fire team?" muttered Taylor.

"What the hell is the problem here?" asked the staff sergeant, catching sight of Harrison. "Why is that man still holding a rifle?"

"That's the problem, Staff Sergeant. Chesty Puller comes running out of his tactical vehicle like he owns the fucking place, saying this guy is exempt. Now he just threatened to waste the entire squad."

"Are you out of your mind? Who do you report to?"

"Your sergeant is slightly twisting my words," said Taylor.

"Slightly? Who's your commanding officer?"

"Lieutenant Colonel Grady, 1st Battalion, 25th Marine Infantry Regiment."

"A reserve unit?" said the sergeant. "Fuck this guy."

"Simmer it, Morales. We're not the only kids playing in the sandbox," he said, turning to Taylor. "Can I see your identification card for verification?"

"I don't look real to you?"

"I have no doubt you're a Marine with the unit you identified. I just need to see if you have the authority to co-opt civilians."

Taylor handed it over.

"Lieutenant, I need an ID check at the intersection. I have a Marine staff sergeant claiming that the civilians guarding the bridge are part of his unit," he said, activating his squad radio. "Let's cool it down, all right? We're all on the same side."

Harrison wondered how blurry those lines might get over the next few months—or years.

"So are the men and women you have lying on the ground," said Taylor.

A group of three soldiers appeared from a concealed position in the dense brush next to the mouth of the bridge, sprinting toward the vehicles. They arrived a few seconds later, raising the total visible soldier count to thirteen, including the four at the far side of the bridge. He assumed they had at least eight more at the other bridge—four to cover the Milton Mills Road intersection and four to cover the bridge. Staff Sergeant Taylor was pissing off a lot of soldiers. Harrison eased next to the Marine, causing the soldiers to tense.

"If you guys freak out like this every time you see a gun, you're gonna have a real problem. This isn't the people's republic of New York. They don't have gun laws up here," said Taylor.

"They do now," said the army staff sergeant.

When the next gaggle of soldiers reached them, a second lieutenant stepped in front of the group, accompanied by a senior noncommissioned officer—probably the platoon sergeant.

"Afternoon, sir," said Taylor.

"Any time you want to salute is fine by the lieutenant," said the sergeant first class.

"Probably not a good idea for the lieutenant's long-term health. Christ, how many noncommissioned officers does it take to run a platoon?"

"Are all Marines this mouthy?" asked the army staff sergeant, handing the ID card to the officer.

"You guys are killing me. All of you," said the officer, staring at Taylor. "Second Lieutenant Matt Poole. Checkpoint commander, 3rd Brigade Combat Team."

"Staff Sergeant Taylor. 1st Battalion, 25th Marine Infantry Regiment out of Fort Devens. This is Harrison Campbell, York County Readiness Brigade commander. Those are his people on the ground."

The lieutenant nodded, scanning his ID card with a handheld device that resembled a GPS receiver. A few moments later, he looked up with a barely contained look of surprise. He handed the card back.

"Staff Sergeant Taylor has situational authority here."

"Over you?" asked the platoon sergeant.

"Over *all* of us," said Poole.

"You've gotta be shitting me, sir? Can they co-opt civilians?" said the army staff sergeant.

"1st Battalion, 25th Marine Infantry Regiment is designated RRZ's internal security. Staff noncommissioned officers and above within the battalion have full authority to co-opt civilians in an armed capacity, though I strongly suggest the staff sergeant works with his battalion to issue provisional ID cards to co-opted personnel. We had no way to verify what Mr. Littner told us, and our orders for border security operations are strict. Disarm and detain armed subjects within designated areas. No exceptions."

"There's always an exception, sir," said Taylor.

"Not when it comes to the safety of my soldiers. Mr. Campbell, I'm really sorry about this," he said, extending a hand. "We didn't expect to find armed militia on the bridge, and I couldn't take any chances."

Harrison reluctantly accepted the handshake, remaining silent. He wasn't satisfied with the lieutenant's explanation of the soldiers' behavior, but there was no point starting an argument. The young officer was following a bizarre set of orders, no doubt crafted by Homeland Security bureaucrats and forced down the throats of the military's senior commanders. There was no point getting mad at a twenty-two-year-old.

"Platoon Sergeant, I want Mr. Campbell's people back on their feet ASAP. If you'll excuse me, gentlemen, I have some apologizing to do," said Poole.

"Lieutenant?" said Harrison, knowing that was a bad idea. "Why don't you let me handle my people? They're bound to be a little hot over this, and I'd rather move them away from your soldiers as quickly as possible. If you could place their weapons in one of the cars, I'd appreciate it. I'll pass on your words."

"Sounds like a plan. Platoon Sergeant, make it happen. And move the soldiers away from Mr. Campbell's people," said Poole.

"Copy that, sir. Back to the intersection, all of you," said the platoon sergeant.

"Mind walking back with me, Lieutenant?" Harrison asked.

"Not at all, Mr. Campbell," said Poole. "I'll be at the CP in a few minutes, Platoon Sergeant."

The soldiers jogged past the intersection as Harrison and the lieutenant walked down the crumbling road.

"I appreciate your patience with the platoon. There was no way for us to know your group's status," said Poole.

"That's what I'm worried about, not just for my people, but for the entire RRZ, or whatever you call it. Are all of the units talking to each other?"

"I have no idea. Maybe at the top echelon? I'm at the bottom of the food chain, reacting to orders pushed down from the battalion commander. We've been working nonstop to prepare the brigade for RRZ deployment."

"Do they explain this RRZ thing in officer's training? Based on my interaction with the Marines, I get the distinct impression that this is relatively new to everyone."

"None of us knew it existed. We drew equipment from specialized bunkers, discarding most of our gear, especially the electronics. They didn't want to take any chances that the circuits had been degraded by the EMP."

"They confirmed an EMP attack?"

"Negative," said Poole. "We made the assumption based on what was discarded and replaced." He glanced back at the Marines. "I guarantee your Marines did the same. They're driving around in a vehicle that hasn't been in service with the Marine Corps for several years. Probably retrofitted and mothballed in a bunker, like most of our stuff."

"Is it possible that nobody knew about the military's role in the RRZ?"

"Someone had to know, but between you and me, it definitely wasn't known at the battalion commander level. The colonel made that crystal clear to the officers and staff NCOs at our first crisis briefing. Nobody expected to leave Fort Drum. We figured one or two of the brigades would be put on ready alert standby, you know, for a foreign mission or something like that. By the end of the week, the entire division will be deployed to major zones within the northeast. Who would have guessed that?"

Harrison watched Dave Littner rise slowly from the grass, glaring at the soldiers backing away. They heard a splash beyond the militia, somewhere along the riverbank. Two soldiers sprinted across the bridge, one of them pointing toward the water hidden by thick undergrowth.

"I don't envy your job, Lieutenant. You're looking at one million plus refugees from the greater Boston area. The border situation is guaranteed to get ugly quick. Most of these waterways are little more than streams at some points."

"Aerial recon is already scoping those out."

"Too bad they didn't take a look at Milton Mills. You might have avoided this little mess," said Harrison.

"We're lucky that didn't happen, or they might have softened the landing zone ahead of us. Good luck, Mr. Campbell," said the lieutenant, chasing after the soldiers that descended the riverbank.

Dave Littner shook his head as the officer passed the group, but didn't say a word. Harrison approached slowly, unsure what to expect. Littner appeared genuinely calm, which surprised him.

"Is everyone all right?" said Harrison.

"Everyone's fine, for now."

"Let's get you back to Sanford. Get everyone cleaned up and fed some warm chow."

Littner shook his head and grimaced. "I'm done. Consider this my formal resignation from the brigade. Same for everyone else here."

Harrison looked past Littner, catching furtive glances and shaking heads.

"I can't see anything good coming out of your arrangement with the government. I thought there might be a chance, but not after this. We're about to have several thousand soldiers and Marines running around like they own the place, which, according to the army heroes that stormed the bridge—they do. We're just commodities. Cogs in this RRZ machine. Fuck that."

"Once everything settles, it'll be a different story," said Harrison, not sure he believed his own words.

Littner's expression softened. "Harrison, you better think really hard about what you're getting the brigade into. Fletcher seems like a straight shooter, but I don't think he has the full picture."

"He knows more about the RRZ than that young lieutenant."

"For now, but what happens when the RRZ is in full swing? You heard what they said about civilians and firearms. Right now they're just taking them away on the street. What happens when they start going house to house, and Captain Fletcher needs the brigade to help? You know, because we have the public's trust. You're smarter than all of us put together, so I know the thought crossed your mind."

Harrison exhaled, searching his thoughts unsuccessfully for a counterargument. It had more than crossed his mind over the past fifteen minutes. In that short span of time, he had encountered two government-sponsored groups conducting operations without the bigger picture, making decisions in a vacuum. He couldn't blame Littner for wanting to sit this one out. The more he learned about the RRZ, the harder he wondered if it was too late to back out of his arrangement with Captain Fletcher.

"I can't convince you to ride this out a little longer?"

"You don't sound convinced yourself," Littner said, finally cracking a thin smile.

"I don't know. I feel like I have to give this a shot."

"If members of the Berwick chapter want to stick it out with the brigade, I won't stand in the way. They can appoint a new leader and carry on. I'll turn everything over."

"This doesn't mean you're out of the brigade, Dave. Let's call it a temporary hiatus," said Harrison.

"No. I think this is it for me. I don't see a good end to any of this. Good luck, Harrison. It's been an honor serving with you. We've done some good."

"Sorry to hear it, Dave. If you need anything at all, no matter what it is, you know where to find me," said Harrison, shaking his hand.

When Harrison turned to walk back to the vehicles, Staff Sergeant Taylor kept a respectful distance. Taylor wore a pained expression.

"Parting ways?" asked the marine.

"Yeah. Dave's been with us since we started. Real shame."

"If we'd been here ten minutes earlier, this could have been avoided," said Taylor.

"Or three days ago, like Captain Fletcher said."

"Or that."

"It probably wouldn't have mattered in the long run," he muttered.

"Why not?"

"It doesn't matter. You said I can make a station-to-station call with the ROTAC, not just a radio-channel call?" said Harrison.

"Yes, sir. If you know the call sign, you can either

scroll down your saved list or input the first few letters using the touchpad."

"Captain Fletcher is Patriot 2 Alpha, correct?"

"Affirmative, but you won't be able to reach him."

"We just saw him less than an hour ago," said Harrison, starting to walk toward the vehicles.

"I just tried to reach him, to see what he can do about getting your folks some ID cards. My Marines say he left the compound twenty minutes ago in a civilian jeep, and he forgot to bring his ROTAC."

"Where is he headed?"

"Nobody will say," said Taylor.

"The Marines won't say?"

"Family and friends won't say," he said, shrugging his shoulders. "It's none of my business."

"Have you been out to this compound?"

"That was my first stop before reporting to the airport."

"What did you see out there?" said Harrison.

Taylor stared at him quizzically. "The whole thing exists, if that's what you're asking."

"I just wanted to know if Captain Fletcher was for real."

"That's not really what you were asking."

"I suppose not."

"Unfortunately, this is all very real. A nightmare—but real," Taylor said. "We should probably hold up until your folks get out of here safely."

Harrison thought hard about what Taylor had just said. He couldn't forget that every one of the men and women deployed to the RRZ had left behind family, some without the chance to say farewell. None of them wanted to be here, even the ones convinced of their mission. They were just too wrapped up in their roles to realize it. They were soldiers, trained to fight wars, not implement a civil disaster recovery plan.

Then again, the government couldn't have possibly planned for a catastrophe of this magnitude. It didn't matter at this point. The RRZ was their new reality, and based on Captain Fletcher's description of the worsening refugee situation across New England, the RRZ was the lesser of two evils. He wondered why Fletcher had left his radio behind. There was no way he forgot it. Taking a civilian vehicle was an odd choice as well, unless...*son of a bitch.* Unless all of the military gear was imbedded with tracking devices.

What are you up to, Captain Fletcher? Or are you just Alex Fletcher right now?

Harrison's money was on the latter.

Chapter 16

EVENT +9 Days

Yarmouth, Maine

Alex emptied the two-and-a-half-gallon plastic gas can into the Jeep's tank, keeping an eye on his surroundings. The shadows grew long across Route 88, enshrouding the tree-covered street in a premature dusk, finally providing some relief from the relentless sun. Their afternoon diversion had taken far longer than he expected, putting them back on the road to Belgrade close to dark. Barring any unforeseen circumstances along the turnpike, they'd arrive at Charlie's camp by nine, well after the last vestiges of light on the horizon had vanished.

Approaching the lake house at night worked out better, in his opinion. He'd drive the final mile without the Jeep's lights, relying on night-vision goggles and his GPS unit to reach the house. They should be able to arrive at the house without attracting much attention. Anyone that heard their arrival would have to go exploring to determine their destination, which was unlikely given the circumstances.

Alex and his dad would thoroughly scout the property before approaching the house, mindful of the possibility that it might have new occupants. He hoped it was empty. Removing squatters presented an unacceptable risk, especially at night. Unless he could scare them into leaving without a fight, he and his group would have to leave. Options would be severely limited at that point, unless he exercised his positional authority to rain down some RRZ pressure on the occupants. He wanted to avoid that, since it would attract attention to the location. Keeping this spot a secret was in everyone's best interest, especially if things went bad and his family needed a backup plan. The trip today had been all about creating options. Time well spent, even if it meant returning at the crack of dawn.

The last of the gasoline drained into the tank. They had started the trip with a full tank, topped off from the house's supply of gasoline. Averaging roughly eighteen miles per gallon, according to the trip computer, Alex calculated they used slightly more than the two and a half gallons to drive fifty-two miles. The rest of their journey would drain an additional ten gallons, leaving them with less than half of a tank. He could justify using thirteen gallons of gasoline, especially in light of the circumstances. They had fourteen gallons split between several containers back at the house, in addition to the three-quarters full tank in the BMW SUV, and they'd need most of it to pull off an evacuation.

With seventeen people, four of whom were injured, they'd have to make at least two runs between locations, burning up most of the gas just to transport personnel and a limited amount of gear. Ideally, they would return a third time to pack the cars with as much food and supplies as feasible. A third trip would require them to start siphoning gas from disabled cars—a dangerous proposition depending on the location of the car. Since the EMP hit at five in the morning, most vehicles were parked on private property or streets within sight of the owners. Few people would react well to the prospect of having their cars drained in front of them. He could always take several empty cans to the airport to fill and make something up about the farm's tractor, hoping nobody knew offhand that his John Deere used diesel.

Alex tipped the container as high as possible, trying to drain the last drops out of the can. His father caught the motion in his peripheral vision.

"Ready?" asked Tim.

"Yeah." He nodded, pulling the clear plastic nozzle out of the gas tank.

His father took a few steps away from the driver's side door and scanned the quiet neighborhood of shingle-style Cape Cod homes. He wasn't visibly armed, but his M-14 rifle lay across the front seat of the Jeep, where he could easily grab it through the open window. Aside from the pistol strapped to Alex's thigh, they had kept their weapons out of sight, finding the journey uneventful. The prevalence of roadblocks seemed confined to southern Maine, which made sense given that most of the mayhem during the Jakarta Pandemic had taken place near the border or along the Maine Turnpike.

They encountered two police checkpoints, one on the outskirts of Gorham and another in South Portland. Alex's provisional security identification and Maine driver's license got them through both with little scrutiny. It helped that Alex had chosen to wear his issued MARPAT uniform, especially at the Coast Guard station, where sentries had barred the gates to keep hundreds of gathering civilians off the base. Upon sighting the mob of people outside of the front gate, they parked the Jeep at a safe distance. Alex had approached a less crowded point along the fence, attracting the attention of a guard. Within thirty minutes he had negotiated the necessary help required to secure another option in the event that the border situation proved untenable.

He screwed the gas cap back onto the tank and looked at the deserted street with his father. The neighborhood looked mostly unchanged, with the exception of missing windows and a few downed tree branches. Yarmouth had been spared the brunt of the tsunami's landfall. Most of the wave's energy had been sapped by the shelter islands of inner Casco Bay. The Royal River had experienced a significant tidal surge, as evidenced by debris and high watermarks far into one of the parking lots, but the docks didn't suffer any direct damage. Physically, the sheltered marina and anchorage remained intact, like he'd hoped.

"Ever get the feeling you have a hundred sets of eyes peeking at you?" his dad asked.

"Not until you just said that," said Alex, throwing the gas can into the back of the Jeep.

"I'm worried she won't be there if we need her," said Tim, nodding down Route 88 in the direction they had just come.

"We can always find another. Plenty to choose from, here or along the coast," said Alex. "It's not like there's anyone around to haul them out."

Alex opened the passenger-side door and waited for his father to move the M-14 to the back before dropping his exhausted body into the seat. He was still running on empty, having slept less than four hours a night since returning from Boston. Even with the Marines on the perimeter, he found it nearly impossible to sink into a restful sleep. He shuddered to think what might have happened if they had arrived in Limerick twelve hours later. Ironically, the Boston-based militia had forced Alex north with Grady's Marines—just in time to save his family from another militia group. It was insanity.

Tim pulled the Jeep off the gravel shoulder. "I like the idea of a land-based escape better. Especially with the weather changing."

"Wait until you see Charlie's place. The term 'cottage' is generous."

"Can't be worse than eight people crammed into a thirty-eight-foot sailboat."

"I'll let you be the judge of that," said Alex, digging through a small rucksack at his feet for a green thermos. "Coffee?"

Alex's dad started to speak, but stopped. He shook his head. "I almost said we should stop at Dunkin' Donuts."

"I catch myself doing that all day. It's a hard habit to break," Alex lamented. "Same thing happened during the pandemic. Getting whatever we want, whenever we want is a deeply ingrained behavior."

Tim stared at the road unfolding in front of them, shaking his head almost imperceptibly. "I wonder if we'll ever see those days again…"

"It depends on how long the government takes to get the electricity flowing. From what I can tell, they planned for an EMP. Let's hope that preparations included stockpiling the big-ticket items like transformers and substation parts. Without those, we'll be watering down the instant stuff within a month or two."

"I don't mind the instant stuff. They use those flavor crystals."

"It's just coffee-flavored water at that point. Not really coffee," Alex said, opening the top of the thermos and wafting steam into the Jeep.

His dad started laughing. "That's all coffee is! Coffee-flavored water!"

"With that attitude, I can't justify sharing any of this with you."

"Smells good, doesn't it?" said Tim.

"Dark roast," said Alex, inhaling the lightly toasted scent.

His dad kept grinning.

"This isn't instant coffee. Kate wouldn't do that to me."

"She didn't want to waste the good stuff on me," said Tim. "Made me promise not to tell...until you couldn't turn back."

"She knows me all too well."

Alex poured a small amount into the thermos cup and tested it. He shrugged his shoulders. "It'll work in a pinch," he said, downing the rest.

"Maybe we should save it for the drive home," Tim said. "It's going to be a long night."

"Let's hope not."

Chapter 17

EVENT +10 Days

Limerick, Maine

Brown's earpiece crackled and went silent. That was the second possible transmission attempt in the past few minutes.

"Liberty Extract, this is Overwatch. Your transmission was garbled. Say again. Over," he stated quietly.

Another burst of static filled his left ear, followed by nothing. It had to be his pickup. The chance of another radio user selecting the same subchannel was extremely low, reduced even further by the late hour. 2:20 AM. He had been told late in the afternoon, via radio relay, that a vehicle would retrieve him a few hours after midnight. He permanently disassembled his hide site a few hours after sunset, stowing the climbing harness in his backpack and descending the tree to wait in the thick bushes near the side of the road. As midnight approached, he started to get worried about the proposed timing of his pickup.

The black Jeep Wrangler had left Gelder Pond Lane in the early afternoon and hadn't returned, creating the possibility of an unplanned meeting between the two vehicles in the vicinity of Limerick. Not a big chance, but even the smallest window of opportunity seized by the enemy represented a possible disaster. He'd learned this lesson the hard way in Afghanistan during 2015 when the Taliban came out of hiding, untouched and unfazed by the pandemic.

Kidnappings had replaced IEDs as the most feared insurgent tactic. With the help of sympathetic or threatened locals, Taliban "skassas," or specters, coordinated the sudden and often inexplicable disappearances of coalition personnel from patrols. The abductions defied explanation, but all had the same thing in common—a short, often unexpected window of vulnerability, like tonight.

Brown tried to contact "Relay One" to delay his pickup until tomorrow evening, but Eli had withdrawn the radio relay vehicle a few days ago, switching to a seemingly random pattern of radio communication to collect Brown's situation reports. He suspected the times coincided with whenever Eli could spare a vehicle to drive close enough to make radio contact. He couldn't blame Eli for making the change. Traffic patterns in and out of the compound yielded little in the way of an exploitable pattern.

One of the tactical vehicles left in the morning, typically before eight, and returned by noon the same day, rarely later. Another vehicle remained permanently absent, presumably based at another government-sponsored compound. This left two heavily armored vehicles and an undetermined number of soldiers at the compound for most of the day.

The situation had grown slightly more interesting today; marking the first time any of the compound personnel had departed in a civilian vehicle, without an escort. Due to Brown's lack of real-time communications with Eli, they had missed an easy chance to eliminate a key player in the government conspiracy without confronting heavily armed ground forces. They couldn't afford to miss future opportunities like this, especially this early in the game. Eli had said it himself. They needed to strike as many critical blows to the regime's fledgling structure as possible to collapse it, but it had to be done right.

At this point, he sincerely hoped Eli wasn't planning to attack the compound. Even trying to drive an explosives-laden vehicle onto the grounds would certainly meet with failure given the amount of firepower provided by the tactical vehicles. Six days after the first attack, he couldn't imagine any scenario in which the government agents hadn't prepared for the possibility of a car bomb, especially after McCulver tipped their hand by harmlessly detonating a firecracker next to a Mine Resistant Ambush Protected (MRAP) classified vehicle.

When he returned to the farm, he hoped to hear that Eli had moved on from this dangerous obsession. If not, he'd consider slipping away and heading north, away from whatever was about to explode in York County. The Maine Liberty Militia had been a good place to land, but he still wasn't one hundred percent sure about Eli.

"Overwatch, this is Liberty One-Zero," he heard over faint static.

"This is Overwatch. What is your ETA for pickup?" Brown requested.

"We just turned onto 160. ETA four minutes."

"Copy, four minutes. I'm headed east on Old Middle Road. Pickup approximately fifty yards past the entrance to Gelder Pond Lane. Right side of the road."

"Roger. We'll be running without lights on the stretch in front of the entrance."

"Copy. Out," he said and lifted himself off the ground.

He walked briskly through the underbrush, keeping parallel with Old Middle Road. A minute later, he turned left and fought his way through to the edge of the road for a quick look toward Gelder Pond Lane. The sheer darkness yielded little beyond a thick, monochromatic curtain. He dug a handheld night-vision spotting scope from one of his cargo pockets and scanned the entrance to Gelder Pond, checking for movement. Satisfied that it was safe to step out of the bushes, he took a few steps onto the dirt road and aimed the unmagnified scope down Old Middle Road. It was empty.

Brown cradled his rifle and shuffled west. He wanted to put as much distance between himself and the Gelder Pond entrance as possible *before* the extraction vehicle arrived. More than fifty yards if possible—enough to determine if they had attracted any attention. Driving this close to the compound represented a moment of vulnerability, and he wasn't taking any chances. He picked up the pace, jogging until he heard the faint hum of a car motor. Through his scope, a dark shape appeared in the middle of the road, well beyond the turnoff.

He watched Gelder Pond Lane carefully as the vehicle skidded to a stop in the middle of the road, directly in front of him. The SUV's engine roared, advertising their presence on the hushed, country road. He watched the entrance to the pond for a few moments until he felt sure that nothing was in pursuit.

"What the fuck? Get in!" yelled the front seat passenger.

The acrid, metallic smell of fresh blood hit Brown's nose when he yanked the door open.

Smells like a slaughterhouse.

He shoved his rucksack through the headrests, dropping it into the rear cargo compartment, barely squeezing into the crowded back seat before the SUV lurched forward at an unadvisable speed.

"You might want to slow down. There's a sharp left turn coming up," he said, pulling the door shut against his leg.

"We'll slow down when we're the fuck out of here," uttered a gruff voice from the front passenger seat.

"At least hit the lights. Trust me."

"Lights? Why don't we honk the horn to scare away the deer? Ever hear of going tactical?"

With the door shut, the coppery stench intensified, forcing him to turn his head and fumble for the button to lower the window. Moments later, the SUV skidded to an abrupt halt, jamming Brown's face into the headrest directly in front of him.

"Take it the fuck easy!" said the guy in the passenger seat.

"You got me driving around in the middle of nowhere with the lights out! What the fuck do you expect!" the driver snapped.

"I think it's safe to use the lights at this point," said Brown, reaching over his shoulder for the seatbelt.

"That's not your decision to make, Ranger Rick. This is my mission," said the man in front of him.

"Does getting back alive fit your mission parameters?"

"This is a courtesy pickup. You can walk back, for all I care."

"I think Eli might feel differently," he said as the car eased forward.

"I don't really give a shit *what* Eli thinks."

"All right. It's your show," said Brown.

"Hit the lights, slick. I'd like to get back alive to enjoy our new toys."

The SUV's interior brightened momentarily as light reflected off the bushes flanking the dangerously narrow road. Glancing to his left, Brown caught a glimpse of the man pressed against the far door. Half of his face was smeared scarlet red. The guy jammed between them had blood all over his neck.

Hunting?

That didn't make any sense. They could hunt in the woods around Eli's farm. Something didn't add up here. He felt a hard thump against the back of his seat, causing him to sit up.

"Did you feel that?" he asked, eliciting no response from either man in the back seat.

The next hit jarred him forward. "What the fuck?"

"We might need to crack one of them over the head again," grunted the man next to Brown.

"If we have to stop this car, I'll do more than knock her over the head," hissed the leader.

"I'll make sure the little one chokes on my dick," grumbled the other back seat passenger. "That should settle her down."

The pounding against the back of the seat intensified.

"Who do you have back there?" asked Brown, quietly unsnapping the holster pressed against the door.

"Some new toys."

"Part of the mission?"

"Eli told us to string up everyone we find at the house, but it seemed like a waste of good pussy. Not like he's gonna complain. We did a real number on the mayor."

"The mayor?" Brown echoed, slipping the Beretta 92FS out of the nylon holster.

"The mayor of Sanford."

Brown paused for a moment, considering his options. It didn't take long for him to reach a decision.

"There's another sharp turn coming up on your right," he blurted, easing the Beretta across his chest as the car rapidly decelerated.

He jabbed the barrel into the middle guy's neck as the SUV's high beams exposed a long, tree-covered stretch of road.

"Looks straight to—"

The pistol's sharp report cut off the driver's protest, catapulting the tight space into pandemonium. He shifted the pistol an inch to the right and fired two 9mm bullets into the next man's face, spider-webbing the blood-splattered window just behind his head.

"Son of a mother—"

The leader turned his body, struggling to push his compact rifle between the front seats. Brown jammed the rifle's hand guard against the roof and aimed the pistol into the back of the man's seat, rapidly pressing the trigger until the man stopped thrashing.

Given an extra fraction of a second to analyze the situation, the driver smartly abandoned the SUV. Brown lurched between the front seats and steadied himself on his side, emptying the rest of his magazine at the fleeing figure. The vehicle started to roll forward, and he let the SUV drift several feet before sliding the transmission into neutral and slipping out of the rear passenger door with his rifle. Brown walked behind the vehicle until it drifted to a stop in the middle of the road.

Bullets peppered the SUV, shattering two of the cargo compartment windows. Pistol caliber, he guessed, judging by the sound of the gunfire and the fact that nothing had passed through the thin metal sides. Brown opened the front passenger door and pulled the leader's limp body onto the dirt road. He reached across the seats and fumbled for the headlight controls. A bullet struck the dashboard above the steering wheel, missing his arm by inches and cracking the LED speedometer display. A second bullet hit the rearview mirror above his head. He caught movement beyond the driver's side door and pulled back into the passenger side.

Fuck this shit.

Brown scurried to the front of the vehicle and quickly fired his rifle point-blank into the headlights, returning the road to darkness. He retreated behind the engine block as bullets snapped over the hood, crackling through the forest beyond the SUV.

Time for a little flanking maneuver.

After backing into the trees, Brown crouched and walked back the way they had come, stopping when he had a clear view around the SUV. He scanned the trees to the left of the vehicle with his night-vision scope, hoping to catch some movement.

Nothing.

The SUV's red taillights washed out the green image.

He'd have to do this the hard way—and quickly. He had no idea how the soldiers at the compound might react to nearby gunfire. Instinct and experience told him they would stay safely tucked away behind their fortifications, but he'd hate to be wrong. For the first time in as long as he could remember, Jeff Brown felt like he'd done the right thing. That he'd chosen the right path on his own. It'd be a real shame to get greased on the side of the road by some twenty-year-old PFC blasting away with a night-vision-equipped "240 Golf."

Staying low, he crossed the road and crouched behind a thick stand of bushes, staying perfectly still. The deep hum of the SUV's idling engine contended with the chirping crickets, eliminating any chance of hearing the soft rustle of fabric against bushes or the faint scraping of boots across dried pine needles.

"The hard way," he mumbled.

Keeping his rifle trained parallel to the road, Brown moved forward, stepping heel-to-toe. He'd covered half of the distance to the SUV when a bullet punched through the side of his abdomen, knocking him to one knee. The gunman had retreated deeper into the forest than he had anticipated. Bullets cracked and hissed around Brown as he scrambled behind a thick tree. He waited a few seconds before leaning around the tree to search for a target.

Muzzle flashes and splintering bark forced him back, but instead of waiting for the fusillade to end, he shifted to the left side of the tree and centered his rifle's canted sights on the flashes. A bullet creased the top of his shoulder as he squeezed the match-grade trigger. The AR-10 repeatedly pounded his shoulder until one of the incoming muzzle flashes pointed erratically skyward, suggesting a sudden, involuntary shift in the gunman's aim.

The forest fell silent against the ringing in his ears, leaving him satisfied that at least one of his .308 bullets had found its mark. Using the rifle as a support, he struggled through searing stomach pain to reach his feet, and stumbled to the back of the SUV. Brown didn't have much time left. He was starting to feel sluggish. Activating the tailgate latch, he swung the door upward, collapsing to his knees in pain. Two figures writhed in the cargo compartment, hog-tied and gagged. He had to free them before all of his strength drained. There was no way to be sure that the man in the forest was dead. He tried to raise himself by the bumper but didn't make it onto his feet. This wasn't going to work.

"Can you hear me?" he yelled.

Muffled screams and more writhing.

"I need one of you to wiggle toward the back of the car! I can cut you free."

The larger of the two figures edged her way to the back of the compartment, contorting far enough for Brown to reach the zip ties interlocking her ankles and wrists.

"Hold still, please," he exhaled, aware that he was fading.

He unsheathed the fixed-blade serrated knife attached to his belt and carefully placed the stainless steel blade against the plastic tie linking the others together. Pressing down firmly, the plastic snapped apart.

"That's just the first part. Your wrists and ankles are still bound. Scoot toward me a little more," he said.

He gripped her ankles and pulled them apart, exposing a quarter-inch of the white zip tie. The razor-sharp blade cut through the heavy-duty zip ties with minimal effort, freeing her legs.

"Hands next."

She worked her way to the edge of the cargo area, extending her hands as far away from her back as possible.

"Pull your wrists as far apart as possible," he said, knowing it might only gain him an extra millimeter of distance to work with.

Brown carefully slid the knife between her palms, easing the knifepoint past her wrists. When the entire five-inch blade had passed safely between her wrists, he lifted the serrated blade upward until it rested against the zip tie. With all of her skin clear of the blade, he snapped the knife upward, parting the plastic. As soon as her hands were free, she crawled back into the compartment like a frightened animal and tore at the duct tape across her mouth.

"I'll leave the knife with you," he said, tossing the blade into compartment before collapsing to the road.

He pressed his hand against his side and felt warm, thick fluid pump through his fingers.

It's probably better this way. Easier.

The woman jumped down from the tailgate, pulling the smaller figure down after her. They paused for a moment.

"The car's still running. You need to get out of here," he said, easing his head against the dirt.

She slammed the tailgate shut, bathing him in a muted red glow from the taillights. Brown raised his head far enough to see that she was standing next to the vehicle, staring at him. He shook his head.

"Get that little girl to safety. I'll be fine."

"You don't look fine," the woman said in a shaky voice.

"There's nothing you can do about that. Pull the bodies out of the backseat and get going. The right rear passenger seat is the best for your daughter. It's the least messy."

"Thank you," she said.

He nodded and lowered his head again. The red light faded from the branches and leaves above him, yielding to blackness and a few patches of star-filled sky. He knew it wouldn't be long before it would all turn black.

Chapter 18

EVENT +10 Days

Forward Operating Base "Lakeside"
Regional Recovery Zone 1

Alex rested his hand on the M1919A6 machine gun's metal buttstock and listened for anything out of the ordinary in the forest. Branches swayed gently with the arrival of a warm breeze that washed over the yard. Beyond that, nothing but crickets. He concentrated for a few more seconds before leaning back in the folding chair with a thermal scope and scanning the forest for heat signatures.

A broad sweep of his field of vision from the back porch yielded nothing but a dark grayscale image of the trees and bushes. He'd found several dozen thermal riflescopes in the battalion's weapons container at the airport. Most of the systems were clip-on types, which mounted in front of the weapon's current day-scope. Unlike dedicated targeting scopes with crosshairs, the clip-on sight could be removed and reattached while maintaining the accuracy of the weapon. He'd issued one to each of the M240 gunners, to sweep their sectors around the house. Diligent use of the thermal scope would make it nearly impossible for anyone to sneak up on them.

The deck creaked, drawing his attention to the sliding screen doors. Kate stood in the middle of the deck, feeling her way around while her eyes adjusted to the darkness.

"Everything okay?" she asked him.

"I think so. Weird, you know? Sounded like a gunfight on Old Middle Road. OP Alpha swears they heard a vehicle on the road right before the gunfire."

"At 2:30 in the morning?" she said, guided by his voice.

"A little before 2:30."

"But nothing for the past two hours?"

"No," he said, reaching out and grasping her hand.

"Any room in there for me?" she asked, pulling a chair away from the porch table.

"There's always room for the love of my life, even if she shows up empty-handed," Alex said, scooting his seat until he was leaning against the sandbag wall.

"Coffee won't make a difference at this point. We need sleep," she said, squeezing in next to him.

"Sleep? I've forgotten the meaning of the word."

"Snug in here," she said, wrapping her arm around him.

They had constructed a three-sided, sheet-metal-reinforced sandbag position in the far corner of the screen porch, facing the northern tree line directly behind the house. The addition of hurricane shutters had severely limited their ability to survey the various sectors around the compound, and Alex didn't want to place the full burden of watching over them on the Marines. They had constructed a second sandbag position on the farmer's porch, to the right of the porch steps. One of the uninjured adults manned each position throughout the night, contributing to the defense of the compound.

"This is about as romantic as it gets for us," he said. "A starlit night behind a sandbag bunker."

"It could be worse..." Kate rubbed his chest with her fingers.

He missed the warmth of her hands. Her lips. Her skin. Everything they shared together as husband and wife. She leaned in and kissed the small of his neck, leaning her head on his shoulder. He pressed his head against hers and exhaled, pretending to relax. How much longer could he pretend? Better yet, how much longer *should* he pretend?

"That's what I'm afraid of. September 1st is three days away. A month after that, our options plummet if this doesn't work out."

"What other choices do we have?"

He shook his head. "I don't know. Head north?"

"Right now?"

"Once the battalion gets here, it'll be hard to disappear," he said, kissing her forehead.

"Where would we go? Charlie's?"

"I don't think that would work out," he whispered.

"I can't believe someone ransacked all of his stuff."

"It wouldn't have made a difference. He had a year's worth of dehydrated food for four people. We have seventeen mouths to feed. That's three months of minimal rations. Not that it matters."

"We can bring enough food to get us through to the summer."

"Then what? We'd have to start from scratch growing food. It's taken us three years to get to this point, and it's not enough to keep us from digging into the reserve supplies by January. Earlier with this many people. We're barely sustainable for the long run if everyone stays."

"We're not kicking anyone out."

"I didn't say we were, but Charlie's house isn't a long-term option. We'd be lucky to make it through the winter. Not to mention we'd probably kill each other before January. It's too small for this group."

"It's not that bad," she said.

"Picture trying to sleep seventeen people in his place. We'd use every square foot of the house just to lie down at night. About the only thing the camp has going for it at this point is abundant fresh water and a wood-burning stove. The neighbors will probably take the stove next."

"That's a real bummer," she said, pausing. "The whole situation sucks."

"If the border holds and we can find that militia nut before he stirs up trouble, we might not have to go anywhere."

"And if we have to leave?"

"I have an idea, but we have a limited window of opportunity before it becomes too risky," said Alex.

"How limited?"

"Early November at the latest."

"Does it have something to do with the nautical charts that appeared yesterday?"

His ROTAC handheld unit chirped, indicating a connection. He read the display. "Patriot Five Alpha." Direct communication from Harrison Campbell. This couldn't be good.

"Hold on, honey," he said, putting the phone to his ear. "Captain Fletcher."

"It's Harrison. We have a problem."

Harrison sounded out of breath, and Alex thought he heard a car door shut in the background.

"What's going on? You sound like you're in a car."

"I am in a car. Greg Hoode has been murdered and–"

"The mayor?"

"Yes. One of my guys down at the storefront went for a smoke. Found the mayor strung up on the statue of Thomas Goodall. Mutilated. They spray painted 'FEDERAL SPY' on the statue's base. I'm headed right over."

"Right across the street from the recruiting station? Fuck. This has to be Eli's handiwork," he said, closing his eyes for a moment. "Has anyone contacted the police?"

"I was going to swing by the hospital on the way downtown."

"Negative. The police will treat this like a crime scene. We need to get the body down before anyone sees it."

"I don't think that's a good idea, Alex. We should let the police take care of it," said Harrison.

"We can't afford that kind of publicity. Eli did this for a reason."

"We don't know it was Eli. Greg had plenty of enemies in town."

"I can't take that chance, and neither can you, for obvious reasons. Remember the gray hatchback that passed in front of the coffee shop when we were talking with the mayor?"

"Two men. Nothing unusual."

"Nothing unusual except the license plate is registered to a F-150 pickup truck in Alfred. We found a pile of Maine license plates at the church outside of Milton Mills. My guess is they're stealing plates from disabled cars and slapping them on the fleet of vehicles they acquired from their little Milton Mills scam."

"Sounds a little thin," said Harrison.

"Why would anyone hang him in the middle of Sanford with the words 'federal spy' spray painted? Eli is sending the town a clear message to stay away from us. We can't afford to have problems filling the provisional security team."

"I'm not touching the body, Alex. Not without one of your staff NCOs on the scene," said Harrison.

"I'm sending a vehicle from the airport. ETA ten minutes. I'll be there in thirty. We have about an hour and a half to clean this up. Thank God nobody's camping out in the park."

"We can't keep this a secret forever."

Kate tapped his shoulder.

"What?" he whispered.

"Did the mayor have a family?" she asked.

"Jesus. Harrison, can you muster a team to visit the mayor's house?"

"Alex, I'm not tampering with evid—ah, *shit.* We're on our way."

"Be careful, Harrison. I'll call you from the road," Alex said, lowering the radio.

"I have to go."

Kate kissed him. "Does he have family?"

"Sounded like it. Harrison is headed straight there," he said, grabbing the thermal scope and his rifle.

"You should put on your uniform in case the police show up," she said.

"Right," he mumbled, his thoughts drifting.

Chapter 19

EVENT +10 Days

Sanford, Maine

They drove to Sanford using night vision, standard operating procedure for an unsecured transit lane. Alex couldn't discount the possibility that this was some kind of elaborate trick to lure them into town, and there was no reason to advertise their arrival with headlights. The Matvee's armor was impervious to small-arms fire and interior damage from basic explosive devices, but the vehicle could be disabled or flipped under the wrong circumstances. Travelling in a convoy, this presented little more than a nuisance. The other vehicles could extract or protect the shaken crew until a "wrecker" was summoned to remove the vehicle. Driving alone, a disabled vehicle spelled disaster. A few well-placed Molotov cocktails could force them out of the armored shell long before help arrived.

Entering the intersection next to the park from the west, Lianez pulled the Matvee across the road and stopped in the opposite lane. Two men dressed in camouflage walked across the road twenty feet in front of them, headed to the York County Readiness Brigade station on the other side of the street.

"I assume those are friendlies?" said Jackson over the

vehicle's internal communications net.

"Roger. Looks like brigade militia."

"Where do you want us, sir?" asked Corporal Lianez.

"Right next to Guardian One-Zero."

The dark shape of Staff Sergeant Taylor's Matvee loomed south of the statue. Bright green, shaky lights at the base of the statue obscured the three figures scrubbing away at the blood and spray paint. Taylor set them to work as soon as the mayor's corpse had been placed in the back of the tactical vehicle. With any luck, the statue would look the same at sunrise, and no one would be the wiser about the mayor's brutal fate. Unless Eli had left a few more displays around town. The mayor's wife and twelve-year-old daughter were missing. Once the park was tidied up, they'd search the rest of Sanford's more commonly used public areas for their bodies.

Lianez drove over the curb and maneuvered them between two trees to arrive next to the other tactical vehicle. Alex flipped up the night-vision goggles attached to his helmet and stepped into the humid morning air, letting his eyes adjust for a moment before meeting Taylor next to the statue.

"What's up with the York County guys?" said Alex, nodding toward the men disappearing into the storefront across Main Street.

"We just got word on the police scanner that two cruisers are heading over from the hospital. ETA any time now. Figured the militia presence might complicate things."

"Good thinking. I should wave off the rest of them. Any idea why they're headed this way—beside the obvious?"

"They were dispatched on a ten-fifty-four. We're pretty sure that means dead body."

"They won't be happy to find us here. Especially with their mayor in a body bag," he said. "How long until we're done here?"

"Ten minutes, tops."

"I guess there's no way to avoid them. Should be fun," said Alex, noticing a set of headlights approaching from the east. "Close up the rear hatch so they don't see the body bag."

"Got it, sir."

Alex activated his handheld radio. "Harrison, is that you approaching from the east along Main?"

"Roger. We're passing the auto parts store. What's the situation down there? My guys said the Marines sent them back inside."

"Looks like we're about to have some company from the Sanford Police Department. Somehow, they know about the body."

"You still want me down there?"

"I'm thinking you should turn it around and head back home. Relations with local law enforcement are likely to sour over this. There's no point in dragging you along for that ride. I'll update you when we're finished."

"Good luck. Buzz Gifford is the line sergeant on duty tonight. He's a ball-breaker," said Harrison, disconnecting the call.

"Great," Alex grunted, catching the flash of a blue strobe light between the old mill buildings to the north.

"Staff Sergeant, put your gunner back in the turret. Keep the other two working on the statue," he said.

"Ooh-rah, sir," said Taylor, dashing over to the statue.

"Lianez, pull your vehicle around the other side of the

statue. Jackson, make yourself visible up top, but keep the two-forty pointed away from the officers."

The police cars sped down Washington Street, their blue strobes illuminating the façades of the tall buildings and marking their progress toward the park. Alex had no idea if any level of coordination had been initiated between the Regional Recovery Zone governing body and the local police department. Judging by the limited interaction reported by the late mayor and the frosty reception by state troopers at the Milton Mills site, he highly doubted it. From what he could tell, the sprawling RRZ bureaucracy hadn't arrived, which was surprising given the large number of soldiers that had recently descended on southern Maine.

The airport was nearly unrecognizable at this point, with dozens of UH-60 Black Hawk and CH-47 Chinook helicopters ferrying soldiers to points along the border. Transport vehicles poured through the area at the same time, depositing combat support and headquarter elements of 10th Mountain Division's 4th Brigade Combat Team at the airport. The rest of the 4th BCT was scheduled to arrive over the course of the next three days, along with the Marines.

Two police cruisers screeched through the turn off Washington Street, skidding to a halt on the north side of the park. The officers hit the pavement yelling, as Corporal Lianez backed the Matvee into place on the other side of the statue, temporarily blocking the verbal onslaught.

"They don't sound happy to see us, sir," said Taylor.

"You think?" Alex said, patting the staff sergeant's shoulder. "Stay right behind your Marines. Keep them working on the statue, no matter how heated this gets."

"Copy that, sir."

"Lianez, I want you out of the vehicle, next to me. Hands off your rifle," he said into his radio mic, placing himself between the onrush and the statue.

"On my way, sir."

Four police officers swarmed past the back of the vehicle, broadcasting a confused slew of commands and threats while shining their lights on the scene. One of the officers slid by Alex and was blocked by Lianez.

"Get away from the statue! Right now!" he bellowed, trying to sidestep the Marine. "Out of my way, son!"

Lianez stood his ground, relenting when the officer pushed him aside. Staff Sergeant Taylor was next in line, presenting a formidable obstacle at six-foot-two, 240 pounds. Alex pointed at the next police officer that rushed forward.

"Stop right there!" he said, his words having the desired effect.

The police sergeant squared off in front of Taylor, took a few steps back, and turned to Alex.

"You do not order my officers around. This is my crime scene, and you will withdraw. Where's the mayor?" he said.

"I think we need to throttle this back a bit, Sergeant."

"I'm not throttling shit back until your soldiers stop tampering with my crime scene," he said, directing his light at the Marines scrubbing the statue.

"They're Marines, and I need you to step back before we continue," said Alex.

"I don't give a shit what they are. What did you do with the mayor's body?"

"What makes you think he's dead?" said Alex.

"Don't fuck with me on this. Greg Hoode was a good

friend of mine. His wife and daughter are at the hospital in hysterics. I don't give a shit who you are or what your orders tell you, but I'm not backing down from this. Where—is—the mayor?"

"I'm sorry about Mr. Hoode," said Alex. "We took him down from the statue."

"Jesus! Why the hell did you do that? Your men need to stop cleaning the statue!" he hissed.

"Greg Hoode's throat was cut from ear to ear, both of which are missing. Eyes gouged out. Fingers missing. Castrated. Disemboweled. Not the kind of scene you want in the center of Sanford when the sun rises."

"That wasn't your call to make," said the police sergeant.

"Yes, it was. This is a Homeland Security matter. I'll turn over the body, but we're scrubbing the scene clean," said Alex.

"Homeland Security? That's a bunch of bullshit," he uttered. "Trust me, you don't want the trouble I can rain down on your ass. Get your men out of here immediately, before this gets ugly."

"How long until we're done, Staff Sergeant?" said Alex.

"About five minutes, sir."

"We'll be out of here in five minutes. I'll deliver the body wherever you want."

"I'm done with this. Help me get them off the statue!" said the police sergeant, trying unsuccessfully to push past Staff Sergeant Taylor.

The rest of his officers started to rush toward Alex and Lianez.

"Touch one of my Marines again, and I'll arrest all of you," said Alex, stopping the officers.

"You don't have the authority," said the police sergeant, jamming a finger in Alex's chest.

Alex needed to deescalate the situation. Alienating the Sanford Police Department would prove to be counterproductive once the battalion's security mission kicked into full gear. With more than forty officers on their roster, the Sanford PD could play a significant peacekeeping and intelligence-gathering role within the immediate vicinity of the RRZ Forward Operating Base. On the flip side, a lack of cooperation by the police might foster passive resistance and heighten unrest. In his experience, nothing was gained by pissing off local law enforcement—in any situation.

"I think we're getting off on the wrong foot here. Normally, we wouldn't interfere in your work, but the mayor's murder is more complicated than you might suspect. If you cut me a little slack here, I'll fill you in on the details."

"What else do you know?" said the sergeant, nodding at his officer to stand down.

"I'm pretty sure this wasn't a locally motivated killing. I think a man named Eli Russell may have ordered it. Does that name mean anything to you?"

"Unfortunately. You think this is militia related? Is that why Homeland is staking a claim?"

"My information strongly suggests the possibility," said Alex. "Very strongly."

"Sergeant Gifford," he said, extending a hand. "This doesn't mean we're friends."

"Harrison Campbell warned me about you," said Alex, accepting his handshake.

"Harrison's a good guy," said Sergeant Gifford. "He could probably help you with Eli."

"We're working together on a few things. Finding Russell is one of them."

"We could throw together the Special Response Team and pay him a visit at his house in Waterboro. Straighten this out immediately," said Gifford.

"I highly doubt you'll find him there. This is the first possible sniff we've had of him in six days. He's gone into hiding with his militia."

"You're not exactly helping efforts to find him."

"Aside from blood and entrails, which won't tell us more than we already know," said Alex, "the only thing they're washing away is a spray-paint tag."

"Possible gang murder? That's not out of the realm in Sanford. Lots of crystal meth gets cooked up around here."

"I don't think so. The tag read 'FEDERAL SPY.' Displaying the mayor's mutilated body in public is Eli's way of scaring the people away from any association with the government or Harrison's militia. I'm not going to bullshit you, Sergeant. We're recruiting local citizens to form a provisional company in support of 1st Battalion, 25th Marine Regiment's security mission. I can't afford any negative PR at this point."

"Was the mayor working with you guys? Our chief got the impression that he had been cut out of the loop."

"Greg Hoode sat down with us at the coffee shop for about ten minutes. We agreed to informally keep each other appraised of any big happenings. It was enough to get him killed."

"Greg was a career politician type, but he took care of the town. One of the good guys, for sure."

"That's the impression I got. At least his family is safe. Small consolation, but at least it's something. How did they manage to escape? Eli doesn't strike me as the merciful type."

"It's weird. Marcia Hoode said they were set free by one of Eli's people—after a shootout of sorts. She was bound and gagged with her daughter in the back of the SUV when it all started. They picked someone up out in Limerick, and all hell broke loose."

"Limerick? Did she say where or what time?" said Alex, looking at Lianez.

"She's pretty dazed. They drove around for a few hours, hiding out in several places before approaching the hospital."

"But she's sure it was Limerick?"

"Pretty sure. They drove on a bunch of unfamiliar back roads right after the shooting. Ended up heading south on 160—took them right through Limerick."

"Shit. I live out on Gelder Pond—a few miles off 160. We heard some gunfire around 2:30 in the morning. Did you call this in to the state police?"

"Not yet."

"Care to take a ride with me out to Limerick?" said Alex.

"That's out of my jurisdiction, but if it relates to the murder here, I—"

"Consider it a peace offering. I'll trade you one crime scene for another. I had to get the mayor's body down," said Alex.

"Let me bring our chief up to speed and try to arrange another shift supervisor. We're stretched pretty thin right now—running extra details to guard the regional communications center."

"Is that normal?"

"Not really. The whole state got put on alert the other

day. Someone knocked out the communications tower at the Cumberland County center."

"That's right next to the correctional facility. Was there a prison break?"

"We don't have a ton of details, but something went down at the prison—and it didn't start on the inside. Armed men broke through the fence," said Gifford, pausing. "Eli?"

"Wouldn't be a bad place to gather recruits."

"No. It wouldn't," said Sergeant Gifford, shaking his head. "I'll meet you at the hospital to take custody of the mayor's body. They still have a functioning morgue."

"Make sure his wife doesn't catch wind of this," said Alex.

"We'll keep it quiet. Work your way around to the back of the hospital. I'll have a squad car and hospital staff by the brick smokestack."

"Sounds like a plan. Staff Sergeant?"

"I think we're done here, sir. The paint's gone, and the blood looks about as washed away as it's going to get. We'll douse it with a few of the five-gallon water cans and call it good. It should pass casual inspection," said Taylor.

"Word's gonna get out. Probably some folks watching us right now," said Gifford.

"Nothing we can do about that, but a few watered-down bloodstains beats seeing the mangled, naked body of the mayor."

"Hard to argue with that logic," said the police sergeant.

Chapter 20

EVENT +10 Days

Limerick, Maine

Alex stood with Police Sergeant Gifford and Corporal Lianez on the shoulder of Old Middle Road, examining the scene illuminated by the Matvee's headlights. A thick ribbon of orange peeked through the forest to their left, melting into the deep blue sky visible beyond the thick canopy of overhanging branches.

"You think this guy was the one that helped her?"

"She said a guy opened the back of the SUV and cut her free before falling on his back. He's the furthest one back—and there's the knife," said Gifford, aiming his LED flashlight at the ground.

Alex walked closer to the body. Unlike the three other bodies lying nearby, this one looked peacefully arranged, eyes staring blankly skyward.

"Check this out, Lianez," he said, pointing his light at the rifle next to the body. "DPMS Panther. .308. Mrs. Hoode thinks the shooting started inside the SUV?"

"She's positive of it. Said the driver braked really hard twice. The second time's when all hell broke loose. There was shooting outside the vehicle, but that came later. Said a few bullets sizzled through the back compartment," said Gifford.

Alex shook his head. "I don't get it. Four members of Eli's militia just get into an argument within a half-mile of my house and end up killing each other?"

"When did they shoot up your place?" said Gifford.

"About six days ago," said Alex.

"They stopped to pick someone up, and the ride ends a few minutes later. Maybe this guy caught a glimpse of the women and decided this outfit wasn't for him. Six days on a surveillance gig takes discipline. Bet he turns up prior military," said Lianez.

"Mind if I take a closer look?" said Alex.

"Now it's my crime scene?" said Gifford.

"I'm not in as big of a hurry here—plus I told you this would be yours."

"You're an interesting fellow, Mr. Fletcher. I'm not even going to ask how you ended up in Limerick with your own detachment of Marines."

"You probably wouldn't believe me if I told you," said Alex, kneeling next to the body.

"Probably not."

Alex ran his light up and down the corpse. MultiCam uniform and boonie hat consistent with Eli's militia. Filthy from what he could tell. Modular tactical vest with double .308 magazine pouches. Matching drop holster—missing pistol. Two additional .308 magazine pouches attached to bottom right side of the chest rig.

"Did your officers find a pistol in the SUV?" said Alex.

"Not sure."

"Might want to have them check," he said, pointing his light at the holster. "You don't want someone stumbling on that in the parking lot. I'm not seeing any brass."

"Ahead of the front most body, sir," said Lianez, walking along the side of the road. "Definitely not .223 caliber. Bigger."

"Probably .308," said Alex, removing the polymer magazine from the rifle next to the body.

He thumbed five rounds onto the road before the magazine was empty.

"How many casings do you have?"

"Two right here," said Lianez, swinging his light around to locate more.

"Then we have thirteen more out there somewhere. I bet we'll find another body in the woods. Did Mrs. Hoode say how many men were involved?"

"You're starting to sound like one of our detectives," said Gifford, leaning over the body with his light. "Best she could guess was three. Looks like dog tags."

"Jackpot," said Alex.

Alex fished the chain out of the man's tactical vest, exposing two plastic-covered dog tags. Giving the tags a quick pull, he separated the chain and held them to the light.

"Brown, Jeffrey A. Social Security number. O positive. No Religious Preference. I know these aren't Marine tags. They stamp USMC right under the social."

"Army?" said Gifford.

"I should be able to tell you in a few minutes," said Alex, rubbing the tags together between his fingers. "I'm curious about the other guys. Mutilation and murder isn't something I'd expect from regular militia—even Eli's group. And the mayor's family? I guarantee they weren't taking them to a bed and breakfast."

"Always a few rotten apples in the bushel," said Gifford.

"True, but four in one bushel? I bet if we pulled prints and ran them through NGI (Next Generation Identification), we'd find a few of these gentlemen on furlough from the prison—compliments of Eli Russell. How long before we can get a crime scene unit out here?"

"No idea. Depends on who's available—and willing to make the trip. NGI won't be much help unless you have a magic connection to the internet."

"As a matter of fact, I do. I also have a biometric scanner back in Sanford. If someone from your department can lift the prints, I can scan them into my system, or we could cut off a few fingers to—"

"Jesus! Remind me to keep at least three towns between you and any of the state's crime scene folks. I assume you're just kidding?"

"I am—sort of. The more my battalion commander knows about Eli Russell's capabilities, the better for all of us," said Alex, contemplating the long-term implications of Eli's latest moves.

"I'm sure we can manage to get you some fingerprints without using scissors. If one of you has a ballpoint pen and a pad of paper, we're in business."

"I think we can arrange that. Let me run these tags through the system and see what I get. We've got about another thirty to forty minutes until we won't need our lights. You want to walk around with Corporal Lianez and try to find the missing man?"

"I wouldn't mind taking a stroll around *my* crime scene—before you start snipping fingers and gouging out eyeballs," said Gifford.

"I didn't realize they retinal scan prisoners," said Alex, laughing. "Try not to stray too far from the tactical vehicle. Eli might be dumb enough to send someone out looking for this crew."

"I certainly hope so," said Gifford, picking up the .308 and removing a few magazines from Brown's vest.

Chapter 21

EVENT +10 Days

Porter, Maine

Eli paced the ground in front of the farmhouse, debating whether he should order the immediate abandonment of the farm. Lowell Sherman and his crew should have returned with Jeffrey Brown more than four hours ago. Even if they got lost picking up Brown and blew a tire on the way back, they should have been here by now. Their absence was conspicuous.

He'd coordinated the night's festivities so Sherman's crew would have ample time to make it back by sunrise. If any of his men had been captured, Eli faced a possible full-scale government assault on the farm. To make matters worse, he couldn't rely on his early warning system to escape. Dozens of helicopters had been spotted over southern Maine, rendering his network of radio-equipped spotters useless. Travelling over one hundred fifty miles per hour at treetop level, the Black Hawk helicopters would close the distance between his most distant spotters and the farm within minutes.

With the sun burning off the morning haze lingering in the shallow valley, they were completely exposed. Escape and evasion tactics would prove useless against government air assets. Hell, for all he knew, they were watching him through the fog with thermal imaging. It wouldn't be the first time the government used drones against the people. The screen door on the farmer's porch creaked, drawing Eli's attention away from the road leading out of the farm. Kevin McCulver stepped onto the dilapidated porch.

"I think it's time to pack up and head to Bridgton. Fuck it. We're too exposed here anyway," said Eli.

"Eli, we're fine. I just talked to Tim Barrett. We're good to go. He just turned off Route 25. Should be here in ten minutes."

"How the fuck did you talk to him! I've been sitting on this radio like it's gonna hatch," he said, raising the handheld to his face.

The LED display blinked "no charge."

"Motherfucker!" he screamed, hurling the radio past McCulver and through one of the front windows.

The sound of shattering glass drew attention from the men gathered under the trees along Norton Hill Road. McCulver rushed down the stairs.

"Eli, why don't we step inside?"

"What the fuck does Barrett know? He's supposed to be hanging out at the hospital."

"He saw a woman drive Sherman's SUV up to Goodall Hospital's emergency room entrance at about 2:50 AM, so he—"

Eli's hand drifted to the Colt Commander on his hip, his face burning. "This isn't making me feel better."

"Bear with me. Barrett hung out long enough to see two police cars head into town about ten minutes later. Police scanner transmissions indicated a possible body in the park off Main Street."

"Sherman took care of the mayor," said Eli, "but somehow fucked up the rest of their mission?"

"He won't be a problem, and neither will Brown. Barrett caught a dispatch requesting a crime scene investigation unit in Limerick. Five bodies. Male. All with fatal gunshot wounds."

"Someone took care of Sherman."

"Apparently," said McCulver. "The question is how?"

"Maybe they spotted Brown at some point over the past couple days and waited for him to make a move," said Eli.

"They would have taken him alive if that was the case."

"Knowing Brown, I don't think that would have been an option."

"What about Jimmy's people?"

"What do you mean?" asked Eli.

"What I mean is we got lucky this time. All five of them are dead. Brown may have taken this secret to his grave, but I'm not so sure about the others. I've been thinking a lot about our plans for Bridgton. Giving the town to Jimmy's Vikings might not be in our best interest."

"Go on," said Eli, checking his watch.

"At first it seemed like a good idea. Putting them in Bridgton gets them out of the way. They're nothing but trouble. Useful trouble, but not at all suitable for our next phase of operations."

"Bridgton will keep them busy while we go about our work in York County."

"But how long will it take for the whole thing to unravel? All it takes is one concerned citizen with a radio transmitter or a working vehicle to bring the whole thing crashing down on their heads—and ours. They'd sell us out in a second to save their own skins."

"And your little genius expedition to the prison just added more of them to the group," said Eli, wondering where McCulver was going with this.

"We needed more people. The prison raid put nearly seventy recruits in the training program."

"Most of them are useless," said Eli.

"We knew that going in. I've identified at least fifteen worth keeping. That's all we needed."

"And the rest?"

"None of them can locate the farm on a map. We made sure of that. We'll drive them an hour north in one of the buses with their hoods on and leave them in a parking lot. They'll scatter to the winds. Problem solved."

"I'm more concerned with the Vikings. What a stupid name. I must have been out of my mind letting Jimmy create that group."

"The Vikings served a purpose—but I think it's time for them to go away."

"Easier said than done. They keep to themselves."

"They took a big hit last night. Two from the original crew and two from the prison. That leaves three in Bridgton—all Jimmy's—and five sitting around here waiting for Sherman."

"And Sherman ain't coming back," said Eli.

"They don't know that, and they probably don't care. More for them to plunder in Bridgton."

"But we're not turning them loose in Bridgton."

McCulver shook his head. "Of course not. Wouldn't be long before that attracted serious attention. We'd have an *Apocalypse Now*-style helicopter raid on our hands before the end of the week. I say we get in and out of

Bridgton as fast as possible. Take the vehicles at the checkpoints."

"We need heavier stuff, including some basic construction equipment. A backhoe loader would be ideal. Something we can use to build trenches and dirt berms—fortify this place a little. I wouldn't mind getting my hands on a fuel truck. I'm pretty sure Bridgton has a public works gas pump, but it doesn't do us much good without electricity. Some of the smaller fuel trucks have their own pumping systems. Don't know if they have one of those. Probably not. We need to keep our eyes open for a big shiny gas carrier. Has to be one stranded somewhere."

"We might have to go actively looking for one soon. Siphoning efforts are barely keeping up with our current consumption."

"We'll figure it out," grumbled Eli, attuned to McCulver's flat, dissatisfied tone.

Maybe he was right. The logistical realities of running a small army proved next to impossible without gas stations, grocery stores, Internet shopping and cell phones. Unless they were willing to attract significant attention. Attention they couldn't afford now, especially with thousands of soldiers running around. He hadn't anticipated such a large, conventional force arriving this soon.

Yesterday evening, Tim Barrett passed a disturbing report. Over a hundred Light All-Terrain Vehicles (L-ATVs), Stryker Infantry Combat Vehicles (ICVs) and armored supply vehicles rolled east through downtown Sanford, preceded by dozens of helicopters. A late afternoon bike ride along Main Street revealed the Sanford Seacoast Airport as their final destination. From the closest allowable point, nearly a half-mile away, he watched helicopters land and take off nonstop for more than an hour. Eli was familiar enough with brigade- and division-sized operations to guess that Barrett had witnessed the arrival of a light infantry battalion, along with elements of a combat aviation battalion.

Over the next several days, they could expect a brigade-sized unit—more than 4,000 soldiers—to deploy within southern Maine. They'd start seeing armored vehicle patrols in some of the planned operating areas within York County. Some new roadblocks. The helicopters were bad enough, but boots on the ground was always the worst. It signified the beginning of the end.

He'd have to rethink their strategy. The Maine Liberty Militia wasn't strong enough or adequately savvy to fight a protracted guerilla war against a brigade-sized, conventional military force. To start, he didn't have the proper surveillance network in place to keep a close enough eye on government forces. Tim Barrett was his only contact in Sanford, and Eli could only talk to him by sending a car south to contact him via handheld radio, which took his message and relayed it to the farm. The system was barely adequate, as evidenced by this morning's fiasco. He'd almost abandoned the farm when it became apparent that Sherman wasn't coming back.

His original plan to connect surveillance posts in York County with his headquarters in Porter proved impractical. Just the fifteen-mile relay to Brown's post in Limerick required four relay stations, consisting of a vehicle, radio and two men—he couldn't trust one to do it right. Sanford was another thirty miles south. No way that was feasible. Driving a car down would have to suffice—until it became too risky because of government patrols. Then what? He didn't have a good answer to that question.

McCulver gave him one of those "all knowing" looks.

"What?"

"You know I'm on your side, right?"

"Aw, shit. Here we go," said Eli. "Can it wait until we hear the rest of Barrett's report?"

"Does his report really matter? A thousand soldiers in Strykers and Black Hawks showed up at Sanford airport, and we lost five men in Limerick. Not exactly a positive turn of events. Game changer, if you ask me."

"I didn't."

Eli glared at him, making it as uncomfortable as possible for him to continue.

"I think it's time to decide what you really want to accomplish with the militia, and if that's possible."

"You don't think the resources in Bridgton represent an opportunity?" said Eli.

"It all depends."

"You're like the fucking Riddler. Spit it out, Kevin."

"I think we snag a few cars at the roadblocks and head back. We use the raid to get rid of a few loose ends—like we discussed earlier."

"And after that?"

"You can't defeat an entire brigade combat team. Not with this army."

"You think I don't know that? It takes time to build up an effective insurgent force."

"We don't have time. Once winter hits, you'll have a hard time convincing folks to stick around. The barn is heated with propane, which won't last. There's plenty of wood to heat the house, but I can't imagine you plan to open the doors to the entire group. Even if we dump most of the prison inmates, we're still looking at forty-plus mouths to feed. Everyone's been eating MREs up to this point. There's no shortage of food in the house, but once again, I don't see you inviting forty folks to join you at the table."

"The new recruits have been eating out of the fields," offered Eli.

"Even if we put an all-hands, concentrated effort into harvesting, we'd still be in deep shit by the end of November."

"A lot can change in a few months."

"For the worse, potentially. If the troops get word that a brigade of soldiers arrived in southern Maine, convincing them to carry out sustained insurgency operations will be a tough sell."

"I can be pretty persuasive," he said, patting his holster.

"That worked once."

"It'll keep working," said Eli.

"Trust me, blowing a man's brains out in front of three dozen armed men has a short half-life as a leadership tactic. Let me know when you plan to kick off that campaign, so I can be on the other side of the state."

"What do you suggest?" he hissed. "I just give up on this whole thing. Find a nice house on the lake and curl up by the fire all winter?"

Just as McCulver stepped uncomfortably close to Eli, a small sedan raced past the vehicles lined up along the dirt road leading out of the farm.

"I'm not suggesting you quit altogether. As your deputy commander, I'm suggesting a smaller, more symbolic target. Something completely in line with the insurgency role you've established. Test the waters with that, and see where it leads."

"Revisit our friends in Limerick," muttered Eli.

"Sort of. I didn't tell you everything Barrett passed over the radio," said McCulver. "The name Fletcher came up."

Eli cocked his head.

"*Captain* Fletcher. Regional Recovery Zone security officer. He established Homeland jurisdiction over the mayor's crime scene. Got the statue cleaned up before sunrise. Seems like he has the Sanford PD in his pocket now."

"Son of a bitch. This Fletcher guy has his hand in everything."

"And he still travels back and forth to Sanford from Limerick," said McCulver.

Eli put his hand on his friend's shoulder. "I know what you're thinking, and I approve, *after* we find a new headquarters. Something much smaller. Suitable for wintering over."

McCulver glanced around furtively. "How much room will we need?"

"Enough for one squad. Roland Byrd's crew."

Chapter 22

EVENT +11 Days

Forward Operating Base "Lakeside"
Regional Recovery Zone 1

Alex opened the front door and shielded his eyes from the halogen lamps illuminating the field across the driveway. The persistent low-pitched growl of a diesel generator bounced off the trees, reaching his ears from multiple directions. The neighbors were going to love this.

Unlike 4th Brigade Combat Team's daytime arrival, Lieutenant Colonel Grady's battalion rolled across the Maine/New Hampshire border at "zero dark thirty," arriving at their designated locations between midnight and 3AM. The battalion's vehicles left Londonderry and linked up with Route 95 near Hampton, driving the vacant turnpike north into Maine. Refugee traffic had been diverted westward several miles before Hampton, in response to the growing crisis at the Seabrook nuclear power plant.

Two Matvees and a medium utility truck detached from the long convoy before it reached Sanford, bringing twelve Marines, a DRASH (Deployable Rapid Assembly Shelter) unit and support gear to "FOB Lakeside" in Limerick. Alex would ride back to Sanford in the truck to meet with Grady, returning later in the day to assume command of the Forward Operating Base. He'd still serve as the battalion's primary liaison with the York County Readiness Brigade, which required frequent trips into Sanford to oversee the recruiting station and guide the training of the battalion's provisional security platoon. His duties threatened to take more time than he'd hoped, but it bought him peace of mind. With six armored vehicles and twenty-four Marines permanently stationed at his house, he could finally sleep easier.

A hand touched his shoulder.

"Looks like one of those eerie scenes in a post-apocalyptic movie. You know, where the government sets up a command post in the middle of hostile territory," said Kate. "The lights attract the zombies or whatever; then they get overrun."

"I'd say that was pretty farfetched if I hadn't spent the last few days repairing bullet holes," he replied, kissing her hand.

"I'd try to hug you, but I can't seem to get my arms around all of your gear."

"Grab lower," he said.

"Nice. I'm sure the Marines wouldn't appreciate the show."

"Quite the opposite. They'd probably turn a few more of the lights in our direction."

"Grady really needs to see you at five-thirty in the morning?" asked Kate, stepping next to him on the porch.

"He'll be running at full speed, 24/7, until the battalion settles into their new role. I'm just hoping he doesn't request my presence every morning at the battalion staff meeting."

"What if he does?"

"He'll have to settle for my smiley face on one of his computer screens. I should get going. I'll ring the satphone when I get a chance."

"When will you be back?"

"I don't know. Depends on how much time Grady wants to spend with me. He'll want to see what we have set up for the recruits, maybe take a trip downtown to the recruiting station. I'd like to introduce him to the chief of police in Sanford. Lots of little things. I'll keep you posted," he said, leaning in to kiss her.

"Why can't you take one of the Matvees? I don't like knowing that those militia nuts are still watching us."

"The truck is armored," he said.

"It doesn't look as safe."

"I wouldn't exactly inspire a lot of confidence insisting that I ride in a more heavily protected vehicle. The truck is fine, trust me."

"Be careful," Kate said, kissing him again.

"I'm always careful."

"That's not exactly what Ryan described in Boston."

"I had everything under control…more or less," Alex said and jogged away before she could delay him any further.

Thirty-five minutes later, the vehicle transporting Alex passed through a reinforced checkpoint at the junction of Route 109 and Airport Road. Two rows of concrete Jersey barriers stretched across the two-lane road, reducing it to a single lane flanked by a modular, armor-plated sentry post. A small generator concealed from the road by one of the barriers powered the portable light towers illuminating the road in front of the checkpoint.

Once inside the Maine Operating Base's outer

perimeter, the driver activated the vehicle's headlights and followed Airport Road to the gate behind the battalion's hangars. A sandbag post framed by a hastily constructed wood structure greeted them at the airport's outer fence. A ranger dressed in full combat gear and helmet stepped in front of the vehicle with a flashlight and a handheld device. On his way to the passenger side of the cab, he placed the device over one of the barcode tags on the side of the MTVR's hood and read the illuminated screen. Alex slid the thick ballistic glass window back several inches and held out his identification card as the soldier approached.

"We're headed to 1st Battalion, 25th Marines," said Alex.

"Copy that, sir," said the ranger, saluting.

"Sergeant?"

"Yes, sir?"

"Aside from your expert marksmanship and superb grenade-throwing skills, how do you stop a hostile vehicle from breaching the airport perimeter without a gate?"

"You really don't want to know, sir," said the ranger.

"Now I *have* to know."

"You're parked over a reconfigured M19 antitank mine. Remote detonated," said the ranger.

"Fucking-A. Can we get moving, sir?" asked the lance corporal driving the MTVR.

"Sorry I asked. Carry on, Sergeant," Alex said, and the MTVR lurched forward.

They turned left on a crumbling asphalt strip and drove behind a dark two-story hangar, continuing to the interior fence separating the Marine battalion's hangar complex from the service road. Bathed in the MTVR's headlights, several Marines manually opened the sliding gate and waved them forward.

"Drive around the back of the rear hangar!" one of the Marines shouted through the driver's window.

Alex leaned across the private first class squeezed between him and the driver. "Where's the battalion TOC?"

"Front hangar to the left, sir," replied the sentry.

He grabbed his rifle and opened the door. "I can take it from here, Marines. Have a detail bring the prisoners from the first raid to the TOC. I have no idea what to do with them. Thanks for the ride."

"Ooh-rah, sir."

Alex jogged toward the first hangar along the airport's westernmost taxiway, taking in the drastically changed runway scene. More tents crowded the five-acre triangle of grass between the taxiway and the airport's secondary runway, completely surrounding the Mobile Tower System (MOTS) deployed by members of the 258th Air Traffic Control Squadron. 4th Brigade Combat Team's Tactical Operation Center lay hidden somewhere in the jumble of tents growing to accommodate the brigade's widening footprint at the airport. Alex had assumed that the brigade staff would occupy the hangars adjacent to the Seacoast Aviation office suite occupied by Captain Adler, instead of going through the trouble of erecting a small city of tents and generators.

When you bring toys, you tend to play with them—and the army had a lot of toys.

Beyond the northern edge of the tent city, rows of quiet, dark shapes lined the distant tarmac, barely discernible as transport helicopters. It was quiet for now. Once RRZ border security and refugee camp operations kicked into full swing, the airport would resemble a beehive, with reconnaissance, troop-ferrying and refugee relocation missions flying twenty-four hours a day. Past the tarmac, over the tops of the hangars, a faint ribbon of light blue sky merged with the star-filled sky. Reveille for MOB Sanford.

Alex reached the hangar and slowed to a walk, not wanting to surprise a tired and edgy Marine sentry near the battalion headquarters. He turned the corner and examined the well-lit, two-hundred-foot-long hangar. The interior had changed drastically since his visit in the afternoon. All of the individual bay doors stood open, likely to ventilate the stifling heat collected in the hangar throughout the previous day.

He didn't envy the Marines quartered under the corrugated tin roofs. Beyond accessing the shipping containers to withdraw a few choice items, he had conducted most of his business outside in the shade. Even the small contingent of Marines that straggled down from Brunswick slept in the grass behind the hangars.

The far left side of the structure, front to back, was occupied by the same tables, display screens and electronics gear he'd seen inside the command tent at Harvard Yard, forming the TOC (Tactical Operations Center). The screens were blank, and only a few of the computers looked operational. Marines stripped down to tan T-shirts, utility trousers and boots worked under the tables, distributing clusters of cables and connecting fiber-optic wire. Lieutenant Colonel Grady, still dressed in combat gear without a helmet, sat alone at a table in the center of the TOC, typing on a laptop. Alex remained unobserved for the moment.

Three recently delivered shipping containers separated the TOC from a fifty-foot-wide area dominated by thick, waist-tall plastic bins and several gray folding tables. A group of five Marines helped offload a utility truck backed up to the hangar opening across from the supply area. The rest of the hangar housed several dozen Marines busy cleaning weapons or checking their personal gear. A few lounged on neatly arranged foam mats.

"Alex!" said Grady, closing the laptop.

Alex hustled into the hangar, stopping a few feet away to salute Lieutenant Colonel Grady. "Captain Fletcher reporting as ordered, sir."

"At ease. Have a seat," Grady said, sliding a chair over from the nearest table. "I was just looking at the after-action report from Greg Hoode's murder. Fucking brutal. Looks like the problem bizarrely took care of itself."

"Bizarre doesn't begin to describe it. The .308 shell casings recovered in the forest belong to the bullets imbedded in one Edward Vega. Jeffrey Brown had the only .308 in the group and reportedly cut the mayor's wife and daughter free. Blood-spray patterns inside the vehicle recovered at the hospital suggest that three of the occupants were quickly killed at point-blank range by the shooter in the right rear passenger seat. Had to be Brown."

"But you found evidence that he had conducted reconnaissance outside of FOB Lakeside?"

"Right. We recovered a notepad filled with information about our vehicle movements. Nothing to indicate direct surveillance of the compound."

"And Brown turned on them"—Grady snapped his fingers—"just like that?"

"He must have heard the women in back and had a change of heart," said Alex, shrugging his shoulders. "The guy had a solid military record and no criminal priors, unlike the rest of the shitbags in that car. Didn't seem like his type of crowd."

"You indicated that two of them shouldn't be on the streets. Tell me a little more about that. I didn't read the full extract portion of the report."

"Lee Hanson and Simon Shaw are—were—registered inmates at the Maine Correctional Facility in Windham, Maine. The facility was abandoned four days ago by correctional officers when a large contingent of heavily armed men broke through the gate. They used explosives to knock out the Cumberland County Communications Center across the street right before the attack."

"Explosives?"

"At the base of the tower. No personnel casualties."

"So, the big question is how did two inmates from the prison raid end up involved in the mayor's murder?"

"I have a theory," said Alex.

"Eli Russell," stated Grady.

"It traces back to him, more or less."

"I don't like more or less," said Grady.

"It's a solid connection, sir. Prisoners from the attack identified Brown as one of the squad leaders used by Eli in the attack on my house. Brown gets picked up by the car used in Greg Hoode's murder. Two of the guys in the car should be sitting in the correctional facility raided four days ago. Brown's the link. If they'd been killed in a car crash before picking up Brown—"

"You'd probably still blame this on Eli Russell. I understand, Alex," he said, putting a hand on his shoulder. "I'd want to get that fucker too. Family is family."

"It doesn't matter who's behind this, sir. Something is

brewing in southern Maine, and that doesn't bode well for the battalion's mission."

"What about these prisoners?"

"I brought them back with the MTVR. They should arrive at the TOC in a few minutes."

"Do they know anything else?" said Grady.

"I highly doubt it," said Alex, hoping Grady wouldn't press for an explanation of his response.

"The prisoners may come in handy if they can identify Russell's crew. I'll talk with the RRZ folks about setting up a temporary detention facility on base."

"Did the Authority arrive?"

"Negative. They're still trying to sort that out. Simultaneously assembling and transporting thirty-six teams turned out to be easier in theory than reality, especially in light of the damage to our infrastructure."

"How many in each team?" asked Alex.

"Two hundred twenty-five, give or take a few."

"Jesus. Sounds like a lot of people."

"Not all of them will be based here. Liaison groups will be deployed to the state capitols and major cities to direct localized efforts. Some forward elements are already in place."

Alex shook his head. "Doesn't sound like they're off to a good start up in Augusta. The governor's office didn't appreciate being told to take a back seat. The word is spreading over HAM radio."

"I stay out of the politics," said Grady.

"Good luck with that. If my suspicions about the RRZ Authority are correct, politics is about to become your top priority. Shoving a cadre of two hundred twenty-five bureaucrats in the state's face is bound to cause friction. Add several thousand soldiers to the mix, none of whom report to local government, and you have the makings of a political disaster. Guess who's going to be the RRZ's front man? I'll give you a hint," said Alex, pointing across runways toward the RRZ Authority's barbed-wire enclosure. "Not them."

"Thanks for painting a bleak picture," said Grady.

"You probably don't want to hear the rest of my predictions," stated Alex.

"The battalion has enough to worry about."

"Like the snazzy uniforms behind door number three," Alex said, nodding at the rightmost shipping container.

Grady paused before changing the subject. "How is the provisional security platoon coming along?"

"Not bad. In two days, we've picked up fourteen recruits. Four signed up under the militia banner. The rest joined as provisional Marines. Gunny Deschane and a few of the Brunswick Marines have been whipping them into shape. It's a bit of a motley crew. We also have the York County Readiness Brigade's training officer, Gary Powers. He's been working closely with Gunny to create a useful three-week training curriculum."

"That's nearly half of a platoon. I'd call that excellent progress," said Grady.

"Don't get too excited. Things slowed down considerably yesterday. Three showed up; two had to be turned away. Despite our best efforts to contain the murder scene, word got out."

"How do we reverse that trend?"

"Community outreach. The recruiting station is located next door to the Readiness Brigade's community assistance center. They distribute limited quantities of food and basic medical supplies on a case-by-case basis to the public. Backing their efforts with a more robust aid package will draw people to the downtown area and the recruiting station."

"I'll see what I can do. I'd like to get that platoon training together as soon as possible. What else do you have on your plate?"

"Something related. I'm working loosely with the Sanford Police Department to ease some of their concerns about the RRZ security situation. I'd like to include a few of their reserve police officers in the provisional platoon structure. We may as well add a local law enforcement element to the mix—especially if we plan to deploy standalone teams within the RRZ."

"Vesting local law enforcement and militia in the military efforts? Sounds like you've done your homework. What about other communities pitching in, or maybe the sheriff's department?"

"I wouldn't count on it. Sanford has the biggest police department south of Biddeford, and they're barely keeping up. The York County Sherriff's department is spread all over."

"See what you can add to the platoon. I like the concept. This is the kind of initiative the RRZ Authority expects from its Marines."

"Speaking of initiative, I'd like to go on the offensive against Eli Russell. My gut tells me he's just getting started. Prior to the attack, he visited several towns around Limerick, stirring up antigovernment feelings. Sounded like a recruiting drive."

"Recruitment couldn't have gone very well. Not if he had to resort to prison inmates."

"You should spend a few minutes chatting with the prisoners I delivered. They believe I was planted in Maine by the government. Part of a false-flag operation designed to subjugate the people. You have to admit, it's a clever story. From an outsider's perspective, all of this looks highly suspect."

"The government didn't conjure an asteroid, then turn out the lights. We were attacked with a low-orbital EMP device."

"How did an asteroid sneak by billions of dollars of technology aimed at detecting near Earth objects one meter in diameter, one hundred years away? I'm just asking a question the RRZ needs to be prepared to answer."

"Whoever detonated the EMP device obviously knew about the asteroid. Both hit us at the same time."

"Still doesn't clear the United States of perpetrating a false-flag operation in their minds," said Alex.

Grady shook his head and walked to the open bay door. "Have you seen the light show up there? It's slowed to a trickle now, but it was particularly active four days ago."

"We caught some of it. Wasn't moving fast enough to be a meteor shower."

"Rumor has it that we knocked out every Chinese satellite in orbit. My guess is the Chinese hit us with an EMP, and the U.S. wasn't taking a chance on a follow-up attack."

"Still doesn't explain how an asteroid the size of a small business park evaded detection for so long. Eli's stories are gaining traction, and we can't afford him gaining some kind of foothold in southern Maine. I'd like to start regular vehicle patrols and aerial reconnaissance extending north of Limerick."

"Air assets are out of the question right now. Every

helicopter is tied up with border surveillance and transport missions. You have six vehicles attached to the FOB. That's the best I can do until we figure out our tasking."

"That's barely enough to scratch the surface! I'm looking at nearly a thousand square miles between Limerick and Route 302, assuming he didn't go further north. Cached satellite imagery shows hundreds of houses buried in the woods off the established roads. He could be at any one of those sites."

"Not if he just liberated a prison."

"We have no idea how many prisoners he took. Without more vehicles and helicopters, we'll be lucky to find him before Christmas."

"Unfortunately, much of the battalion's mission is rather strictly defined by RRZ protocol. Checkpoints, patrol routes, VIP security—the list goes on. You're lucky to have six vehicles at your disposal. I'm not sure I can meet the battalion's baseline obligations with the remaining inventory."

"Russell's the only internal security threat on our radar right now. Just saying, sir, if we wait too long, this'll bite us in the ass. Bite the RRZ in the ass. I can feel it."

"I'll give you what I can, when I can," said Grady. "I hope it's enough to make a difference."

Chapter 23

EVENT +12 Days

Bridgton, Maine

"Slow down a little," said Eli, nestling a pair of binoculars between the dashboard and the windshield.

The *Welcome to Bridgton* sign stood several hundred feet ahead of them, marking the start of a sharp curve that would dump them into the roadblock.

"You ready?" he asked, looking over his shoulder at McCulver.

"Strong signal. Ready to go."

A red SUV followed closely behind them, filled with the remaining Vikings. As Eli predicted, the last of Jimmy's criminal brethren had chosen to ride together as the raid's shock troops. Once through the checkpoint, they would ride ahead into town and attack the police station, cutting off communications to the officers on patrol, or so they thought.

"You sure we'll be safe?" Eli asked.

"Duck if it makes you feel any better," said McCulver, holding a garage door remote control.

Eli slid his Colt Commander out of the holster on his thigh and cocked the hammer with his thumb.

"Start flashing your high beams so we don't have a

blue-on-blue engagement here," he said, noticing Grizzly's nervous glance toward the pistol. "Can't be too careful."

Grabbing the binoculars with his free hand, Eli scanned the roadblock. A scoped rifle without a shooter sat on the hood of the same blue pickup truck they had encountered a week ago. A figure dressed in MultiCam utilities and a tactical vest stood behind the roadblock, firing a pistol at someone obscured by a two-door, silver sedan. The sound of gunfire reached the car, causing Grizzly to brake.

"They're firing at us!" he blurted.

"Keep going. It's something else," Eli said, pretending to care about what he saw through the binoculars.

"I told you, Eli. They're up to something," said McCulver.

"Son of a bitch, Kevin. You were right," muttered Eli.

"Right about what?" asked Grizzly.

"Griz, I need you to do exactly what I say. I'll explain when it's over."

"When what's over?" he protested, stopping the car.

"Keep us going, or we're all dead. Stop right in front of the roadblock, and don't move the car."

"Jesus," said Grizzly, glancing at the rearview mirror.

"We have this under control," said Eli, raising his pistol to the bottom of the door frame. "Please drive forward, and stop at the roadblock."

Grizzly eased the car forward, breathing rapidly between panicked statements. Eli hated to put the man through this kind of fabricated stress, but his perception of events, when recounted among the troops, would prove important to his credibility as a morally honest leader and shrewd tactician, two traits he needed magnified to pull off the next phase of his plan. As the car approached, Craig Page squeezed between the roadblock vehicles, grinning wickedly.

"Eli, I could run him over," said Grizzly.

"Negative. We have to do this right, or we're dead men. Stop right here."

Pistol along his right side, Craig jogged forward and leaned in Eli's window.

"You see that shit?" he yelled, unaware that Eli's pistol was pointed at his face.

"Unfortunately," said Eli, jamming the pistol beneath Craig's jaw.

Before Craig could register a look of surprise, or betrayal, Eli pressed the trigger, blasting a hole through the top of his skull and snapping his head backward.

"Duck!" he said, throwing his head down as a deep thump shook their car.

Eli swung the door open and aimed down the side of his car, sliding against the metal until the red SUV came into view. Through the billowing gray and white smoke, the roof appeared punctured in several places, warped upward from the cabin. The vehicle's shattered windows littered the road with pieces of bluish-white safety glass. He kept his pistol sighted on the cabin, unable to determine the true effects of the blast through the smoke billowing out of the windows.

"They're dead, Eli. Trust me on that. There's a head on the road about thirty feet back," said McCulver, pointing beyond the smoldering car.

"Remind me never to piss you off. I thought you'd blow the whole car," said Eli.

"I don't like to waste explosives. That was a small thermobaric charge, which fit snugly inside the center console compartment. I basically detonated a racquetball-size quantity of magnesium powder inside the car. Nasty shit."

"Holy shit. You weren't kidding about the head," said Grizzly, stepping out of the car. "We need to get out of here."

"Griz, why don't you drive back to Porter and warn the others? We'll take the pickup and head to the other checkpoints manned by the rest of these psychopaths. You tell the sentries to shoot on sight if any of them try to get back to the farm."

"How many are there?"

"Only two left after this, but I've got regular troops at five other checkpoints. I need to get to them immediately before this spirals out of control. Don't stop for anyone. Don't fuck up the passcode on the way in, or they'll turn the SUV into Swiss cheese."

"Roger that. Good luck, sir."

"Carry on now, Griz. Hey, sorry you had to see this, but I won't tolerate the murder of civilians. We're all in this fight together."

"That's right, sir. I'll pass the word."

"What's the code?" Eli prompted.

"Code?"

"The code to keep your ass from getting shot."

"Born to Run. Backstreets," stated Grizzly.

"How many flashes?"

"Track number four. Four flashes."

"Good man. Get out of here," he said, patting him on the back.

When Eli's SUV swerved to avoid the blackened head in the middle of the road, McCulver shook his head.

"He's not coming with us, is he?"

"To the new place? I don't think so. He wouldn't fit in with that crowd," said Eli, removing a handheld radio from one of his vest pouches.

"All cleanup units, this is Liberty Actual. Over."

Staticky voices responded, acknowledging his transmission.

"The northern checkpoint has been neutralized. Commence your runs. Stick to the script. No improvising. I want all units headed back to base within ten minutes. Out," said Eli.

"You want to hit the route three-oh-two checkpoint on the way out?" McCulver asked.

"Not a bad idea. Byrd's men are good, but you never know with Jimmy's old crew."

Chapter 24

EVENT +15 Days

Porter, Maine

Alex stood in the shade of the two-story pavilion next to the Ossipee Valley Fairgrounds, hiding shamelessly from the late afternoon sun. Transitioning from the Matvee's cool, crisp environment to the humid August air proved infinitely uncomfortable in full combat gear. He wasn't sure how he'd managed to pull this off in Iraq, where the temperatures routinely soared twenty degrees higher than the hottest day on record in Maine, made worse by a complete lack of air-conditioning in any of their vehicles.

"Guardian Four-Zero inbound with local contact. ETA one mike," his squad Motorola crackled.

"Roger. Break. Guardian Two-Zero, this is Guardian Actual. What is your ETA with Guardian Three-Zero?" radioed Alex.

"This is Guardian Two-Zero. Five mikes. Over."

"Copy. All units meet by the white pavilion inside the front gate."

"Sounds like we might have a break," said Staff Sergeant Evans, scanning deeper into the fairgrounds with binoculars.

"I hope so. Three days without a sniff of Russell is a little discouraging."

"We've barely scratched the surface, sir. This is going to take time unless we get lucky."

"Tell me about it," Alex muttered.

They'd spent almost every daylight hour driving the three main roads heading north toward Route 25. Most of their effort had been focused on areas directly north or northwest of Eli's previous headquarters, leading them to the towns of Porter and Cornish. Alex planned to stay south of Route 25 and sweep east, canvassing rural roads until they hit Standish. Canvass was the operative term. Each team of two vehicles set out to explore dozens of sites selected the night before using archived satellite imagery. If the team leader spotted an unmarked dirt road or trail, they radioed their position and took a closer look.

The process was slow and tedious, requiring an entire day to thoroughly investigate a fifteen-square-mile area. By his calculation, they had nine hundred square miles to search before reaching Route 302. Sixty days. Eli Russell wasn't going to wait sixty days.

A tan Matvee appeared on Route 25, racing toward the fairgrounds' entrance with a promising lead: a local claiming to have seen a few vehicles pull deep into the fairgrounds eleven days ago. Same day as the attack in Limerick. Alex highly doubted Eli Russell picked the fairgrounds as his headquarters, but he wasn't discounting the possibility that a small cell had remained behind for surveillance or to serve as a radio relay. Jeffrey Brown's notebook suggested the use of a mobile communications network, which made sense given the geographic separation between Sanford and points north of Limerick. They'd sweep the grounds and surrounding trees with all four vehicles just to be sure.

The most likely scenario here involved Eli using the

fairgrounds as a staging area or rally point while a new base of operations was established. It suggested they would find Eli north of Route 25, but that wasn't a guarantee. The Ossipee fairgrounds could have been established as a fallback point well before the Limerick raid. Unless the eyewitness saw the bulk of Eli's vehicles headed in a particular direction, Alex couldn't draw any conclusions or make any assumptions about the location of Eli's hideout.

Alex walked into the scorching sun and met Sergeant Keeler's tactical vehicle in front of the pavilion, noticing a mountain bike strapped to the side. Keeler hopped out of the front passenger seat and opened the door behind him. A stocky, gray-haired man wearing faded jeans and a yellow short-sleeve button-down shirt jumped down to the dirt road, kicking up a shallow cloud of dust.

"Perry Gerson. Hope I can be of some help with this, Captain," said the man, extending a hand, which Alex gladly accepted.

"Alex Fletcher. Any help at this point is highly appreciated. Prior service?" said Alex, shaking his hand.

"Army staff sergeant. Infantry. Last tour was with 1st battalion, 6th Infantry. An IED sent me home with two broken legs and a permanent back injury."

"Ramadi 2006?"

Gerson nodded with a confused look on his face.

"He's like a walking encyclopedia of the Iraq War," said Staff Sergeant Evans, shaking his hand.

"Insurgents took over Ramadi after the fall of Fallujah. Not a fun area of operations. They relieved 3rd Battalion, 8th Marines. One-Six had a rough go of it."

"The good captain fought with Regimental Combat Team One in Iraq."

"Now I'm really confused," said Gerson. "I thought they eventually put officers out to pasture if they didn't pick up major."

"Apparently, if you wander too close to a group of Marines during a national crisis, they hand you a rifle and restore you to your old rank," said Alex.

"I'll keep that in mind if I see any army units. So, the sergeant here tells me you want to hear more about the vehicles I saw last week?"

"Yes, please. Why don't we step behind the pavilion before I die of heat exhaustion," Alex suggested.

Staff Sergeant Evans checked his watch.

"Yep. He's been out of the air-conditioning for twelve minutes. Ten's the limit."

"That's what happens when you strap sixty pounds of armor and gear to a forty-eight-year-old body," said Alex.

"Point taken, sir. You are getting a little old," retorted Taylor, flashing a smirk.

"See what I put up with?" said Alex, guiding them to the shade.

Getting out of the sun was only part of the reason Alex moved Perry Gerson behind the pavilion. If Eli had left a surveillance team behind, the less time Gerson spent in the open, the better.

"So, you're sure about the day you saw vehicles here?"

"Definitely. I bike to Porter every day to check on my mom. Up until that day, I could count the number of running vehicles I'd seen on my two thumbs. All of a sudden, I got three pulling into the fairground."

"They came from the west?"

"Definitely. Two SUVs and a smaller car. I took a side road off Route 25 to bypass the fairgrounds. Seeing three cars pull in at the same time made me nervous."

"Good instinct. This is a particularly nasty group," said Alex. "Were you able to see into the fairgrounds?"

"I stopped a little ways up the side road behind the Quick Mart and hoofed it over to those bushes. Watched them for about fifteen minutes through my rifle scope."

"That's why we stopped him," said Sergeant Keeler. "Carrying a hunting rifle over his back."

"And I really didn't appreciate that. There's a lot of talk about Homeland confiscating firearms. We've been hearing about it all over the HAM radio frequencies," said Gerson.

"We're not following that directive. I ordered my Marines to stop and question any civilians carrying firearms because anyone carrying a gun is more likely to observe their surroundings."

"Either way, it's a little unnerving being pulled over by an armored vehicle, though I have to admit, it's good to see the military. Beyond a visit from the state police six days ago and a flight of Chinook helicopters headed north, we haven't seen anyone in a position of authority since this whole thing started. What's happening out there?"

Alex glanced at Taylor, who imperceptibly nodded. They had agreed to share details with the public on a case-by-case basis. Information regarding the battalion's RRZ mission was strictly off-limits, but general information about the event was fair game. Neither of them felt this was a violation of information security, since most of it was conjecture and theory. Alex had scoured the information available through his link to the classified SIPRNet, trying to find an official release verifying some of Lieutenant Colonel Grady's rumors. His search came up empty. Neither the government nor the military confirmed an EMP attack, or any of the follow-up action suggested by Grady.

"Here's what I know for sure. An asteroid or large meteorite hit somewhere in the Gulf of Maine, causing significant blast and seismic damage up and down the New England coast. It triggered a tsunami, which did even more damage. Boston was hit the hardest by the blast effects, but the tsunami devastated the entire coastline. I saw Portland Harbor firsthand. It's a mess."

"Good God," Gerson said incredulously.

"Obviously, we were hit by an EMP, but I have no official confirmation," said Alex.

"This couldn't be related to the asteroid?"

Alex shook his head. "No. The timing might suggest it, but I've researched EMPs pretty extensively. Atmospheric breach by a sizable near-Earth-object contains no scientific mechanism to create an electromagnetic pulse. I'm not saying it's impossible, but the EMP effects are mostly confined to the United States. Evidence suggests a more localized, North American event."

"Invasion? I have to admit, that's the first thing that came to mind when I saw that vehicle."

"I haven't seen anything to suggest that. The soldiers and Marines are here to keep the peace and speed along the recovery," said Alex. "Which brings me back to what you saw through your rifle scope. What are we looking at?"

"I couldn't see the whole gathering without exposing my position, but you're looking at maybe two dozen vehicles. All makes and models. I counted about twenty men in camouflage. MultiCam pattern with matching boonie hats."

Alex shared a look with Evans. Luck had arrived in the form of a medically retired, army staff sergeant.

"Most of them were armed with AR-style rifles. A few shotguns. I spotted two hidden sentries at the entrance back there. I was pretty happy about my decision to take a side road. I would have ridden right by the sentries. God knows what might have happened."

"I'd venture to say you made the right call. Did you see any of them leave?"

"A gray Suburban left a few minutes after the other cars arrived, headed east on 25. I didn't stick around long after that. Had to get over to my mom's place. She's not handling the heat so well. When I made the return trip a few hours later, the fairgrounds were empty. They left at some point between 1:30 and 4 PM. You might want to head into Cornish and ask around. Be damn near impossible to drive twenty cars through town without attracting attention, and that's really the only way to head east without getting really creative. Sorry I can't be of more help."

"This is fantastic, Mr. Gerson. One way or the other, we should be able to narrow our search focus. Would you mind accompanying us into town? Your presence would go a long way toward loosening tongues, if you catch my drift."

Two Matvees sped into view from the east, roaring into the fairgrounds and skidding to a halt behind the other vehicles. A thick plume of dust followed and enveloped the entire group.

"Damn, I miss shit like that!" Gerson said and covered his eyes as the dust cloud intensified. "I suggest we park your fleet of armored trucks on the outskirts of town and walk it in. Might be a little less imposing."

Alex coughed and let the dust pass before responding. "Probably a good idea. Crazy question for you. Can we help you move your mother, or is she hell-bent on staying in her own house?"

"Seriously? That would be fantastic. I've been making the trip because I didn't have a way to get her from point A to point B. Thank you."

"It's the least I can do. We'll head over to her place and let you break the news. Then we'll make the rounds in Cornish. Sound like a plan?"

"Best plan I've heard so far. I think this officer might be a keeper, Staff Sergeant Evans."

"The jury's still out, Mr. Gerson." Evans winked.

***

Alex wedged his rifle against the utilitarian dashboard and removed his helmet, bathing in the cool air pumped out of the Matvee's vents. He was glad to be out of the stagnant, humid air, having spent the past hour and a half walking through Cornish.

"Guardian units, this is Guardian Actual. RTB via Route 5. Standard interval. 360-degree sector coverage. Good work out there. I think we have something. Guardian standing by this channel."

Once each Matvee responded, Corporal Lianez pulled onto Route 25, headed toward the Route 5 bypass just west of downtown Cornish.

"What do you think, Staff Sergeant? Is it enough to focus the search north by northwest from Cornish?"

"It's enough to justify starting our search north of Route 25 near the border, but I don't think we can definitively clear the areas southeast of Cornish. Gerson spotted a gray Suburban heading east. Could have been a final scouting run."

"But nothing passed through Cornish, including the back streets—unless they miraculously slipped through town with twenty-plus vehicles without anyone noticing. They either turned south on Route 5 and burrowed east into the zone we haven't searched, or they headed west and turned north on Route 160."

"They hit the correctional facility in Windham. That's a helluva lot closer to the eastern side of our search grid than the west. They drove two correctional buses out of there. Hard to miss those. Not easy to hide either," said Evans.

"I don't want to spend three more days south of Route 25," said Alex, shaking his head. "It doesn't make sense for Eli to head back toward Limerick."

"We can't make any assumptions," Evans countered. "For all we know, he has two or three locations. He'd be smart to split up the group. Less traffic in and out. Less exposure if one of his men was captured. Might explain how he was able to pull off the murder in Sanford. That's a long-ass way from here."

"Are you doing this to fuck with me?" said Alex.

"I'm just here to make sure you don't try to jam the square peg in the round hole, sir."

"All right. Pull out your tablet, and we'll take a close look at the satellite imagery east of Route 5—mark off roads to hit tomorrow. I'll give this one day; then we start looking north of Cornish."

Chapter 25

EVENT +15 Days

Porter, Maine

Eli unzipped the green duffle bag and descended the sturdy wooden plank stairs into the clammy cellar. The change in temperature was a welcome relief from the stagnant, overheated air trapped inside the farmhouse.

No wonder Kevin spends most of his day down here.

Halfway down the stairs, McCulver's workshop came into view. Three long folding tables covered with various electronics devices and tools stood parallel to each other, illuminated by two standing lamps placed next to each end of the middle table. The lamps were connected to a portable generator they kept running for several hours at a time.

For all of McCulver's bitching about gasoline consumption, he put a sizeable dent in their supply with his own little operation down here. Not that Eli was complaining. Kevin's bomb-making expertise was critical to their operation, especially now.

"How's it coming along?" Eli asked, his feet hitting the hard-packed dirt floor.

McCulver sat on a wooden stool taken from the kitchen island, hunched over a small object on the center table. A thin tendril of gray smoke rose between his hands. He answered without looking up.

"Not bad. I'm working on the remote detonation mechanisms for the car bombs. I should finish up in three to four days."

"I don't think we have that much time. The surveillance team in Kezar Falls spotted two military vehicles crossing the Ossipee River Bridge, driving east on Route 25."

"Jesus, that's kind of close."

"That's not the worst of it. Guess where they stopped?"

McCulver looked up from his work and shook his head.

"Ossipee Valley Fairgrounds. To have a chitchat with one of the locals and join up with two more military vehicles."

"Four tactical vehicles? That's enough to roll us up for good. We can't resist that kind of firepower. Not with rifles and shotguns. Do we know who they talked to?"

"Negative. The team took a big enough risk driving down to Cornish. They didn't stick around for long."

"Fuck, Eli. Route 25 is more than thirty miles from Sanford. This isn't a random event. Was this part of the brigade that arrived in York County?"

"That's the interesting part. The team said they were dressed differently than army soldiers. Wore a darker green uniform."

"Marines wear MARPAT in either desert or woodland. Army uses a universal pattern. Lots of gray and tan. Could be part of the detachment based out of Limerick."

"Brown reported four vehicles total at the Limerick site. Gives me an idea."

"The plan is ambitious enough, Eli."

"Either way, it has to be modified. Previous intelligence indicated this Fletcher guy left every morning with one vehicle. Sometimes two. The plan can handle two vehicles."

"One is better," said McCulver.

"And four is impossible. We need to split them up, which is where you come in," said Eli, patting McCulver's shoulder.

"What's the timeline?"

"Three days, but we move everyone out of here to the forward staging areas tomorrow night."

"Forward staging areas?"

"I'm sending Harry Fields' squad to find suitable locations near our targets. The rest will follow tomorrow night. I want everything out of here by midnight. Once the troops depart, Byrd's squad will help us move all of the remaining shit to our new place up north. We'll be in position with the Limerick team before the sun rises."

"Lots of moving parts, Eli. Sure we can trust Byrd's men to keep this quiet?"

"They don't know shit about shit. All Byrd knows is that his squad gets to sit this one out. I didn't hear him complaining."

"And Fields?"

"He's eager as a motherfucker to get in on the action."

"Uh-huh. What about the inmates? I assume we won't be busing half of them north to be released?"

"I have something special lined up for the jail-break battalion," he said, grinning wickedly.

"I assume it has something to do with the rigged-up buses?"

Eli nodded. "I wish I could be there to witness your masterpiece."

"I don't—wait. What do you mean *my* masterpiece?"

Eli pulled a wide-brimmed, dark green campaign hat out of the duffel bag, placing it on McCulver's head.

"Deputy Sheriff McCulver, welcome to the York County Sheriff's Department."

McCulver stood up and removed the hat. "You do remember that I know this is a suicide mission, right?"

"Oh. Did we talk about that already?" said Eli, trying desperately to maintain a straight face.

McCulver's eyes darted to the table, presumably looking for a weapon.

Eli broke out in a sudden fit of laughter. "Jesus, Kevin. You're one paranoid son of a bitch," he said, grabbing the hat out of McCulver's hands. "I just need you to get the buses past the first checkpoint on Route 99 and coordinate the fireworks, from a distance. You need to relax a little, brother."

"I'll relax when I'm tipping back a few cold ones up north."

"The first round's on me."

"First and last," said McCulver.

PART III

"Reengage"

Chapter 26

EVENT +17 Days

Main Operating Base "Sanford"
Regional Recovery Zone 1

Alex's vehicle rolled past the rangers' outer perimeter checkpoint and turned toward the Marines' hangar complex. The six-foot-tall chain-link fence separating the battalion staging area from the rest of the airport had been reinforced since his last visit. A thick coil of concertina wire ran along the ground, extending the entire length from the outer perimeter to the edge of the taxiway. Tan HESCO bunkers flanked the battalion access gate; the left barrier sporting a bipod-mounted M240G machine gun. The airport was slowly transforming into an isolated firebase.

A dark gray blanket of clouds dominated the sky beyond the green hangar, a stark change from the long stretch of sun-blasted weather that would have marked a successful Labor Day weekend—if weekends mattered anymore. The Marines at the gate waved them through, directing them toward the rear hangar, which housed the battalion's motor-transport section. When they reached the hangar, Alex received a call via ROTAC from "Patriot."

"Captain Fletcher," he answered.

"Alex, I'm in front of the hangar with Major Blackmun."

"Roger. Heading your way now," he said, turning to Staff Sergeant Evans in the back seat. "Why don't you and Jackson take a little break? I need to make room for Colonel Grady and Ops."

He picked up Grady and Blackmun, giving up his seat to the battalion commander and joining the battalion operations officer in the crew compartment.

"Major Tim Blackmun," said the marine, shaking his hand. "The colonel's been singing your praises since Boston."

"All part of my propaganda campaign to keep you on board," said Grady.

The battalion commander turned in the front seat and forced a grin through the exhausted exterior of his weathered face. Alex wondered if he looked as bad as Grady. He hoped not. His former platoon commander looked half dead.

"Good to have you at this meeting, Alex. The bulk of the RRZ Authority arrived yesterday afternoon, and they didn't waste any time tearing into things. Apparently, RRZ New England North is way behind schedule."

"What does that mean?" Alex asked.

"Somewhere inside the Beltway, someone with a few PhDs and no clue opined that most of the RRZs would be fully operational within fifteen days of receiving the executive order."

"Looks like the place is up and running to me," said Alex, staring out of the compact window at three Chinook helicopters rising from the tarmac.

"The MOB is mostly operational. It's the rest that has them worried. The FEMA camps are massive gaggles of humanity sleeping in the open. They haven't begun to ship tents and supplies south. Border security is marginal at best." Grady sighed. "Frankly, I don't know if that will ever get better. Supply and fuel logistics are another story altogether. With most of the port facilities in the region destroyed, we're running our vehicles on fuel farm reserves. RRZ contingency planning didn't include the possibility of a tsunami."

"Why would it?" Alex remarked.

"Exactly. We spent the entire night and much of the early morning all trying to explain, with minimal success, that they'd be lucky to see a fully operational RRZ by the end of September."

"What were these people before the event?"

"Mixture of everything as far as we can tell. Former governors and mayors, consultants, industry types, career government employees. Lots of smart people, so I was told—over and over again."

"D.C. loves to throw smart people at a problem. Anyone with any real experience running refugee camps or humanitarian aid missions?"

"Each region has a fully staffed FEMA team," Grady said. "They might be the only full-timers in the bunch."

Alex rolled his eyes. "How often did they train as a group?"

"They met once a year in D.C. to run a three-day field scenario at Andrews Air Force Base, followed by four days of briefings."

"Then everyone went back to their day jobs?"

"Sounds like it."

"No wonder they're pissed. They actually have to *do* something."

"Better than nothing, I suppose," said Grady.

"Let's reexamine that statement in a few weeks, sir," Alex said as they stopped at the edge of the eastern taxiway.

An airfield controller stood at the entrance to the tarmac, holding up a hand to stop the vehicle for two Black Hawk helicopters. Soldiers loaded down with full combat gear and field kit streamed single file under the spinning blades.

"Did you read my summary of the Bridgton report?"

"Sounds pretty conclusive," said Grady.

"Irrefutable. Eli's building up his vehicle fleet. Most likely to outfit the prisoners he snagged from Windham. We're not going to catch him with two vehicle teams working a thousand square miles of territory."

"Every helicopter is tasked for border missions," said Grady, exhaling deeply. "We can bring it up this morning, but I'm not sure how well it will be received. Their heads are spinning."

"We need to try."

The Black Hawks rose above the hangar and dipped south, speeding away from the airport. Cleared to proceed, their vehicle continued past the vacant Sea Coast Aviation building and raced across the empty blacktop toward the "Authority Complex." The fence surrounding the series of small hangars and office structures was topped with concertina wire and lined with evenly spaced Jersey barriers set several feet in front of the fence. A modular, armored guard post sat behind the right side of the fence, buried behind several, waist-height HESCO barriers blocking the entrance to the compound. A white sign with bold black letters attached to the left side of the fence read "RRZ AUTHORITY. Authorized Personnel Only. No Vehicle Traffic."

"Jesus, the engineers could have built their own port facility in the time it took to construct the RRZ's Green Zone," said Alex, eliciting a quick laugh from Major Blackmun.

"Don't laugh. Long-term plans require a twelve-foot-tall HESCO barrier with cameras and elevated guard positions," said Grady.

They parked next to a row of four-door Jeep Wranglers with "RRZ1/NEN" painted on the sides and hood. A JLTV (Joint Light Tactical Vehicle) with 4th Brigade Combat Team/10th Mountain Division markings pulled alongside as Alex dismounted the Matvee. The turret in the army vehicle swiveled, pointing the M240 toward Route 109 beyond the perimeter fence. For all of their security concerns, the RRZ Authority had picked one of the worst possible locations for their "secure" compound. Located less than four hundred feet from the road passing the airport, the cluster of hangars could be taken under accurate, concentrated fire from vehicles outside of the outer perimeter. Maybe the HESCO wall wasn't a bad idea.

An army captain and staff sergeant emerged from the JLTV, saluting Grady and Blackmun.

"You guys drew the lucky straw?" said Grady, returning the soldiers' salute.

"I was volunteered, sir," said the officer. "Captain Van Tassel. Assistant ops."

"I'm just here to make sure the good captain doesn't stick a boot in his mouth, or up one of their asses," said the staff sergeant, nodding at the compound.

"Good luck," said Grady. "I brought two to keep me in check."

Alex ran his hand along the rear bumper of one of the vehicles.

"Brand new," he announced. "Did they fly in with these?"

"Negative," Captain Van Tassel answered. "The security team delivered them from one of the warehouses. Armored J8s. Blast and small-arms resistant. The Diplomatic Security Service uses these all over the world."

"One of our security teams?" asked Alex.

The captain and Grady shared a brief, pained look.

"Mercenaries," responded Major Blackmun, nodding at the compound's security checkpoint.

"Contract security, Major," Grady replied dryly.

Three serious-looking men wearing hiking boots, khaki pants, assorted dark T-shirts and olive-green tactical vests stood in front of the HESCO barriers, short-barreled assault rifles at the ready.

"Big business," muttered Alex.

"What was that?" said Blackmun.

"I'm just thinking about the business behind all of this. The RRZ concept must have made some people rich."

Grady stopped, halting the group in front of the first set of Jersey barriers.

"Careful what you say in there. Hell hath no fury like a bureaucrat scorned."

A second contract security team escorted them to a conference room on the second floor of a run-down building in the center of the compound. Rows of mismatched chairs sat facing a worn wooden conference table at the front of the room. Unopened boxes of electronics equipment were stacked floor to ceiling against the inner wall of the thirty-foot-long room. Flat-screen monitors, wireless router gear, computers—enough off-the-shelf gear to set up a full-scale operations center.

"Doesn't look or feel like they're setting up," said Major Blackmun.

"I saw a few people working on laptops in the offices downstairs. Not exactly a beehive of activity," said Alex.

"I think they expected this to be assembled prior to arrival," said Grady.

"I'm sensing a trend with these expectations," said Alex.

"You and me, both."

A man dressed in jeans and a long-sleeve collared shirt walked into the room and squinted, nodding at Colonel Grady.

"Fantastic. You're early. We're trying to iron out a few last minute changes. I'm Ian Day, assistant chief of staff," he said, remaining near the door.

"We met briefly last night. Lieutenant Colonel Grady, 1st Battalion, 25th Marines. This is my operations officer, Major Blackmun, and one of my intelligence officers, Captain Fletcher."

"Perfect. I'll let the governor know you're here," he said, stepping out of the room.

"The governor?" whispered Alex.

"Governor Medina. RRZ governor," said Grady, tilting his head. "I think I hear her now. She's kind of hard to miss."

"Do we have to call her governor?"

"I just call her ma'am. She hasn't complained about it yet—and she doesn't seem to be one to hold back on complaints."

Voices grew in the hallway, reaching a peak outside of the door.

"Colonel, I don't care who you have to displace. My people are taking over the hotel. Start making arrangements," ordered a sharp female voice. "Ian, tell Eric that this whole operation is moving across the street. I don't give a shit what they have to do to make that place secure. I'm not spending another night in one of these dirty offices."

A male voice mumbled something.

"I don't care if they have to surround the place with an entire battalion until the barriers are up."

A muted response yielded another shrill retort.

"Everything! Move everything! Put the operations center in the fucking restaurant. I don't care. Just get it done!"

This should be interesting.

A few seconds later, a tall Hispanic woman in navy blue business attire strode into the room with her entourage of security guards and staff. Grady stood up when she entered the room, furtively signaling with his right hand for the rest of them to do the same.

"Lieutenant Colonel Grady, why are you still wearing those uniforms?" she said, putting out both hands in a stop gesture. "Please sit down. I hate faux respect more than a complete lack of it."

"We're still sorting out the sizes, ma'am," said Grady, taking a seat.

"Look, I know you don't want to wear the new uniforms, but it's non-negotiable. Someone put a lot of time and thought into the color scheme. As internal security, your troops need to be instantly recognizable as such. Just like the police," she said, taking a seat with her staff at the conference table.

"Only Russian internal security troops wear blue camouflage uniforms. Secret police types," said Grady.

"Then I guess it's a good thing the people don't have access to the Internet, or they might make the connections. Figure out the sizing issue, Colonel. You have enough uniforms to refit a full battalion—last time I checked, you have half of a battalion," she said, her eyes narrowing on Alex. "I assume this is your militia expert?"

"Alex Fletcher, ma'am," said Alex, nodding.

"You suspect the mayor's murder is militia related?" she asked.

"We know it's connected to a growing militia based in southern Maine called the Maine Liberty Militia, most likely perpetrated to discourage civilian cooperation with the military and RRZ Authority."

"Yet we're actively admitting militia volunteers onto the base for training?"

Grady saved him from airing a sarcastic response.

"Part of a provisional security detachment, designed to operate under battalion supervision in the southern Maine zone. I've successfully implemented this type of program before in Afghanistan. Active partnerships with recognizable civilian institutions serves to ease fear and engender trust," said Grady.

"We're talking about U.S. citizens, not tribal Afghans. I'm a U.S. citizen. You're a U.S. citizen. This isn't an invasion force. It's a humanitarian mission. I'm not sure why you're treating this like the Helmand Province."

"Six deployments taught me to work closely with the

locals, preferably before arriving. I sent Captain Fletcher and a small contingent of Marines ahead of the battalion to liaison with the York County Readiness Brigade, an upstanding militia group."

"And his community outreach efforts have resulted in the murder of Sanford's mayor?"

Alex shook his head and muttered, "This is fucking pointless."

"I'm sorry, I didn't catch that," Governor Medina said.

"I said this is fucking *pointless*."

"Colonel?" she stated, shooting Grady a nasty glare.

"I'll work on Captain Fletcher's language, ma'am."

She regarded him for a moment, a thin grin forming on her pressed lips. "Message received, Colonel. I'm taking this in the wrong direction. Let's start over. Captain Fletcher, what are we dealing with? Who's running this Liberty group?"

"The Maine Liberty Militia is run by Eli Russell. Surprisingly, he has no criminal record. Former army, discharged honorably. Worked for a local auto parts company as a salesman for fifteen years prior to the event. According to Harrison Campbell, York County Readiness Brigade commander, Eli was kicked out of the brigade three years ago during a purge of ultramilitaristic types. Unfortunately, the purge gave Russell a head start forming his own group. The MLM."

"And he's perpetrating crimes in the security zone, using this group," she said.

"Correct. We've linked him to a growing number of disturbing incidents within the southern Maine zone. Most recently, he raided a correctional facility thirty miles north, adding an unknown number of hardened criminals to his organization. Five days later, he hit Bridgton, less than forty miles away, killing more than a dozen checkpoint volunteers and stealing several vehicles."

"It sounds like he's taking his business north," she said.

"The mayor was mutilated and tied to a town landmark about two miles from here," said Alex.

"Seven days ago. The Bridgton incident occurred after the murder."

"Trust me, ma'am. He's still active in the area."

"Either way, I'm seeing this as more of an annoyance than a viable threat to security," she stated.

"He has a guy that knows how to build bombs. Big bombs. Police reported a large quantity of slurry explosives stolen from an excavation company in Windham."

"Slurry explosives?"

"Water gel-based explosives used for mining and excavation. They can be poured into common objects, completely evading detection, or used to create shaped charges. We're talking high order detonation stuff. Trust me, Eli Russell has the immediate capacity to be far more than an annoyance."

"And his whereabouts are a complete mystery?"

"I have a few solid leads regarding his general location. If I had dedicated helicopter support, I could better exploit those leads," he said, glancing at Grady, who took his cue.

"Ma'am, freeing up some of the battalion's vehicles from rural patrols and checkpoints south of Sanford would be a solid investment in our security mission."

One of the governor's staff whispered and pointed at a printout on the table. She examined the paper and shook her head.

"None of that is going to happen right now. Brigade air assets are maxed out with current mission requirements, and I have additional tasking for your battalion."

"I'm at 55% manning, with ten vehicles down. I'd suggest leaning on 4th Brigade for additional tasking," said Grady.

"RRZ protocol strictly delineates areas of operation. Even if I could deviate from the protocol, I wouldn't. 4th Brigade has its hands full with the border areas."

Grady pulled a handheld tablet device out of his tactical vest. "What am I looking at in terms of tasking?"

"We'll need 24/7 security for the CISA Camp being set up at Sanford High School. Helicopters should start ferrying personnel from New Hampshire to the MOB within a week. Count on security for transport back and forth to the airport."

"CISA?" said Grady.

"Critical Infrastructure Skills Assembly. Refugees processed through FEMA checkpoints outside of the security area are screened for backgrounds and skills that can assist in the recovery. We fly them here for further evaluation. The goal is to assemble teams with the expertise to tackle projects focused on restoring essential services like electricity and communications. The list is pretty exhaustive."

"The process sounds exhaustive—and manpower intensive," said Grady. "What level of security do you expect at the high school?"

"CISA is essential to the recovery effort."

"I don't doubt that, but securing several hundred civilians in a fluid environment will eat up Marines, especially with a known explosives threat in the area. A more proactive approach to the militia is preferred."

"Then we'll have to focus on hardening all potential RRZ targets against explosives. Engineers will build a HESCO barrier to assist with CISA security," Medina said.

"You can't put a twelve-foot HESCO barrier around the entire state and hope for the best," said Alex.

"We have a lot of HESCO material and—"

The conference room windows rattled, followed shortly by a distant sound resembling thunder. Chairs scraped the linoleum floor as Alex and the military contingent stood.

"Thunderstorms predicted for the morning," one of the staff members offered. "Sixty percent chance."

"That wasn't thunder," said the staff sergeant.

Grady's ROTAC chirped. "Send it," said Grady, listening for several seconds before responding. "Deploy the quick reaction force. I'll catch up with them on Route 109. Order all checkpoint units to maintain their positions. Defense posture Red. Nothing gets in or out."

"What happened, Colonel?"

"Units in Sanford report a massive explosion near the downtown area."

The recruiting station.

Chapter 27

EVENT +17 Days

Sanford, Maine

From Alex's elevated vantage point in the Matvee's armored turret, he caught the first glimpses of the devastation ahead. The four-story brick building appeared through the cloud of gray-black smoke enshrouding Sanford's central park area. Smoke from the blast should have cleared by now. The vehicle decelerated in front of Town Hall, the driver approaching cautiously. Flashing red lights cut through the murk at the western end of the park area across from the building, headed toward Main Street.

As they passed Town Hall, the scene took shape. Windows on the second floor directly above the recruiting station poured smoke and flames skyward. Broken glass and crumbled brick debris littered the street and sidewalk. Deeper in the park, small groups of people huddled over injured bystanders, waving frantically for the inbound ambulance. The Matvee slowed to a standstill. A jagged, scorched hole encompassed the entire right half of the building's storefront.

"What are you seeing?" Grady asked over the vehicle net.

"I'm not seeing the remains of a vehicle. Probable

remote detonation, like at Harvard Yard. We need to lock this area down hard, sir."

"Copy. How many people did we have in the station?"

"Eight. Three Marines and five of Harrison's people."

"You better let him know," said Grady.

The vehicle edged forward, pulling over the curb and stopping in the park. The rest of the quick-reaction force raced by, deploying at even intervals across from the burning building. One of the vehicles continued to Washington Street and turned left, headed toward the back of the building to check for survivors. Alex swiveled the turret to cover the road heading back to the airport, digging through his vest to retrieve his ROTAC.

***

The binoculars started to tremble when the convoy of four heavily armed tactical vehicles appeared through the haze. He knew the heavy machine guns mounted in the turrets could tear through the brick wall in front of him with little effort, and every time one of the barrels shifted past his window—he flinched. He'd been happy to leave the general ranks and return to Sanford, especially after the massacre in Limerick. They needed someone to keep an eye on the county seat of York County, and nobody knew the town and the people better than Sanford's top realtor, Tim Barrett—but this was too much! Too risky.

This particular spot had been his best idea. Overlooking the central commons, the empty corner office on the third floor of the Sanford Trust Building gave him a bird's-eye view of the town's main thoroughfare. As a realtor, nobody questioned his presence in the office buildings, especially downtown, where most of the buildings remained empty from the recession. He'd felt safe, almost untouchable until a few minutes ago. Something had gone wrong with the bombing.

A guy wearing a gray T-shirt and red hat was supposed to stuff a small package into a city trash container outside of the storefront, remotely detonating the device from a pickup car on Washington Street when Barrett confirmed that the sidewalk and street were clear of innocent bystanders.

Nothing had gone according to the plan relayed by Kevin McCulver. The man showed up wearing a dark orange student backpack, and walked into the recruiting station. The building exploded before the glass door closed behind him. The blast turned out to be far more powerful than he expected, injuring citizens gathered in the park.

Had the plan changed? What else had changed?

The whole point of the operation had been to draw the Marines to the recruiting station so Barrett could observe the marine's response. The vehicles continued down Main Street toward his building, and he considered abandoning the mission.

If he stayed and the Marines captured him, he could be forced to divulge information critical to Eli's plans. He suspected elements of the Maine Liberty Militia had been moved closer to Sanford, since he no longer had to drive north to make his reports. McCulver took them directly, every four hours. He'd even met with McCulver two days ago on his last trip north. Combined with the targeted information McCulver had just requested, he had no doubt they were preparing an imminent strike. On the other hand, if he deserted his post before delivering the information, Eli would no doubt hunt him down and kill him and his entire family. It wasn't much of a choice.

Tim steadied the binoculars against the windowsill and searched for the face he'd seen on numerous occasions in front of the recruiting station. Hampered by the thick smoke hanging over the street, he still hadn't located his target. Shifting from vehicle to vehicle, he studied the dismounted Marines, muttering curses. This was taking too much time. He started to envision slipping down the stairwell and disappearing into the parking lot behind the building before the shock of the bombing wore off and the Marines started to process their options. The turret gunner in the most distant vehicle yelled down to four huddled Marines helping a group of wounded civilians at the edge of the park. When he started pointing at the buildings surrounding the commons, Barrett almost lost control of his bladder.

Fuck this. I'm out of here.

He started to lift his head from the binoculars when a familiar silver sedan materialized on the street behind the tactical vehicle. Harrison Campbell's car. The gunner waved at the car and dropped into the vehicle. Breathing rapidly, Tim looked through the binoculars, focusing on the Marine that emerged from the armored transport.

Gotcha.

He stared at the symbol painted on the hood of the tan vehicle and wrote them in a small notebook taken from his pants pocket: *Six-one-one inside an octagon.* He had no idea what the numbers meant, but who gave a shit. Mission accomplished.

Tim slowly withdrew the binoculars, careful not to disturb the blinds. He stuffed them in his backpack and started for the door, faltering before opening it. McCulver had been really clear about passing the information immediately. He hesitated with his hand on the doorknob. They were probably worried about him being captured without passing the numbers. Ten more seconds wasn't going to kill him. McCulver answered his radio transmission immediately.

"Sanford Overwatch, please confirm the following. Vehicle marked as six-one-one, surrounded by an octagon," said McCulver.

"Affirmative. Solid copy. Over."

"Roger. Proceed to extract point. Don't leave anything behind."

"Copy. Heading to extract," Tim said, switching the radio off and stowing it in the high-end daypack McCulver had given him when they met.

Tim opened the door and walked down the dim hallway to the stairwell leading to the back exit, suddenly very aware of the backpack in his hands. He'd been very excited to get the backpack, instantly recognizing the expensive brand. His thoughts flashed to the dark orange backpack carried by the bomber.

Stop. You're being ridiculous.

Tim pulled a flashlight out of his pocket and pushed the fire door open, illuminating the empty stairwell. He stepped inside, and the door closed behind him.

***

Alex rushed out of the Matvee, wanting to get between the arriving vehicle and the building. There was nothing anyone could do for the men and women inside. Harrison Campbell burst out of his car and ran toward the building, stopping to shield his face from the heat. His driver, the tough-as-nails woman he'd met at Campbell's compound, sprinted to catch up, grabbing his arm. He shook it free and pushed Alex out of the way.

"They're all gone, Harrison. Nothing we could do," said Alex.

"All of them? They can't *all* be dead," he said, peering at the storefront through the smoke.

"I have a vehicle around back. Nobody made it out."

"My wife's cousin is in there," he said.

"I'm really sorry, Harrison," said Alex, stepping behind the vehicle to escape the heat, pulling Campbell with him.

"You know what we have to do," Campbell stated emphatically.

Alex nodded gravely. "I'm working on it."

A deep, muffled thump reached Alex's ears, and he reflexively crouched, scanning the buildings for signs of gunfire or an explosion. Marines yelled, "Secondary!" and scrambled for their vehicles.

"Get inside the Matvee," Alex said, pushing Campbell toward the armored vehicle.

"Second floor, west of park," he heard through his headset.

Grady's and Blackmun's rifles swung in the direction of the Sanford Trust Building. Alex searched through the smoke for evidence of an explosion, noticing a cloud of smoke, or possibly drywall dust, drifting out of the third-story windows and floating toward the park.

Internal blast? Accidental detonation?

Whatever it was, it signified a dangerous shift in tactics. Two bombs in one place represented a concentration of focus. The first blast changed the rules. The second changed the entire game. Eli was on the offensive. Governor Medina couldn't bury her head and hope for the best. That ship had just sailed.

Chapter 28

EVENT +17 Days

Main Operating Base "Sanford"
Regional Recovery Zone 1

Alex examined the RRZ Authority parking lot through his binoculars, noting the same number of tactical vehicles lined up next to the evenly parked row of conspicuous white Jeeps. The fact that he hadn't been summoned with Grady left him feeling uneasy. If the RRZ Authority didn't want the battalion's counterinsurgency officer present at a meeting to discuss the targeted bombing of RRZ personnel, he suspected Grady would return with unpleasant news.

Distant thunder echoed through the hangar, drawing his attention to the western sky. A thick band of thunderclouds dominated his view through the hangar door, occasional branches of lightning breaking up the dark, featureless wall of rain rapidly approaching the airfield. He wondered how the house in Limerick would hold up under the storm.

As a short-term fix, they had patched up the exterior holes in the house and barn using a crate of all-weather sealant taken from the Home Store in Sanford. Theoretically, the sealant should be all they needed, but Alex's dad wanted to reinforce the job by nailing strips of board over the heavily damaged areas to reduce weather-induced wear on the sealant. It was a project Alex suggested they delay until the long-term viability of remaining at the compound had been decided. Today's attack represented a major setback to staying in Limerick. Lightning illuminated the hangar's interior, followed by a single, explosive crack that rattled the building's metal frame. A few dense raindrops smacked the asphalt taxiway in front of the hangar.

"Lower the doors halfway!" yelled Sergeant Major Howard.

"I got it, Sergeant Major," said Alex, jogging toward the automatic controls to the left of the TOC.

Alex lowered each of the five doors separately, not wanting to overload the battalion's primary generator. The wind intensified before the door in front of the TOC reached the halfway mark, blowing rain sideways into the hangar. He let the door continue to the end of the track, then glanced over his shoulder at the battalion sergeant major.

"Close it up, sir! Rain's coming in sideways!"

Alex felt the humidity level rise even before the last door nestled against the painted concrete floor. At least it was ten degrees cooler than yesterday. He joined the battalion intelligence officer, Captain Paul Bernstein, who had just returned from the supply station.

"Any luck?" Alex asked him.

"The sensors are in the supply system. It's just a matter of getting them here under the circumstances. The lieutenant wasn't hopeful, even with our CO pushing for delivery. Then there's the issue related to the parent gear required to monitor passive sensors. We don't have anything like that at the battalion level. This is a theatre-specific, division-level asset."

"What about the RRZ supply system? Every time I close my eyes, they drag something new out of those warehouses."

"No surveillance gear, unless it's classified or named differently," said Bernstein.

"Can the supply officer see the full inventory of gear hidden away out there?"

"Negative. She can search by name or specific supply system number. And she isn't keen on searching for gear that doesn't bear directly on our mission, so don't get any ideas."

"Maybe we can get Grady to lean on 4th Brigade's commanding officer. I know they have acoustic sensors."

"Not the kind you're looking for. Mostly low power, localized stuff monitored by a nearby station. One thousand meters or less."

"Then we'll have to put LP/OP teams in the field," said Alex.

"Patriot's en route. He wants to meet with ops and intel staff immediately," announced one of the Marines monitoring the battalion tactical along the back wall of the hangar.

"We can barely cover the battalion's checkpoint requirements," stated Bernstein, waving for his staff sergeant to join them.

Alex took a seat in one of the folding chairs facing a table-mounted sixty-inch flat-screen. Major Blackmun, a first lieutenant and the operation's first sergeant joined them a few moments before Grady burst through the side hangar door next to the monitor. They stood and waited for him to approach.

"As you were," said Grady, hanging his rifle on a rack

of hooks bolted to the wall next to the door.

He stared at them, his weathered, battle-scarred face betraying no emotion. "Here's the situation. The RRZ Authority has changed our tasking to focus on immediate area security, with a major emphasis on—you guessed it—the airport. The Route 109 corridor from the airport to Sanford High School will be secured by vehicle checkpoints and foot patrols. Goodall Hospital is now our responsibility. I've convinced them to consider moving the CISA camp to one of the structures across the street, where it will be easier to defend. Our security mission will remain compacted until the militia threat has been neutralized."

Alex started to form a question.

"I know what you're going to ask," said Grady, preempting him. "How can we neutralize the militia threat if everything is tied up in Sanford? I haven't figured that out yet. They're aware of the dilemma, but all of their Ivy League think-tank analysis paperwork suggests that domestic-based militias do not have the strength or resolve to address a hardened, tighter security posture."

"Long term, the Green Zone approach doesn't work, sir. We've proven that time after time," said Major Blackmun. "That's in the record books."

"They're not looking at this long term. They think if we can keep the militia threat from disrupting RRZ operations for the next three to four months, the winter will slow them down, if not bury them. There's some truth to that."

"Four months is a long time. I've read the RRZ protocols," said Alex. "If we can't secure southern Maine, they'll shift the security area north. We have to be more proactive about Eli Russell. I don't think it will take much. He blew up two of his own men today, which leads me to believe he doesn't like loose ends. If we get enough vehicles searching north, we're bound to find something. All we need to do is grab a few of his people to unravel the whole group. The guys we captured at my house were eager to give up Eli's original headquarters."

"Unless I can get Authority to scrap the high school idea, I can't spare additional resources," Grady said. "I barely convinced them to keep FOB Lakeside, and that fight isn't over. They aren't convinced of its short-term ROI."

Alex paused for a second, staggering mentally from the thought of losing the Marines protecting his house. If the RRZ forced Grady to dismantle FOB Lakeside with Eli on the loose, he'd have no choice but to evacuate north, with or without Grady's permission.

"ROI? This isn't a publicly traded company. Fuck it. We'll accelerate the provisional security group's training and get them out there shaking the trees alongside *any* Marines we can spare."

Grady winced, his stoic face clearly pained to proceed. "Governor Medina ordered all militia removed from the base—effective immediately. She doesn't want any unfriendly militia slipping into the group, especially in light of the fact that the Maine Liberty Militia isn't mentioned in Homeland's database."

"Can I train them off base?"

"Not with RRZ personnel or equipment."

"What about the provisional Marines? They're not militia."

"They don't want any new personnel involved in RRZ security matters," said Grady.

"So the program is scrapped."

"Essentially."

"All right. I'll need to borrow one of the Armadillos to return the volunteers, unless Medina plans to make them walk home," said Alex, resolved not to say another word.

"Operations will secure a vehicle for their return," said Grady, nodding at Major Blackmun.

"Got it, sir," said the major.

"Anything else?" said Grady, looking at Alex, who shook his head.

"Nothing? Very well. Alex, I need to speak with you before you leave. Ops, gather up the rest of your staff plus all of the company commanders. We need to redeploy the battalion by twenty-hundred hours, which doesn't give us a ton of time."

Alex approached Grady as soon as the group broke apart.

"Sir?"

"Guardian represents the battalion's only dedicated search assets," said Grady, referring to the vehicles and Marines stationed in Limerick.

"It's not enough, but we'll do what we can. If Harrison Campbell agrees, I'll try to field a few of his vehicles. Not sure how he's going to take this. It's kind of a slap in the face after what happened today. I sold him pretty hard on the cooperative aspect of working with the RRZ."

"If he's willing to help, we'll keep his vehicles fueled. I completely understand if he isn't interested."

"He understands what's at stake if Eli destabilizes the RRZ."

"Just do me a favor and keep their involvement out of your digital reports. I'm not the only one reading them—and make sure you recover all of the ROTAC gear."

"It makes sense to let Campbell keep one of the

ROTAC sets. It's the only way we can get in touch with him in the field. He doesn't have access to any of the battalion or RRZ traffic."

"I was specifically told to recover the ROTAC gear," stated Grady.

"I never recorded the ROTAC transfers in any of my reports. You didn't tell them, did you?"

Grady shook his head.

"They're tracking the phones? Fuck, there's something wrong with all of this. The whole RRZ set up seems like one giant clusterfuck, except for surveillance. No problems there. What else are they tracking?" demanded Alex.

"Vehicles. ID cards. But you didn't hear that from me," said Grady.

"ID cards? They can track these?" said Alex, pulling out his card and examining it.

"No, but they can track when and where they've been swiped. I received a digital message eight days ago notifying me that Captain Alex Fletcher had accessed the Northeast Sector Coast Guard base in South Portland, Maine."

Alex didn't know what to say. He hadn't prepared an excuse for visiting the Coast Guard station because he'd underestimated the depths of the government's paranoia.

Never again.

"This is fucked up, Sean," Alex whispered. "They spend more time watching and analyzing our movements than trying to fix the shit storm out there."

Grady contemplated Alex's statement, lowering his voice to respond. "I'm not sure how much of a difference any of this will make in the long run, but we have to try. It's our best option."

"Maybe," said Alex, rubbing his sweaty face with both hands.

"Promise me you'll stick around until this Eli Russell business is finished. Whatever you do decide to do after that, I'll make sure nothing stands in your way."

"I'll need some leeway with this. More Marines would help," said Alex.

"I can't give you more vehicles. They're tracking our deployment carefully."

"If I had an additional squad of Marines at the FOB, I'd feel comfortable releasing the rest of my vehicles to search for Russell."

"We could probably spare a few fire teams from Alpha Company. Would that work?" said Grady.

"We'll make it work."

Chapter 29

EVENT +17 Days

Sanford, Maine

Alex selected Harrison's ROTAC channel and pressed "lock." He wasn't looking forward to this meeting.

"Harrison Campbell."

"Harrison, it's Alex. I'm sitting on the road in front of your property with Gary, the Kleins, and the twelve volunteers that decided to stay with the brigade. I can drive them up if that's all right."

"Probably not a great idea right now. Not everyone took the RRZ's move in stride."

"I understand, but I do need to talk with you in person. Trust me, it's important."

"I'll meet you at the first checkpoint," said Campbell.

"Is that the one where your folks pop out of the woods with guns, or the fortified bunkers a little further down the road?"

"I'll call ahead and make sure they don't shake you down."

"I appreciate that. I've hit my shakedown limit for the day," said Alex.

"That bad?"

"It's not good. See you in a few minutes."

Alex trailed the group, drifting back as they disappeared around the bend leading to the gate. A gust of wind unleashed a cascading shower of water from the drenched leaves above. The drops pelted his helmet and uniform, tapering off as the breeze died. He removed his helmet and let the damp, shaded air wash over his head. A purposeful rustling of the bushes to the right drew his attention to a familiar face.

"Ms. Nunya." He nodded. "Glad to see you back on point."

"Harrison wants you to wait here," she said, resuming her watch of the forest's edge through the thick trees.

"Back where we started, huh?"

She didn't respond.

Message received.

When Harrison arrived a few minutes later, they walked slowly back toward the rumbling military vehicle.

"Sorry I dragged you into all of this. I should have known the RRZ would do this."

"No need to apologize. I knew exactly what I was getting into."

"Still," he said, glancing behind them. "They seem pretty pissed."

"They had hoped this would turn out very differently. We took a vote after you came to visit me the first time. The decision to partner up with a government entity was far from unanimous. I gave everyone the option to decline participation and remain in good standing within the brigade. Nobody took me up on the offer."

"The York County Readiness Brigade isn't out of the fight yet," said Alex. "I need your help searching for Eli."

"Doesn't the RRZ have several thousand soldiers and dozens of helicopters in southern Maine?"

"Most of the battalion's assets have been re-tasked with protecting the area immediately surrounding Sanford. 4th Brigade Combat Team units are off-limits unless it has something to do with the border."

"You've got to be kidding me. They're just holing up at the airport and hoping for the best?"

"Pretty much. I still have the Marines stationed at the Limerick FOB, but Grady's not sure how long that will last. The more teams we have searching for Eli, the better. Grady authorized me to refuel any vehicles used in the search effort."

"I'll bring this up a little later today and get back to you," said Campbell. "What's your plan if Grady recalls the Marines from your property?"

Alex shook his head. "I'd have to leave."

"Well, you're always welcome here. Plenty of room in the barn, and it has a nice fireplace. Not a bad place to spend the winter."

"That's a generous offer, Harrison. In light of what I put you through—put your wife through—very generous. Thank you."

"My wife isn't angry with you or any of the folks dug in at the airport."

"Eli Russell," stated Alex.

"And Kevin McCulver. He wasn't a bad guy when he was part of the brigade. Just couldn't stop playing with things that go boom. Hard to believe Eli twisted him that far. Then again, I never suspected Eli was warped enough to murder his way across the county. Did your people figure out what happened with the second bomb?"

"Hard to say. State police are sending an evidence team to work with the Sanford department. From what I could tell, the bomb detonated inside the rear stairwell on the second floor. Big hole in the brick wall facing the parking lot."

"Accidental detonation?" said Campbell.

"Once again, hard to tell. Timing suggests the bomber might have been on his way down to detonate a secondary device among the arriving Marines."

"Suicide bombing? Doesn't sound like Eli's people. We're not talking brainwashed Jihadis."

"My thoughts exactly, but witnesses report a man with a backpack walking into the recruiting station seconds before the bomb detonated," said Alex.

"Bizarre. They could have thrown the backpack through the door and remotely triggered the explosive with the same result," said Campbell.

"Unless they have something bigger in the works, and they're not taking chances with a slipup," said Alex.

"You think the second explosion was deliberate?"

"We'll probably never know. There wasn't much left to examine. How are you set for security? Eli might have a sizeable group."

"We're good. Most of the chapter members have brought their families over until this Eli thing blows over. Not taking any chances that he might remember some names."

"Smart move. We'll monitor the HAM radio 24/7 in case you run into a problem. You know our station ID, so don't hesitate to call," said Alex.

"Be a lot easier with one of these," he said, holding out a translucent shopping bag containing the ROTAC handhelds.

"Trust me, these are more trouble for you than they're worth. The RRZ can track these," said Alex. "I didn't want to tell you when I called, because I suspect they can listen to our transmissions."

"Shit. I put a tracking device in the hands of every chapter."

"Take this as a good sign. If they wanted to keep a close eye on the brigade, they wouldn't have asked me to collect them."

Campbell barely smirked.

"I'm trying to find anything positive about the RRZ."

"Good luck with that," said Campbell. "I'll get back to you later about a possible joint search effort."

"You know where to find me."

Chapter 30

EVENT +17 Days

Forward Operating Base "Lakeside"
Regional Recovery Zone 1

Fiery orange rays of late afternoon sunlight crowned the tree canopy surrounding the clearing, distinct from the shadowy forest behind the Marine encampment. Kate peered into the growing dusk, waiting for Alex's vehicle to emerge. News of the attack in Sanford was unwittingly delivered to the house by Staff Sergeant Taylor, who momentarily forgot that the house Motorola was tuned to the FOB's security channel.

After sending a Matvee to reinforce the HESCO position guarding the entrance to Gelder Pond Lane, Taylor was bombarded with questions when he delivered one of the Marines to the sandbag position on the back deck. He cracked easily under the pressure of three mothers demanding more information.

This led to a heated daylong debate about the pros and cons of staying at the compound, dominated by Ed's end-of-the-world predictions and sudden outbursts demanding that the Marines immediately escort them north to the Thorntons' lake house. Charlie and Linda stayed mostly neutral, but Kate could sense that they wanted out of FOB Lakeside just as much as the Walkers.

She understood why. The Limerick property had turned into a mental and physical prison, despite the robust protection delivered by the Marines.

The discovery of Jeffrey Brown's surveillance post on Old Middle Road had unnerved everyone, rendering the simple pleasure of sitting on the porch impossible. Every glance at the impenetrable forest left you wondering if you'd just taken your last breath. Forget about letting the kids out of the house. Same problem—but worse. Logically, Kate knew the forest was clear of intruders. The Marines patrolled regularly during the day and took up positions in the forest at night. Odds were stacked against anyone slipping through the Marine security perimeter.

Daily, she tried to convince the group that staying here was everyone's best option, but her faith in the option had waned. Even Alex, who had lobbied heavily against leaving, seemed less enthusiastic about defending his position. They had reached the inevitable crossroads. Should they stay, or should they go? Ed had been ready to go six hours ago, but she asked him to wait until Alex returned before reaching a decision—or leaving. She made sure to reinforce the danger of running into Eli's men on the road, which seemed to cool him off temporarily.

She heard the Matvee's deep rumble, then spotted the grayish-tan vehicle racing through the trees. She waited for Corporal Lianez to execute a three-point turn and park the Matvee facing the exit road before jogging across the gravel driveway toward the assembly area. Alex rushed out, hugging her tightly, and the Marines disappeared into the tent.

"I really missed you today," she said, kissing him.

"It wasn't a good day to be away. I'm sorry. The shit never stopped rolling in my direction."

"Same here. Ed's on the verge of a nervous breakdown. The rest aren't too far behind."

"How are you holding up?" he said.

"I'm fine, I guess."

"You guess?" he said, his eyes shifting to the DRASH tent. "Let's check out the lake."

"Uhhh, sure," she said, taking his arm.

The fact that Alex felt uncomfortable discussing their situation in front of the Marines didn't boost her confidence. Neither did her reluctance to take a sunset stroll on her own property. Something had to change. He waited until they had put about thirty feet behind them.

"What's going on?"

"I feel like we're back on Durham Road during the pandemic. Trapped, just waiting for the inevitable."

"Yeah," he said. "I'm feeling the same way, but on a bigger scale."

"My perspective is confined to the house. I'm afraid to step outside. We're all afraid."

"I know we're safe here, honey. I wouldn't stay if I didn't believe that," he said, hesitating to continue.

"But what?"

"We met with the RRZ Authority today," he said and shook his head. "If Eli Russell blows up their headquarters compound, along with everyone inside, the RRZ might have a chance."

"Don't say that. They left behind families and other responsibilities for this. They're just like the rest of us," she said.

"I know. I know," he mumbled. "But something's off with the overall picture. Grady said something that really got me thinking. The RRZ Authority arrived thinking all the initial work had been finished, or should be. Seems like one hell of a disconnect from reality."

"Maybe they weren't getting reports from the ground units," said Kate.

"Wouldn't surprise me given the chaos of assembling the RRZ teams, but that doesn't ease my worries. How could anyone with any experience in disaster-response planning think that a system of FEMA camps designed to handle hundreds of thousands of displaced New Englanders would be up and running sixteen days after an EMP attack? Not to mention the sheer impossibility of executing a camp structure that enormous. I don't care how many warehouses they have stocked with dehydrated food and propane heaters. This isn't going to work."

"What are they supposed to do? Say fuck it and stay home?"

"At least pretend not to be surprised when an understaffed National Guard engineering battalion can't build forty camps, each designed to hold several thousand refugees, in sixteen days. That's all."

"And that would make you happy?" she asked, hoping his rant was over.

"No. I'd still be wondering if trying to stay here long term was a mistake."

"Even if you find and kill Eli?"

"Even if we hunt down and kill everyone in his militia. A million-plus people are streaming toward the Maine border. The only thing standing between them and us are about four thousand soldiers and a few easily fordable rivers. Once the refugees start trying to cross en masse, the whole thing will fall apart, leaving us to fend for ourselves."

"Unless you stay with the Marines. We can move with the battalion."

"And live where? In a tent next to the battalion's hangar? Take over someone's house?"

"I'm just thinking aloud. Trying to make this work," said Kate.

"I know you are. I'm sorry. We don't have to make this decision yet. One step at a time. What's the consensus in the house?"

"The Walkers want out of here pretty badly. I pulled the Eli card to keep them in place until you got back," said Kate.

"I can't send any of the Marines north. All of the vehicles and satellite-enabled radios, like this one," he said, tapping his ROTAC, "can be tracked by the RRZ and Homeland. That's the other thing that has me skeptical. There's a disturbing Big Brother aspect to the way Homeland has been running things."

"They can't drive up by themselves. Three of the four adults can't drive. The kids have their licenses. I mean, maybe—"

"I have an idea," said Alex.

"I don't want you out there in one of those cars," said Kate.

"Something different. Tell Dad to get Harrison Campbell on the HAM radio. I'll be right inside. I need to check on something," he said, kissing her.

"Wait. What's the plan?" she said, pulling at his arm.

"Something I should have thought of earlier."

Chapter 31

EVENT +18 Days

Forward Operating Base "Lakeside"
Regional Recovery Zone 1

Alex opened the door for Harrison Campbell and Gary Powers, motioning for them to step inside. The two men stopped a few feet into Alex's mudroom, examining the walls. Campbell extended his hand to the doorframe next to Alex, putting his finger through one of the bullet holes.

"Good heavens. I had no idea it was this bad," he said, shaking his head.

"It gets worse in the kitchen. We killed twenty-nine of Eli's men, most of them trying to rush the house. He probably escaped with a half dozen."

"Thirty-six shooters? All with semiautomatics? I don't see how any of you survived this," Campbell said, walking into the bathroom to inspect the sandbag position. "Steel reinforced. Clever."

"Sheet metal. Didn't stop the .308s."

"Good thing he never put the thirty-cal into action against you. Would have sawed right through the house, sheet metal and all."

"We got lucky with that," said Alex. "It was bad enough with a squad peppering us from the trees behind the house. In a strange sense, Eli's tactics kept us in the game long enough to repel his final attack. He went for a two-pronged assault. One squad from the eastern tree line, another from the barn. If he'd added one of those squads to the base of fire pouring into the back of the house, we wouldn't be having this conversation. The volume of fire would have been overwhelming. We could barely move around with twelve men emptying magazines into the house."

"Looks like you have some work ahead of you," said Campbell.

"New toilet?" said Powers. "No way the other one survived."

"Priorities. Grabbed two from the Home Store. Not much demand for plumbing items these days," said Alex.

"Basic, yet inventive. Not a bad idea for the house and barn," said Powers, patting the sandbags.

"And most importantly, effective. The only improvement I'd make is to double up on the sheet metal. A few of the positions experienced breakthrough. Step this way, and I'll introduce you to the walking wounded," he said, guiding them through the kitchen to the great room.

Charlie tried to stand up as they approached.

"Charlie, save your strength. You'll need it to deal with Linda during the ride," he said, winking.

"I have to be in the same car?" said Linda.

"Funny."

"Everyone, this is Harrison Campbell, founder of the York County Readiness Brigade, and his training officer, Gary Powers. They'll lead the convoy north, along with yours truly," said Alex.

The room broke into a disharmony of questions.

"I'll explain the details in a moment. From left to right,

we have Charlie and Linda Thornton, both wounded in the attack. Charlie's close to walking again, but Linda has a ways to go. She needs surgery, which I don't see happening any time soon. Need to be careful with her foot."

"Don't worry about me, gentlemen. Damn foot can't get any worse," she said. "I can still shoot, so don't count me out of the game."

"You got an empty trunk?" asked Charlie.

Campbell laughed. "Sorry, sir. We're packed to the gills. I can put you in separate cars if that would help."

"Families ride together," said Ed.

"You're just trying to keep him out of *your* car," Linda groused.

"Is it that obvious?" said Ed, winking at Campbell and Powers.

"After all we've been through," said Charlie.

"Especially after all we've been through," said Ed, and they all laughed.

Alex gestured toward the Walkers. "Ed and Samantha Walker. Ed was wounded saving my hide—again. They have three children, ages fourteen through nineteen. Overall, you're looking at a highly capable group."

"I can still shoot out of a window," stated Linda.

"I want her in my car," said Gary.

"Sold, to the man in jeans and woodland camouflage jacket!" howled Charlie, receiving a shoulder punch from his wife.

"Hey, careful," Charlie said, "I'm injured."

Alex turned to Campbell. "You sure you want to do this?"

"Too late to turn back now," he said.

"Let's get this wrapped up," Alex said. "The cars are

packed and waiting. I'll ride in the lead vehicle with Harrison. The Walkers will follow in their Jeep. Gary and the Thorntons will be in the third vehicle. The last two cars in the convoy will carry the bulk of the convoy's supplies."

"Maybe the Thorntons' car should be in the rear," Ed suggested.

"I'm not that loud," said Charlie. "Jesus."

"All the more reason," he said. "No. I'm more concerned with the supplies. Sorry to put this out there, especially since you guys are doing us a huge favor, but that's a lot of temptation. Especially the truck pulling the utility trailer."

"No offense taken," Harrison said. "I'm way ahead of you. I'm breaking up the groups that drove up together from Sanford. I'll have a good mix of old and new members in each vehicle. I trust everyone implicitly, but we can't change human nature."

"Plus, it would be pretty damn hard to make an escape pulling the trailer," said Powers.

"Sounds good," said Ed. "I guess we should get rolling."

"Before we leave, a couple of critical points to remember," said Alex. "Five cars travelling in a convoy will attract attention. I expect to be stopped. Keep your weapons out of sight at all times. I'm riding in full uniform with my magic badge, but we can't count on that solving all of our local law enforcement problems. Weapons need to be stowed out of plain sight, but easily accessible. Take some time to work on this once everyone is situated. Safeties engaged at all times. Harrison, I'll need you to brief your people on this."

"I'll take care of it," said Powers.

"If we're stopped by law enforcement or the military, I do all of the talking. Everyone stays in their vehicle unless I direct otherwise by hand signal or radio. I don't expect trouble, but you never know. If we run into any non-authority-based—"

"You can use the word. We're all grownups," said Campbell, eliciting a few muffled laughs.

"If we run into any *militia* blockades, we stop and turn around. Drivers have been briefed on those procedures. Samantha, you execute a simple three-point turn, and we all proceed in the opposite direction in a group until we can safely stop and figure out an alternate route. I made this trip with my dad a little over a week ago, and we didn't have a problem. One police checkpoint in Westbrook. A lot can change in a week. We just have to be careful and keep communicating over the handhelds. Easy enough?"

"Easy enough," said Ed, followed by the rest.

"Guys, can you start getting everyone situated? We'll be ready to transport the walking wounded in a few minutes," he said to Campbell and Powers.

"Gotcha. You know where to find us," said Campbell.

When Alex heard the mudroom door close, he sat in one of the chairs facing his friends.

"I trust Harrison and Gary, but I don't know the other guys—which is why I'm keeping them separate from the families. I recognize a few of the faces from the volunteers we started training at the airport. At least I know they cleared criminal background checks and passed Gunny Deschane's interview, which was more like an interrogation."

"How well do you know Gary?"

"I worked with Gary a couple of times at the airport.

Harrison vouches for him."

Charlie and Linda didn't look convinced.

"He'll be driving, so you'll be able to watch him closely. Keep the radio in the back, along with a readied pistol. If he's not acting right, give me a call and mention John Wayne. This will be our distress code. Say, 'Hey, Alex, I feel like John Wayne riding off into the sunset,' or something similar. If I hear John Wayne, we stop the convoy."

"Roger. John Wayne."

"I picked that because of your Daniel Boone cap and tiger-striped camouflage. Easy to remember."

"Jesus, Alex. I got it," said Charlie.

"What else?" said Alex.

"You should really consider sending the kids up with us. At least until you take care of this Eli Russell character," said Samantha Walker.

"Ethan and Kevin won't go without my parents, and Kate won't let any of the kids out of her sight."

"Maybe they should all come up while you sort things out with Eli Russell and the RRZ," said Ed.

"I won't separate us. We're safe here," said Alex.

"For now," said Ed.

"For now," he agreed. "If I can't find Eli or the RRZ implodes, we'll leave."

"You know where to find us," said Charlie.

"I certainly do. Save me some sleeping bag space away from the bathroom," he said, getting a few laughs.

"Yeah, we'll need to build an outhouse or steal one of those Porta-Johns. Charlie can take his newspaper out there," said Linda.

"There won't be any newspapers, sweetie," said Charlie.

"Point is, you aren't conducting your morning business inside," she said.

"That's more than enough. I can see where it's going," said Alex.

"You started it," said Charlie.

"My bad," said Alex, his mind drifting to the realities of the topic.

Alex hadn't thought about the cottage's sanitary situation. Most septic systems are designed to accommodate the expected purpose of the dwelling. He couldn't imagine the builders had anticipated seventeen people using the small lake house indefinitely. Even without the addition of the Fletchers, they'd be lucky if the system survived the winter. Life on Great Pond in Belgrade would degrade fairly quickly without the use of an indoor bathroom. Another reason they were better off elsewhere. He had to be practical about this decision, and seventeen people crammed into an 800-square-foot cottage designed primarily for three-season use was far from practical.

"Let's get out of here before I rethink the bathroom situation," said Ed.

"You might want to stuff a few extra packs of toilet paper in each car," said Alex, extending a hand to lift Ed out of his seat.

"Trust me, I thought about it," Ed said, resting his arm on Alex's shoulder. "Another week, and I should be able to get around on my own without any help."

"Sounds about right," said Alex. "I got him, Samantha. We'll see you at the Jeep."

"I'll get everyone situated," she said, sharing a concerned look with Ed.

Alex helped Ed out of the door, purposely letting

Charlie and Linda pull ahead.

Ed leaned over and whispered, "You don't have any plans to head north—do you?"

Alex shook his head. "I don't think it's in the group's best interest."

"It could work," said Ed.

"I appreciate your optimism, but we both know Charlie's place can't sustain seventeen people. It'll be tough enough with nine of you."

"What are you gonna do?"

"Ideally, I'd like to stay right here," said Alex. "But it's not looking hopeful."

Ed snapped his head toward Alex.

"You'll be fine up north. If the security situation in York County implodes, for whatever reason, they'll reestablish the security area border at the Saco River."

"What if that fails?"

"It can't," stated Alex.

Ed shrugged his shoulders. "Why not?"

"Because I didn't see a plan for a tertiary security border," he said, grimacing.

"Come hell or high water," muttered Ed.

"Charlie has a good plot of land next to a pristine lake. I packed up a kit with enough seeds for two seasons and a slightly worn copy of a book we've used to figure out a lot of this homesteading stuff. Sort of a dummies guide to self-sustainability."

"I can't take the book from you," said Ed.

"If we stay here, I'll borrow it back from you in the spring. If not, the book is better off in your hands. I don't think we'll have much need for it where we're headed."

Chapter 32

EVENT +21 Days

Kennebunk Road
Sanford, Maine

The trees flanking Kennebunk Road disappeared, exposing a well-lit labyrinth of concrete barriers designed to funnel traffic through a single opening next to the armor-plated guard post. Darkness lay beyond the halogen lights mounted to the roof of the shadowy structure. Kevin McCulver slowed the York County sheriff's car as they approached the checkpoint. One of the sentries stepped onto the road, motioning him forward. The second guard was nowhere in sight—presumably still inside the impenetrable enclosure.

He'd read about these modular armor designs a few years ago, when they were widely fielded by the U.S. military at entry points to most outposts and bases in Afghanistan. Afghan National Police units based in remote areas had begun to install larger versions at police stations to serve as "safe rooms" during frequent Taliban raids. Impervious to heavy-caliber bullets and bomb fragments, occupants could safely fire on attackers and call for reinforcements, which was exactly why this morning's plan required both guards to step out from inside the bunker.

He drove between two rows of concrete Jersey barriers and dimmed the cruiser's headlights as they pulled up to the sentry post. Light penetrated the car's windows, casting serious doubt on their charade. McCulver wore a freshly pressed York County sheriff's uniform, but stepping out of the car wasn't an option for him. The uniform hung on his meager frame like a scarecrow; the bullet-resistant vest worn underneath doing little to improve the situation. A shadow moved behind one of the ballistic glass windows set high in the enclosure.

This isn't going to work.

"Change of plans," he whispered to the passenger next to him. "We talk our way through and stop just past the checkpoint. Make up some excuse to draw the second sentry out."

The stone-faced former inmate slowly shook his head. "Eli's orders were clear. No improvising."

"Eli isn't here. If we don't take them down at the same time, one of them will radio ahead."

"You let me worry about that," he said, adjusting his grip on the suppressed pistol tucked between his right thigh and the door.

When the bright light started to fill the cabin, McCulver stole a closer glance at his passenger and nearly stopped the vehicle. A stain several shades darker than the hunter green uniform shirt covered most of Karl Pratt's left shoulder, an anomaly somehow overlooked when they distributed the dead sheriffs' gear by flashlight at the staging area. The blemish continued past the yellow patch sewn into the upper sleeve, covering half of the York County emblem with a crusty maroon film.

"Jesus, Karl," he hissed. "You look like you dressed a deer in that uniform."

Karl glanced at his shoulder patch as the sentry approached. "Change of plans," he said, raising his handheld radio. "Shooter, this is Raider Lead. Fire at the sentry next to our car. Fire now."

"What the fuck are you doing?" said McCulver, putting the cruiser into park.

"Saving the operation," said Pratt, tossing the radio on the dashboard.

The ranger's body language didn't change when Pratt stepped out of the car. He kept his rifle aimed at the ground in a patrol ready position.

Maybe this will work.

Despite McCulver's initial reservations, the police cruiser and uniforms got them close enough without drawing suspicion.

"Deputy, please wait inside the vehicle while I clear you with dispatch," he said, removing one of his hands to activate his radio.

A sharp crack spun the soldier flat against the guard post wall. Pratt was already in motion, sprinting in front of the car with his pistol aimed across the hood. A second bullet hit the sentry, knocking him to the ground and spraying a bright red line across the police cruiser's windshield. Bullets clanked off the thick armor as Pratt disappeared behind the guard post, relentlessly firing his suppressed pistol at an unseen target.

Through the thick glass windows imbedded high in the armored wall next to the car, successive flashes illuminated the sentry station's interior, followed by muffled gunshots. The night fell silent for several moments until a single flash and muted crack inside the guard post temporarily jolted McCulver out of his fear-induced stupor. He fumbled for the door handle, spilling onto the asphalt next to the downed sentry.

The wounded soldier reacted to his arrival by clawing at the Motorola attached to his tactical vest. Lurching forward, McCulver ripped the radio free before the sentry could send a warning. Karl Pratt poked his head around the corner of the guard post.

"What the fuck are you doing?" he hissed, stepping into view. "Start the attack. No way this went unnoticed."

"Did you get the other sentry?"

"What do you think?"

McCulver grabbed the radio Pratt had left on the dashboard, settling into the driver's seat. Two sharp reports caused him to duck and reach for the compact pistol hidden in the door panel. Groping for the door, he peeked over the dashboard. Pratt's pistol was aimed downward at the sentry—slide locked backward.

"All Raider units, this is Raider Lead. Commence your attack runs. I say again. Commence your attack runs."

Pratt ran up to his door. "Are you going to move the car?"

"Douse the lights," McCulver said, shifting the car into drive.

He pulled the cruiser through the opening and parked behind the armored enclosure. In the rearview mirror, he watched the checkpoint darken. Pratt's shadowy figure emerged from the back door a few seconds later, sprinting for the car. McCulver climbed over the center console, twisting into the passenger seat. He reached between the seats and pulled a red plastic toolbox into his lap.

"You didn't have to park fifty feet away," said Pratt,

crashing into the driver's seat.

McCulver didn't respond. Something was off with this guy. He didn't like the mercurial shift from respectful to insolent when they arrived at the guard post. Eli would never tolerate shit like that. Not from a piece of shit like Pratt. Unfortunately, there was nothing he could do about it right now. Pratt had demonstrated enough competence under pressure to buy him a second chance—or at least another five minutes.

***

Specialist Gabriel Martinez froze, straining to listen over the leaves rustling in the faint breeze. Nothing for several moments, then two barely audible cracks from the west. He turned his head in the direction of the airfield and processed the green image provided by his night-vision goggles. Nothing. He flipped the goggles upward and completed the same sweep with his rifle's thermal scope. They were still alone as far as he could tell.

"You hear any of that?" he whispered to Staff Sergeant Mark Jensen, his patrol leader.

Jensen edged closer.

"Just the one sound."

"Nothing out there?"

"Negative. I thought the relief team had arrived early," said Martinez.

They were an hour away from completing a six-hour shift patrolling the 1,500-foot strip of forest bordering Route 109, along the eastern edge of the airfield. The woodlands lay just inside the airport's security fence, representing a possible security risk from insurgent teams wishing to approach the airfield unseen.

"Wishful thinking. Suppressed weapon?"

"Hard to tell. Thought it came from the airfield."

"The Marines have a shit ton of those suppressed HK rifles," said Jensen.

"I haven't seen them carry any on patrol," replied Martinez.

"Call it in. We'll make our way to the airfield."

"Roger that, Staff Sergeant."

***

Second Lieutenant Kyle Walker sat on a rusty folding chair inside the Seacoast Aviation hangar, watching the steam rise from the metal canteen cup perched on a WhisperLite camp stove. He'd pulled the mid-watch again, putting him in front of Bravo Company, 2nd Ranger Battalion's radios for eight hours, starting at twenty-two hundred hours. The eight-hour stretch was brutal, but he'd fall out of the rotation for the next twenty-four hours, giving him a chance to patrol with his platoon and catch up on rest. With five officers in the company, including the company commander, they had enough flexibility to meet the RRZ's requirement to keep an officer and staff NCO on dispatch duty at all times.

"That water ain't gonna boil any faster with you eyeballing it, sir."

"How did I get stuck with you, First Sergeant?"

"Captain asked me to keep an eye on you," said First Sergeant McMillan, glancing deeper into the hangar. "Speaking of the good captain…"

A muscular African-American man dressed in running gear emerged from the shadows, walking toward the tables of electronics gear pushed against the hangar wall.

"Morning, gents. I'm headed out for a quick run and some PT before the RRZ briefing. Brought this for you, First Sergeant," Hines said, tossing the MRE at McMillan. "Briefing's at 6:15."

"I don't like to eat on duty, sir. Sets a bad example for the more impressionable members of the company," said McMillan, nodding at the lieutenant.

The radio squawked. "Rogue Watch, this is Rogue Three. Over."

Walker glanced at his watch before answering. 5:12. Perimeter teams checked in at the bottom of the hour. This wasn't a check-in.

"This is Rogue Watch. Over."

"Interrogative. Did any other Rogue units report noise to our west?"

"Negative. What did you hear?"

"Distant crackling noise. Best guess is suppressed gunshots."

The amplified words hung in the air for a moment.

"Tell them to stand by," said Hines. "What's Rogue Three's location?"

"Stand by, Rogue Three. Out."

Walker turned to the laptop on the table in front of him, forgetting about the boiling water on the concrete floor next to him. After a few mouse clicks, he had zoomed in on Rogue Three's passive tracking beacon.

"Moving parallel to Route 109, less than one hundred feet from the western edge of their patrol zone."

"Where's Rogue Two?"

"Sweeping the woods adjacent to the RRZ Authority compound," said Walker.

"Contact Rogue Two and the Outland Four," Hines ordered. "I want to know if they can corroborate any of these sounds. First Sergeant, may I borrow your NVGs?"

The seasoned ranger handed the captain his helmet with NVGs attached while Walker contacted the units. Rogue Two had nothing to report. He grabbed the radio handset tuned to the outer perimeter checkpoints and transmitted.

"Outland Four, this is Rogue Watch. Over."

No response.

"Outland Four, this is Rogue Watch. Over."

He waited a few seconds before checking the radio set to make sure he was still transmitting on the Outland frequency. He tried one more time before calling out to Captain Hines, who stood in the middle of the open hangar door twenty feet away.

"No response from Outland Four."

"I don't see their security lights," said Hines.

"I recommend we send QRF out to the checkpoint, sir," said First Sergeant McMillan, standing with his rifle.

"Send QRF. Raise alert status to Red for all stations. Contact Patriot and pass the alert. Wake the troops, First Sergeant."

***

Specialist Martinez held up a fist, stopping their progress.

"Vehicle. Up ahead," he whispered.

"Let's go," said Jensen, sprinting past him.

They stopped at the edge of the woods and crouched, searching the open landscape next to the airfield for the source of the engine sounds.

"Two buses and several smaller vehicles headed toward the airport from Outland Four. Running dark," said Jensen, turning his head east. "What the fuck happened to Outland's lights?"

"They should be on. I'm calling this in," said Martinez.

"Hold on. I see a police cruiser behind the buses."

Martinez watched the darkened convoy speed toward the empty intersection ahead. The buses showed no signs of slowing.

Something's way off.

"Staff Sergeant?" said Martinez.

"Send it as a SPOTREP," said Jensen, disengaging his rifle's safety.

Before Martinez could transmit, his earpiece activated.

"All Rogue and Outland units. Alert Level Red. Outland Four not responding to radio calls. Any unit with eyes on Outland Four—report immediately."

"Rogue Watch, this is Rogue Three. SPOTREP. Fifteen vehicles headed west on Kennebunk Road. Outland Four is dark. Over."

"Copy fifteen vehicles. Are you reporting them as confirmed hostile?" said Rogue Watch.

"Uh—wait one," said Martinez, releasing the transmit button. "Staff Sergeant, what do you—"

"Confirmed hostile!" interrupted Jensen. "They're ramming the fence!"

The lead bus slammed into the gate directly across from the intersection, snapping the padlocked chains and barreling through the fence like it didn't exist. He thumbed the Motorola button as the second bus passed through the new opening, headed toward the runway.

"Confirmed hostile! I say again, confirmed hostile! They just breached the gate in front of the Kennebunk Road intersection."

Chapter 33

EVENT +21 Days

Main Operating Base "Sanford"
Regional Recovery Zone 1

Standing in the stairwell next to the folding doors, Matt Gibbs gripped the steel handrail and ducked when the front of his bus smashed into the fence. A quick jolt, followed by several halfhearted cheers, told him that McCulver had been right. The brute force produced by a fifteen-ton bus travelling at thirty-five miles per hour had snapped the gate like a twig, leaving a few spider cracks in the windshield.

"I can't see the runway," said the driver, slowing the bus.

Gibbs opened his eyes and peered through the windshield, quickly reaching the same conclusion. The shapeless black view ahead gave him no indication if they were on the dirt access road leading to the runway. Logic told him the runway was dead ahead, but he couldn't afford to be wrong. Eli had stressed the importance of timing and speed on this operation, especially if they hoped to return alive. Any delay reaching the primary targets could doom them to failure, and failure was not an option—especially with Eli. He hated to give up the element of surprise, but he needed to be sure.

"Hit the lights for a second."

"Don't you have night vision?"

"Did you see me bring any on board? All of the night vision is in the cars. They need it to get to their targets."

"We turn these lights on, they'll see us coming."

"We're not driving the whole way with the lights. Just long enough to reach the runway. Hit the goddamn lights," said Gibbs.

"Whatever," the driver said and flipped on the headlights.

They were twenty or thirty feet to the right of the dirt road. The runway lay several hundred feet ahead.

"Get us back on the road," he said. "Careful turning in the grass."

As the bus eased left, his radio squawked.

"Raider One, this is Raider Lead. Turn your lights off immediately."

"This is Raider One. We're off the road. We can't see where we're going," said Gibbs.

"Turn your lights off—immediately. You're compromising the mission. I'll guide you to the runway. Follow the green light," said Raider Lead.

"Told you," said the driver, killing the lights.

Before the view ahead disappeared, he caught a glimpse of McCulver's police cruiser speeding past. A few seconds later, a subdued, green glow lit the cruiser's interior. Through the bus's windshield, the familiar shape of a chemlight waved side to side.

"Follow that car," Gibbs said.

Ten seconds later, the chemlight flew out of the cruiser's window and bounced twice before stopping.

"Raider Two, this is Raider Lead. Green chemlight is your mark to turn right and proceed down the taxiway to your targets. Good luck and God bless America. Rally at the same chemlight for group extract to staging area. Raider One stay on me. The main runway is dead ahead. Out."

The bus continued past the green mark, driving blind until the cruiser's interior reappeared, bathed in green light. McCulver had clearly thought this one through. Gibbs had a good feeling about it, despite the audacity of Eli's overall plan. Casualties would no doubt be high, and there was no guarantee he'd survive to celebrate their victory, but the price paid in blood today would be well worth the sacrifice. This morning's attack would deliver a strong message to the government, rallying patriots throughout New England and ultimately sparking a countrywide revolution. He was proud to play an integral role in a battle that would be compared to the "shot heard round the world" fired at North Bridge in Concord.

"Raider One, this is Raider Lead. Mark your turn at the chemlight and commence your attack run. Good luck and God bless America. Hit them hard and rally at the chemlight."

The second chemlight sailed in a shallow arc, landing on the runway ahead of the bus. Gibbs pulled the door release handle, retracting the bifold door and bathing the stairwell in a cool gust of moist air. Peering through the open doorway, he could vaguely identify the dark shapes of Raider Two racing down the taxiway toward the hangars crowding the airfield's main tarmac. As the bus started its wide turn onto the runway, he tightened his grip on the vertical handle in the stairwell and triggered his radio.

"Raider One units, this is Raider One Lead. Once you

hit the runway, proceed at best speed to the hangars along the western edge of the airfield and return to the chemlight. We need to be back on Kennebunk Road in less than five minutes. Respond. Over."

By the time Raider One-Six, the sixth vehicle in Gibbs' formation, responded, the bus had completed its turn, accelerating on the open runway. He could barely believe they were doing this. Gibbs climbed the stairs and studied the view ahead. The obsidian murk still hid the distant hangars, but he knew the bus was headed in the right direction. A dark gray strip, several times wider than the bus, cut through the sea of black ahead. A dark shape appeared in his peripheral vision as one of the Raider vehicles sped past the bus.

"How fast are we going?" he yelled over the wind blowing into the doorway.

"Fifty-five!"

"Kick it up to seventy. I don't want to fall too far behind the cars."

"This thing isn't designed for drag racing," said the driver.

Gibbs felt a weak burst of acceleration as the rest of his attack force zipped by on both sides of the bus.

"I got the damn thing floored. This is it!"

He patted the driver on the shoulder.

"Keep it going as fast as you can," he said, watching the dark shapes pull away.

Raider One Lead had the same problem. Three hundred feet away, running parallel to the main runway, the long, gray shape of the second correctional bus drifted further behind the pack of smaller vehicles, which had nearly disappeared in the darkness ahead. Gibbs didn't like the separation between the buses and the cars.

It was the one aspect of Eli's plan that left him uneasy.

With the faster vehicles arriving ahead of the buses, they would bear the brunt of the return fire from the stirred-up hornets' nest at the other end of the runway. Eli spun the situation differently, which rallied the troops but did little to quell his apprehension. He described the buses as battleships, which would shatter the confused enemy's morale with a broadside of concentrated gunfire. A little overstated, Gibbs thought, but not a bad image.

Much like the battleship Eli described, a mixed group of militia and inmates would simultaneously fire a medley of semiautomatic rifles, bolt-action hunting rifles and shotguns at the hangar. The volume of fire exiting the slatted security windows might be impressive, but it hardly qualified as a fearsome broadside. Firing into the dark from a moving platform, his team of twenty-three men would be lucky to hit anything. Despite Eli's elevated claims, Gibbs understood that the buses functioned more as a show of force than a force multiplier. The car bomb would do most of the damage.

"Raider One Lead, this is Raider One-One. I'm seeing a ton of shit up ahead. Looks like some kind of tent city in the area between the runway and western taxiway."

"This is Raider One Lead. Is this before or after the turn?"

"Pretty sure it's after the turn. Jesus, I have a dozen, possibly more helicopters on the tarmac. Are you sure we're just looking at a company of soldiers? This looks a lot bigger."

"Intelligence reported a company-sized infantry unit housed in our target hangar, along with elements of the National Guard in Raider One's target area. How far until the turn?"

"Coming up in a few seconds. This is not a company-sized unit. Shit, I have troop movement around the tents and vehicles. Holy fu—"

The radio transmission abruptly ceased, and a stream of red tracers raced from left to right across the black horizon, ricocheting skyward when it reached a point a few hundred feet in front of the bus. Some of the tracers continued uninterrupted on their slightly parabolic trajectory across the airfield.

"Raider One-One, this is Raider Lead!" he yelled.

No response.

Damn it!

One-One carried the explosives, and he didn't have communications with the rest of the vehicles. Eli wanted to keep command and control simple. The rest of the cars were supposed to follow One-One to the hangar and provide covering fire while they triggered the car bomb. Lines of tracers erupted from both directions, stitching the darkness ahead of them and deflecting in wild, high arcs. He lurched forward as the bus decelerated.

"What are you doing?" said Gibbs.

"It's a fucking ambush, man!"

He stared through the windshield at the intensifying maelstrom of crimson streaks crisscrossing their intended path. He knew each tracer represented four projectiles, which meant the space ahead of them was filled with hundreds of 7.62mm bullets.

"Keep your speed until I get clarification."

"Clarification? They're getting the shit pounded out of them!" screamed the driver.

"Just give me a few seconds!" Gibbs yelled, grabbing his handheld radio.

"Raider Lead, this is Raider One. Taking heavy fire

from both sides of the airfield. Lost contact with Raider One-One. Request permission to abort mission."

"Negative, Raider One. Your lead vehicle has made the turn. Proceed to target and provide covering fire for extract. Do not abandon your men!" said McCulver.

"Roger. Proceeding to target."

"He's full of shit," said the driver, slowing the bus. "We're driving into a kill zone."

Gibbs drew his pistol and jammed it into the inmate's shoulder. "You keep this fucking bus moving forward."

Before either of them could process the situation, tracers skipped wildly across the runway thirty feet in front of the bus, engulfing the last Raider Two vehicle in a brilliant storm of high-velocity streaks. The SUV abruptly swerved when tracers penetrated the vehicle and ricocheted through the interior, briefly illuminating the blood-splattered rear windshield.

"Stop the bus!" screamed Gibbs, unaware that he'd just killed himself.

The driver slammed on the hydraulic brakes, propelling Gibbs through the windshield.

***

McCulver watched the battle unfold through night-vision binoculars with a tinge of disappointment. Soldiers from the tents and hangars had responded faster that he'd expected, with lethal results. Few of Raider's vehicles made it off the runway or taxiway, striking deeper into the airfield as he'd hoped. Eli told him it didn't matter. As long as they got close to the business end of the runway, Eli was satisfied—mission accomplished. McCulver wanted more. He'd put most of the explosives into the airport phase of the operation and hated to see it wasted. He inwardly cheered them on, urging them to break through the hail of machine-gun fire to deliver one of his creations.

The buses had been his biggest hope, but one of them had faltered, the driver a victim of "cold feet," according to the most recent radio transmission. He focused on the stalled bus, watching bright green streaks pour into the metal coffin from both sides of the airfield. Two figures piled out of the front door, stumbling several steps before a stream of tracers swept through their bodies and dropped them to the asphalt. Through the horizontal security bars affixed to the outside of the corrections vehicle, he witnessed a bizarre light show inside the bus as tracers bounced around inside, exiting at dozens of different angles like a Fourth of July sparkler.

Glancing at the taxiway, the second bus lumbered forward, somehow miraculously continuing its doomed journey toward the end of the airfield. If it survived the next fifteen seconds of concentrated gunfire, McCulver might get secondary explosions from the fuel-laden helicopters crowding the tarmac.

He zoomed in on the cluster of protected hangars closest to the taxiway, searching for evidence of the pickup truck assigned to ram through the fence and shoot up the mini-compound. Based on the extra layer of security surrounding the buildings, they guessed this had to be some type of headquarters. He spotted the pickup truck buried halfway through the chain-link fence next to a long hangar. Figures scurried across the inner perimeter firing into the wrecked vehicle, presenting an opportunity he couldn't resist.

A quick check on the second bus confirmed that it

wasn't going to reach the helicopters, so he tuned the handheld radio to the first of three preset frequencies and pressed the transmit button. The view through his binoculars flashed bright green, followed by a sharp explosion that rattled the police cruiser. Temporarily blinded, he panicked and jabbed at what he hoped was the button that advanced the preset. He hit the transmit button. Nothing.

"Pratt, I can't see. Dial this to preset channel two and press transmit. Repeat for preset channel three," he said, holding the radio out.

"What do you mean, you can't see?"

"Night-vision flare. I need you to do this fast," said McCulver.

Really fast.

Their car was two thousand feet away from the nearest hangar, still within range of the heavy-caliber machine guns reported by Tim Barrett.

"Jesus, you're a regular clusterfuck," said Pratt, snatching it out of his hand.

A few seconds later, with his vision slowly returning, he still hadn't heard the explosions.

"I can't figure this cheap piece of shit out. Where the fuck did you buy these?" said Pratt.

"It's a basic handheld radio! How hard can it be?"

Several blurred flashes passed the windshield, followed by loud cracks.

"They're ranging us!" McCulver shrieked. "Hurry the fuck up! It's a radio not a Rubik's Cube!"

"I can't make any sense out of these buttons. Who the fuck buys a radio with only three buttons?" said Pratt.

"Someone who's working with a bunch of dipshits. Give me the radio and get us out of here!"

"I'm done taking orders from you," said Pratt, pressing something metallic against his left temple.

"What the fuck do you think you're doing?" said McCulver, gripping the binoculars tightly.

"What I was ordered to do—by Eli."

McCulver jammed his left hand upward, pinning the pistol to the roof of the car, while he slammed the binoculars into Pratt's head. He repeatedly pummeled Pratt until the pistol clattered against the center console. Opening the door, he jumped onto the runway and slammed the door, feeling his way to the back of the car. Risking a glance over the trunk, he registered movement and ducked, barely avoiding two suppressed bullets. The sound of scuffling along the asphalt on the other side of the trunk forced him to scramble to the front of the car. A line of red tracers arced over the car, illuminating Pratt's figure kneeling by the trunk.

Shit!

He rolled in front of the car as bullets snapped by his head.

Peering under the front bumper, he spotted feet shuffling down the side of the car. Before he could react, a bright red flash tore through one of Pratt's feet, followed by a torrent of bullets striking the cruiser. Lying flat, he watched Pratt's body crumple to the runway in a hissing pile of battered flesh and clothing. McCulver scrambled behind the engine block and crouched on shaky legs, listening to the distant crackling of small-arms fire over his thumping heart. He waited for another burst of machine-gun fire to rake the cruiser, but several tense seconds passed with no incoming fusillade.

McCulver weighed his options. Driving the car would attract bullets. If the cruiser had been pointed at the fence, it might work, but they had parked facing the other direction so he would have a clear view of the attack through the passenger-side window. The time required to turn the vehicle spelled the difference between life and death, eliminating that choice. The only hope of escape lay in the trees due east of the car. He didn't know the distance to the tree line, but he knew it was far enough away to present a serious challenge. Crossing several hundred feet of open terrain with night-vision-equipped M240 machine guns at his back sounded like a bad bet. Unless he could distract them.

Rising slightly, he shuffled past the open door and kneeled next to the driver's seat to search for the radio detonator. The car held a sharp, coppery smell mixed with a faint ammonia odor. Feeling around the wet, sticky interior, a flush of anger warmed his face. Fucking Eli. He should have known better than to trust that self-serving snake. His hand hit the radio in the driver's foot well. Lying prone several feet away from the cruiser, he examined the radio, which appeared to be dead. He pressed the power button next to the antenna, and the radio buttons and channel LED display glowed muted orange. The dumb fuck had turned the radio off. Without hesitation, he pressed the button labeled "Preset" until the LED displayed "Preset 2."

***

Specialist Martinez dropped to the ground as a stream of tracers raced past to his left.

"Rogue Dispatch, this is Rogue Three. Cease fire on the police cruiser at the end of the runway. Friendlies in contact. I say again, cease fire on the target at the eastern end of the runway. Friendlies in contact."

"What the hell are these two doing?" whispered Staff Sergeant Jensen lying several feet to his right.

"Trying to kill each other," said Martinez, staring at the grayscale image through his thermal scope.

The heat signature kneeling behind the trunk of the car fired two shots before moving down the right side of the car. A burst of white streaks ripped through the figure, passing through the car. Martinez ripped his head away from the scope in time to see another line of red tracers shoot by less than twenty feet away.

"Goddamn it!" yelled Martinez, grabbing his radio microphone.

"Rogue Dispatch! This is Rogue Three. Cease fire on target at eastern end of runway. Friendlies in contact! Acknowledge. Over!"

"This is Rogue Dispatch. Cease fire acknowledged by airfield units. Out."

"Stay low," said Jensen. "No way every shooter out there got that order."

One hundred feet from the cruiser, at the edge of the runway, the two rangers watched the surviving heat signature crawl around the front of the vehicle and pause. A few snaps passed overhead and to the side.

"Told you," said Jensen. "We stay right here until the snap, crackle, pop is over."

"Sounds good to me," said Martinez. "Should we drop him?"

"Negative. This looks like a command and control target. He isn't going anywhere."

When the figure started frantically digging around the driver's seat, Martinez zoomed in, interested to see what the man needed so badly.

A handheld radio? Shit!

"Possible detonator," he hissed.

"Got it," said Jensen. "Stand by to take him out."

Martinez concentrated on the gray image, which crawled away from the vehicle and stopped. He kept the scope's crosshairs on the figure's head.

"Take the shot," said Jensen when the figure raised the handheld radio.

Martinez steadied the sight picture and pressed the trigger, exploding their relatively calm corner of the airfield.

"You missed," said Jensen.

"Uh-huh," replied Martinez, watching the man writhe in pain holding his mangled fingers.

Chapter 34

EVENT +21 Days

Forward Operating Base "Lakeside"
Regional Recovery Zone 1

Alex leaned over the map stretched across the folding table in the DRASH tent, matching satellite image features on his digital tablet to paper. He drew small circles on the map, each representing a field or some kind of clearing in the woods that held a structure. When he finished, his vehicle leaders would use the tactical tablets assigned to each Matvee to snap digital pictures of assigned search sectors. They'd keep the quick reference images of the paper map minimized on their tablet screens, "checking off" each location after it had been cleared.

The Marine seated at the communications table next to him suddenly sat up, adjusting his headphones and grabbing a pen. He scribbled furiously on a pad of paper before responding.

"Copy all. Passing to Guardian Actual now," he said, turning to Alex. "Sir, MOB Sanford is under coordinated attack by car bombs and small-arms fire. Patriot wants our vehicles on the road ASAP, heading south to intercept retreating hostile forces."

"Acknowledged. Will contact Patriot en route. Send it."

Alex grabbed his rifle and burst out of the tent, nearly colliding with Staff Sergeant Taylor.

"You're up earl—"

"MOB Sanford is under attack. Car bombs and small arms. I need four vehicles, four Marines each, including gunners. Full tactical load outs. We roll in two minutes. Staff Sergeant Evans!" he said, sprinting toward the house.

He met Evans on the gravel driveway in front of the porch. "I just heard!"

"I'm taking four Matvees and fifteen Marines to Sanford. Pull the forest LP/OP's back to the house immediately and set up 360-degree coverage. Send one Matvee with four Marines and a two-forty to reinforce the Old Mill Road LP/OP. The other Matvee sits right here on the driveway."

"Copy. What about the LP/OP at the entrance to the compound?"

"Keep them in place in case something slips through," said Alex, holding up a finger to Kate, who had just arrived. "One second, hon."

"ROE?" said Evans.

"Weapons free. Assume all unidentified vehicles or ground personnel are hostile. They're using car bombs. Don't let any vehicles near the OPs," he said, slapping Taylor on the shoulder. "Get your men situated."

"I'm on it, sir," said Evans, disappearing for the command tent.

The Matvees parked in front of the DRASH tent rumbled to life in the darkness, followed immediately by the vehicle east of the house.

"Where are you going?" said Kate, turning her head to Matvees. "Where are they going?"

"South to cut off Eli's retreat. He'll be long gone before the Marines deploy the quick-reaction force. If we're lucky, we might catch him heading north."

"He's up to something," she said.

"I'm leaving two vehicles and more than half of the Marines. You'll be fine," said Alex, quickly kissing her.

"I'm not worried about *us*—I'm worried about you."

"He can't take on four armored tactical vehicles."

"Then why would he attack the airport?"

"Because he's crazy," said Alex.

"Crazy doesn't mean stupid," she said. "Be careful."

***

Houses peeked through the trees along the road, marking the outskirts of Limerick's downtown area. Alex searched the green image for anything out of place. A church steeple rose above the trees. First Baptist stood at the intersection of Routes 160 and 5. He'd split the convoy in less than a mile.

"Slow us down until we get to Route 11," said Alex.

"Copy," said Corporal Lianez, and Alex felt the Matvee downshift.

His ROTAC chirped. "Alex, what's your plan?" Grady asked.

"I'm sending one vehicle down Route 11 in case he heads west. We'll hit the Route 4 junction in eight minutes, where I'll send another Matvee east to intersect with 35. I'll proceed down Route 4 with the rest. What makes you certain he didn't die in the attack?"

"A solid hunch. Half of the cars involved in the attack

exploded simultaneously. 4th Brigade had a car rigged with explosives pile right through their tents surrounding their TOC. Miraculously, it didn't detonate. Either it malfunctioned or the triggerman was killed. Rangers think they nabbed the guy setting off the explosives, but it wasn't Eli. My guess is he watched from a safe distance and bolted when it became clear that the attack had failed. That was five minutes ago."

"Do you have units in pursuit?"

"I'm waiting for clearance. The Authority compound got hit pretty hard, and they're not keen on sending heavily armored vehicles away from the MOB. Work up a search plan for ten vehicles."

"That's it? They should have every vehicle at their disposal looking for this lunatic," said Alex.

"Ten is all I could convince them to consider. They think this is a diversion to draw everyone away."

"How big of a militia do they think he has?"

"It just got a lot bigger in their minds. Contact me when you have a plan. I have to go," said Grady, disconnecting the call.

"Punch it, Lianez. We need to make up lost time."

***

Eli peered through one of the First Baptist Church's steeple windows and counted the tactical vehicles speeding past Duvall's Market. Four oversized armored baddies headed south through town. He steadied his handheld night-vision scope on the hood of the lead vehicle, studying the infrared markings.

Bingo. Six-one-one.

The Matvees roared past the church, running the

intersection and quickly disappearing down the narrow, two-lane road.

His first instinct had been correct. The large-scale attack on the airfield drew the compound vehicles out. Now to test his deepest instinct.

"Liberty One, this is Liberty Actual. Four tactical vehicles headed south through Limerick. The nest is empty. Commence your attack."

Chapter 35

EVENT +21 Days

Forward Operating Base "Lakeside"
Regional Recovery Zone 1

Corporal Eugene Merrick leaned against the back of the armored turret, studying the road through his night-vision goggles. Four white glows, infrared chemlights spaced evenly along the right side of the road, broke up the green-scale image. The entire scene seemed noticeably brighter, prompting him to raise his NVGs and examine the road unassisted. The dark blue-gray image deteriorated rapidly, forming a murky screen a few hundred feet down the road. Better than the last time he checked, but still twenty to thirty minutes away from transitioning to daytime optics. Merrick lowered the NVGs, immediately spotting a distant, grainy vehicle in the center of Old Middle Road.

"SPOTREP. Vehicle approaching from the west. Running dark. Estimate twelve hundred feet. Definitely beyond the one-thousand-foot marker. Request permission to engage," said McCall, lowering himself into the gunner's sling and nestling the M240G into his shoulder.

"Negative," said Sergeant Keeler, his vehicle leader. "Report number of vehicles."

"Stand by," said Merrick, lifting his goggles.

He looked through the 6X ACOG scope mounted on the machine gun, hoping the magnified view might provide the answer. Staring through the illuminated red reticle, he found the lead vehicle and quickly confirmed a total of four in the convoy.

"Four vehicles. Lead is an SUV. I can't make out the rest," he said, lowering his NVGs.

"Copy. Engage lead vehicle at the five-hundred mark. Groves, move your two-forty closer to the road and watch the western approach," said Keeler.

Merrick lifted his head above the scope, keeping the metal stock buried in his shoulder. The furthest glow disappeared momentarily as the convoy sped past the one-thousand-foot marker.

"Mark. One thousand feet," he said, disengaging the safety.

"Copy. One thousand," repeated Keeler.

A few seconds passed before the second marker vanished.

"Mark. Seven hundred fifty feet."

"Copy. Three point four seconds. Vehicle speed estimated at fifty-plus miles per hour. Commence firing," said Keeler.

Merrick triggered the infrared laser mounted to the machine gun and nudged the gun right, connecting the bright green line with the hood of the lead SUV.

***

Harry Fields scanned the road through his AR-15's night-vision scope, pressing the rubber eyepiece against his eye socket. The SUV jolted, and the barrel of the rifle struck the windshield, jamming the scope into his cheekbone.

"Damn it," he hissed, a sharp pain radiating down his face.

Using rifle optics from the cramped seat made little sense, but Eli had only issued his team one pair of NVGs, and it made a hell of a lot more sense to equip the driver with those. He hesitantly returned the scope to his face and searched for the target. The turn onto Gelder Pond Lane was somewhere up on the right. The scope bounced into his face again, causing him to wince—but he kept staring ahead. A bright green line hit their hood, deflecting through the windshield.

"What the—shit!" he screamed, yanking the steering wheel right.

Red streaks flashed past down the left side of the SUV, illuminating the interior as they rumbled along the gravel shoulder of the road. Fields turned his head in time to see the tracers ricochet off the next vehicle in line, which abruptly swerved left and disappeared.

"Keep us right here and slow to ten miles per hour."

He raised his rifle and tried to locate the concealed machine-gun position. A second burst of tracers lit the road, barely missing the next car in line, which maneuvered behind Fields' SUV to avoid the fusillade. Momentarily safe, he decided to call for the reinforcements waiting in Limerick. With a second threat distracting the machine gun from the opposite direction, he could get close enough to use the explosives against the emplacement.

"Liberty Actual, this is Liberty One. Request reinforcements from your direction. I have a machine gun—hold on," he said, squinting through the scope.

An armored vehicle lurched into view, blocking Old Middle Road.

"That's not supposed to be there," he whispered before his SUV swerved off the road.

Red flashes chased them off the shoulder, striking the back end of the SUV and bouncing around the cargo compartment. His driver slammed on the brakes, grinding them to a halt in front of a thick tree trunk. One of his convoy's vehicles raced past on the road, engine revving at maximum RPMs, tracers pouring through the cabin and igniting the interior. He stared at the flaming car until it fishtailed and veered off the road, vanishing in the thick foliage ahead. He fished the radio out of the foot well and opened his door.

"This is Liberty One. Abort mission. Tactical vehicles sighted in road. They knocked out two of our vehicles before we could reach the intersection. Cancel reinforcements. We're gonna try to get out of here on foot."

He waited several moments for a response.

"Outstanding, Liberty One! Reinforcements en route," replied Eli.

"What? Negative. Gelder Pond Lane is blocked by a tactical vehicle. My entire convoy is out of action," he said.

"Roger. Clearing inner checkpoint with explosives. Reinforcements ETA three minutes. Give 'em hell! Out."

Fields gawked at the radio as everyone abandoned the vehicle.

"What the fuck is he talking about?" said Fields.

"Don't you get it, Harry?" said his driver.

"Get what?"

"He set us up! We're on our own!"

"No. I saw Brown's notebook. The count is right. Four tactical vehicles. They all left."

The deep sound of a powerful diesel engine reached their ears.

"Doesn't sound like it," he said, crouching behind the door. "We need to get away from this heap as fast as—"

Tracers tore through the door, ripping through the driver's body and spraying Fields' face with blood. He tumbled out of the SUV as bullets slapped into the hood and shattered the windshield, crawling on all fours through the brush. Projectiles and tracers snapped overhead, followed by piercing screams, as the vehicle gunner cut down the rest of his men. Fields slithered into a muddy ditch and pressed himself flat, hoping they might have escaped undetected.

He started to lift his head up to take a quick look when a deafening blast, followed by a sharp concussive wave, shook the ground and echoed off the trees. For a moment, he thought they had fired a grenade or some kind of shoulder-fired rocket at him. A second explosion left him covered in dirt and debris, his ears ringing. He curled up in a fetal position, fully expecting the next one to land on him.

***

Corporal Merrick aligned the laser with the man crawling through the bushes and started to apply pressure to the trigger. He was a breath away from dispatching the last of Eli Russell's attack force when the man dropped out of sight.

Shit.

The twenty-two-year-old gung-ho Marine in him said

pull the trigger and bury the fucker in hot steel, but the combat-experienced noncommissioned officer told him to give it a few seconds. He eased the laser to the top of the ditch and waited. His patience was rewarded when he detected movement a few inches below the green beam. Before he could adjust his aim, a brilliant explosion appeared through his port-side ballistic screen, followed by a sharp blast that rattled the turret.

"What's happening out there?" Keeler asked.

"Explosion south of the road. Vicinity of the flaming car. Looks like a car bomb," said Merrick.

"Copy. Mop 'em up so we can get off this road," Keeler said.

Merrick said, "I got one left playing hide and seek."

"Hit him with a grenade if you have to," said Keeler.

"Don't think that'll be necessary," he said, centering the laser on the top of his target's head.

A second explosion pelted the turret's armor and ballistic glass with debris and shrapnel. Merrick instinctively ducked, though his life had already been spared by a combination of chance and probability—less than 5% of his body had been exposed to the fragments thanks to the turret's design. He gripped the sides of the turret hatch to stabilize himself as the Matvee rocked violently on its suspension. A muted voice sounded in his right ear.

"You okay up there?" asked Keeler.

Merrick slipped out of the gunner's belt and dropped into the Matvee. Dirt and small branches poured through the hatch with him.

"I'm fine!" he yelled, barely able to hear himself. "SUV blew up! I think all the cars are rigged!"

Keeler turned in the front passenger seat to face him.

"We're heading back to the OP. Cover our six."

"There's still one out there," said Merrick.

"We'll pick him up later," he said, turning to the driver. "Get us back to the OP."

Chapter 36

EVENT +21 Days

Limerick, Maine

Alex's ROTAC chirped twice and displayed "Dagger," the call sign given to the FOB's perimeter security team.

"Captain Fletcher," he answered.

"Sir, the OP situated on Old Middle Road just engaged four vehicles approaching from the west. Two vehicles confirmed destroyed. The other two swerved into the forest just beyond the two-hundred-fifty-foot marker. Guardian Four-Zero is in the process of mopping up the survivors."

"Do you require assistance? I can be there in five," said Alex, hoping Taylor waffled on the decision.

He was looking for any excuse to head back. Logically, he knew Taylor had enough firepower at the compound to repel any attack thrown at them by Eli, but Kate's words had stuck with him: *He's up to something.*

"Negative. I have a night-vision-equipped, two-forty team watching the opposite approach. We can handle anything that approaches from either direction."

"Copy," said Alex. "Advise if the situation changes."

"Affirmative. Sounds like Keeler's gunner is chewing them—whoa! Jesus!" yelled Staff Sergeant Taylor, momentarily ceasing his transmission.

"Staff Sergeant?"

"Stand by, sir."

Stand by? What the fuck?

"Slow us down, Lianez," he said, retransmitting. "Taylor. What the fuck is going on?"

"Taking a report from Guardian Four-Zero. Wait one," said Taylor.

"Pull us over," said Alex, switching to Guardian's tactical frequency. "Guardian Two-Zero. This is Guardian Actual. Lakeside was attacked. We'll wait here for Dagger's status report. Watch your sectors."

"This is Two-Zero. Copy."

Through the oversized side mirror, Alex watched Sergeant Copeland's Matvee nestle in several yards behind them. He raised the ROTAC to his face.

"Taylor, you're making me nervous. Do I need to turn around?"

"Negative. Keeler reported two explosions in the forest. No friendly injuries. Sounds like a repeat of the airport."

Alex shook his head. *Four explosives-laden vehicles?* What was Eli hoping to accomplish?

"How many men did Keeler report in the forest before the explosions?"

"His gunner reported seven kills. They left one alive—crawled into a ditch near one of the explosions. If he isn't gone, he's pretty fucked up," said Taylor.

"It's not enough to get through," muttered Alex.

"Say again, sir?"

"Something's not right. I'm bringing Guardian One-Zero back to the FOB. Advise Keeler and all Dagger units of the change. ETA five mikes."

"Copy, sir. One vehicle returning. Redeploying

LP/OPs. Will advise Dagger and Guardian Four-Zero," said Taylor.

"Taylor?"

"Yes, sir."

"Get my family into the basement."

"I'm not sure Mrs. Fletcher will comply, sir. She relieved the Marine I had watching the remote sensors."

"I don't care if you have to drag them down the stairs and sit on them. I want them out of the line of fire," he said, lowering the ROTAC.

Kate was right. Eli *was* up to something. Throwing explosives-laden cars and armed inmates at the airport accomplished nothing beyond momentarily tightening a few RRZ sphincters. With spies in the Sanford area, Eli knew what his militia faced at the airport, and he'd sent them anyway. Nothing added up so far, and Alex couldn't shake the uneasy feeling that Eli had bigger plans for FOB Lakeside. He wasn't taking any chances with his family.

"Take us back to the FOB."

***

A second, distant burst of automatic gunfire filled the steeple, followed by an urgent transmission in his headset from Harry Fields.

"This is Liberty One. Abort mission. Tactical vehicles sighted in road. They knocked out two of our vehicles before we could reach the intersection. Cancel reinforcements. We're gonna try to get out of here on foot."

More tactical vehicles?

This changed things. Brown had been confident about

the vehicle count. Four total. Now he had mobile threats in two directions. He'd have to sacrifice the rest of his men to buy some time.

"Outstanding, Liberty One! Reinforcements en route," replied Eli.

"What? Negative. Gelder Pond Lane is blocked by a tactical vehicle. My entire convoy is out of action," he said.

"Roger. Clearing inner checkpoint with explosives. Reinforcements ETA three minutes. Give 'em hell! Out," he replied, turning to Jim Hunt and grabbing the barely visible squad leader by the shoulders.

"Son of a bitch, Harry broke through! They left their guard down, and now we're gonna fuck them up. Take your vehicles west on Old Middle Road and link up with Liberty One."

"Hot damn!" said Hunt, scrambling for the trapdoor near the back wall. "You sure you don't need our help here?"

"Negative. We got the easy part," said Eli, removing his backpack. "Not much can go wrong. Pay attention to the radio. Once we're done here, I'll be headed in your direction. Don't want to get fragged."

"We'll be ready for you," said Hunt, disappearing through the steeple floor.

Eli rifled through his backpack, pulling a handheld radio from a zippered internal pouch. He pressed the power button and checked the bright orange LED as another burst of staccato gunfire echoed through the quiet, rural town of Limerick. Verifying the radio was set to "Preset 1," he pushed transmit and waited. The windows rattled, followed by a deep, reverberating boom.

Perfect.

He quickly selected "Preset 2" and hit transmit. Nothing. He pressed it again. Silence. "Preset 3" yielded the same disappointing stillness.

No worries.

McCulver had warned him that substantial damage to the car might disable the bomb, and Fields reported two out of the four cars out of commission. He calmly cycled to "Preset 4" and was immediately rewarded with a steeple-shaking detonation. Eli carefully changed the channel to "Preset 8" and gingerly set the radio on the windowsill facing south. McCulver had skipped three channels as a safety precaution against prematurely detonating the grand finale.

"Time for the real show," Eli mumbled, focusing his night-vision scope on the furthest visible point along Route 5.

Chapter 37

EVENT +21 Days

Limerick, Maine

Alex leaned forward against the five-point harness and scanned the approaching intersection. His eyes flickered between the structures racing by, searching windows, parking lots and driveways for signs of human activity. Brake light reflections, cigarette glows, car door lights, flickering curtains—anything that could signify a hidden threat. He sensed the Matvee easing into a shallow left turn after the gazebo marking the center of town.

"Keep your speed," he said. "One more intersection, gents."

A small hill rose behind the gazebo, crowned by a stand of trees. A steeple peeked over the broken canopy of branches, drifting right and quickly disappearing behind them. When the road straightened, a second church appeared directly ahead, marking the next intersection.

"Route 5 coming up on the right. Stay left and watch for inbound."

Racing into the Y-shaped junction at seventy miles per hour, he spotted a faint glimmer of light in the steeple. Before he could warn the driver, his ROTAC illuminated, drawing his attention to the center console. When he looked up again, they were halfway through the intersection.

"This is Dagger. Hostile vehicles inbound from the east. I say aga—"

***

Eli's index finger twitched over the transmit button while his other hand pressed the night-vision scope into his face. The timing had to be perfect. McCulver told him to expect a half-second delay between transmitting the signal and the detonation, which had to build into the equation based on the approach speed. Kevin helped him work out a chart to calculate the speed, but the tactical vehicle was moving too fast for him to put it to use. If he took his eyes off the scope, he might miss his chance. The attack was a one-shot deal. They had buried two charges along the north side of the road, separated by thirty feet.

Eli raised the handheld radio next to his face and held his breath, finger pressed against the textured rubber button as the armored car raced through the intersection. At the last moment, Eli panicked, not trusting himself to time the detonation correctly. Instead of waiting to target the vehicle with the more powerful of the two IEDs, he pressed the button early and ducked.

The blasts shattered every window in the steeple, splintering the wooden window frame with hissing asphalt fragments. Donning the backpack, he took a quick look out of the missing window with his scope. A thick cloud of dust billowed through the town, rendering the green image useless. Unable to make an immediate assessment of the situation, he swung his rifle into the ready position and descended the ladder.

"Viper team, where are you?" he said, unable to locate them in the haze.

"Over here," someone croaked, the voice muffled.

"Where is here?" he demanded. "Speak up!"

"By the front windows, all the way to the right!"

"What the fuck are you doing there?" he said, running down the center aisle, still unable to see them through the veil of dust.

"We wanted to see the explosion," one of the men mumbled. "I think Ronnie's dead."

Eli followed his voice to the rightmost front window of the church, where he found the two of them in a heap on the glass-covered floor. Triggering his rifle light, he confirmed the man's suspicion. Ronnie had a three-inch piece of jagged metal protruding from his scalped forehead. Joe didn't look much better; his face and neck were shredded by glass fragments that had miraculously missed his carotid artery. He kneeled in front of him.

"Did you see the explosion?" asked Eli, slipping his razor-edged KA-BAR out of the sheath attached to his belt.

"Fucking thing flipped right off the road," rasped Joe. "You did it, man. Help me up."

In a blur of hands, he grabbed Joe's long, knotted hair and yanked his head forward, jamming the seven-inch blade into his neck. Joe's body went slack immediately, his spinal cord severed near the base of his skull.

"Sure. I got all day to deal with fuckers that can't follow directions," replied Eli, pulling Joe off the glistening blade and tossing him aside.

He rushed to the front door, not wanting to waste the time backtracking through the church. After throwing a few latches, he wrenched open the right side of the warped door and squeezed onto the concrete steps. The dust-choked air smelled like ammonia and charred wood. He stood there for a moment, searching through the haze for an outline of a vehicle. There was nothing. Several small fires burned brightly near the intersection, bushes and trees ignited by the superheated blast.

He hesitated on the stairs, not keen on rushing into the unknown. The Matvee was designed to withstand roadside bombs, and he couldn't take the chance that the damn thing flipped over and landed right side up. The dampened sound of distant machine-gun fire reached him, prompting him to abandon caution. Fuck it. Even if the thing landed on its wheels, nobody inside would be walking a straight line anytime soon. He ran blindly toward the intersection, activating his radio.

"Griz, bring the car directly to the intersection. Lights on. I need the Molotovs right away. We don't have much time."

***

A strong ammonia smell permeated the Matvee's cabin, competing with the industrial stench of diesel fuel. Alex shook his head and rubbed his eyes, initially confused by the counterintuitive feeling of moving his hands downward to reach his face. Something was different. An intense pressure strained against his shoulders, and one of his legs dangled freely; his Kevlar knee pad was looming inches from his flushed face. He released his hands, surprised when they flopped upward, striking the shattered ROTAC on the roof of the vehicle.

Fuck. We flipped.

He stared at the spiderwebbed windshield, trying to

make sense of what had happened. The dark, fragmented view didn't offer any clues, aside from the very fact that a ballistic window designed to withstand IED fragments and .50-caliber armor-piercing projectiles had been shattered. He grabbed a flashlight from the clutter of gear littering the roof and directed the beam at Lianez.

The corporal's left forearm was wedged into the steering wheel, his elbow hyperextended at least forty-five degrees. His right hand lay uselessly against the roof, most of his fingers twisted at odd angles. Alex didn't see any blood, which was a good sign. Busted-up limbs could be fixed. Lianez moved his lips, but Alex didn't hear anything. He tried to respond, but the words came out as vibration, like the Matvee had been submerged underwater. He couldn't hear.

The fuel odor intensified, stinging his eyes and spurring him into action. The Matvee wasn't flame resistant, and he detected a flickering orange glow through the driver's window. They needed to get out of here immediately. He eased his right leg out of the foot well and let it hang in front of him with the other, his feet inches from the roof. Alex triggered the harness buckle and dropped to his knees and elbows.

He gripped the flashlight and turned his attention to the rear compartment. The Marine behind him hung unconscious in his seat harness, suspended with no obvious external injuries. Moving the beam to the right yielded a ghastly sight. PFC Jackson lay crumpled against the roof in the rear cargo compartment, his neck bent at an unnatural angle against the rear hatch. Lifeless eyes stared back into the passenger cabin.

Shit.

Light poured through the driver's side windows,

distracting him. He squeezed along the roof to the window behind Lianez's seat and peered through the small, ballistic-glass window. An SUV sat in the middle of the road, illuminating the Matvee with its headlights. Alex thought about banging on the door with his flashlight, but quickly abandoned the idea. The vehicle wasn't there to rescue them. He grabbed the radio handset dangling between the seats.

"All units, this is Guardian One-Zero. Troops in contact. We've been hit by a roadside bomb. Request immediate assistance at the intersection of Route 5 and Route 160."

In a panicky voice, Alex repeated the call, unsure if anyone responded. He could barely hear his own voice, let alone the digitized, staticky voices often heard over the VHF radio net. When he checked the window again, a face blocked his view of the SUV. He immediately recognized Eli Russell's grinning, pockmarked face from the DMV photos downloaded to his laptop. The man looked even scarier in person.

***

Eli stopped short of the intersection and gawked at the damage done by McCulver's largest IED. A jagged, three-foot-deep crater, centered on the gravel shoulder, extended several feet into the asphalt road. Wide, gaping cracks continued beyond the hole, reaching the far side of the blacktop surface. The asphalt fissures closest to the crater's epicenter hissed and crackled from superheated bitumen, the petroleum-binding product used to shape modern roads. All that remained of the telephone pole that stood behind the roadside bomb was a splintered stump just outside the crater; the remainder of the pole and the wires it suspended were nowhere in sight. He'd never seen anything like this. The devastation was perfect.

He jogged south along the road until he found the second crater. Long fractures reached into the southbound lane, connected to a sizzling hole half the size of its sister IED.

He muttered obscenities until he spotted the tactical vehicle upside down in a thick cluster of bushes next to a used car lot. The truck had flattened a path through the brush, rolling from the road to its resting site. He eyed the lush undergrowth surrounding the vehicle.

That'll burn nicely.

Skirting the massive crater, he crossed the road and examined the wreckage in the dancing light cast by the small fires. Every external feature had been blasted off by the explosion or crushed by the rolling motion of the vehicle. A strong diesel smell hit his nose, competing with the ammonia, telling him that the monster's fuel tank had been ruptured. All the better. Beams of light cut through the dust to his right as the SUV slowly navigated the intersection. Eli motioned for Grizzly to bring the vehicle forward and point its headlights at the vehicle.

"Watch for anyone crawling around the sides. I'm gonna light this thing up like the Fourth of July," he said, hurrying around to the rear lift gate.

He pulled a plastic milk crate filled with Molotov cocktails out of the cargo compartment and shuffled toward the overturned vehicle. A light flickered through the compact door window, causing him to instinctively stop halfway between the road and the charred armor hull. If one of the occupants opened the door, he'd be caught in the open. He sprinted past the windows and kneeled next to the armor junction behind the rear driver's side door, breathing heavily. The SUV eased over the shoulder of the road and poured its high beams over the wreckage.

He dropped the crate of clinking bottles behind him and crawled along the side of the steel hull until he reached the rear driver's side window. A face appeared in the window, disappearing moments later. Eli centered his face on the window and watched a Marine fumble with something on his vest. The marine's lips moved rapidly, and Eli realized he was calling for help.

He needed to get this over with. The machine-gun fire north of here had stopped just as quickly as it started, which meant Liberty Two was finished. He checked his watch. One minute and they needed to be on the road. Just as he was about to pull away from the window, the Marine turned his head and they locked eyes. A flash of recognition passed over the marine's face, replaced by rage.

Fletcher.

Eli grinned and winked.

"Cover that door!" he yelled over his shoulder to Grizzly, who kneeled behind the driver's door and leveled his rifle at the vehicle.

Shaking with excitement, he returned to the crate and removed two Molotov cocktails. McCulver had conveniently stuck a camping lighter in the crate, which he used to light the kerosene-soaked cloth wicks on both bottles. He scurried around the other side of the vehicle just in time to see the rear passenger door open.

"Burn, motherfucker!" he screamed, heaving one of the bottles at the rear-facing door.

The bottle hit the armored hatch squarely, engulfing

the door in flames when the gas and motor oil mixture ignited. Eli hurled the second bottle at the flat armor above the hatch, showering fire between the door and open interior. The hatch slammed shut, cutting off a scream of agony, and the dense bushes next to the door burst into flames.

He pulled out three more bottles from the crate and returned to the burning side of the vehicle. The mixture still burned against the armor, the thickened concoction sticking in place like napalm. He lit the wicks and walked along the vehicle, smashing two of the Molotov cocktails against the front door and throwing one under the hood against the partially buried, cracked windshield. Thirty seconds later, he had expended every bottle in the crate, completely enshrouding the armored vehicle in flames.

"Get the next crate!" he yelled, jogging up to the shoulder of the road.

He met Grizzly in front of the SUV, yanking bottle after bottle out of the tray and tossing them in an arc toward the burning vehicle. Each bottle exploded, adding to the inferno until the hull nearly disappeared behind a wall of flames. He pulled the last bottle, stepping next to his driver.

"Griz, I saved the last one for you," he said, cocking his arm back.

"You should be the one to—"

The petroleum-filled wine bottle swung in an arc, shattering over his head. Grizzly stumbled forward, clawing at his eyes and screaming curses. Eli kicked him in the back, sending him in an uncontrolled fall toward the burning vehicle. He rolled to the edge of the firestorm and had started to get up when his head and torso burst into flames, turning him into a human torch. Eli watched with depraved satisfaction while Grizzly twisted and flailed, disappearing inside the inferno. The fire caught in the trees and spread through the bushes.

The temperature inside Fletcher's sealed metal coffin would soon reach intolerable levels, forcing the Marines to abandon their bulletproof cocoon and venture into the fire, but he didn't have time to savor the glory of shooting them down in person. He'd far overstayed his welcome in Limerick. In the end, it didn't matter; Eli had a better way to make Fletcher suffer.

Chapter 38

EVENT +21 Days

Limerick, Maine

Alex lunged at the door, pounding the heavy armor plating after Eli's face disappeared. He considered opening the door, but decided to lock it instead. He had no idea where Eli had gone.

Crawling under Corporal Ragan's unconscious body, he drew the Heckler & Koch P30 compact pistol from his drop holster and gripped the rear passenger door handle. He opened the door with his left hand, pointing the pistol toward the front of the vehicle with his right.

Clear.

Before Alex could check the back of the vehicle through the window, flames consumed his arms. He screamed and dropped the pistol inside the vehicle, as fire rained into the vehicle compartment.

Without thinking, he slammed the door shut, locking it to prevent Eli from tossing an incendiary bomb inside. Within milliseconds of the door closing, the Automatic Fire Extinguishing System (AFES) activated, instantly saturating the enclosed space with a dry chemical that extinguished the fire before it burned through his uniform. Alex lunged through the cloud of chemical dust to lock the two front doors. He didn't feel like testing the

AFES against the full contents of a Molotov cocktail.

While locking the front passenger door, flames erupted beyond the ballistic window. Seconds later, a bright yellow flash consumed the windshield. He slid into the empty back seat and studied the SUV through the window, calculating his chances of breaking out and killing Eli. Beyond the powerful headlights, a lone figure crouched behind the open driver's side door, no doubt covering the Matvee with a rifle. Before he could further analyze the situation, flames obscured his view.

This fucking lunatic is trying to burn us alive!

Thick black smoke started to seep into the cabin from the open turret. Alex reached down and tried to raise the hatch, but extensive damage to the turret structure trapped the metal hatch in place. Alex had no idea how long they could stay inside the vehicle, but he knew it wasn't long. Beyond the caustic smoke, which had no way to escape, the temperature had risen at least twenty degrees since the first Molotov exploded. They were sitting inside an oven.

"Lianez! Can you hear me?" he said, squeezing into the space next to the corporal.

The corporal's words came out slurred. "I hear you, sir. I think I'm all fucked up!"

"You're fine, but I have to move you!" he said, studying Lianez's hyperextended arm. "First I need to untangle that arm!"

"Hold on, sir! Let's think about this for a—"

Without warning, Alex straightened the marine's arm and pulled it clear of the steering wheel at the same time, extracting a prolonged, expletives-filled scream.

"Sorry I had to do that! No time to fuck around! Ready for round two?"

"What?"

"Keep your left arm straight!"

"What? No!"

Alex grabbed the top of Lianez's tactical rig and released his harness. He pulled the Marine onto his right side as the buckle detached, keeping his head from hitting the roof and snapping his neck. Unfortunately, there was no way to prevent his mangled arm from bouncing off the steering wheel and hitting the door. With Lianez cursing and screaming, he dragged the Marine into the cargo compartment, sliding him next to Jackson's lifeless body in front of the rear hatch.

He'd forgotten about this egress point earlier, which allowed them to exit the vehicle without exposing himself to the shooter next to the SUV. He'd still have to worry about Eli, or anyone else that arrived in his entourage, but at least he didn't face a guaranteed firing squad. It was their best chance at this point, and they needed to get out. He could barely see through the smoke.

"Ragan! Let's go!" he said, slapping the unconscious Marine still hanging in his harness.

The Marine stirred, regaining some motor control, but Alex didn't have time to nurse him along. He pulled the corporal toward the middle of the Matvee and released his buckle, jarring him back to consciousness with a short fall.

"We need to get out of here!" said Alex, starting to cough.

Corporal Ragan squinted with a confused look. "Why can't I hear?" he yelled, scanning the cabin. "What the fuck happened?"

Alex grabbed the marine's vest and pulled him close. "Ragan!" he said. "Look at me!"

Ragan's wild eyes settled on Alex.

"We're trapped inside a burning vehicle! Jackson is dead, and Lianez is fucked up!"

A thump hit the door behind Alex, distracting him long enough to see a burning hand press against the window.

"Fuck!" said Ragan, fumbling for his door handle.

Alex dove across the vehicle, stopping him. "It's not safe! Hostiles! We have to exit through the rear hatch, together! Find your rifle!"

Snatching his HK416 from the front of the vehicle, Alex crawled over Jackson and leaned against the scorching hatch, waiting for Ragan to join him. When they were both next to the door, he lifted the handle and nodded at Ragan, who kicked the hatch open. Alex scrambled clear of the blaze, kneeling in the grass and aiming toward the road. The SUV was gone.

"Right side clear!" he yelled, feeling the ground sway under him.

"Left side clear!" answered Ragan.

"We have to get them out!" said Alex, taking a few wobbly steps toward the fire.

His vision blurred, narrowing as the familiar dark shape of a Matvee roared into the intersection.

Chapter 39

EVENT +21 Days

Forward Operating Base "Lakeside"
Regional Recovery Zone 1

Alex bolted upright, coughing—trying to make sense of his surroundings. He sat in a dark space on a hard floor. The floor jolted, bouncing his head off of something hard and fixed.

My helmet's gone.

A pair of hands pushed against his chest. He reached for his pistol, suddenly remembering that he'd dropped it in the Matvee.

"Sir, I need you to lie back down!" said a familiar voice. "God damn it, Allen, will you watch the fucking road! He might have a head injury!"

"I'm trying! We're almost there," replied the driver.

Sergeant Keeler. Corporal Allen.

He was in friendly hands. For a moment, he thought Eli might have captured him. He hated to think what the man would do to him or any of his family if they were captured.

"Lianez and Ragan?" asked Alex.

"They're fine, sir. Both up front. Jackson's with Guardian Two-One, back at the site."

"Jackson," mumbled Alex, shaking his head. "Any sign of Eli?"

"Don't know yet. We saw one crispy critter next to your Matvee, but we couldn't get close. We barely got your guys out."

"I won't stop until Eli Russell is dead. That's my promise to Jackson."

"Wish I could be there to see it," said Lianez, leaning in his seat to nod at Alex.

"We all want to be there for that one," said Keeler from the shadows of the compartment.

The vehicle jolted to a stop.

"We're at the FOB, Sergeant," said Corporal Allen.

The back hatch opened, filling the compartment with cerulean predawn light.

"Alex!" yelled Kate, pushing past Staff Sergeant Taylor, who held his hands up.

"Easy, ma'am, they got rattled pretty bad," said Keeler, kneeling in the doorway.

"I'm fine," said Alex, sliding through the hatch, barely able to stand on his own.

He held Kate tightly, burying his head in her shoulder.

"You don't look fine—or sound fine," she said, kissing the nape of his neck.

"Where are the kids?" he whispered.

"In the basement with your parents and two Marines. The place is swarming with Taylor's men," she said.

"Good," he said, kissing her lips briefly. He whispered in her ear, "Start packing up the trailer and roof carrier. Everything on the list. Just in case."

She pulled back a few inches, staring at him quizzically. "We'll get started on that, *together*, after you get medical attention and a little rest."

Alex kissed her again and stepped back, reaching into the Matvee for his helmet and rifle. "He's still out there."

"You don't know that. It doesn't sound like anybody survived the attack, either here or at the airport. Odds are good that he was killed."

"He looked fine when I saw him—right before he tried to burn us alive," he said, clipping his rifle into the sling points integrated into his Dragon Skin vest.

"You can barely stand up on your own! Let the Marines deal with this!"

"I can't!" he snapped, turning to her. "He's still out there. And if he's still out there, you and I aren't safe. The kids aren't safe. None of us are safe."

"Then we pack up, *together*, and go. He can't follow us where we're going," she said.

"He went through a lot of trouble to get at me, again. What makes you think we'll ever be safe? He's obsessed."

"He's not the only one," she said, frowning.

"That's not fair," Alex said, pointing at her.

"Neither is this," Kate said, grabbing his helmet. "Your family needs you *here*."

Alex let go of the helmet, exhaling deeply. He hated fighting with Kate, especially when she was right. He could leave this to Grady and slip away. The Marines might think less of him, which would sting, but ultimately, he had a duty to protect his family.

"He could have stayed and finished the job. There's something else up his sleeve. Something we can't predict. I have to finish this. It's the only way to be sure."

Kate embraced him, pressing her head into his neck. "You're gonna get yourself killed."

"No. Someone's watching out for me," he said.

Kate pushed back, shaking her head in disbelief. "Really? I'd hate to have your guardian angel."

"I'm still standing, right?"

"Barely. Make sure you stop by and see the kids before you take off. Emily hasn't stopped crying since the bombs started going off. Amy's not crying, but I know she's worried."

"I'll be there in five minutes," he said, kissing her passionately on the lips. "I love you."

"I love you more. You better not leave me with your parents," she said.

Alex laughed. "Might be in your best interest to loan me your guardian angel. Double duty."

"Tempting. See you inside," she said. "Don't forget."

"Never," he said, searching for Staff Sergeant Taylor, who had mysteriously disappeared with the rest of the Marines when they started arguing. "Staff Sergeant!"

"Yes, sir?" Taylor said, appearing from the side of the Matvee.

"I want a two-vehicle convoy to transport Lianez, Ragan, and Jackson back to Sanford," he said. "Sorry, Staff Sergeant. Jackson was my responsibility. I should have taken him down from the turret when I returned. I was convinced we'd run into Eli's follow-on force, and I—"

"Sir, Jackson didn't belong anywhere but in that turret. We don't drive around with gunners strapped into seats. Jackson pulled a bad card," Taylor said, his eyes glistening.

Alex grabbed both of his shoulders. "We're gonna find that fucker. Trust me on that."

"I have no doubt about that, sir. Just don't piss off the old lady too much. You get to drive out of here in ten minutes. Some of us don't have that luxury. She's an ass kicker," said Taylor, brightening up slightly. "Don't tell her I said that."

"She'd take it as a compliment," said Alex, walking them toward the DRASH tent. Guardian Two-Zero is at the bombsite. What about the rest?"

"Six-Zero replaced Four-Zero at the OP on Old Middle. I sent the rest to the bombsite. They should be there by now."

Alex nodded, looking back at the Matvee. "Keep Lianez and Ragan in place. We'll use this vehicle and Five-Zero to make the trip to Sanford. Departure in ten minutes. Has Grady called?" he asked, feeling his vest pockets for his ROTAC.

"He was headed into an emergency RRZ meeting a few minutes ago. I briefed him on the situation before he had to cut me off."

Alex nodded, picturing the broken handheld radio on the roof of the Matvee. The memory triggered a daisy chain of images.

"Son of a bitch," he muttered.

"Sir?"

"Have the Marines at the bombsite scour the church. I remember seeing a light in the steeple. After that, pull everyone back to the FOB. Tell Evans we're heading out later this morning. When I get back with the ten Matvees Grady promised, we're going on a little overnight trip."

"The Marines will be happy to hear that," said Taylor.

"Just keep it quiet around my wife, or guess who's gonna stay behind to watch over the place."

"Mum's the word, sir."

"That's what I thought," Alex said.

He jogged toward the house to catch up with Kate.

PART IV

"Revenge"

Chapter 40

EVENT +21 Days

Main Operating Base "Sanford"
Regional Recovery Zone 1

Alex craned his head forward as they approached the outer perimeter checkpoint on Route 109, staring skyward. A staggered formation of military helicopters crossed the road far ahead, heading north. Six Black Hawks and two Chinooks. Someone was having a party.

"I wonder what that's about," he remarked.

"Looks like a company-sized raid," said Corporal Allen, slowing the vehicle at the entrance to the maze of concrete barriers.

"Maybe they found our man," said Sergeant Keeler from the back.

Alex shook his head. "They wouldn't need eight helicopters."

When the formation disappeared over the trees, he turned his attention to the checkpoint. One of 1st Battalion's Matvees was parked next to the concrete-barrier-lined entry road and opposite the armor-plated sentry post.

The Matvee's gunner peeked over the turret with binoculars, yelling down to the rangers, who remained out of sight. A few seconds later, the gunner held a hand out, signaling for them to stop. Sergeant Keeler reached forward and grabbed the hand microphone attached to the VHF radio set.

"New procedures, sir. Outland Four was wiped out by two guys in a stolen police cruiser last night. That's how they got onto the airfield. Switch me over to channel eight, sir?"

Alex reached over his lap to select the requested channel on the AN/VRC-110 radio receiver mounted next to him.

"It's all you, Sergeant," he said.

"Outland One, this is Guardian Four-Zero, in formation with Guardian Five-Zero. Requesting permission to approach."

"This is Outland Four. Pull up to the stop sign and send your vehicle commander forward. We need to verify ID."

"Copy. Moving forward," said Keeler, unbuckling his harness.

"I got it, Sergeant," Alex said. "I want to ask a few questions."

When the vehicle stopped, Alex hopped out and jogged up to the guard structure. His body felt sluggish on the short run up the road, like he'd just finished a long run. Combined with a dull headache, the full body stiffness wasn't a good sign. He'd barely paid attention to the effects of the IED explosion at the FOB. Fueled up on adrenaline and the thought of smashing Eli Russell's head in with his rifle stock, Alex had moved on autopilot until he settled into the Matvee's seat for the thirty-minute drive. He'd almost fallen asleep twice, which was unusual for him during the morning, especially after a few cups of coffee. Maybe Kate was right, and he needed to throttle it back a little. Maybe he needed to throttle it back all the way and get checked out by one of the corpsmen.

"He's good to go!" yelled the Marine in the turret. "That's Captain Fletcher."

One of the rangers appeared, shaking his head at the gunner as Alex handed over his ID card. The ranger vanished for a few seconds.

"You're clear, sir," he said, handing the card back.

"I just heard about Outland Four. Sorry," said Alex. "What happened?"

"Two shitheads dressed like cops jumped them at the checkpoint. Fuckers had a York County Sherriff's car and everything. We caught one of them at the end of the runway, trying to set off the rest of the bombs. RRZ snatched him up real quick."

"What did they do with him?"

"He's in some kind of solitary lockup at the detention center. 4th Brigade nabbed a few more on the runway."

"Where's the detention center?" said Alex.

"One of the hangars next to the northern end of the runway," said the ranger.

"Any idea where the helicopters are headed?"

"Negative, but that's the first time I've seen more than two head north at the same time."

"That's what I was thinking. I'll get out of your way," he said, turning to the turret gunner.

"Marine, does Grady have one of these at every checkpoint?"

"Yes, sir, and all over the inner perimeter. Half of the battalion's vehicles are tied up," said the corporal.

Alex didn't like the sound of that. With most of the Matvees tied up with airfield security, his chances of squeezing *any* support out of Grady dropped into the single digits.

When Alex stepped into the TOC, Lieutenant Colonel Grady was glued to one of the widescreen monitors at the command table, talking into his ROTAC. He didn't notice Alex until one of the Marines slammed the door to one of the storage containers, drawing his attention away from the screen. Grady held up his index finger and winked, nodding at the chair next to him. Alex mouthed, "I'm fine," and waited for the battalion commander to finish the call. From Grady's harsh tone and hushed voice, he guessed the RRZ Authority was on the other end of the line. Less than a minute later, Grady shook his head and slammed the radio down on the table.

"Good news, sir?"

"No. The good-news fairy walked off the fucking job. More shit about the blue uniforms. Good to see you in one piece, Alex," said Grady, shaking his hand and slapping his shoulder. "Sorry about Jackson."

Alex was struck by the last part of Grady's comment. He thought of himself as an outsider in the battalion, just a temporary stakeholder. Even this morning, when he apologized to Taylor for Jackson's death, he still viewed himself as an outsider. Grady didn't see it that way. Alex had been put in command of FOB Lakeside, and all of the Marines assigned. They were *his* Marines. He'd somehow forgotten.

"You all right?" asked Grady, snapping him out of the deep thought.

"Yes, sir. Hearing's still a little fucked up. Ringing coming in and out," he said, tapping his helmet. "Jackson was a good kid. Good Marine. How do they handle next-of-kin notification?"

"Given the circumstances, I don't know," said Grady. "Nobody seems to know."

Alex watched a lone Black Hawk helicopter approach the outer tarmac, slowing to a hover in front of the lone two-story hangar north of the Marines' compound.

"Where did they send the helicopters?"

"North. To raid Eli's compound," said Grady.

"What? Fuck!" yelled Alex, running toward the open hangar door. "I need to be on that raid! I can't believe you didn't tell me about this."

"Alex!" said Grady, chasing him out of the hangar. "The mission was given to 4th Brigade. No Marines involved per RRZ orders. We need all hands on deck."

"I saw, sir. How many of our vehicles do they have tied up with perimeter security?"

"We had a major breach here, if you hadn't noticed!"

Alex shook his head. "We knew the York County Sheriff's Department was missing a few cruisers. I had one of them show up at my house two weeks ago, right before Eli threw an entire platoon of men at my family."

"I submitted that intelligence through the RRZ data system and personally briefed the rangers. We did our part," said Grady. "Surveillance camera footage indicates that the car was used to get close enough for the militia team to get lucky. We've modified the procedure to prevent a repeat."

Staring at the northern horizon, Alex balled his fists. "Where's Eli's compound?"

"About five miles north of Route 25, off 160," said Grady, wincing.

"Imagine that. Right where I wanted to search a several days ago," said Alex. "How did they figure it out?"

"A few of the militia prisoners saw the light when we

showed them that *all* of their cars had been rigged with explosives, including the buses. They were under the impression this would be a quick hit spearheaded by a few diversionary car bombs. Apparently, nobody signed up for a suicide mission."

"He won't be there," said Alex.

"What makes you so sure?"

"Eli's too smart for that. He knew there was a chance someone would end up talking. They'll find the place emptied out. At most, he left a small crew of expendables behind. They won't know a damn thing about Eli's next move."

"I don't think there's another move, Alex. Eli's done. We identified seventy-three bodies at the airfield. Five prisoners. Taylor just called in with the count in Limerick. Thirty-one dead. For all we know, Eli burned up in his own fire at the intersection."

"Don't count on it. Did they find anything in the church?"

"Two bodies. One stabbed through the throat. The other took shrapnel from the explosion."

"Brilliant," muttered Alex.

"Brilliant?"

"Killed two birds with one stone. Got at me while shedding his own dead weight."

"He only killed one of those birds," said Grady, patting him on the shoulder.

"Which is why we need to go after him right now. He doesn't strike me as the type to give up on a grudge."

"You look like you could use a seat," said Grady, pointing to the makeshift briefing area. "I need to discuss something with you."

Alex turned his head, staring directly into Grady's

grizzled, tired face. "Sounds like I'm not getting ten vehicles to hunt down Eli."

"Worse. The RRZ ordered me to shut down the FOB," said Grady.

"When?"

"I'm stalling on them on this," said Grady.

"When?"

"Effective immediately. They've compressed the RRZ Security Area," he said, looking around, "and there's talk about declaring martial law."

This sealed Alex's decision. The only thing standing between his family and a return visit from Eli was a twenty-four-hour security shield provided by 1st Battalion, 25th Marines. Even that had proven to have its limitations.

"Martial law? I didn't see that on the RRZ menu."

"Neither did I. Apparently, there's a private menu, which requires approval from Washington. Governor Medina didn't seem to think her request would be denied."

"What are we looking at?" said Alex, crumpling into one of the folding chairs.

Grady dropped into the chair in front of Alex, facing backward.

"They've drawn a five-mile circle around Sanford, then a straight line through it from the coast to the New Hampshire border. Anything in the circle, or south of the line, is subject to restricted daylight hours, strict nighttime curfew, random searches, RRZ ID card registration."

Alex hung his head in his scorched Kevlar-weave gloves and started laughing. "How are people supposed to register for IDs when they don't have any way to get to their designated registration point? Nobody has a car. Someone needs to pull those fuckers out of their compound and drive them around. They might be surprised to see we got hit by an EMP."

"They won't be coming out of there anytime soon. Not after this morning's attack. As for the ID card program, someone had the foresight to design mobile card-making equipment. 1st Battalion, along with a full battalion from 4th Brigade, will go door to door in the Security Area. We start training on the gear tomorrow."

"I suppose you'll be confiscating firearms at the same time," said Alex, stifling a laugh.

Grady just stared at him, his face betraying no reaction.

"Jesus, Sean. This isn't Washington, D.C., where guns are banned. More than fifty percent of this population owns a firearm. You start asking for guns, and you better be prepared for a gunfight."

"I know, and the 4th Brigade CO agrees. We're waiting for heads to cool down over in the Green Zone before we try to talk some sense into them. People might have to live with the curfews and restricted hours, even the unconstitutional searches. Our goal is to stop the insanity there."

"What if Medina won't listen?"

"We'll cross that bridge when we get there."

"Better not let Eli cross it first. He'll be back in business within the week if you start taking the guns away. The entire state will turn against the RRZ," said Alex. "How the fuck don't they see that?"

"You're preaching to the choir," said Grady.

"What about Harrison Campbell's folks? I can't envision this playing out well for them."

"You need to give him a heads-up. All known or suspected militia types within the Security Area have been designated as high threat. The York County Readiness Brigade was mentioned by name. They'll be at the top of the gun confiscation list if the measure is approved. I wouldn't be surprised if the RRZ issued a detention order."

Alex stood up. "Damn it. I feel like an asshole for getting his people into this."

"They would have been targeted anyway. If anything, your short collaboration with the brigade will help the situation. Harrison's folks did some good work on the RRZ's behalf. That gives me leverage to keep them from being treated like criminals. That said, they might have to hang up their guns for a while, or at least keep them out of sight if we pay them a visit. I need you to explain this to him. I'll do everything in my power to protect them, but I need them to play along when the time comes."

"I'll pass this along, but you need to sit down with Harrison and work this out, sir. Passing along good intentions isn't the same as directly shaking on them," said Alex.

"I copy you loud and clear on that. Ask Motor-T for a clean vehicle to visit Campbell."

"I'm sure Campbell won't mind a little mud," said Alex.

"Clean, as in we've disabled the tracking devices. They're watching us closely. Leave your ROTACs behind and don't activate the vehicle data system. Use the VHF if you have to pass traffic," said Grady.

Alex smiled for the first time since he woke up. The fact that Grady was finding ways around the RRZ system gave him hope that he wouldn't leave Campbell at the mercy of the government. It also left him with the distinct impression that Grady was more interested in honoring his Oath of Office than playing federal shell games with the people's constitutional liberties. He distinctly remembered raising his right hand at the Navy Marine Corps Memorial Stadium in Annapolis and swearing to "defend the Constitution of the United States against all enemies, foreign and domestic."

"I'll be back shortly," said Alex, moving a chair out of his way.

"You should stick around. We're patched into the 4th Brigade's radio feed for the raid. Time on target is zero-seven-twenty. Twenty-one minutes from now."

"He won't be there," said Alex, shaking his head.

"Never know," said Grady.

"I know."

Chapter 41

EVENT +21 Days

Sanford, Maine

Alex met with Harrison Campbell at the edge of the forest leading into the property, under the watchful eyes of several heavily armed men and women. He sensed something was different. Campbell's people looked tense.

"Keeler, why don't you head down the road about three hundred meters, until you're out of sight."

"Copy, sir. We'll point the Matvee in your direction in case you need a quick extract," he replied, over the intrasquad radio.

"I appreciate that. The reception is looking a little frosty. Out," said Alex, turning to Campbell.

"Frosty?" said Harrison, extending a hand. "No, cautious. Glad to see you in one piece. I talked with your dad a little earlier on the HAM."

"Eli really outdid himself this time. He threw close to a hundred of his people to the wolves, including inmates from the correctional facility. Most of the cars were rigged with explosives. Some were remote detonated, still containing the occupants."

"We knew something big was going down. Sounded like the Battle of Gettysburg toward the airport. What about the compound?"

"He sent a total of seven cars, in two waves, at the compound. None of them got past the checkpoint at the turnoff. The second wave sped down Old Middle Road like nothing happened to the first wave."

Campbell shook his head. "All to get at your sorry ass?"

"Apparently. He buried two roadside bombs in downtown Limerick. My vehicle was hit by the smaller of the two," said Alex.

"Two in one place?"

"He wasn't taking any chances that I might return with a second vehicle. This was a well-planned attack. I'm worried it's not his last."

"Well, he can't have much of an army left," said Campbell.

"It only takes one person to press a button. Who knows how many IEDs he has planted around southern Maine?" said Alex.

"You should be fine driving around in one of those things," he said, nodding toward the Matvee disappearing behind a stand of trees down the road.

"I might not be driving in one for very long. The RRZ is making some changes after the attack."

"This doesn't sound good," Campbell said, stepping into the sun. "Should we take a walk?"

"Probably a good idea."

When they were far enough away not to be overheard, Alex explained the full situation. Campbell listened impassively, showing little response to his revelation. When Alex finished, he stopped walking and rubbed his face, exhaling hard.

"You really trust Grady?"

Alex nodded. "I trust him to do the right thing with

his battalion. Unfortunately, the RRZ has another five thousand soldiers at their disposal. It sounds like the 4th Brigade commanding officer is on the same page as Grady, but I don't know where his loyalties will fall if the RRZ doesn't bend on this."

"We're not giving up our guns, Alex. You know that."

"I wouldn't expect you to, but I'm sure you can work something out with Colonel Grady if he's required to pay a visit, especially if any RRZ observers tag along."

"They have no right to pay us a visit," said Campbell, crossing his arms over his rifle-magazine-laden vest.

"Harrison, don't be a stubborn ass. Work with him on this. Bury the damn rifles for an hour when he comes to inspect, or whatever he's required to do."

"This is going to be a tough sell. Disarm while the government walks through the camp armed to the teeth? You see the problem, right?"

"Very clearly. I also know the RRZ has designated your organization as high threat. You're one classification level away from a direct action raid. I watched eight fully loaded helicopters head north to Eli's compound. You don't want that kind of visit. Sit down with Grady and hash this out," said Alex, raising his voice.

"Most of us feel more comfortable working with you," said Campbell.

"Well, I can't make any promises that will amount to anything. Grady has a battalion of Marines that'll follow him through the gates of Hell. He's your man moving forward."

"I think you're making a mistake taking off. You're more than welcome here. It'll be a bitch of a winter, but we'll come out on top," said Campbell.

"The offer is tempting, Harrison. Thank you," said

Alex. "But I'm not so optimistic about the bigger picture. I think it's time for a change of scenery."

"Northern Maine is a change of scenery. I have a feeling you're headed for a bigger change. Will we see you again?"

"Probably not," Alex said, holding his hand out.

Campbell took his hand and surprised him with a quick bear hug.

"Good luck out there. Stay safe."

"I will, and you do the same. I wouldn't be surprised if Eli turned his full attention to the York County Readiness Brigade. Frankly, I'm amazed he left you out of this morning's festivities."

"Funny you mention that. We had a guy go missing last night. He took off around eight to check on his mom and never returned. At first we figured he had second thoughts about the brigade and split, but maybe he ran into Eli's crew on the road last night."

"Second thoughts? Was he new?"

"Yeah, he was one of the guys that joined through the recruiting station. He drove up with us to Belgrade. Skinny-looking guy with a buzz cut. Local kid. Rob Duhaime."

"I remember him. Knew his way around a rifle. He had one of your cars?"

"No. He had his own car. That's why we brought him along for the trip to Belgrade. Rob's pickup was the only vehicle with a tow hitch for your trailer. Not all of the brigade was keen on driving your friends up north."

"I'll pass a description of his vehicle to the police and our battalion operations staff. They can keep an eye out for his truck. If he ran into Eli's group somehow, he's probably dead on the side of the road," said Alex. "Silver pickup. Do you remember the make and model?"

"Nissan Frontier."

"If the Nissan returns, make sure Duhaime's driving. Never know," said Alex.

"Way ahead of you. We planned on searching it thoroughly, regardless of who's driving."

"Take care, Harrison. I hope our paths cross again."

"Same here, Captain Fletcher."

Alex walked across the tall grass field connecting with the dirt road leading to the gate. He pressed the remote transmit button on his vest and recalled the Matvee, which raced out of the tree line to meet him on the road. Looking over his shoulder at Campbell's property, he tried to picture what would have happened if Eli had concentrated his attack on the York County Readiness Brigade headquarters. A hundred men armed with rifles and explosives-laden vehicles could have punched through the defenses fairly easily unless Campbell had a few surprises he hadn't disclosed.

He wondered if the Marines back in Limerick would notice if the thirty-caliber machine gun disappeared. Maybe another trip to see Campbell was in the very near future, bearing a proper farewell gift. As one thought triggered another, he settled on the silver pickup truck, imagining one of Eli's unwitting followers driving it toward Campbell's people in the woods. Something bothered him about the mental image. He kept picturing Duhaime behind the wheel. Duhaime. The twenty-three-year-old kid that knew his way around an AR-15—and happened to own a brand-new pickup truck.

"Oh, shit," he muttered, sprinting behind the Matvee to the passenger side.

He jumped in and slammed the door shut.

"Is this set to Patriot?" he asked, grabbing the VHF handset.

"Yes, sir. Is everything all right?" said Keeler.

"Hold on, Sergeant," he said, triggering the radio. "Patriot, this is Guardian Actual. Over."

Static filled the Matvee for several moments.

"Patriot, this is Guardian Actual. Over," he said, releasing the transmit button. "Where the fuck are they! Allen, get us moving. RTB. Don't stop for anything."

The Matvee lurched forward as the radio speaker crackled. "This is Patriot Three," replied Major Blackmun.

"Ops, have they started identifying the suspects from this morning's attack?"

"They've identified three of the five prisoners. Not sure about the rest. They're still trying to get the vehicle wreckage off the runway."

"Copy. Any chance one of those vehicles is a silver Nissan pickup truck?"

"Wait one. I need to call 4th Brigade. They're collecting all of this information."

"Standing by," said Alex.

Sergeant Keeler leaned between the driver and passenger seat. "Anything we need to be worrying about, sir?"

"Get Peterson out of the turret. Make sure everyone is strapped in tight," said Alex, fumbling with his harness while trying to hold onto the radio handset.

"Gunner stays in the turret, sir," said Keeler.

"You can't shoot an IED. Get him down now. I'm not having a repeat of this morning."

"Roger that, sir," Keeler said, pulling PFC Peterson down through the hatch.

"This is Patriot Three," Blackmun's voice said over the radio. "Good guess on the pickup. We have a silver Nissan Frontier with Maine plates sitting in the grass between the main runway and the outer taxiway."

"Was the vehicle rigged with explosives like the rest?"

"Affirmative."

Alex froze for a moment, terrified by the possible implications.

"Did they find all of the occupants? I'm looking for someone specific," said Alex.

"Three dead inside the vehicle. A fourth cut down about twenty feet away. 4th Brigade sent me a list of names they've collected. What's the name?"

"Rob Duhaime," Alex said, his heart pounding.

"Bingo—two for two. Robert Duhaime. Source of ID is a Maine driver's license. Age twenty-three. Springvale address. Right up the road."

Shit. Eli knew about the Belgrade house, and Alex had no way to warn Charlie and Ed.

Eli wouldn't head up to Belgrade alone, not after his spectacular failure at the Limerick compound. He'd head to a predetermined rally point and link up with whatever remained of his militia army. If Alex acted quickly enough, he might be able to nail Eli before they left the rally point. Someone had to know where he was headed. Alex started thinking about possible links to Eli, starting with the most obvious.

"The ranger at Outland One mentioned a guy they captured by the police cruiser. Can you read the names of the prisoners?"

"Pinette, McCulver and Bowen. Two unknowns," said Blackmun.

"What was the middle name?" said Alex.

"McCulver. Kevin McCulver. There's a note attached to his name. Rangers picked him up by the police cruiser at the far end of the runway. Says the driver had chased him around the car, trying to kill him with a suppressed pistol."

They have Eli's bomb guy.

"Interesting. Which unit is running the detention center?"

"262nd Engineering," said Blackmun.

"Copy. Striker Two-Two is inbound. ETA five minutes. Out," said Alex, pulling the vehicle commander's data tablet out of the docking station attached to the dashboard.

"Sergeant Keeler, can I use this thing offline?"

"Yes, sir. Select 'local mode' on the first screen."

After following the sergeant's directions, he chose "navigation tools" from a list of offline applications and opened a map of Maine. By the time they reached MOB Sanford, he had a plan. A desperate plan with no guarantees outside of the fact that September 8th, 2019, would most likely be his last day in Maine.

Chapter 42

EVENT +21 Days

Main Operating Base "Sanford"
Regional Recovery Zone 1

Alex grabbed his rifle and turned to Sergeant Keeler in the back seat. "If anybody asks, I'm trying to get a little more information about the two unidentified prisoners. One of them might be this Duhaime guy."

"*If* anybody asks," said Keeler.

"*If* being the operative term," Alex said, closing the door.

He walked through the dusty parking lot, slipping between a pair of Humvees parked in front of a corrugated steel hangar. A handwritten sign was taped to the inside of the glass door leading into the building that read "262nd Engineering." A gray-haired, slightly overweight soldier typing at a laptop greeted Alex inside, barely looking up from his work.

"How can I help you, sir?"

"I'm here to see Captain Adler," said Alex, looking at the empty computer stations spread throughout the sparse office. "Where did everyone go?"

"All hands on deck reinforcing the RRZ compound. Captain Adler's across the tarmac, trying to unscrew that situation. They want Jersey barriers around the whole thing. Both sides of the fence."

"Where's the good captain going to find that much concrete?"

"Where else? The perimeter checkpoints. RRZ's orders," said the soldier. "Robbing Peter to pay Paul."

"Perfect."

"I'm sure we can expect even brighter decisions in the future. Do you want me to contact the captain, sir?"

"Yes. I need to see one of the prisoners."

"You can see them right on this monitor, if you'd like," said the staff sergeant, pointing to the laptop next to him on the desk.

Alex walked behind the desk and examined the green image. Five men sat next to each other along a wall, hands behind their backs.

"Where are they?"

"Locked inside a storage container at the back of the hangar. We had them under guard in the open until Captain Adler mobilized the company."

"Why do they have engineers watching prisoners?"

"The RRZ didn't want the rangers watching them, or any of the Marines. My guess is they'll be transferred over to 4th Brigade. There was some talk of building a fenced-in area past the main runway for detainees. Some kind of tent city setup."

"Sounds like they're expecting more guests," said Alex, turning from the screen to the soldier. "I can't make an ID with this night-vision image. I need to see them in person."

"I'll have to clear that with the captain. The RRZ threw a fit when they found out the ranger guys went to town on the prisoners," he said, grabbing his ROTAC.

"Sounds like they got solid intel on the group responsible for the raid."

"Old intel. The place was empty," he said, raising the handheld radio. "Sir, I have a Marine captain here requesting to see the prisoners. He needs to make an ID, and the night-vision camera view isn't cutting it."

The staff sergeant looked up. "He wants to know if it can wait, sir?"

"The prisoner I'm trying to locate may be able to shed some light on Eli Russell's location," he said, staring at the screen while the staff sergeant relayed his response.

"He'd like to talk with you, sir," he said, handing over the ROTAC.

Alex considered his approach and decided to go with direct.

"Rick, it's Alex Fletcher. I need a favor. One of your prisoners might have information that can lead us to Eli Russell. I need to see them immediately."

"Alex, I can't grant you access to the prisoners. The information shaken out of them this morning didn't pan out. The RRZ wants a proper interrogation team handling this. They're flying in a team from somewhere. Nobody is allowed to handle the prisoners until they arrive."

"This is a personal favor, Rick. The asshole responsible for the airport raid is the same psycho responsible for two attacks against my family. He's disappeared, and I think he might be targeting friends of mine. I don't have much time here. Eli has a three-hour head start."

"They'll throw me into one of those containers next if they find out about this. Something tells me you're not planning on a quiet sit-down with the prisoner in question."

Alex walked deeper into the office and whispered his response.

"I don't think I'll need to take it that far. Sounds like he had a little falling out with the other guy in the police cruiser. Instinct tells me it was more than an argument about who was driving. Just give me some time with the guy. Ten minutes. If I can't get the information I need in that time, I'll approach this from a different angle."

"I know I'm going to regret this," said Adler. "Put Staff Sergeant Gates on the line. The clock starts as soon as Gates steps through the door. Ten minutes."

Alex jogged back and handed the ROTAC over to Gates, who listened to Adler's instructions.

"I don't think we should leave the prisoners unattended, sir," he said, glancing nervously at Alex while Adler responded. "Understood, sir," he said, setting the ROTAC on the desk.

"Captain Adler needs me to run a new laptop over to him at the RRZ compound. He wants you to watch over the hangar while I'm gone," said Gates, raising an eyebrow. "The keys to the prisoner container are hanging there. In case something happens that might require you to evacuate them in the next ten minutes."

"I suppose I could hold down the fort for you," said Alex, suppressing a grin. "I should probably keep your ROTAC. Do you have a directory for the MOB?"

Staff Sergeant Gates stood up. "Who do you need to call?"

"Combat Controllers. Tech Sergeant Gedmin, if you know his station."

"Preset nine," said Gates, running his hand over his balding head. "Ten minutes."

"Make it thirty. Please."

"I might make it four hours…go home and have a drink. Something tells me I'm going to need one," he said, walking toward the door with a black nylon laptop case. "Good luck, Captain. I hope whatever you got planned is worth it."

"It's more than worth it," Alex said, selecting preset nine.

"Tech Sergeant Gedmin," the phone squawked.

"Tech Sergeant, this is Captain Fletcher."

"Good to hear your voice, Captain. Word on the street is you had a close call this morning."

"Too close. I lost a Marine in the attack," said Alex.

"Sorry to hear that. It wasn't a good morning, and it just got worse," said Gedmin. "NOMAD's raid was a bust."

"I heard. What if I told you I know how to find Eli?"

"I'd tell you to grab Lieutenant Colonel Grady and head over to the RRZ compound ASAP."

"That won't work for a number of reasons. I have something different in mind, but it requires a huge favor. One I can't pay back."

"Define huge."

"The size of a Black Hawk helicopter."

"That's one hell of a favor," said Gedmin.

"And I need it delivered to Captain Adler's hangar in less than ten minutes, fueled and ready for a 115-mile, maximum-speed transit to the Belgrade Lakes area. This is a one-way trip for me, and I'm running out of time. There's more at stake than just losing Eli Russell."

Gedmin didn't respond for a few seconds. "What's your alternative plan if I can't pull this off?"

"You don't want to know," said Alex.

***

Kevin McCulver thumped the back of his head against the metal wall, creating a steady, low-grade pounding rhythm to compete with the self-hating voice inside his head. The distraction technique hadn't proven very effective. Sitting in the dark on the coarse plywood floor, all he could think about was how stupid it had been to think he was indispensable, part of Eli's inner circle.

He kept trying to rationalize Eli's decision. Maybe Eli had ordered him killed if it looked like they might be captured, to keep the Rangeley Lake house a secret. Possible, but deep inside, he knew it wasn't true. Eli had used him to cull the herd, and he'd never once suspected that he was being played. None of them, including Karl Pratt, had a place at Eli's next table. He quietly laughed at the irony of the situation. He sat in a hot, unventilated shipping container, zip-tied to the floor next to four men he had readily betrayed. They'd tear him to pieces if they discovered the truth, just like he'd stab Eli in the throat if he ever saw him again.

"Quit banging your fucking head against the wall!" someone shouted, startling him.

"Sorry," he mumbled, resting his head against the corrugated steel.

A voice to his left started the same angry line of questions they'd rehashed at least a dozen times since their capture. He was thankful everyone was handcuffed to the container tie-down bolts. Two of the prisoners were from the correctional facility, and there was little doubt they would beat him to a pulp given the opportunity.

"How the fuck didn't Eli know they had this much

shit here? He *had* to know!"

McCulver stayed silent, hoping the question would go away.

"I'm talking to you, shit stain! Don't act like you don't know that!"

McCulver cleared his throat. "I told you. Reports from our guy in town indicated one company of Marines and a few vehicles. That's why we planned a run-and-gun operation. A quick shake-up."

The container jolted as the inmate pulled on his restraints.

"More like a shake and bake! Our cars were rigged to explode!" he said, kicking the plywood floor with his heels. "First chance I get, you're a dead man."

The guy next to him, one of the men assigned to Matt Gibbs' squad, spoke for the first time since the soldiers locked them in the container.

"You knew everything was rigged, right? I mean, you're Eli's bomb guy."

Time for some tap dancing.

"Not all of the cars were fitted with explosives. We had a primary and a secondary, in case the first car didn't make it to its objective. Everyone driving in one of those cars knew about the explosives."

"GI Joe said *all* the cars had explosives," said a gruff voice at the back of the container.

"They made that up so you'd give them Eli. You didn't tell them anything, did you? A bunch of helicopters took off right after they finished pulling us one at a time into the office."

McCulver hoped floating a few of his own accusations might put a stop to this line of questioning. Nobody like being called a rat.

"I didn't say shit!" yelled the prisoner who had started the inquisition. "Maybe I should have."

The container door swung open, causing him to squint. With the sun blazing through the doorway, he couldn't see who had opened the container. The outline of a combat helmet appeared briefly.

"Which one of you is McCulver?" said the figure, stepping into the enclosure.

"The piece of shit right in front of you," said an angry voice.

A gun barrel pressed into his right temple, lukewarm against his skin. "Is that right? Just nod or shake your head."

He nodded swiftly, concerned about the situation. The gun barrel jammed into his head represented a significantly disturbing setback in their treatment. All of them had been abused upon capture, subject to sudden, short-lived beatings while they were corralled into the hangar. The situation changed quickly with the arrival of some government-looking types. The civilians put a stop to the blatant physical abuse, removing their captors from the scene. The group that took responsibility for their custody seemed less intense, like they didn't do this for a living. The soldier pushing the business end of his rifle into McCulver's head looked deadly serious, and he was alone. Not a good combination for someone wearing a dead sheriff's deputy's uniform.

"I'm going to cut you loose. If you do anything besides sit there quietly, I'll use the same knife to spill your guts on the floor. Understood? Nod or shake."

He nodded, spurring the soldier into action. A second later, with his shoulders nearly pressed out of their sockets, a sharp pain seared through the top of his left wrist, causing him to writhe against the floor. McCulver howled as the pain continued, burrowing into the top of his hand. A moment later, his hands snapped free.

"What the fuck is wrong with you?" yelled McCulver, receiving a bloody fist to the side of his head for the question.

"You're lucky I didn't cut off one of your thumbs and slide the zip-tie off," said the soldier, kicking him in the solar plexus and knocking the wind out of him.

McCulver was yanked to his feet and kneed in the right quadriceps muscle, causing an agonizing spasm. His leg felt immobile from the blow, and he couldn't put weight on it. A second strike to the side of the thigh collapsed his leg in a series of unbearable cramps, and a forearm locked under his neck. The soldier's hot breath washed over the right side of his face.

"You won't be able to run, not that you're going anywhere," he said, tightening the grip against his neck.

"You're choking me," gasped McCulver, struggling to breathe.

"Not even close. We're moving forward now," he said, manhandling him out of the container.

Once clear of the makeshift prison, he marched them behind the container, out of sight from any observers on the airfield. The soldier shoved him against the hangar wall, knocking him to the ground. Glancing around, McCulver noted the hangar looked empty.

Not a good sign.

"This isn't an officially sanctioned visit, if that's what you're wondering," said the soldier.

McCulver lifted his trembling left hand, examining the damage. A deep gash ran from the bottom of his hand to the knuckle under his middle finger, bleeding profusely into his lap.

"What do you want?"

"I want Eli."

"I already told them where to look," McCulver whispered.

"Let me see your other hand," said the soldier.

McCulver kept the previously bandaged hand pressed against his spasming right thigh. He'd momentarily forgotten about the throbbing pain of his mangled fingers.

"They already know everything."

When the soldier squatted a few feet in front of him, he immediately recognized the digital camouflage pattern.

Now I'm really fucked.

The marine's uniform looked filthy, like he had spent the past week crawling through the forest. Patches of frayed, blackened material covered his arms, and his face was smeared with a gritty black film. A faint, charred rubber smell filled the air between them.

"The place was abandoned," said the marine, staring at him impassively.

"That's because we threw everything we had at the airport. There's nobody left," said McCulver.

The Marine checked his watch, fiddling with the buttons. "One minute before I start slicing and dicing, and there's no going back from that."

McCulver swallowed hard, not doubting for a second that he meant it. He didn't see any other option. Maybe he'd be willing to trade information.

"What do I get in return…if I knew where you might find him?"

The Marine glanced at his watch. "For saving me a little time? I won't cut the rest of that *Deliverance* crew loose and toss you back in the container with them. I need an answer in the next five seconds."

"What happened to the minute?"

"I'm on a tight schedule," he said, standing up and drawing a black serrated knife from a scabbard on his belt.

"I know where to find him," said McCulver. "We secured a place on Rangeley Lake."

The Marine leaned over and grabbed his collar, pulling him to his feet. The knife bristled against his neck.

"You and I are going on a field trip," he said, dragging McCulver to the front of the hangar.

The marine's radio chirped when they reached the left side of the open hangar door.

"Captain Fletcher," the Marine answered.

Fletcher? This can't get any worse.

"Just in case you're curious, sir. I saw you walk the prisoner to the side of the hangar. At least make some kind of an effort to conceal yourself until the helicopter arrives. I'm not the only one keeping an eye on the situation."

They don't know he's taking me? It's worse.

"Does that mean you found me a helicopter?" Fletcher inquired.

"Medical bird from the 126th Aviation Medevac unit based out of Bangor. They just returned from a trip ferrying two of the RRZ casualties to Central Maine Medical Center. I didn't see any follow-on tasking, so I took the initiative."

"What's my cover?"

"Vehicle injury sustained during routine patrol in the vicinity of Belgrade Lakes. Transport to Central Maine Medical Center and RTB."

"I need to stop in Limerick on the way up. Any way you can help with that?"

"I'm staying clear of the control tower for a while, sir. Any add-on services are your responsibility. Good luck out there."

"Thanks for taking a chance on me. Sorry I won't be around to return the favor."

"It's all about building good karma, sir. Remember that when you're thinking about pushing your guest out of the helicopter."

"I'll try," said Fletcher, pushing McCulver's face into the hangar wall.

His cheekbone ground into the corrugated metal, the cheaply fabricated sheets of steel scraping his skin.

"I think I see our ride spinning up right now," said Fletcher, turning him around.

"Here's the way this works. You're an injured sheriff's deputy who will accompany the injured Marine to Central Maine Medical Center."

"How was I injured?" asked McCulver.

"Car accident, from what you can remember. You hit your head pretty hard on the door," said Fletcher before yanking his head back by the hair and slamming it against the hangar—twice.

Cheers echoed from the shipping container as he spat bloody tooth fragments onto the concrete floor.

"One more for the crowd?" said Fletcher, pulling his head back.

"No. No. Please," he begged. "Please."

His head raced forward, abruptly stopping less than an inch from impact.

"Take a seat. I need to make a few calls," said Fletcher, releasing his grip.

McCulver quickly lowered himself to the ground, wincing at the pain caused by using his hands. He looked up at Fletcher, who held the olive-drab tactical phone to his ear.

"Don't think I'm not watching you," said Fletcher, never looking down at him.

"Staff Sergeant Taylor, I need a twelve-marine assault team assembled in five minutes. This is not an authorized mission, so volunteers only. I guarantee this will be a career killer."

"Can I assume this has something to do with Eli Russell?"

"This has everything to do with Russell."

"I don't think career progression is on the front burner at the moment. I shouldn't have much trouble rounding up a few eager Marines for some payback, sir."

"I didn't think you would. Find a suitable location to land a Black Hawk helicopter and pass me the grid. Red smoke marks the LZ. I need to talk to my wife."

"I'll get her a ROTAC after we pick the LZ, sir."

"Roger, see you in less than fifteen minutes. Out," said Fletcher, peeking out of the hangar. "I hope you don't get airsick."

McCulver kept his eyes on the bloody pile of teeth and saliva on the floor in front of him. He'd finally met the one person that scared him more than Eli.

Chapter 43

EVENT +21 Days

Medevac flight over southern Maine

Three minutes out of MOB Sanford, Alex pretended to receive a call on his ROTAC, writing on a green notepad that already held the location of a baseball field in Limerick. He tore the page from the pad and held on to it tightly as it whipped around in his hand from the wind generated by their high-speed transit. The pilots were pushing the helicopter's speed envelope, flying them north at close to one hundred eighty miles per hour. He stood up, holding onto one of the straps attached to the ceiling, and walked forward, passing the medevac litter restraining "Deputy" McCulver.

Reaching the cockpit, he thrust the paper between the seats and activated the headphones connected to the helicopter's communication system.

"I just received information that the vehicle accident may have been caused by a local militia group. My CO wants us to set down at the FOB in Limerick to pick up a squad of Marines. They're at this ten-digit grid. Red smoke will mark the LZ."

The copilot reached up and took the paper, clipping it to his kneeboard.

"Copy. Inputting grid coordinates. We can take six-combat loaded Marines. Any more than that is pushing the cabin configuration," said the copilot, pushing buttons underneath one of the color displays in front of him.

"We don't mind squeezing in," said Alex.

"Hang on back there," said the pilot, and the helicopter banked sharply left.

"ETA five minutes. Tell them to pop smoke as soon as they hear us," said the copilot. "We'll try to fit as many in as possible."

"Copy. I'll take as many as you'll give me," said Alex, kneeling next to McCulver, who stared at him wide-eyed.

The helicopter descended a few minutes later, heading toward a distant swirl of red smoke past the outline of a baseball diamond.

"ETA one minute," said the copilot.

Alex removed his headset and replaced it with his helmet. He kneeled next to McCulver, patting him on the head. "Don't go anywhere."

When the helicopter touched down behind second base, Alex jumped down onto the flattened grass and jogged toward Staff Sergeant Evans, who kneeled behind the pitcher's mound at the front of a column of combat-loaded Marines. Sand from the infield pelted Alex while he yelled over the thunderous drumming of the helicopter's rotor blades.

"Load them up, Staff Sergeant! It's a medevac bird, so we might have to leave a few behind. Priority goes to the automatic riflemen. I want them closest to the doors!"

While Evans led the Marines toward the helicopter, Alex ran toward the third base dugout, where Kate sat out of sight behind a translucent privacy screen fixed to the chain-link fence.

"Sorry about the cloak-and-dagger stuff," he said, kissing her quickly. "I'll explain later."

"How sure is this?" she asked.

"One hundred percent."

"How will you—"

"Honey," he interrupted. "I need you on the road within the hour."

"Alex, we can't be ready in an hour! We haven't started loading the trailer!"

"You *have* to be on the road in an hour. This is a one-way trip for me. I can't predict how the RRZ will respond to this stunt. I kidnapped one of the prisoners held in the detention center, and this mission isn't exactly legitimate."

She stared vacantly at the helicopter loading the Marines. "I can't believe this is happening."

"We'll be fine. It's just happening a little faster than we expected. Everything on the list is packed and ready to move. You have plenty of able bodies to help."

Four Marines started jogging away from the helicopter.

"I have to go. If I don't show up by this time tomorrow, you have to leave."

"We're not leaving without you," she said, her face regaining confidence.

"Twenty-four hours and you push off. If all goes well, you'll see me this afternoon," he said.

"Say good-bye to everyone for me," she said, kissing him once more.

He nodded, then ran across the sand swept infield toward the helicopter.

Chapter 44

EVENT +21 Days

Rangeley, Maine

Alex glanced nervously at Staff Sergeant Evans. He'd caught a glimpse of Rangeley Lake through the compartment door, which meant their medevac mission cover story was a few seconds away from completely unraveling. They needed to move McCulver into a position next to him, where he could see the lake and guide them to Eli's exact location. Sitting a wounded sheriff's deputy near one of the doorways during the approach would invariably raise questions that Alex couldn't answer. The pilot's voice filled his headset.

"Captain, I just received orders to return to base immediately. Breaking off the approach."

Alex felt the helicopter pitch right, exposing the entire lake through the port-side troop compartment door.

"Negative. My unit on the ground reports possible militia movement near the accident site. I need you to set us down as close as possible to their location," he said, nodding at Evans.

Evans tapped Sergeant Copeland's forearm, and the two Marines slid across the helicopter from their positions along the starboard hull, behind the copilot's seat. They started loosening McCulver's safety restraints.

"Captain, my orders are to bring everyone back to MOB Sanford. This is straight from the top," the pilot said, looking over his shoulder at the Marines huddled over McCulver. "Why are your Marines releasing our patient?"

"He needs some fresh air," said Alex, putting his hand out to stop the helicopter's crew chief from standing up. "We have this under control, Sergeant."

The crew chief looked around the helicopter at the scene unfolding, then glanced sharply at Alex.

"Is this a hijack situation?" he yelled over the wind buffeting the back of the cabin.

Alex withdrew his arm. "Not yet!"

Evans and Copeland manhandled McCulver into position next to Alex.

"Who is he?" yelled the crew chief.

"He's one of the prisoners captured at the airfield! Killed two rangers while impersonating a cop! Give me two more minutes of flight time!" said Alex. "It's important."

"Everything all right back there, Sergeant?" he heard over the headphones.

"Good to go, sir," the Air National Guard sergeant said, glaring at Alex. "I strongly suggest we give these devil dogs a quick aerial tour of the southeastern shore. Looks like they brought a guide to point out the more important features."

"Fuck, I knew something was off here. When we land, I want your team off my helicopter. This is bullshit," said the pilot.

"Fair enough. Just get us close to our target," said Alex, feeling the helicopter bank right.

"This better be a valid target, Captain, or we're out of here."

"We're hitting the suspected location of Eli Russell, the militia leader responsible for this morning's attack."

"4th Brigade's air cavalry already hit that target," said the pilot.

"They hit an abandoned site. Deputy Dog here provided a more current location."

"That's not a sheriff's deputy?"

"He's Eli Russell's second in command. Captured in the raid on the airfield. I'm borrowing him for a few hours, along with these Marines."

"No wonder the RRZ is frantic," said the pilot, starting their descent. "What are we up against on the ground? In case you haven't noticed, we're not armed for a combat mission."

"Unknown number of hostiles armed with semiautomatic rifles. We'll keep them busy during the approach and departure. Set us down as close to the objective as you feel comfortable."

"I see a nice flat spot right below us," said the pilot.

"Just a little further. Sorry to drag you and your crew into this," said Alex. "I'm going to transfer my headset to Deputy Dog, so he can guide you to the objective."

"Roger. I'll do what I can to get you close. Feet wet in one minute."

Alex removed his headset, leaning close to McCulver's face. "This better be fucking real, or you're going skydiving. Understand?"

McCulver nodded, and Alex slipped the headphone-equipped aircrew helmet over his bleeding head.

"Press this button to transmit," he said, placing McCulver's hand on the remote trigger hanging from the headset below his right shoulder.

"Staff Sergeant Evans! Get the gunners ready!"

Alex readied his own gear. The helicopter dropped toward the trees, banking left along Rangeley Lake's southeastern shoreline. A hand forcefully tapped his shoulder.

"Sir, the pilot thinks your target is that point jutting out into the lake! We'll make a two-hundred-foot, high-speed pass down the port side and look for an LZ!" yelled the crew chief.

Alex gave him a thumbs-up, then transmitted over his intrasquad radio, "Target coming up on the port side! Weapons hold until I give the order."

The two Marines next to McCulver nodded, shouldering their M27 Infantry Automatic Weapons. Alex leaned his head forward and located the spot where the gently curving shore protruded into the dark blue water. From this altitude, he couldn't see a break in the trees indicating the presence of a house or field, but that also meant Eli's people would have the same issue scanning the horizon to locate the helicopter.

The helicopter turned a few degrees to port, lining up for a pass directly over the point. As the trees approached, the outline of an open area appeared, starting at the neck of the landmass and extending to the roof of a massive cedar shingle, craftsman house situated on the water's edge. Alex leveled his rifle at the house as they passed, seeing nothing on the expansive deck facing the lake. A steep wooden staircase led from the deck to a dock and covered boathouse that contained a bow rider powerboat and three yellow kayaks. The house and dock disappeared when the helicopter banked left. The two Marines stationed in the doorway lowered their rifles slightly, each of them looking at Alex and shaking their heads.

"I didn't see anything through binoculars," said the crew chief. "We'll make a second run across the field in front of the house. Looks like plenty of room to set down."

The helicopter eased out of the turn, settling on a low-level run that would bring the front of the house down their port side.

"Six vehicles parked in front of the house. People in camouflage running toward the vehicles!" yelled the crew chief. "The pilot is widening his approach to open the distance."

Alex passed the information to the Marines and steadied his rifle. The helicopter swayed right and slowed as it crossed the field. Through his ACOG scope, he spotted four men headed for the vehicles parked fifty feet from the house, all of them carrying military-style rifles. The helicopter rapidly drifted toward the far end of the clearing, seconds away from reaching the water.

"Weapons identified. Request permission to engage," said one of the gunners.

"Stand by," Alex said, grabbing the crew chief's binoculars and shoving them into McCulver's face. "I need a positive ID on someone!"

McCulver stared through the binoculars for a moment. "Roland Byrd! He's one of the squad leaders."

"Weapons free!" Alex yelled through the cabin, flipping the selector switch on his rifle to automatic.

The cabin exploded in a discordance of gunfire. The Marine gunners fired repeated short bursts of automatic fire from their M27s. Pressing the trigger rapidly, Alex tried to keep the scope's bouncing reticle on the torso of a man next to a black SUV. A red cloud burst behind the man's head after the hail of bullets shifted across the windshield and found their target. A crack passed through the compartment, followed by the distinctive, repetitive clang of bullets hitting metal. The helicopter tilted forward and surged over the trees, robbing them of targets. He turned to the crew chief.

"Tell the pilot to put us down at the entrance to the clearing! I don't want any of the cars getting off the point! We don't know if Eli is here!"

A few seconds later, the helicopter banked hard left, causing everyone to grab on to something bolted to the helicopter. Alex let his rifle hang by its sling and put an arm around McCulver, whose legs dangled freely over the edge. He caught the staff sergeant's eye as the helicopter leveled.

"Tempting!" he said, pulling McCulver toward the cockpit, where the assault team secured him to the fixed medical litter with zip ties.

The crew chief grabbed him while he repositioned. "Tell your gunners to concentrate on the ground level of the house during the approach. There's an automatic weapon in one of the windows. This is a one-shot deal."

"Just get us low enough to jump!" said Alex.

"Team, we're on final approach. Assault team exits on the port side. Out the door in less than two seconds. Starboard-side gunners, concentrate your fire on the ground floor. Possible automatic weapon in one of the windows or doors. Starboard gunners stay with the helicopter and provide cover for their departure."

"Ten seconds!" yelled the crew chief.

Alex reloaded his rifle, mentally counting the seconds. He'd exchanged rifle magazines and reached seven when the starboard-side automatic rifles erupted, tearing into the windows partially obscured by the home's wraparound porch. A red pickup truck lurched forward, speeding down the dirt road and closing the distance to the helicopter.

"Concentrate all fire on that vehicle!" said Alex, sliding past the crew chief to help.

The two gunners tracked the moving target with short bursts of fire, and the road exploded around the truck. Alex canted his rifle and lined up the iron sights with the hood, hoping to lead the target enough to send all of his bullets into the front seat. The rifle bucked repeatedly against his shoulder. The pickup truck's tires exploded, and the windshield disintegrated from the concentrated fire of three rifles. The red vehicle swerved off the road and rolled to a stop, smoke pouring out of the crumpled hood, its lifeless driver visible through the shattered passenger-side window.

"Time to go, sir!" yelled the crew chief, pulling him away from the starboard opening.

Alex followed the last Marine out the door, jumping several feet to the hard-packed road. Bullets snapped past as the helicopter rapidly climbed out of the way, heading for the cover of the eastern tree line. The Marines wasted no time sprinting for the remnants of a crumbling rock wall fifty feet in the direction of the house. Several closely spaced cracks exploded overhead, confirming the crew chief's warning about an automatic weapon. They slammed into the knee-high pile of rocks, bullets striking all around them. He crawled next to Evans, keeping his head well below the rocks.

"Hit the house with 40 mike-mike until the incoming automatic fire stops, then move your men forward," he said, as another burst of gunfire whipped overhead. "I'll see if I can find your target."

"Copeland, Derren, 40 mike-mike at the windows. Now! Kennedy, Bradley, put the targets hiding behind the vehicles out of business," said Evans, pulling a gold-tipped 40mm grenade from the Velcro pouch attached to his tactical vest.

Alex crawled along the stones until he reached a break in the wall. He nestled the vertical fore grip against a rock and scanned the house through his scope. All of the ground-floor windows were partially broken or missing. Gunfire reached his ears, immediately followed by stone fragments and dirt striking his face.

"Leftmost bottom window!" he said, lining up his scope's reticle with the corner of the house.

He fired steadily until he heard three nearly simultaneous thumps from the Marines' M320 grenade launchers. A few seconds passed before the high-explosive, dual-purpose grenades struck the house. The first projectile hit the roof of the porch, penetrating several inches before exploding the overhang above the corner window. The second and third grenades hit milliseconds later, passing through the shingle siding under the porch roof and detonating inside the house. The three windows spaced evenly to the left of the front door ejected a cloud of wood fragments and drywall twenty feet into the front yard.

With the automatic weapon neutralized, the M27 gunners tore into the bullet-riddled silver sedan hiding two men. A short burst of automatic fire knocked one of the men into the open, where he dropped to his hands and knees. A second burst stitched across the side of his torso, collapsing him in a cloud of dust.

"Hold your fire!" yelled Alex, spotting two empty hands held palms forward through the car's missing windows.

"Hold your fire!" repeated the Marines, up and down the rock wall.

"How far away are the cars? Rough guess."

"One hundred yards."

"All right. Here's the plan," he said, talking loudly enough for the entire team to hear. "We're gonna move up with Kennedy and Bradley covering the front of the house with their M27s. We'll move them up after we secure the prisoner and clear the house. Ten seconds. Do not fire on the man behind the vehicle unless he presents a weapon. Clear?"

"Clear, sir," they responded.

"Reload and get ready," he said, dropping the magazine from his rifle and stuffing it in one of his cargo pockets.

The Marines reloaded their weapons and inched forward against the rocks, waiting for his signal. Alex pushed off the ground and jumped over the wall, motioning for them to follow with his left hand. He wanted to be the first Marine over the wall, in case a sniper watched them from the house or trees, but he also needed a head start. Most of the Marines in the battalion were twenty years younger than Alex, and he didn't want to arrive at the cars embarrassingly far behind the rest of his team.

Halfway across the field, the Marines overtook him, yelling for the lone survivor to step into the open with his hands above his head. He arrived a few seconds after the first marine, sliding between the leftmost cars and scanning the front of the house. Dark gray smoke poured out of the windows on the ground level, indicating a secondary fire caused by the grenades. A quick look at the second floor showed a few broken windows, with all of the shades closed. He turned to Evans.

"Keep the M27s in place at the rock wall. I don't think we'll get the chance to clear the house."

Evans nodded, grabbing the zip-tied prisoner delivered by Corporal Derren and shoving him to his knees against the black SUV's hanging bumper. Alex approached the scruffy, bearded man, who spit a combination of dirt and blood onto the ground, keeping his head low. He squatted and used his rifle barrel to lift the man's face.

"Look at me, you piece of shit. Is Eli here?"

"No," he croaked, shaking his head and avoiding eye contact.

We beat him here?

Alex didn't think it was possible. The Matvee's navigation software calculated the driving distance between Limerick and Rangeley Lake to be one hundred twenty-nine miles, roughly three hours utilizing the most obvious roads north. He doubted Eli would take a predictable route, so he adjusted the course through rural western Maine and added another thirty minutes to the trip. Eli should be here, unless he drove straight to Charlie's place.

"Have you seen him this morning? Feel free to expand your answer beyond yes or no," Alex said, jamming the barrel into the soft spot above his trachea.

The man coughed. "He left about fifteen minutes ago with the other half of the squad. Two cars."

"Do you know where he was headed?" said Alex, moving the rifle barrel to his forehead.

He closed his eyes and shook his head, "No. He drove in and sped off. Said he'd be back later this afternoon."

Eli wasn't wasting any time.

"He said that?"

"Yes."

"Later this afternoon. Exact words," said Alex.

"Exact words. Are you gonna kill me?"

"I haven't decided yet," he said, watching the man's eyes tear up. "Do you have a way to get in touch with Eli?"

"Handheld channel 11, subcode 33. If he asks you to jump stations, go to channel 14, subcode 21."

Evans wrote the codes on the top of his wrist with a black marker. "Got it."

"Is there anyone left in the house?"

"I don't know. Ron had the drum-fed AR. He stayed behind to cover us."

"I think it's safe to say Ron is out of the picture. How many more?"

"Five."

"You better hope the math works out," said Alex, pressing the barrel against the man's left eye. "We should have four bodies, Staff Sergeant. I see one to the left of this SUV and at least one in the pickup that tried to escape."

"Pretty sure there's two more over here," said Evans, scooting to the far right vehicle and poking his head over the hood. "Two dead!"

"That makes five. Where are the keys to these cars?"

"I have the keys to the Honda over there," he said, tilting his head to the left. "Everyone had different keys. The plan was to split up."

"We'll start searching the bodies, sir," said Evans.

Alex stood. "Roger that, Staff Sergeant. I want to be on the road in two minutes, assuming we didn't disable every car in the lot."

"We'll figure it out, sir," Evans said, mustering the Marines.

Alex yanked the prisoner to his feet by his shirt. "I need one of your radios."

"Byrd had the squad's radio," he said.

Alex shrugged his shoulders. "Which one is Byrd?"

The prisoner nodded at the bullet-riddled red pickup truck burning in the middle of the field.

"That figures," said Alex, rubbing his face.

"Sir?" said the prisoner, still avoiding eye contact.

"Yes?"

"I assume you're using a PRC-153 radio to communicate with your squad?"

"Go on," said Alex.

"Your radio is basically a spiffed-up version of Motorola's XTS-2500 line. It can access the same UHF frequencies used by Eli's radio, with the same coding functionalities. I used to work at the Radio Shack in Windham."

The black SUV behind them roared to life, startling the prisoner. He dropped to his knees, pleading for his life. The gray, four-door sedan to the left of the SUV started next, followed by the pickup next to it. A rifle stock punched through the milky-white windshield, knocking hundreds of safety glass particles onto the hood and dashboard. Staff Sergeant Evans dragged his rifle over the dashboard and grinned.

"I think we're ready to roll, sir. Is he coming with us?"

Alex kicked the prisoner's feet, gaining his immediate attention.

"If you can show me how to access those UHF channels, I promise we'll slow to ten miles per hour before we toss you out of the car. Deal?"

The terrified man nodded.

"He'll be along for part of the ride."

Chapter 45

EVENT +21 Days

Belgrade, Maine

Alex raised a hand to cut down on the gale-force wind battering his face between the front headrests. At least he wasn't in one of the front seats. He'd eaten his lifetime quota of bugs on the way to Boston in Ed's Jeep. Boston felt a lifetime away.

"Take a right after that collapsed barn," said Alex. "That should be North Pond Road."

He picked up the computer tablet on the seat next to him and checked the map, making sure this turn was correct. They couldn't afford the slightest delay. Despite the severely unsafe speeds endured during the Grand Prix-style, sixty-seven-mile drive between Rangeley Lake and Charlie's lake house, Alex's convoy didn't have a shot at catching up with Eli. A twenty-minute head start guaranteed Eli would arrive first. He just hoped Kennedy's driving had closed enough of the time gap to catch Eli in the planning or surveillance phase of his attack. If Eli opted to skip the prudent course of action and drove his Bronco right through Charlie's front door, the Marines might arrive too late.

"North Pond Road, sir! Hang on!" said Private First

Class Kennedy, yanking the steering wheel right.

The oversized SUV skidded into the turn, barely slowing as it fishtailed toward a utility pole on the other side of the crumbly asphalt road. Alex dropped the tablet in his lap and braced himself. The tires screeched, and the wooden post loomed in the rear driver's side window. The SUV's tires quickly regained traction, propelling them forward. The utility pole swiftly disappeared behind them in a cloud of dust, and Kennedy floored the accelerator. He twisted in his seat, peering through the rear cargo hatch window. The pickup truck and sedan carrying the rest of his team slid into the turn, successfully emerging from the dust cloud unscathed.

"One point two miles to the turn onto Crane Road. Let's slow down for that one so we don't alert the entire lake," said Alex, patting Kennedy on the shoulder.

"Got it, sir," said Kennedy, flashing two thumbs-up from the steering wheel.

"I can't imagine we're too far behind him, sir. Not with Formula One's driving," said Evans, shaking his head. "They're probably still sitting around tying their boots and adjusting their gear."

Alex nodded. "I don't think he'll wait around too long. He knows exactly what he's up against."

"Which is why I doubt he'll rush the process. He's facing some of the same folks that kicked his ass the last time."

"I hope you're right, Staff Sergeant," Alex said, focused on the computer tablet.

One mile until we find out.

He thought about the layout of Charlie's cottage. The 800-square-foot A-frame's first floor was an open-concept design with floor-to-ceiling windows facing the lake. A spiral staircase situated in the middle of the house led to a suspended loft. Front to back, the only closed room in the house was the bathroom, which was located behind the kitchen next to the pantry. Two small windows and a door adorned the street-facing side of the house, which mostly shielded them from direct observation, but also restricted their view of the most logical approach. The steep roofed sides of the A-frame design came down to the ground, creating wide blind spots next to the house. From a tactical perspective, Charlie couldn't have chosen a more difficult house to defend. Now Alex understood why Eli only brought half of the militia squad. Eli could effectively surround the structure by taking up positions on opposing sides of the house.

The only feature of the house that might work in his friends' advantage was the cellar. Robert Duhaime never set foot in the house, and cellars were not a common feature in lake houses, unless you were a prepper. Charlie had insisted on buying a plot of land high enough above the water table to dig a suitable cellar to store his supplies. With a little warning, they could take shelter underground and keep Eli at bay. Part of him wanted to fire an entire magazine out of the window at the trees, hoping that the gunfire might warn them of the impending danger, but he knew this might also warn Eli. With a threat at his back, Eli's best chance of survival was to attack immediately and secure hostages. If he hadn't killed them already.

His decision to attack Eli at Rangeley Lake put his friends at risk. The choice had been clouded by a selfish desire to put an end to this once and for all. He just hadn't counted on losing the helicopter and missing Eli by twenty minutes. The RRZ's return to base directive had arrived at the worst possible moment. He didn't have time to consider how they would reach Charlie's if they missed Eli.

He glanced past Kennedy's arm at the speedometer. Ninety miles per hour. Several seconds later, they passed a long, tree-wrapped gravel road, which satellite imagery showed to be the last driveway on their right before the Crane Road turnoff. He'd know really soon whether the decision to take the helicopter to Rangeley had been a mistake he'd live with for the rest of his life.

"Start slowing down. The turn is five hundred feet on the left. It's the only turn showing on the map," he said, lurching forward in his seat from the car's immediate deceleration.

"All stations, prepare for dismount. Coming up on the turn," said Evans over the squad radio.

"I got it," said Kennedy. "Green street sign right next to the utility pole."

"Let's try to miss that pole, Kennedy," said Alex, searching the woods surrounding the turn. "Looks clear."

"And I don't hear any shooting," added Evans. "We need to roll in quietly. Take the turn extra slow, Kennedy."

The Marine nodded, gently easing the SUV onto a smooth asphalt road flanked by signs announcing "Private Road. Dead End." They cruised past the signs, slipping into the shadows cast by the tall pines bordering the road. Alex slid across the rear bench seat to the driver's side and angled his rifle out of the window. The tires crackled over acorns, twigs and pebbles strewn across the asphalt, each sound exploding in Alex's ears.

"We're looking for a black Bronco and a red Chevy Tahoe," said Alex.

"Or seven guys in woodland camouflage with rifles," said Evans.

"That too," said Alex, peering through the trees.

He risked a quick glance at the computer tablet, gauging their progress.

"The road angles to the right, then goes straight about two hundred feet until it splits. We go left at the split, carefully," said Alex.

"Copy, sir," whispered Kennedy.

"Why are you whispering?" said Alex.

"Because you're whispering, sir."

Alex felt the SUV change direction, turning slightly right.

"I see the split," said Evans. "No sign of Eli's vehicles. Still quiet."

"Take the turn as close to the left side of the road as possible, Kennedy," said Alex, leaning over to view the turn.

He caught a sparkle between the trees and a few slivers of blue. Patches of North Bay widened as they approached the "T" intersection. Kennedy skirted the right side of the road and executed a gradual, shallow left turn, cutting the corner as close to the shoulder as possible. The tactic minimized the car's exposure before Evans had a chance to scan the road.

"Red SUV ahead. Two hundred feet. Facing north," said Evans, settling in behind his rifle.

"Stop!" said Alex, hitting Kennedy on the shoulder and sliding to the middle. "What about Eli's Bronco?"

"Hold on," said Evans, staring intensely through the ACOG scope on his rifle. "Got it. Black SUV in front of the Tahoe. No passenger movement."

"The house is another two hundred feet past Eli's

vehicles. Time to dismount," said Alex, pushing the door open and jumping into the road.

Sustained machine-gun fire shattered the quiet, followed by the sporadic pop-pop of semiautomatic fire. Alex dropped to the road and rolled next to the SUV, just as a shorter burst of automatic fire ripped through the lakeside community. Evans leaned out of his window.

"They're firing at the house!"

Alex pushed off the ground, crouching behind the door. Another long, staccato burst echoed through the street, devoid of the telltale hisses and cracks.

Shit!

"Drive!" he screamed, hopping into the car.

They roared past Eli's Bronco, as long bursts of automatic fire continued.

We're too late.

Based on the feeble level of return fire, he doubted many of his friends had survived the initial fusillade.

"Dismount! Take your Marines down the road on foot and push through the yard. Weapons free!"

Before Kennedy hit the brakes, Alex pushed off the seat in front of him and leapt out of the SUV, skidding across the shoulder into the bushes on the right side of the road. Without pausing, he lurched forward, breaking through the dense brush and tumbling onto a well-manicured lawn. He scrambled to his feet and sprinted for the thick wall of evergreens that marked the boundary of Charlie's property, cringing with every devastating burst of rifle fire.

"Staff Sergeant, you got anything on the road?" said Alex, his rifle barrel entering the wall of pine needles.

"Negative. We're almost in position in front of the house."

"Advise when ready. I'm entering the bushes on the right side of the property. Out."

The gunfire stopped, dropping a heavy silence over the yard. Gunfire meant his friends were still in the fight.

Please. No.

Alex shouldered his rifle, advancing cautiously in the face of the unbearable silence. When a few seconds passed without another shot, he stopped in the middle of the evergreen hedge and switched his squad radio to the first frequency programmed by the militia prisoner. He needed to distract Eli long enough to save anyone left alive in the house. It was all he could do at this point.

"Eli, I'm going to kill you just like your piece of shit brother and nephew," hissed Alex. "Make a bullet in the head a new Russell family tradition."

"Good luck with that."

The bush in front of him exploded, discharging a bloodied man in camouflage.

Charlie!

He collided with Alex, knocking them both to the lawn under bullets snapping through the branches. The sound of sustained automatic gunfire kept Alex pressed to the ground while the man desperately clawed at the grass beside him to get away. Alex twisted onto his side and reached out to calm Charlie, his hand knocking a Motorola radio out of the way. *What the*—Eli Russell stared back at him, stunned for moment, before his blood-splattered face morphed into a demented grin.

"You!" he screamed, flipping onto his back and fumbling with the pistol holster on his belt.

Alex rolled onto Eli, jamming his left hand against the top of the holster while driving his knee into his groin. Eli bellowed and planted his left foot under Alex's lower abdomen, propelling Alex into the evergreen bushes. He tripped over the sturdy branches of a dwarf spruce and crashed to the ground, smashing the back of his helmet against a landscaping boulder. The blow left him stunned, until the first bullets from Eli's gun whipped through the pine boughs, passing inches overhead.

Alex rolled to his right in a desperate attempt to evade the storm of bullets chasing him. He collided with a tree trunk as Eli crashed through the bushes, screaming and firing his pistol until the slide locked back. One of the .45-caliber bullets struck the top of Alex's helmet, snapping his head backward against the ground. The second bullet pounded his upper sternum—one inch below the top of the Dragon Skin vest. The impacts stopped him cold, freezing him in place for the kill shot. Eli crouched a few feet away, quickly reloading the pistol's magazine and leveling it at Alex's face.

"What were you saying about my brother?"

Alex kicked his right foot in an arc over his body, hitting the pistol but failing to knock it out of Eli's grip. Eli backed up and extended the pistol forward, his eyes darting nervously to the left. A rifle barrel protruded through the bushes, hovering inches from Eli's temple. A single, point-blank shot snapped Eli's head sideways. His body remained upright for a moment, then crumpled to the ground next to the dwarf spruce, a bright crimson fountain pulsing skyward from the neat hole punched through his head. Charlie limped into the open, keeping his AR-15 aimed at Eli's motionless body. A Marine shouldering a bipod-equipped M27 burst through the bushes a fraction of a second later, sweeping the smoking barrel left and right for targets.

Corporal Almeda? He'd stayed behind in the helicopter,

or so Alex thought.

"Hostile is down. Say again. Hostile is down," said the marine, crouching over Alex. "That was stupid, Mr. Thornton. You all right, Captain?"

"The rest of your squad is hidden along the road," he rasped, still struggling to breathe from the sternum shot.

"Copy that, sir," said the marine, activating his microphone. "Friendlies on road in front of the house. Hold fire. I repeat. Hold fire."

Charlie kneeled next to him, slowly shaking his head. "What the hell happened to you?"

"What the fuck hasn't happened to me?" Alex grumbled, clasping Charlie's hand. "Is everyone all right?"

"Ed fell off the deck trying to follow me. He's the only casualty I'm aware of."

"I'm fine, jackass!" said Ed, hobbling stiff-legged into view. "You knocked me down the stairs."

"You were moving too slow!" said Charlie. "Everyone's fine. We moved the kids into the cellar after the Marines arrived."

Alex stared quizzically at Almeda. "How did you pull that off, Corporal?"

"You owe that crew chief a few bottles of something expensive," said the Marine. "He convinced the pilots to drop us off at the second set of coordinates."

Staff Sergeant Evans squeezed between the bushes next to Alex, his eyes drawn to the blood-soaked corpse on the ground.

"Is that him?"

"That's him," said Alex, staring at Eli's lifeless, bloodshot eyes.

"I'll snap some pictures so they can confirm his ID," said Evans. "Almeda, escort these gentlemen back into the house until we secure the perimeter. I don't want any surprises."

"Affirmative."

"I got them, Staff Sergeant," said Alex, using Ed's hand to pull himself up.

"You got us?" said Ed. "I'm losing track of the number of times we've saved *your* ass."

"Me too," said Alex, brushing off the pine needles. "I don't know what I'll do without you guys watching over me."

An awkward silence enveloped the group.

"There's an empty house at the end of the road. The owners live in Hartford. Doubt we'll ever see them," said Charlie. "We can make it work up here—together."

Alex unfastened the nylon straps against his chin and removed the three-pound ballistic helmet, accepting the sun's warm rays on his face. He liked the sound of that.

Together.

"Does the other house have more than one toilet?" asked Alex, raising an eyebrow.

Charlie and Ed broke into laughter, knocking down more of the wall Alex had spent the past six years building around him. He flipped the selector switch on his rifle to "safe," and clipped the helmet to the side of his vest.

"Can't be any worse than a thirty-eight-foot sailboat," said Ed.

Alex smiled, shaking his head. "I'll be the judge of that."

Chapter 46

EVENT + 22 Days

Penobscot Bay, Maine

A crisp, north Atlantic gust penetrated his jacket, providing a stark reminder of the family's decision. Instead of warm trade winds and endless summer days, they unanimously decided to steer the *Katelyn Ann* north, toward a bitter cold winter in Belgrade, Maine, relieved to keep the sturdy bonds of hard-earned friendship intact. Doubts still lingered about the Federal Recovery Plan's long-term impact on New England, but they all agreed that northern Maine provided adequate geographical isolation to keep them out of harm's way for the immediate future.

Alex raised the binoculars hanging from his neck and scanned the wispy fog ahead for the signs of Belfast harbor. His handheld GPS receiver indicated they were less than a nautical mile from the town docks. White specks materialized in the distance, announcing the outer edge of Belfast's extensive mooring field. From what he could tell, the field was intact, untouched by the wall of water that had devastated coastal facilities further south in Casco Bay.

Sailing the *Katelyn Ann* out of Yarmouth through petroleum-covered inner Casco Bay had reintroduced

Alex to the extent of the tsunami's damage. Marinas and town facilities they'd frequented on family sailing trips had been wiped out of existence, now marked by little more than bobbing clusters of discarded boats, heavy debris and the occasional decayed body. Alex steered them as far away from land as possible until they passed Monhegan Island, where he pointed the bow in a northeasterly direction for the transit into Penobscot Bay.

He tracked a steady flow of merchant vessels and petroleum carriers headed in the same direction, maintaining a cautious distance from the behemoths. The sight of inbound maritime traffic was encouraging, signaling the first real steps toward recovery he had seen since the morning of the event. The unusual volume of ships plying the bay's restricted waters meant one thing: Searsport's Intermodal Cargo Terminal had power and was open for business. Good news since petroleum and durable goods reaching Searsport could be transported by pipeline and truck to points south, easing recovery efforts in the most damaged areas of New England.

As the field of swaying sailboat masts came into focus ahead, the familiar deep growl of a throttling lobster boat reached him. Scanning the mist, he spotted the ancient wooden contraption cutting across the bay for open water and its crustacean harvest. On the surface, Belfast harbor appeared unchanged in the wake of the disaster. Alex knew better, but seeing the waterfront emerge unscathed gave him hope. He'd seen nothing but one devastated harbor after another on the trip up the coast.

"Mom, bring the kids topside!" said Alex. "We're getting close."

Amy Fletcher appeared through the open cabin hatch. "How close?"

"Ten minutes from tie up."

"That close?" she said, climbing into the cockpit and peering over the ripped dodger. "Belfast looks completely untouched," she said.

"On the outside. It's a different story behind every door. We need to offload as quickly as possible and get out of here. Two vehicles and a loaded trailer are bound to attract attention."

"What about the boat?" she said.

"I'll find an empty mooring and do a ten-minute winter prep. Throw a little fuel stabilizer in the diesel tank. Pump the water from the lines and run a jug of antifreeze through the system. Same with the engine. If we need to leave, we can have the boat running in less than two minutes."

"We won't need to do that. I have a good feeling about this," said his mom.

"Me too, Mom, but it's always good to have options."

"I'll leave you to your options while I get the kids up to help," she said, climbing below deck to send the kids topside.

Alex pulled back on the stainless steel throttle lever, slowing the sailboat for their transit through the crowded mooring field. Most of the boats appeared empty, devoid of the telltale signs of a cruising family or couple: towels and bathing suits draped over the boom, or dinghies swinging lazily from a line tied off to an aft cleat. Occasionally, a head peeked through a hatch or appeared in a cabin window. He wondered if they had been there since the day of the event or if they had fled north seeking refuge. Either way, they couldn't stay on the water much longer.

Studying the rapidly developing image of Belfast's

waterfront in his binoculars, he spotted the first marina on the edge of town. He'd arranged to meet Kate at the first dock that could handle a five-foot draft at low tide. Extending a few hundred feet into the harbor from a concrete pier at the end of a dirt parking lot, the slips looked full—and Kate was nowhere in sight. He struggled with a rising sense of anxiety. He'd been out of radio contact with Kate for more than a day. A lot could happen in a day.

The decision to join the Walkers and Thorntons in Belgrade came with a few logistical requirements, which they decided should be handled by splitting up in Yarmouth. The most critical necessity was food. They had stocked the boat with a two-month supply of dehydrated food packets and MREs, which represented more than enough sustenance to reach South America, but nowhere close to the amount required to survive a Maine winter. The earliest they could expect to start eating modestly from a garden was mid-June. Nine months. He came up with a plan, utilizing the Marines, to transport the rest of their long-term food stores from Limerick to Belgrade.

Since Alex needed to keep a low profile in southern Maine, he agreed to take the sailboat north, ferrying the younger kids and his mother to the Belfast harbor. Kate, Tim and Ryan split up between the two vehicles in Yarmouth and returned to the compound in Limerick. With Lieutenant Colonel Grady's blessing, Alex had arranged for the Marines at FOB Lakeside to stuff two Matvees with most of the remaining dry foods in their basement. Additional survival gear, ammunition and domestic supplies would be packed in the two SUVs, which would join the convoy of tactical vehicles headed north. Grady justified the deployment of the Matvees to recover his "stranded" Marines.

Alex scanned the dock again, still not seeing any signs of human activity. She was probably at the next dock. At the far left of his visual field, a car door opened in the parking lot. Two figures ran across the concrete pier, waving with both hands as they sprinted down a steep metal ramp toward the floats. They stopped three-quarters of the way down the dock, jumping up and down to draw his attention. The empty slip appeared as soon as he cleared the last cluster of boats in the mooring field. He lowered the binoculars and steered toward the dock, curious and eager to start a long chapter with his new Band of Brothers—as long as it didn't involve sharing a bathroom.

Epilogue

EVENT +45 Days

Main Operating Base "Sanford"
Regional Recovery Zone 1

Lieutenant Colonel Grady pressed orange earplugs into his ears and muttered a few obscenities. The noise from the C-17 Globemaster III's massive quad turbofan engines cut through the foam as the beast taxied in front of the battalion's hangar and stopped. The table vibrated under his laptop computer, and papers started to flap on the clipboards fixed to the tables.

"Sergeant Major!" he said, standing up and knocking his chair back. "Close the hangar doors."

According to the air operations task list, MOB Sanford had twelve hours of continuous heavy airlift scheduled, which guaranteed one of these noisemakers parked right in front of his TOC for the rest of the day. When the last hangar door clanged against the concrete hangar deck, he risked removing one of the foam earplugs. It was better. Sort of. The high-pitched scream of the engine had been replaced by the rattle of the metal bay doors, which he could tolerate. He turned his attention to the computer screen and read today's tasking report, shaking his head. Maybe Alex had the right idea.

020245Z OCT 19
FM NSC WASHDC IMMEDIATE
TO DIRECTOR FEDREC/HOMELAND WASHDC
INFO RRZ AUTHGOV IMMEDIATE
INFO RRZ MILCOMMAND
SECRET NOFORN SECTION 1 OF 1 WASHDC
DECL: NDA
FEDRECBULLETIN
SUBJECT: TASKREP OCT19
GENTEXT/REMARKS/
1. URGENT//RECALL INITIATED 010001Z OCT 19 FOR ALL FORWARD DEPLOYED MILITARY COMPONENTS OF FOLLOWING UNIFIED COMMANDS: A. USCENTCOM B. USPACOM C. USEUCOM D. USAFRICOM. RETURNING UNITS WILL BE REDEPLOYED IAW CATEGORY FIVE PROTOCOLS WHEN 80 PERCENT READINESS ACHIEVED. ESTIMATED REDEPLOYMENT DATE FOR PHASE ONE RECALL UNITS 010001Z DEC 19. ESTIMATES ON LATER PHASES TBA.
ACTION//START PROCESS OF EXPANDING FOOTPRINT WITHIN RRZ TO EMPLOY UNITS. PRIORITY TO SECURITY AND HUMANITARIAN MISSION.
2. HIGH PRIORITY//INFRASTRUCTURE REPAIR BELOW EXPECTED LEVELS. ACTION//EXPEDITE IDENTIFICATION OF KEY CRITICAL PERSONNEL FOR REPLACEMENT/REPAIR OF TRANSFORMERS AND LOCAL LEVEL ELECTRICAL GRID SUPPORT EQUIPMENT.

ACTION//SUBMIT CRITICAL TRANSFORMER REPLACEMENT REQUESTS TO FEDREC/HOMELAND DIRECTLY. SEE PRIORITY TABLES IN FEDRECINST1057.3B
3. HIGH PRIORITY//DOMESTIC TERRORISM EXPECTED TO INCREASE IN NORTHERN LATITUDE RRZS AS WEATHER DETERIORATES.
ACTION//EXPEDITE EXPANSION OF REFUGEE CAMP SYSTEM BEYOND CURRENT AUTHORIZED CAPACITY.
ACTION//INITIATE FRONT LOADING NUTRITION PROGRAMS WITHIN CAMP SYSTEM TO ENCOURAGE COMPLIANCE AND PARTICIPATION IS AUTHORIZED. USE OF LONG TERM FOOD RESERVES IS AUTHORIZED. DO NOT EXCEED 70 PERCENT INVENTORY DEPLETION LEVELS WITHOUT APPROVAL FROM FEDREC/HOMELAND.
4. PRIORITY//COMMUNICATIONS BANDWIDTH EXPECTED TO DECREASE WITH CONTINUED LOSS OF LOW EARTH ORBIT SATELLITES DUE TO ANTI-SATTELITE MISSILE ATTACKS BY PRC.
ACTION//IMPLEMENT SATELLITE DATA COMMUNICATION RESTRICTIONS ALPHA THRU DELTA EFFECTIVE 030001Z OCT19.
5. PRIORITY//HUMANITARIAN AIRLIFT FROM EUROPE EXPECTED TO CEASE WITHIN NEXT FIVE TO TEN DAYS. MILITARY PRESSURE FROM RUSSIAN FEDERATION INVASION OF FORMER SATELLITE NATIONS

CITED BY EUROPEAN COUNCIL AS PRIMARY REASON. CHINESE ECONOMIC PRESSURE SUSPECTED TO PLAY A SECONDARY ROLE.
ACTION//REFOCUS CURRENT HUMANITARIAN AID MATERIALS TO TASKS CRITICAL TO SECURITY.
BT#3459
NNNN

***
*

Acronyms and Terminology Used in *The Alex Fletcher Books*

ACOG – Advanced Combat Optical Gunsight. A telescopic scope commonly issued to troops in the field.

ACU – Army Combat Uniform

AFES – Automated Fire Extinguishing System

AFV Stryker – Armored Fighting Vehicle used by U.S. Army

AN/VRC-110 – Vehicle based VHF/UHF capable radio system used by U.S. Marine Corps.

AR-10 – 7.62mm NATO/.308 caliber, military style rifle

AR-15 – 5.56mm/.223 caliber military style rifle

BCT – Brigade Combat Team, U.S. Army

Black Hawk – UH-60, Medium Lift, Utility Helicopter

CISA – Critical Infrastructure Skills Assembly

CQB – Close Quarters Battle, urban combat

CH-47 Chinook – Twin engine, tandem rotor, heavy lift helicopter

CIC – Combat Information Center

CONEX – Intermodal Shipping Container. Large metal crates typically seen stacked on merchant ships or in shipping yards.

C-130 – Propeller driven, heavy lift fixed wind aircraft capable of short landings and takeoffs.

C-17B Globemaster – Heavy Lift, fixed wing aircraft

C2BMC – Command, Control, Battle Management and Communications

DRASH – Deployable, Rapid Assembly Shelter

DTCS – Distributed Tactical Communication System (satellite based network)

EMP – Electromagnetic Pulse

ETA – Estimated Time of Arrival

FEMA – Federal Emergency Management Agency

FOB – Forward Operating Base

GPS – Global Positioning System, satellite based

GPNVG-18 – Panoramic night vision goggles, wide field of vision.

HAM radio – Term used to describe the Amateur Radio network

HBMD – Homeland Ballistic Missile Defense

HESCO – Rapidly deployable earth filled defensive barrier

HK416 – 5.56mm Assault rifle/carbine designed by Hechler & Koch.

Humvee – Nickname for High Mobility Multipurpose Wheeled Vehicle (HMMWV).

IED – Improvised Explosive Device

KIA – Killed in Action

L-ATV – Light Combat Tactical All Terrain Vehicle

LP/OP – Listening Post/Observation Post

MARPAT – Marine Pattern, digital camouflage used by U.S. Marine Corps

M-ATV – Medium Combat Tactical All Terrain Vehicle. MRAP

Medevac – Medical Evacuation

MOB – Main Operating Base

MP – Military Police

MP-7 – Personal Defense Weapon designed by Heckler and Koch, submachine gun firing armor penetrating ammunition

MRAP – Mine Resistant Ambush Protected vehicle

MRE – Meals Ready to Eat, self-contained field rations used by U.S. military

MR556SD – 5.56mm assault rifle/carbine with integrated suppressor.

MTV M1078 – Medium Tactical Vehicle used by U.S. Army, 5 ton capacity

MTVR Mk23 – Medium Tactical Vehicle Replacement used by U.S. Marine Corps, 7 ton capacity

M1919A6 – .30 caliber, belt fed medium machine gun fielded during WWII and the Korean War. Fully automatic.

M240G – Modern 7.62mm, belt fed medium machine gun used by U.S Army and U.S. Marine Corps

M27 IAR – Heavier barrel version of the HK416 used by U.S. Marine Corps. Replaced the M249 belt fed machine gun. Issued to one member of each fire team.

M320 – Rifle-mounted, detachable 40mm grenade launcher.

NCO – Non-Commissioned Officer (Corporal and Sergeant)

NEO – Near Earth Object (asteroid or meteorite)

NVD – Night Vision Device (used interchangeable with NVG)

NVG – Night Vision Goggles

PRC-153 ISR – Intra-squad radio. Motorola style radio (usually strapped to tactical vest) for squad communication.

ROTAC – Tactical Satellite Radio

RTB – Return to Base

Satphone – Satellite Phone

SNCO – Staff Non-Commissioned Officer (Staff Sergeant E-6 and above)

SUV – Sport Utility Vehicle

Two-Forty – M240 machine gun. See M240G

UH-60 Black Hawk – Medium Lift, Utility Helicopter

YCRB – York County Readiness Brigade. Harrison Campbell's group.

Complete the saga with the final installment:

DISPATCHES

Book 5 of the Alex Fletcher series

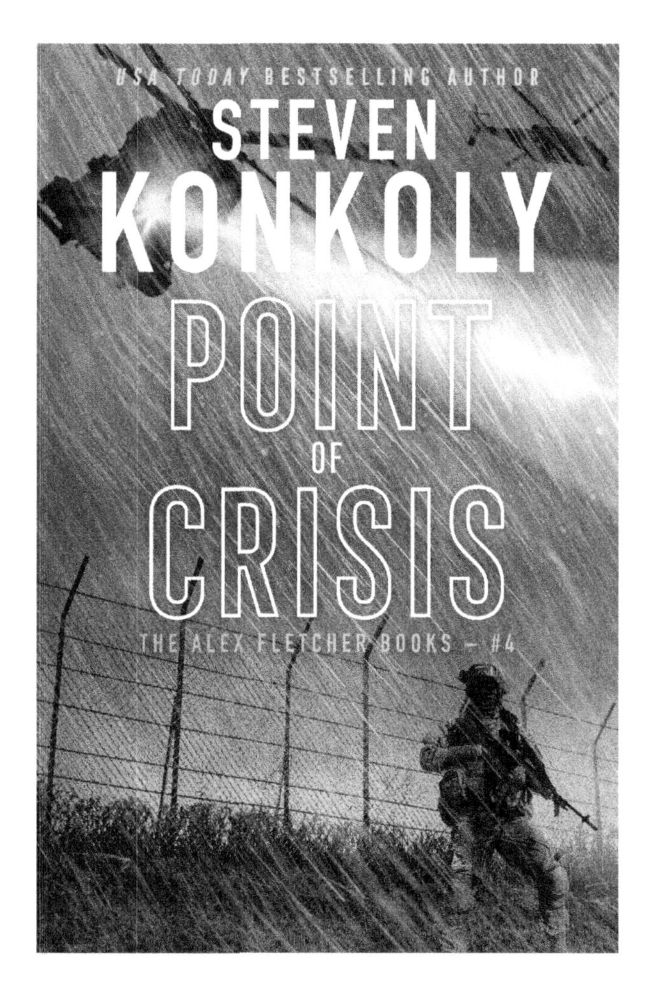

Available at Amazon Books

Please consider leaving a review for Point of Crisis. Even a short, one-line review can make all of the difference.

Thank you!

For VIP access to exclusive sneak peeks at my upcoming work, new release updates and deeply discounted books, join my newsletter here:

eepurl.com/dFebyD

Visit Steven's blog to learn more about current and future projects:

StevenKonkoly.com

About the Author

Steven graduated from the United States Naval Academy in 1993, receiving a bachelor of science in English literature. He served the next eight years on active duty, traveling the world as a naval officer assigned to various Navy and Marine Corps units. His extensive journey spanned the globe, including a two-year tour of duty in Japan and travel to more than twenty countries throughout Asia and the Middle East.

From enforcing United Nations sanctions against Iraq as a maritime boarding officer in the Arabian Gulf, to directing aircraft bombing runs and naval gunfire strikes as a Forward Air Controller (FAC) assigned to a specialized Marine Corps unit, Steven's "in-house" experience with a wide range of regular and elite military units brings a unique authenticity to his thrillers.

He lives with his family in central Indiana, where he still wakes up at "zero dark thirty" to write for most of the day. When "off duty," he spends as much time as possible outdoors or travelling with his family—and dog.

Steven is the bestselling author of nearly twenty novels. His canon of work includes the popular Black Flagged Series, a gritty, no-holds barred covert operations and espionage saga; The Alex Fletcher Books, an action-adventure thriller epic chronicling the events surrounding an inconceivable attack on the United States; The Fractured State series, a near future, dystopian thriller trilogy set in the drought ravaged southwest; and THE RESCUE, a heart-pumping thriller of betrayal, revenge, and conspiracy.

He is an active member of the International Thriller Writers (ITW) and Science Fiction and Fantasy Writers of America (SFWA) organizations.

You can contact Steven directly by email
(stevekonkoly@striblingmedia.com)

or through his blog:
StevenKonkoly.com.

Printed in Great Britain
by Amazon

28265645R00260